The Secret War Report of The OSS

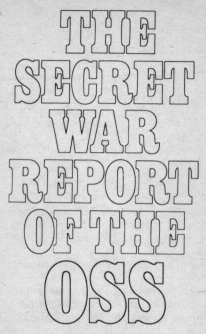

THE SECRET WAR REPORT OF THE OSS

Edited and with
an introduction by

ANTHONY CAVE BROWN

A BERKLEY MEDALLION BOOK
published by
BERKLEY PUBLISHING CORPORATION

Brandt and Brandt
101 Park Avenue
New York, N.Y. 10017

SBN 425-03253-1

BERKLEY MEDALLION BOOKS are published by
Berkley Publishing Corporation
200 Madison Avenue
New York, N.Y. 10016

BERKLEY MEDALLION BOOK ®TM 757,375

Printed in the United States of America

Berkley Medallion Edition, JUNE, 1976

The spearhead of the invasion of Europe will be secret intelligence and psychological warfare operations.

General William J. Donovan
Director, Office of Strategic Services

Table of Contents

*mation (COI).....OSS supplants COI in June
1942.....Early difficulties.....OSS both
wartime expedient and rehearsal for a peacetime intelligence-gathering organization.....Donovan letter of August 1945 sets
forth principles to underlie future CIA*

*General Counsel.....Special Relations Of-
fice.....Board of Review*
*Technical Branches: Communications - Re-
cruiting and Training.....Research and Development Division ("suitcase" radio, Joan-
Eleanor air-to-ground communication system).....Message Center (cryptographic
methods and security).....Research and Development: special devices (pocket incendiary,
weapons silencers, train-derailing techniques,
sabotaging gasoline engines); agent authentication (production of false documents).....Research and Analysis*
*Secret Intelligence: Geographic
desks.....Labor section (Ship Observer Unit,
utilization of seamen for intelligence gathering)*
*Counter-Espionage—X-2: Registry (gath-
ered 400,000 items).....Liaison with other
agencies.....Special units (countered use by
enemy intelligence of insurance company
covers; art-looting investigation).....Field
operations (manipulation of captured enemy
agents; double and triple agents)*
*Foreign Nationalities (analysis of U.S.
foreign-language press; indications of policies
of foreign countries)*
*Censorship and Documents (obtained back-
ground data for counterfeiting agents' documentation)*
*Special Operations (physical subversion of
the enemy through sabotage, infiltration, support of resistance groups; recruiting and training Jedburghs)*
Morale Operations—"Black" Propaganda

(bribery, blackmailing, poisoning, black mar-keteering, etc.; rumors planted of Hitler's death; newspapers, radio stations falsely pur-porting to be German)

Operational Groups (designed to be used in small units behind enemy lines for harassment; Army personnel recruited for OG's in Italy, France, Balkans and Norway)

Maritime Unit (infiltration of agents by sea; marine sabotage)

Special Projects Office (research on enemy secret weapons, including radio-guided missiles; development of radio-guided Javaman craft for destroying ships in enemy harbors)

Schools and Training (initial dependence on British for staff and methods. . . . . Training (em-phasis on maintaining "cover," handling a "blow," "safe houses," avoidance of rote learn-ing, specialized intelligence activities). . . . . As-sessment (holding areas to screen prospective trainees; psychological and psychiatric apprais-al of agent candidates using novel meth-ods). . . . . Training areas set up

PART II   OSS—OPERATIONS

Operation Torch (invasion of French North Africa): The Vice-Consuls (State Department cover for intelligence agents operating in French-controlled territory after February 1941). . . . . Clandestine radio stations . . . . . Chains of informants (divine leader "Strings", and Berber adventurer "Tassels" marshal their large native following; RAF as-signed targets based on intelligence gath-ered). . . . . Sabotage groups (smuggling in of British arms from Gibraltar). . . . . Propaganda (Arabic translation of Roosevelt's "Four Free-

doms" speech)..... *Preparations for D-Day (U.S. General Mark Clark secretly landed; Germans deceived into expecting invasion at Dakar, little resistance encountered)*

Tunisia (with signing of armistice with Frence forces on 11 November 1942, OSS headquarters moves to Algiers; Brandon mission assists in attempts to oust Germans from Tunisia; OSS takes hostages)

Oujda Base Operations (from this Moroccan base near Algerian border, intelligence work concerning Spanish military activity and cooperation with Germans coordinated; enemy intelligence schools and spy rings uncovered; OSS establishes camp near Oujda to train Spaniards as intelligence agents; Banana operation launched in Spain proves failure and arouses U.S. Ambassador's hostility to OSS)

Eire (chief agent "Hurst" continues activities despite U.S. Minister's disapproval; OSS obtains, through official Irish source, intelligence about bombing targets gathered in Tokyo by Vatican representatives)

Spain and Portugal (German occupation of Spain feared)..... SI—Secret Intelligence (verifies Spanish military and economic cooperation with the Axis Powers, prepares detailed mapping and intelligence survey of the country; scheme to evacuate Free French by ship from Spain largely unsuccessful; useful contacts established among neutral and enemy diplomats in Madrid and Lisbon; hostility of U.S. Ambassador in Madrid; tungsten smuggling from Spain and Portugal to Germany traced and stopped)..... X-2—Counter-Espionage (agents under State Department cover in Lisbon, Madrid, Barcelona, Bilbao and San Sebastian identify enemy agents and double some; deceived by Jean Charles Alexandre; OSS burglary of Japanese embassy in Lisbon; following German col-

Greece by November 1944.....Recruitment
and training.....Infiltration (caiques, small
seacraft, chiefly used).....Secret intelligence
(Donovan rules main OSS target in theater
Russian threat to the Balkans; exploits of three-
man Horsebreeders team—500 sub-agents recruited).....Morale operations.....Special
operations (sabotage of bridges; achievements
of Smashem).....Complications caused by
Greek civil war

Yugoslavia: 15 Reichswehr divisions operating against Partisans; Donovan disposed to support both the Communist Tito and his royalist
opponent Mihailovich, leader of the Chetniks;
problems of Partisan supply; mystery of Tito's
identity; withdrawal of support to Chetniks in
early 1944; arrival of Independent American
Military Mission to Marshal Tito on 9 October
1944; Tito forces OSS withdrawal on 31 March
1945

Rumania: OSS team conducting Operation
Bughouse enters country 29 August 1944 following anti-Nazi coup; adventures of SOE Colonel Gardyne de Chastelain; OSS priority tasks
comprise evacuation of downed U.S. fliers, determining damages to Ploesti oilfields, uncovering Axis intelligence officials and agents (over
4,000 identified), investigating Russo-
Rumanian relations.

Czechoslovakia: Premature Slovak Independent Army revolt in late 1944 disastrously in-
volves OSS team

Bulgaria: OSS operations quickly terminated
by Russian objections

Albania: Teams Tank and Bird and later
Tirana city team operate

Relative success of OSS operations in Stockholm and Bern contrasted with poor record in
Istanbul

Turkey.....''Dogwood,'' chief agent of
Cereus circle, establishes contacts in four coun-

tries: Austria, Germany (with member of Hitler assassination conspiracy), Hungary (Gestapo plot to infiltrate OSS; failure of Duke Mission to German-occupied Budapest), Bulgaria.....''Dogwood,'' if not German-controlled double-agent, guilty of self-confident garrulity.....Mrs. Hildegarde Reilly, German double-agent, penetrates Istanbul OSS

Sweden: Secret intelligence (OSS disputes with U.S. minister in Stockholm; spying on Russian intelligence services; surveillance of Swedish shipping to Germany; coverage of SKF shipments of ball bearings to Germany; Japanese attempts to buy ball bearings).....Special operations (''Birch'' infiltrates Germany, reaches Berlin).....Morale operations (publication Handel and Wandel attempts subversion of German business leaders).....X-2 (3,000 agents and officials of intelligence interest identified)

Support to Norway and Denmark.....Resistance movements under control of native intelligence services.....Norway: SO Westfield Mission supplies groups in north; OG Rype Team led by Major William E. Colby, later a chief of the CIA.....Denmark: Railroad sabotage; pinpoint aerial bombardment of Gestapo headquarters to destroy files; 13,000 resistants organized

Switzerland.....Main Allied wartime listening post.....Allen W. Dulles, OSS Bern chief, makes contact with anti-Hitler German underground.....Shipment of microfilm through occupied France.....Relations with dissident diplomats of German satellite countries: Hungary mission fails; Austrian underground reached.....German Foreign Office contact ''Wood'' provides secret cables by the pound in official wrappings.....Abwehr contact Gisevius reveals planning of putsch (aborted 20 July 1944) against Nazi regime.....Industrial intelligence gathered includes data on rocket bombs. ...West Front intelligence....Japan's surrender offer received

double-agent or merely loud, free talker?)

Special Operations/London (principal task, building, with British, a strong resistance force in France; preference for guerrilla as against conventional warfare; "Alfred's" radio operator "Narcisse" escapes Gestapo by shamming death, and subsequently they undertake Operation Sacristan; Marksman circuit arms and directs a thousand Maquis)

Bern Chains (black market goods enable agents to cross French frontier from Switzerland; intelligence on railroad conditions in France)

Agent Processing.....Special Force Headquarters (SFHQ)/London: Training (rigorous selection standards, silent-killing instruction, parachute school, peculiarities of each radio operator's "fist" noted as security measure against doubling, specialized schooling); Cover and Documents (new French identity card at first baffling; "aging" documents; best cover one corresponding to agent's actual occupation); Briefing (agents angered at deliberate deception on dubious points in their cover); Infiltration into France (usually effected by air into prearranged target area).....SI/Algiers recruiting (on far smaller scale than in London; training emphasises personal relationship between teacher and student; clothing and documents present difficulties; dispatching of agents mostly blind air drops into France)

Planning for D-Day (resistance uprising to coincide with invasion of Normandy; close co-operation with British and French established).....Building French resistance (OSS officers and Jedburghs participate in organizing 300,000 French resistants, help in sabotage of factories, transport; Team Stockbroker invents "phantom train" technique of railroad sabotage; Union, Justine and Eucalyptus teams participate with Maquis forces in Vercors against efforts of 22,000 German troops; "Ludovic" of Team Beggar survives two arrests in Paris). . . . . Supply (air deliveries by OSS steadily increase until British totals finally are overtaken; BBC broadcasts code names (messages personnels) *of next day's air drops; daylight vs. night-time supplying). . . . . Jedburghs (in intention each three-man team to comprise a French, British and American member; sample Jedburgh operation order of 2 June 1944 detailing mission, resistance elements to be encountered, German order of battle, etc., reproduced; various Jedburgh activities summarized; after-action report of Team Frederick in Brittany covering June-August 1944 reproduced; report of activities of Team Bruce, led by William E. Colby, former director of the CIA, reproduced; Jed Team Alexander almost embroiled in rivalries of Gaullist and Communist resistance forces). . . . . OG's (Operational Groups) in France (most military of OSS units, they participate in sabotage operations, help improve morale of resistants; exploits of sections Emily, Louise, Betsy and Patrick). . . . . SI (Secret Intelligence)/North France (British in London, at first objecting to American secret intelligence activities, finally agree to joint Sussex operation of 120 agents organized into two-man American Ossex and British Brissex teams; pathfinders for later Sussex teams dropped "blind" into France on 8 February 1944; intelligence from Ossex team Vitrail on D-Day minus 1 establishes German unawareness of invasion plans; activities of Teams Jeanne, Foudre and Dentelle; Proust project serves as Sussex auxiliary to carry out low-priority tasks); Army detachments in North France (OSS detachments provided to First Army, Third Army, Ninth Army and 12th Army Group). . . . . Resistance aid to Overlord (French resistance destroys 800 strategic targets*

Army G-2's support.....SSS mediates with local French populace for G-2.....Concerned with tactical intelligence "just behind the fighting zones".....Intelligence gathering during early phase of rapid advance contrasted with that during later slower movement.....Reliance upon "civilian reconnaisance".....Adventures of Marianne and of the clergyman, "Joe-1912".....Mayfair team provides fresh information

Special Counter-Intelligence (SCI) units established to provide rapid distribution of information to field staffs of swiftly advancing military forces.....Capture of Abwehr agent "Jigger" yields data on German sabotage methods.....German agent "Keel" played back for six months after his death.....German agents Dragoman and Skull captured and played back to Abwehr to provide false intelligence.....Use of Skull as bait results in unintended killing of high German agent Kaulen .....Witch an outstanding case of agent doubling

Joan-Eleanor provides means for agent on the ground to communicate by voice with OSS representative in a plane flying 30,000 feet overhead.....First J-E operation, employing agent "Bobby" in Holland, saved when "Bobby" transmits control signal after capture by Gestapo

West Front and 12th Army Group.....Vain attempts at infiltration into Germany..... "Sleepers" (stay-behind agents) not activated as German Ardennes offensive is turned back.....Ninth Army.....First Army .....Third Army.....6th Army Group

Note: While some less interesting or repetitive material has not been included in this reprint, much of the Official War Report of the Office of Strategic Services (OSS) concerning European operations is reproduced exactly, though not necessarily in the original order. The additions and commentaries of Anthony Cave Brown, Editor of this reprint, have been scrupulously distinguished from the Official text. In cases where the Editor's material might not readily be identified as such, it has been enclosed in square brackets ([/]). Square brackets have been used also for the more interesting explanatory footnotes in the text and the word "footnote" added. Editorial deletions are shown by the word "deletion" in square brackets, except that insignificant textual changes such as references to exhibits and the like are unnoted. Where material has been officially obliterated from the transcript furnished, the word "excision" appears in square brackets. Some discrepancies of usage will be found between the Official text and the added editorial matter.

INTRODUCTION

When I was engaged in collecting the material for *Bodyguard of Lies,* which was a history of strategy and stratagem for the invasion of France by Allied forces on 6th June 1944, I was conscious that there was a large gap in my research, one that could not be filled. Just as *Bodyguard* was published, however, it was filled, although it was too late to include any of the material in my volume. That gap was the War Report of the Office of Strategic Services, prepared under the direction of Kermit Roosevelt, in 1948, and kept securely under lock and key at the Central Intelligence Agency until its declassification in February 1976.

I think now as I did when I was working on *Bodyguard:* the OSS official history was and is a vital and important document concerning the participation of the United States in one of the most secret aspects of World War II—the clandestine war with the ideologues of the Third Reich. This was not the account of the movements of great armies and vast air and sea fleets, nor of the immense clashes of arms that wrecked a continent. It is the history of what went on in the shadows to outwit and undermine the will of a mighty power —Germany—to impose its will on the rest of mankind. The secret war was as much a part of that vast conflict as it was of any other in history, except that this time, with ideologies sharpened and technology improved, its outcome was even more decisive than it was, shall we say, in the war waged against Europe by the Lord of Asia, Genghis Khan. Nor was the prosecution of the secret war of 1939-1945 any less bloody and violent than that of orthodox campaigning. General Sir Colin Gubbins, the chief of the British Special Operations Executive (SOE), which existed to set Europe ablaze, told me that per capita the secret war was bloodier than the Somme. The only difference was that the cries were muffled and, in many instances, the corpses were never found.

The secret war of which OSS was part was largely the outcome of the dictum of Winston Churchill, the Prime Minister of Great Britain during the great conflict:

Battles are won by slaughter and manoeuvre. The greater the general, the more he contributes in manoeuvre, the less he de-

mands in slaughter.... Nearly all the battles which are regarded
as the masterpieces of the military art...have been battles of
manoeuvre in which very often the enemy has found himself
defeated by some novel expedient or device, some queer, swift,
unexpected thrust or stratagem....There is required for the
composition of a great commander not only massive common
sense and reasoning power, not only imagination, but also an element of legerdemain, an original and sinister touch, which
leaves the enemy puzzled as well as beaten....There are many
kinds of manoeuvres in war, some only of which take place
upon the battlefield. There are manoeuvres far to the flank or
rear. There are manoeuvres in time, in diplomacy, in mechanics, in psychology; all of which are removed from the battlefield, but react often decisively upon it, and the object of all is to
find easier ways, other than sheer slaughter, of achieving the
main purpose.

When Churchill became Prime Minister in May 1940—a time
when the German Army stood on the English Channel and in effect
Europe from the North Sea to the Russian frontier was under the
Nazi flag—he took the measures needed to employ clandestinity
on a very large scale, a scale hitherto not perceived in the western
world. Out of these measures came the phenomenon of the 20th
Century—total war, the sum total of the wits, energy and resources
of one group of nations against the sum total of the wits, energy
and resources of an opposing group of nations. Several historians
of the period—notably Professor Hugh Trevor-Roper, the Regius
Professor of Modern History at Oxford, a man who was a junior
officer in the Secret Intelligence Service of England at that time
and privy to little, and whose opinions, concerning secret service, while accepted on a very wide scale, must sometimes be regarded as suspect—have said that Churchill's concept did little
more than provide the upper classes of England with the means to
consolidate their rule. This, we now know, of course, is exactly the
opposite of the truth. In historical terms, what the secret war of
1939-1945 did release were large numbers of popular movements
of all political colors from which the postwar world emerged. In
very real terms, the war of the shadows was a class war in which
the main aim of those fighting was to sweep away all that was
shabby, decadent, corrupt and infamous, and enable the world to
start again. In this context, I am much taken with a statement in a
letter to his parents from Major Frank Thompson, an SOE agent
on operations in Bulgaria. It echoed precisely the statements of his
American colleagues, for example Major Donald Downes, of the

OSS in North Africa and Italy, a typically idealistic American whom the reader will encounter later.

> My Christmas message to you is one of greater hope than I have ever had in my life before. There is a spirit abroad in Europe which is finer and braver than anything that tired continent has known for centuries, and which cannot be withstood.... It is the confident will of whole peoples, who have known the utmost humiliation and suffering and have triumphed over it, to build their own life once and for all.... There is a marvellous opportunity before us—and all that is required from Britain, America and Russia is imagination, help and sympathy.... Four years of Nazi occupation have made the issues very clear... 1944's going to be a good year, though a terrible one.

Like all good revolutionaries, it will be interesting to note, Major Thompson was prepared to die in the fight; he was sold and shot four days after this letter went out to London in the courrier.

Here then was the theory and principle behind the war of the shadows, the strategy of the campaign. We must now attend to the tactics of the secret war. Churchill, again, was the man who had the most to say about the secret conflict:

> In the high ranges of Secret Service the actual facts in many cases were in every respect equal to the most fantastic inventions of romance and melodrama. Tangle within tangle, plot and counter plot, ruse and treachery, cross and double-cross, true agent, false agent, double agent, gold and steel, the bomb, the dagger and the firing party, were interwoven in many a texture so intricate as to be incredible and yet true. The Chief and the High Officers of the Secret Service revelled in these subterranean labyrinths, and pursued their task with cold and silent passion.

In short, the secret war was an odyssey which required a Homer. It came from an improbable quarter. The first official work on clandestinity in modern history surfaced in 1966. It was called *S.O.E. in France,* and the chronicler was M.R.D. Foot, of Manchester University, a former captain in the Special Air Service (the model for the Green Berets) who was captured (and almost shot) while on an intelligence mission in France just after the invasion. It was a marvellous work of high adventure, scholarship and wit. It was also a surprising work because, for centuries, the British have held successfully that to be successful a secret service must be secret. Nothing of its activities might be revealed, whether those activities concerned the past or the present, and especially if they concerned the future. The British Government enforced this belief with a law—the Official Secrets Act—that made wise men do no more with secrets than a cat does with a hot stew—circle it, sniff it enviously, and leave it alone. The reason for the publication of *S.O.E.* was politics. Harold Macmillan, the Prime Minister, saw some problems with the French. The French resistance movements, or the survivors, believed that some of their organizations had been deliberately betrayed to the Germans by perfidious Albion in order that surprise might be obtained on D-Day in Normandy. These men were now determined to make England pay for her cold-bloodedness by keeping England out of the European Common Market. And so, to show the French that the British did not betray France and, indeed, only nurtured the French underground, *S.O.E. in France* was released.

As important as this volume was, it was only part of the official history of the secret war. It told little or nothing of the activities of the Secret Intelligence Service (SIS or MI-6). There were rumors that an official history of SIS was to be published, and that its author was Peter Fleming. This seems to have died for the moment with the elegant death of the author on the grouse moors in 1968. There were rumors that General Sir Stewart Menzies, the chief of the SIS, left a 60,000-word report on SIS in World War II, to be published after his death. His motive was to defend himself posthumously against his critics—notably Trevor-Roper—and show that if he did nothing else with his stewardship he did destroy the German intelligence service. Neither of these two documents has surfaced so far, though it is likely that Menzies's report will arrive on newspaper editors' desks at any time, given the pride of his Scottish family. This will certainly cause an enormous storm and place certain reputations where they belong.

Between the publication of *S.O.E. in France* and *Bodyguard of Lies,* a ten-year period, one other work of great importance came into the public domain. This was Sir J. C. Masterman's *The Double-Cross System in the War of 1939 to 1945.* This splendidly dry little work was Masterman's after-action report of activities in which the British in England first captured and then put into its own service the German intelligence organizations at work in England. There were two other works of less importance, but which should be mentioned: Donald McLachlan's *Room 39,* a semi-official history of British naval intelligence, and F. W. Winterbotham's *The Ultra Secret,* a minor work which dealt with a major subject—Ultra, the British (and later Anglo-American) code-and-cipher-breaking service.

But, it will be noted, all these works are British in origin. Nothing was said at all, at least officially, about the American secret services, and especially about the OSS and the Signals Intelligence Service. Now, at long last, and to the delight of modern historians, the CIA has declassified *The War Report of the Office of Strategic Services*. It is a work of great importance in modern affairs, for it shows how one of the world's two leading powers once worked—and, at least to a certain extent, the methods employed by it since the end of World War II. While it lacks much of the literary style that characterizes the British publications—it is, after all, not a history but an official report—the lengths and breadths of the murderous game are not concealed; and it does not lack candor. Of importance is that it displays how the American intellectual works when he is angry; that the American is every bit as cold-blooded and deadly as his Russian, Chinese, Korean, French, British, Czech, Zionist and North Vietnamese friends and enemies.

The chief of the OSS project was Kermit Roosevelt, who, before joining OSS, became a history professor at the California Institute of Technology. Roosevelt was a grandson of President Theodore Roosevelt, and his first assignment in the OSS was that of assistant to Dr. Stephen Penrose, the chief of OSS Secret Intelligence (SI) in the Near East. Roosevelt was a Near East specialist and the sort of man who knows a thing or two about the game of nations—it was he, for example, who engineered the *coup d'etat* that rid Iran of Mossadegh for the Shah and for the CIA in 1953; who became vice-president for governmental relations for Gulf Oil; and who now represents the Shah (among other Near Eastern potentates and governments) in Washington.

Roosevelt's central figure is General William J. Donovan, the founder of OSS, a queer figure who comes off three-quarters Machiavelli and one-quarter boy. A lawyer, soldier and rich man, we now know that behind Donovan was Francis Cardinal Spellman, a case for medieval scientists if there ever was one, a creature who seemed to believe that the only thing to do with Communists was to burn them alive, a priest who saw eternal damnation in anything pink. Also behind General Donovan, helping this fervid Catholic in his intrigues against and with the Joint Chiefs of Staff, was Kermit Roosevelt. Whether Donovan was really the right man for the post of chief of America's first secret service is very questionable. Successful clandestinity demands good bureaucracy and excellent judgment, and Donovan did not always display both. His politics, always those of the right, were useless internationally, for while he did recruit Communists to kill Krauts, as he put it, he feared and distrusted Communists in places where they counted. In Italy and France, he could never quite make up his mind what to do politically; and, since political belief was the clandestine's primary motive (money, adventure, self-aggrandizement, all played lesser parts in the struggle than contemporary historians insist), his policies often failed and, even when they succeeeded, led to interminable muddle. Likable, even admirable on occasions, he was in fact an Elizabethan man, swaggering about capitals in beautiful cords, displaying a fine calf for a riding boot, but forever dependent really upon the British for the finesse which that secret struggle demanded. Dr. William Maddox, the OSS/SI chief in London, of Harvard and Princeton; Colonel the Honorable David Bruce, that amazing, cultured and unflappable jack-of-all-trades; Allen Dulles, the OSS spymaster in Switzerland—all would have done the job better than Donovan. None of these men would have risked that most vital of all commodities of clandestinity—security—by rushing ashore with the assault troops at Sicily, Salerno or Normandy, as did Donovan. What would have happened had Donovan been captured? All men—even one so backboned as Donovan—have their breaking point and, with the experience they had acquired in making men talk, the Germans would surely have kept Donovan suspended carefully between life and death until he did talk. What then? Would he have blown Ultra? Would he have blown the atomic bomb? Would he have blown the structures of the Anglo-American intelligence services? Would he not have babbled the truth about his government's attitude towards the Kremlin, thereby precipitating the greatest of crises between Washington and Moscow? Donovan was very close to the crater's edge at Normandy; he was wounded in the throat, very close to the jugular, and very close to the front line.

And yet, to be fair, Donovan was the OSS and the OSS was Donovan, at least at first. There were some ghastly blunders, in which agents by the score died cursing the United States. Only when it was well and truly blooded after Normandy did the OSS begin to lose its reputation as a "fly-by-night civilian outfit headed up by a wild man who was trying to horn in on the war." Only then —and especially in X-2 (the OSS's counterespionage service) and its counterintelligence (CI)—did Washington really begin to take seriously these "bourbon whiskey colonels" with "cellophane commissions (you could see through them, but they kept the Draft off)." Only when the service started Witch, Joan-Eleanor, and the agent penetration of Germany—three of the most outstanding espionage operations of modern history, told here for the first time—

did the field agents begin to get a reputation for being other than "rah-rah youngsters to whom the OSS was perhaps an escape from routine military service and a sort of a lark." Only then do we find extraordinary young men like B.M.W. Knox (who would become Director of Hellenic Studies at Harvard) and William E. Colby (director of the CIA, replaced in early 1976 by George Bush) doing feats of courageous work behind the enemy lines of such magnitude that one is left in awe of what the human intellect is capable of when times are bad and perilous.

But in the end, it was too late: because of Donovan's personality, his conduct of office, it was made plain to him that he was not wanted at the end of the European war, and that his service was to be placed in a state of suspended animation until Washington decided what to do about the Kremlin. He went away, very disappointed, to write long memoranda to public journals about the glories of his service and the need for a secret service in peacetime. His men scattered to the four winds, leaving the great game in Europe, at least for the time being, to the British, even though it was obvious they were exhausted by the effort of nearly half a century of legalised thuggery against just about everybody. Anybody but Donovan would have kept the service intact; but he had made too many enemies among the Joint Chiefs. Neither had he made too many friends elsewhere; the British had tired of him long since, and even if Churchill had been in a position to ask Truman to keep him on and help the British play the ball with the Russians, nobody in fact stepped forward from the grimy London headquarters of SIS to speak well of Donovan.

Yet, of course, the service survived, largely because of the excellence of the men that Donovan had recruited. The list is very long, quite as long as that brilliant crop that the State Department produced to manage the Russians at the end of the war. There was Stewart Alsop, Tracy Barnes, Andrew Berding, Bill Boggs, Tom Braden, Franklin Canfield, Allen Dulles, Arthur Goldberg, Joe and John Haskell, Archibald MacLeish, Peter Tompkins, Arthur Schlesinger Jr., Russell Forgan, Milton Katz, and so on and on.

The War Report of the OSS does not claim that it won the secret war with Germany; it does not claim that it won the secret war with Germany in concert with the British; it places credit where credit belongs—with the British services—and acknowledges the great debt that the United States had and has to Great Britain. But it does show that a relatively young country can create a service that had taken other countries centuries of experience to create and perfect, and then take those older countries on and give them a bad time. It also shows that in the closing months of the war with Germany the OSS began to outstrip the British services in penetrating Germany. When it is kept in mind that Himmler had in the Third Reich the most proficient police force in human history, the full magnitude of this accomplishment will be realized. The dexterity with which X-2 handled its controlled agents will doubtless bring a knowing smile to the hard and wise old features of Masterman. It is also reasonable to suppose that the German who wrote these words about the first American agents into the field in 1942 has (assuming that he survived the conflict) regretted them:

> Since all their thoughts are centered on their social, sexual, or culinary interests, petty quarrels and jealousies are daily incidents with them. Altogether they represent a perfect picture of the mixture of races and characters in that savage conglomeration called the United States of America, and anyone who observes them can well judge the sort of mind and instability that must be prevalent in their country today.... Lack of pluck and democratic degeneracy prevails among them, resulting from their too easy life, corrupt morals, and consequent lack of energy.... They are totally lacking in method, organisation and discipline.... We can only congratulate ourselves on the selection of this group of enemy agents who will give us no trouble.

This patronising attitude was not confined to the Germans; it was shared by the British, as this statement by Malcolm Muggeridge, the British commentator, shows of the first arrivals in London after Pearl Harbor:

> Ah, those first OSS arrivals in London! How well I remember them, arriving like jeunes filles en fleur straight from a finishing school, all fresh and innocent, to start work in our frowsty old intelligence brothel.... All too soon they were ravished and corrupted, becoming indistinguishable from seasoned pros who had been in the game for a quarter of a century or more.

It is a profoundly interesting commentary on Anglo-American secret relations of those times that, for their part, the Americans could recall in common a single startling factor—the length of the lunches and the amount of liquor and wine consumed. Lyman Kirkpatrick, who would become Executive Director of CIA, would express that common recollection:

> Almost immediately on my arrival in London I found myself

plunged into a series of lunches that would last from 1 p.m. through a good part of the afternoon, and dinners that lasted well past midnight. Our European friends were formidable consumers of alcoholic beverages, with apparently little effect, and I always wondered whether they also put in the same long office hours that we did. The entire routine was quite a strain on the liver.

The verbatim OSS report has many virtues as an historical document; and among them is that, with only the briefest of censorings, it discusses frankly and for the first time the whole question of finance in the secret world as it was then and, presumably, at least to some extent, it remains today. For reasons of space, I will deal with the budget topic here in my introduction. An agency such as OSS, engaged in secret and unorthodox activities, is peculiarly liable to difficulties in its relations with other parts of government. Secrecy inevitably creates a psychological attitude of distrust and suspicion on the part of others. Moreover, and especially with finance, this attitude is aggravated by the clash with established procedures and regulations which the performance of irregular and unorthodox activities often entails.

An agency such as OSS must necessarily, therefore, enjoy high trust if it is to perform its operations successfully and secretly. This is especially the case where money is concerned, for the nature of clandestinity demands special funds which cannot be accounted for in the usual fashion since detailed explanations would destroy the secrecy required for safe and successful execution of an operation.

The main device employed by OSS was almost the same as that employed by the British—a Secret Vote or Unvouchered Funds (UFs). This was money made available by the President without reference to the legislature and which was accounted for by Donovan's signature alone on a certificate that read in part:

I certify that expenditures were actually made in the amount on this voucher according to reports in this office and that it would be prejudicial to the public interest to disclose the names of the recipients, the dates and the names of places in which the expenditures were made. The expenditures were made incident to collecting and analyzing confidential information and data bearing upon the national security of the United States.

Plainly, almost unlimited opportunities for fraud existed in this arrangement. In a moment, we shall see that, except for one mysterious case in Italy, no major case of fraud ever developed concerning

OSS UFs.

The question of secret banking is worth some elaboration here, not only because the funding of secret operations is the first step in their implementation, but also because the magnitude of the OSS's banking arrangements demonstrated how rapidly OSS had matured into a first-class espionage service. To handle UFs, OSS formed an organization called Special Funds. This existed to provide finance for the maintenance of cover, whether of a corporation, a training installation, a recruiting office or an agent or group of agents in enemy or enemy-occupied territory. "Unvouchered funds," says the Report, "constituted the modus operandi of the most secret operations in which OSS was engaged." In order to provide this service, Special Funds "engaged in world-wide operations for the procurement of more than 80 different currencies which proved necessary for the undercover activities of OSS." Special Funds kept "intelligence files on these and other currencies" and "It devised and put into effect intricate procedures by which the procurement and disbursement of (UFs), both in the United States and abroad, were camouflaged so that the connection of OSS or its agents with a given transaction was not revealed." This required "the most minute attention to detail" and alertness to the financial maneuvers of the enemy, who tried frequently to trap agents through financial regulations and the marking of currency. As the Report put it:

> Basic to the understanding of Special Funds is realization of the fact that the money carried by an undercover agent is essentially an operational supply. Upon the security of the currency he uses depend not only the agent's life but the success of the operation in which he is engaged. The procurement of currency for use in undercover operations was therefore subject to the most stringent security precautions.

This necessity laid OSS open to large-scale fraud, for as the Report went on: "While every attempt was made to procure the necessary foreign funds as cheaply as possible, the security of the transaction and of the currency itself was the governing factor rather than the legal rate of exchange." It is important and significant that in the area of foreign exchange, where crookery abounds, there was not a single case of an OSS paymaster lining his own pockets.

The first allocation of UFs came out of the President's Emergency Fund in September 1941, in the amount of $100,000. When OSS was formed out of its parent organization, the Coordinator of

Information (COI) in June 1942, another $3 million was granted for the fiscal year 1942-43. Then came a further $10 million in UFs. When OSS went to Congress for a formal appropriation for 1943-44, it received $21 million, of which nearly $15 million was classified as unvouchered funds. For the period 1944-45, $57 million was obtained, $37 million of which

> may be expended without regard to the provisions of law and regulations relating to the expenditure of Government funds or the employment of persons in the government service, and $35 million of such $37 may be expended for objects of a confidential nature, such expenditures to be accounted for solely on the certificate of the Director of the Office of Strategic Services and every such certificate shall be deemed a sufficient voucher for the amount therein certified.

These millions were in a real sense "mad money," for almost all essential housing, transportation, food and communications expenses were largely borne by other agencies such as the Army and its Air Force. If the purchasing power of the $57 million is multiplied by ten—$57 million bought about as much in the forties as $570 million in the seventies—then it will be seen that OSS was well endowed indeed.

While it is true that war is a remarkable stimulus to organization and change, one is compelled to marvel at the speed with which Donovan and his staff formed an international banking organization to finance America's clandestine activities. One is also compelled to marvel at the dexterity with which he managed the illegalities without such characters as Drew Pearson getting to know. Nowhere are these points better illustrated than in the OSS Foreign Exchange Division.

The FED was established in August 1942 to arrange "the transfer of such secret funds abroad as were necessary to maintain OSS intelligence and other special operations, and also for providing foreign balances in some areas in such manner as not to disclose the fact that the United States Government had sizable cash deposits in those areas." If, for example, the German intelligence service had learned that the United States was surreptitiously buying up large quantities of French North African paper the Germans might reasonably assume that the United States intended some military action in that theater. At least, therefore, they would be obliged to keep an eye on that area, by sea, air and human intelligence, thereby lessening the possibility that the attack forces would obtain surprise and thus increase the possibility of heavy

American casualties.

The monies sent overseas fell into two categories: (a) work funds, (b) task funds. The former were those used to pay salaries and to maintain undercover agents who were ostensibly engaged in legitimate business. As the Report points out: "Unless a man so engaged was openly paid, his cover would soon become suspect, since he would appear to have no source of income. Task funds were those used (often by the same individual) to obtain confidential information, or for bribes and other secret operational purposes."

The complexities of funds transmissions were of the first order. "All countries in Europe, whether belligerent or neutral," says the Report, "censored communications and strictly regulated movements of capital. In most countries all banks were required to report to the government any sizable or unusual bank transactions, particularly cable transfers of money from outside the country for the benefit of resident aliens." This difficulty required the service of a secret service within the service, one as security-conscious as the cryptographic branch. Transfers had to be "laundered" through seven or eight countries before they reached the agent as the German intelligence services were aware that the Achilles' heel of the American service was the bank. As the Report shows, "Special Funds learned early that the enemy was sending agents into all neutral countries to ferret out black market and other undercover financial operations. Such agents were specially trained and in many cases held responsible positions in the local banks."

Nor was the financial operation ended when the draft reached the agent. The Report tells how

> [FED] took every precaution to see that the currency notes which were acquired through many devious channels were not traceable to the United States Government or to OSS. In order to protect the secret agents who would use the moneys, Special Funds endeavored to avoid repetition of successful operations, and not to rely upon any single pipeline for the movement of funds longer than absolutely necessary.

As the Report admits, this required that FED engage in black market transactions, while at the same time forbidding the agent concerned to obtain the foreign exchange himself. FED acquired very large stocks of foreign exchange of all descriptions through various black markets, usually Lisbon, Tangiers or Bern. No doubt the brokers made fortunes, and the OSS lost some through the ever-changing rates of exchange in the world's "sludge" currencies—but, as will be seen, while the French, for example, lost many agents because they did not have a financial structure such as FED, OSS lost none through maladroit financial operations.

As 1943 came and went, and FED reported that foreign currencies stocks being held were depreciating fast (very few currencies then seemed to appreciate), OSS went in for gold and diamonds on large scales. Special Funds officers worked marvelous deals in 1943 with $800,000 in gold, using French and British specie to buy foreign currency. This practice was termed "unorthodox methods of acquisition," and usually involved such worthless currencies (outside their own frontiers) as the Spanish peseta and the German reichsmark. But at no time did OSS ever acquire sufficient reichsmark through either conventional or unconventional methods of acquisition, and it was compelled to use foreign diplomats stationed at Berlin. They were "induced" to take large quantities of notes with them when they left Berlin on leave or diplomatic missions. These missions were "performed at great personal risk, since the German internal fiscal controls were strict and any infraction was punishable by death." Yet it was in such a financial operation that OSS succeeded in financing one of the outstanding human intelligence feats of the war in Europe—the agent penetration of Germany on a large scale. It is difficult to see how this operation could have been undertaken without such illegal methods; checkbooks and credit cards were useless in those days as, no doubt, they are today in Russia.

In all this, of course, there were great dangers, for the Germans were perfectly well aware that agents needed money, and without money agents could soon be arrested. To speed that day, in 1944 they released 90 million francs onto the Lisbon market, knowing that the British and American intelligence services would buy them in anticipation of the intelligence needs in France after D-DAY. It was clear to FED that the Germans had taken the serial numbers of the currency and that they intended to use these serial numbers to prove that those found in possession of the notes in France must be agents—and bundle them off to Buchenwald. OSS was just as smart: they directed that the notes, which they did buy, were not to be released until after the breakout from the bridgehead in Normandy. The Germans were checkmated; but their agents in Lisbon and Madrid were nothing if not nimble. They began to use specially marked money and issue special notes. As the Report tells the story:

The Gestapo made every bank and post office in France its unwitting assistant in an attempt to trap Allied agents. A particular issue of notes, the numbers of which had been recorded by the Gestapo, was sent into the black market, which was practical assurance that the notes would eventually find their way into the hands of agents being sent to France. The Gestapo sent warnings to all banks and post offices in France that a bank robbery had been perpetrated and that notes of a specific series had been taken. All banks and post offices were notified that the Gestapo was to be informed immediately if any notes of this issue were passed. The banks and post offices, operating in good faith and innocently supposing that they were assisting in the apprehension of bona fide bank robbers, made every effort to comply with this request.

OSS was, it seems, especially careful of new notes. As the Report goes on:

All new notes with serial numbers running in sequence, and which were obviously direct from the Bank of France, were segregated, put through an aging process and properly pinholed....OSS knew that fresh and unmutilated notes were available in France only to banks or accredited government agencies. The mere fact that an individual possessed a new note would make him suspect. It was customary in French banks to count notes on receipt from the Bank of France and to pin the notes together with a common pin into small bundles or packets. Therefore, any bank note which had proper circulation in France through regular channels would show at least two pinholes.

And how were the notes aged?

The aging of new notes in order to simulate ordinary circulation presented another problem to Special Funds.

Bank notes could not be aged with ordinary garden dirt because the soil left a residue which was easily detected and would render the agent in possession of such notes immediately suspect, if he were placed under close scrutiny. It was discovered that one of the best ways to age bills was to scatter them about the floor of a room in which persons were carrying on routine duties over a period of hours and to have the notes walked on and generally scrubbed about underfoot. It was the practice of Special Funds/London to lock one of its offices against intrusion, scatter one to five million francs about the floor, and go on with the usual work of the office. A day or two of this type of treatment generally served to smudge, rumple and tear the notes sufficiently to render them innocuous in the hands of an agent operating in the field.

The Report admits that some agents were dishonest and cached funds for their own use after the war. For example, 32 diamonds were issued in early 1945 to SI (secret intelligence) agents going into Germany. Of these, not one was reported sold or exchanged, and yet only nine were returned. All the rest were listed as lost. In one of the "lost" cases the diamond was subsequently found in the agent's possession. But as the Report observes: "When considered in relation to the total amount of money handled by Special Funds, such losses may be regarded as almost inconsequential." The Italian loss was made the more serious because it involved $17,000 and the murder of the American OSS officer who was carrying the UF. The subsequent court cases held in this matter left the general impression that OSS was staffed by wildly extravagant, licentious and dishonest agents. This was far from the truth; and there is no reason to doubt that OSS/SO agents were just as trustworthy as were SOE agents in the field. Here the record is known and is remarkable. Between November 1943 and July 1944, the period when guerrilla in support of the invasion was at its most intense, one section of SOE concerned with France (and not the largest of the sections by any means) parachuted to Anglo-Franco-American agents on the ground in France a total of 1.35 billion francs. Not a centime went astray, though 25 million francs disappeared and was found a day or two later under some waste paper, presumably awaiting its turn at the incinerator.

Since by law secret financial transactions may not be discussed publicly in England—M.R.D. Foot, for example, states that, even though his was an official history, he was not permitted access to Secret Vote accounts—I have dealt at some length with the financial operations of a secret service. After all, this is the first time in history that such information has come into the public domain (I believe the accounts of the German intelligence services vanished in the holocaust at the end of World War II). Therefore it is interesting to examine the generosity of the OSS. How much did they pay their agents? Was it enough? Did the Germans turn any agents because the American government was being niggardly?

The truth is that good agents are in as short supply as good writers, editors, reporters; in consequence Donovan paid his best agents well, or at least those agents who required payment at all. One of the best agents in the service of the United States was "Wood," Allen Dulles's leading spy in the German foreign ministry. "Wood"—real name Fritz Kolbe—was ideologically motivated and would probably have broken the contact if Dulles had insisted that he accept cash for his services. This was wise, for Kolbe happily supplied Dulles with the innermost secrets of the German foreign office, and the Wehrmacht generally, for the critical period of the war. As it was with Kolbe, so it was with Hans Bernd Gisevius, the former Gestapo agent attached to the German diplomatic mission in Switzerland who kept Dulles supplied with the most intimate and dangerous secrets of the Schwarze Kapelle, that small group of German nationalists and Christians who were seeking ways and means to end the war by killing Hitler. He, too, never asked for, or got, a pfennig even for his expenses.

There were, of course, cases of venality, but SI agents in the field received on average $300 a month—good but not handsome pay by the standards of the times. No agent was paid more than $5,000 a year, exclusive of task funds. X-2 rarely paid any salaries at all, paying lump sums for such information as the estimated time of arrival and pinpoint of an incoming agent, or an enemy agent's home address. Sometimes this type of information was expensive —men's heads usually are. I have heard the sum of $10,000 as being dispensed in the case of Mr. Desire at Avranches—but then Mr. Desire tipped X-2 off that the German army was to make a massive counterstroke at Mortain in August 1944. Since Bradley was able to defeat the attack (though not through Mr. Desire's information alone—Ultra played a large part in that epic), it may be argued that $10,000, if it was paid at all, was a small sum to disburse. As for task funds, there was no average. One agent who was in the field in France for almost a year and produced much valuable ground intelligence spent 136,728 francs (approximately $300 at the rate of exchange then prevailing). Another, a man who was in for only a month and acquired little information, spent 1.150 million francs (approximately $2,500). And it should not be imagined that OSS paymasters, for all their apparent wealth, could be suckered. As the Report states: "Special Funds...was often successful in scaling down agent bills, as well as claims of Allied espionage agencies for services rendered."

Special Funds' last claim is perfectly acceptable:

> Responsible for a service function vital to the organization and execution of secret activities, the Special Funds Branch operated in a field without precedent in America. The type and scope of OSS operations for which unvouchered funds were necessary provided a challenge to the ingenuity of the Special Funds Branch in developing methods of undercover financing

both in the United States and throughout the world.... It is worthy of note that no OSS mission was ever cancelled due to the lack of proper funds previously screened for safe use.... The money used by an agent was potentially one of the most vulnerable points in his cover. It constituted the one commodity which he was forced constantly to use and which was inevitably subject to close scrutiny. The Germans were fully aware of this fact and used this knowledge in endeavors to detect and neutralize Allied espionage and subversive activities in territories which they controlled. Their methods of financial tracing by marking money, recording serial numbers, issuing special notes and withdrawing entire currency issues from circulation were continually subject to refinement. Further, they influenced the promulgation by satellite or subject governments of various financial regulations designed to trap Allied agents.... The record with regard to the financing of OSS agents was impressive. Every OSS operation which resulted in an agent capture was carefully investigated to ascertain whether improper funds were in any way responsible. No statement of the success or failure of Special Funds in this regard can be categorical, since several agents were lost without trace. However, as of August 1945, no case had been found of an OSS agent who was captured due to the fact that he had been supplied with insecure funds.

This last is a very considerable claim to make—and one that illustrates just how deadly the game was in those days. While it is perfectly true that comparisons are odious—after all, the British were playing the game on a much grander scale than the Americans, at least until September of 1944, and had played it much longer under much more difficult circumstances—there seems no doubt that this is one claim neither SIS or SOE would make.

But what was this extraordinary organization that sprang, virtually, out of clubby conversations between Donovan and Sir Stewart Menzies, the chief of SIS from 1939 until 1945, and Colin Gubbins, the chief of SOE? It was a little bit of everything to be found in London—secret intelligence, sabotage, guerrilla warfare, political warfare, deception, cryptanalysis, special forces, irregular maritime warfare, playing double agents, technical intelligence of various kinds. In reality, the British system was better, and more effective, although this may have been mitigated by the intense and bitter rivalry that marked interservice relationships in England. There, it was Hobbes' war. Donovan's organization was too big for comfort, too big for safety, and its size was a monument to his own ambitions and salesmanship. In the end, of course, it collapsed into several fragments, all interdependent but separated by staff, geography, finance, even politics. Nor did Donovan escape the bitter rivalry that marked the English services' relationships; Donovan's worst enemies in Washington were two, and in the end they got him. The first was General George V. Strong, the army chief of intelligence, and the second was the ubiquitous J. Edgar Hoover, whose FBI was responsible for "the active pursuit and liquidation of the enemy intelligence services in the zone of the interior"— which meant the United States. Strong thought that Donovan was a gamekeeper turned poacher, which was fairly accurate; and Hoover wanted no agents at work in the United States unless they were under *his* control—no matter which nation they worked for.

OSS, which began with a few men wandering uncertainly about the Library of Congress looking for remote documentation about such places as Aquitaine, Istria and Transylvania, reached the peak of its strength in December 1944, when it employed some 13,000 people, 5,500 of whom were to be found at headquarters in Washington. In general, this work force may be called "high grade personnel," and it is therefore important to establish how effective they were, especially in the area of secret intelligence (SI). Two factors seem to have been always present to prevent OSS from flowering fully—the British and Ultra. In every theater of the world, OSS encountered varying degrees of trouble with the British. At the top relations were unusually warm and close, with OSS executives to be found dining at special tables in the St. James's clubs, in the boxes of SIS chiefs at the theater, at the hunt, on the grouse moors, at dazzling little dinner parties in Belgravia and Mayfair, on the Avon and the Test. The trouble lay on the middle rungs and just below the top, where OSS officers soon perceived that SIS was not only a military instrument but also one fashioned to serve Britain's interests—especially the preservation of the British Empire. They found the British masters at the art of committee work and were being outwitted constantly, as this letter by General Albert C. Wedemeyer, one of the intellectuals of the U.S. Army, demonstrates:

> They swarmed down upon us like locusts with a plentiful supply of planners and various other assistants with prepared plans to insure that they not only accomplished their purpose but did so in stride and with fair promise of continuing in their role of directing strategically the course of this war. I have the greatest admiration for them...and if I were a Britisher I would feel very proud. However, as an American I wish that we might be

more glib and better organized to cope with these super negotiators. From a worm's viewpoint it was apparent that we were confronted by generations and generations of experience in committee work and in rationalizing points of view. They had us on the defensive practically the whole time...we came, we listened and we were conquered.

The purpose of much of this maneuvering was, of course, to obtain the moral and actual support of America in the task of preserving the British Empire when the last trumpet sounded—especially in such places as Egypt, Africa, India, Burma and Southeast Asia. It did not take the Americans very long to realize what the game was all about; and in the field OSS agents began actively to conspire against British rule, especially in India. In turn, this led to considerable friction with the British. The younger OSS officer, usually a man with too little experience to envision what the postwar world would be like without the empire, to perceive who would try to fill the vacuum left behind if Britain was forced to abdicate as a world power, evinced quite definite fits of Anglophobia. This Anglophobia was particularly important in London, where OSS had its main base overseas.

OSS, SO and X-2 worked closely with the British at all times, and apparently harmoniously, at least until OSS came into its own in Europe after September 1, 1944, when American military power began to dominate operations. The friction came mainly in the sphere of secret intelligence (SI).

The British argued that SI should come under their control to avoid wasting resources, to prevent the accidental blowing of agents, and to assure maximum coverage of necessary targets. They asserted that SIS was the more experienced of the organizations, they had more agents in place, and they already controlled the apparatus for infiltrating and exfiltrating agents and for communications. Donovan, in September 1943, perhaps shocked by the massive collapse of the French resistance nets around Paris through a clumsy strategic deception scheme in which the French were used as pawns, rejected this viewpoint very unceremoniously. The British proposals for "coordination" of SIS-SI operations meant "control," and he warned that: "Physical circumstances permit the British to exercise complete control over United States intelligence. . . . The habit of control has grown up with them...through their relations with refugee Governments and refugee intelligence services....We are not a refugee government." He conceded the necessity of having SOE and SO cooperating in field operations, and indeed at headquarters, but he successfully rejected SIS blandishments with the words: "But the attempt of the British...to subordinate and control the American intelligence and counter-intelligence service is short-sighted and dangerous."

On 27 October 1943, the U.S. Joint Chiefs of Staff acted upon Donovan's recommendation and gave OSS full and unqualified authority to conduct SI. It may be said that this date and this decision marked the point at which the CIA concept was born—a worldwide intelligence service devoted solely to serving the interests of the American government and people. On that date, so to speak, OSS left school and went out into the wide, wide world to fend for itself.

SI now came to its second stumbling block—Ultra. With the penetration by the British of the German Enigma machine-cipher system in its military, air, naval and secret intelligence modes, conventional spying was compelled to take second place in the business of acquiring intelligence about the enemy. Ultra was so uniformly successful, so quick, and so reliable, especially when related to other forms of intelligence such as the "Y" wireless traffic analysis and HF/DF, that it could do the job of informing the Allied high command about what the enemy was up to far faster and more reliably than any spy. Consequently, British agents overseas were able to spend a great deal of time on two types of intelligence operations which were important to the success of the invasion— the "active pursuit and liquidation" of the enemy intelligence services, to prevent those organizations from learning the secrets of the invasion, and to sow the thousands of fragments of deceptive information which, when assembled by the enemy high command, presented Hitler and his General Staff with a logical and plausible —but wholly wrong—picture of Allied intentions.

By the end of the year 1943, the British had become so expert at these games—games that Lawrence of Arabia once called the "witty hors d'oeuvre before the main battle"—that OSS/SI found itself being overshadowed in London in all three types of intelligence activity. This, of course, was expected: the British had had an intelligence service for centuries and, in its modern form, SIS was at least 30 years old; OSS was only 30 months old.

However, once Eisenhower took command and the Americans became responsible for their own intelligence and counterespionage, they began with surprising speed to overtake the British at the game, although they never quite obtained a parity of reputation. Happily, after September 1944, when OSS got a larger share of the game in Europe, relations settled down to one of amicable support. The enemy intelligence services were pursued and liquidated and the basis of the postwar intelligence alliance between England and America was cemented so effectively that it was able, after a brief period of hand-wringing, to withstand such shocks as Fuchs and Philby. Contrary to popular belief, this alliance was super-successful against the Russians and their intelligence allies.

Something needs to be said about X-2. This U.S. counterintelligence organization barely existed when OSS grew out of COI in June 1942. The essence of successful counterespionage work is a good central registry. This America did not have, although the FBI registry on hostile and subversive organizations and individuals in the United States and associated territories was very comprehensive. The importance of the files is self-evident. Whereas secret intelligence is of value only so long as it is "hot," counterintelligence files have a perennial use. Hostile agents have been known to slip into countries and lay low for years before emerging to burrow away at the keel of the ship of state. By the end of the war, therefore, X-2 had 400,000 carded names on file—men, women, even children (the Hitlerjugend is a case in point) who might one day again be dangerous. These cards, obtained in large part from the British, but also from the German records, retained their value after the war. Nobody could be sure that the German intelligence services had not merely gone to ground and would sometime in the future emerge to trouble the world again. As the Report puts it: "These files did not lose their value at the conclusion of a given operation, or of a war. Individuals or relationships which have seemed dormant for a long period may become active again and provide the key to detection of widespread intelligence activities."

OSS engaged in a third area of clandestinity on a wide and successful scale throughout the world. This was SO—special operations. As the maps in this volume will show, England and America were engaged in SO on a gigantic scale at D-Day, primarily to delay the German build-up while the armies of America, Britain and Canada were consolidating their bridgehead and building up for the breakout. The War Report describes this dangerous activity, but does not always capture the *spirit* of the times. This, of course, was almost as remarkable as the courage of the participants; and it should be recorded in the words of one of the men who dropped in behind German lines. Although it is referred to in the body of the War Report, I have selected the report of Jedburgh team Giles from my own files, not because the prose is in any way unusual, nor because the exploits demand space. The main reason why I selected Giles to illustrate SO is that the team was a true Jed —it was composed, as it was intended, of an American, a Briton and a Frenchman.

Jed team Giles consisted of Captain B.M.W. Knox, the American; Captain Paul Lebel, the Frenchman (who had been very badly wounded in action in North Africa); and Sergeant Gordon H. Tack, the Englishman (Giles' wireless operator). They were all under thirty, and their mission was to parachute into France and raise and supply an army of Bretons in the area of Finistère. Their mission instructions directed that they were not to engage in open warfare with the German army in Brittany until they heard the BBC broadcast this signal at a prearranged hour: "Le chapeau de Napoléon, est-il toujours à Perros-Guirec?" When they heard their signal, they were to emerge from the shadows and, with their maquisards, help secure the approaches to the great port of Brest. While awaiting an aircraft at Langham Place in west London—it was a memorable wait because somebody left the party a demijohn of rum—they heard who their opponents would be in Brittany: the 2nd Parachute Division, which included a strong cadre of the Hitlerjugend, and which had arrived for rest and reformation after heavy fighting in Russia.

The Drop, July 8/9, 1944. The jumping order was Knox-Tack-Lebel. The pilot (of the USAAF Liberator) reported seeing the lights about 0100 hours and the hole was opened. For the next twenty minutes we circled round trying to find the lights again but since we had agreed with the pilot that he would drop us blind if necessary, we were not too worried, as we were going to get out anyway. Finally he saw the lights, and dropped us in as good a run-in as I have ever seen. Knox and Tack landed fairly close together—Captain Lebel joined us after two or three minutes. We were welcomed immediately by a group of very excited, very young Frenchmen, all of whom we had to kiss in turn.

They were met by the chief of the R(eception) C(ommittee), M. Arzel on a meadow near les Trois Chapelles between Briec and Laz. Arzel explained that the FFI (Free French) in Finistere was "rather disorganized as a result of the capture and execution of twelve of their leaders during the previous week." They learned that the Germans had ordered that all unauthorized males between 16 and 60 found on the streets at any hour would be shot on sight. Males of any age who had a *laissez-passer* were compelled to walk on the streets with their hands on their heads, or with both hands on the handlebars of their cycles. The passage of all motor transport was forbidden except to those with a *laissez-passer,* and any one caught in charge of a motor vehicle after dark was liable to be shot on the spot. In some areas of Brittany, the Germans were raiding houses and confiscating all men's boots and shoes. All farms found to be housing people who were not members of the family, or who did not carry correct identification documents, were burned to the ground, the menfolk shot along with the guests.

Meanwhile the RC had been gathering up the [arms and supplies] containers [which had been dropped with Giles], and we were just preparing to break out our rucksacks and move off in true Jedburgh style, groaning under the weight of pack, weapons, and wireless set, when we noticed three cars and a large truck. This maquis [the French word for guerrilla, derived from the dense undergrowth of the Corsican hills], it seemed, was motorized. They loaded the containers onto the trucks, chutes and all, and about 4:30 in the morning the convoy moved off, German rifles sticking out of all the windows, in the direction of Chateauneuf. We kept to the back roads, but the three of us were not a little worried, especially by the truck, which made as much noise as a Sherman tank.... The last part of the journey was done in broad daylight. The maquis, when we finally reached it, turned out to be a group of approximately fifty men, living in a small wood about three kms. west of the village of Laz.

Between 9 July and the 12th, Giles unpacked and distributed the arms, stripping the Stens, carbines and Brens of a thick antirust grease called cosmoline, broke out the ammunition, and showed the maquisards how to clean and use their weapons. Legal, the short, strong, taciturn second-in-command of the maquis, went into Chateauneuf to call out fifty more men to complete Giles' company. "We were very happy," wrote Giles in the after-action report, as if they were characters out of *For Whom the Bell Tolls.* "And we were very busy." They listened on their hand-cranked Jed wireless set to the BBC to see whether London had any messages for them. This service was at once the simplest and most secure form of communication between an agent's controller and the agent in the field. The messages sounded like gibberish. "The rhubarb is excellent at Perignan" meant to the agent that he was to blow the railway lines at Lyon. "The cat has two heads" could mean that an agent was to proceed to a rendezvous in the station at Beauvais to meet an incoming agent. "Howard embraces Juliette" might mean that agent Gingembre would be landing that night at Paray-le-Monial. The import of the *messages personnels*—as they were called in the clandestine services—was known only to the agent and his controller.

That afternoon we listened to the BBC messages, and heard the message which had warned the Breton maquis that we were arriving. It was "La lune brille sur le dolmen" and in this case it meant that a supply aircraft would be over the D[rop] Z[one] we had used to land to bring us in more containers of arms and ammunition. We were rather worried at the prospect of going back to the same DZ because we suspected that the ground might have been blown, in which case the Boche might be waiting for us. How we got away with this second reception I shall never know. It was a much heavier load this time, the men were exhausted—and we were still loading containers on the truck when daylight came. We finally got away, and safely back to the CP. We found out later that morning that the ground had been blown and that 300 German paratroops had arrived in Laz five minutes after we had gone through and that they were searching all the farms in the area. We sent this information off to London by pigeon, since we were afraid to use our wireless on the grounds that the paratroops might have a D[irection] F[inding] car with them. The pigeons had been parachuted all over the area the night before. This message apparently never reached its destination. The paratroops didn't find us, and during the course of the day we armed another maquis which was based on the woods around Plessis, to the east of Laz.

The two most dangerous moments in the life of an agent were at the DZ and while transmitting. Safety depended on absolute silence, but the noise of the aircraft engines on a dark, still night made it almost impossible for the Germans—and the French not in the maquis—not to know that "une parachutage"—as a supply drop was called—was afoot. Both Germans and French would then hurry towards the light cast by the bonfires lit to guide the planes in. What was more, the noise of the maquisards working was often enough to wake the dead. "There was nothing either quiet or clandestine about my first parachutage," wrote one Jedburgh officer.

Once the containers were released from the aircraft there was considerable drama. The local Maquis chief began the proceedings by shouting, "Attention everyone, the bidons [containers] descend." Everyone present repeated this, adding advice to Bobo or Alphonse or Pierre, or whoever was nearest, to "have a care that the sacred bidons do not crush thee." Once the con-

tainers had landed the parachute stakes were on. The winner
was whoever could roll and hide away the most parachutes
before being spotted by someone else. The bullock carts then
came up with much encouragement from the drivers such as
"But come, my old one, to the bidons advance." Then began the
preliminary discussions as to how the first container would be
hoisted on to the cart and who should have the honour of com-
mencing. I found I had to go through the actions of beginning to
hoist one end myself before, with loud cries of "But no, my captain, permit," or, for example, "My captain, what an affair!"
would my helpers then get on with the job. Once, however, the
drill of clearing the DZ was understood these helpers were of
the very greatest value and we succeeded one night in clearing
the DZ in 70 minutes. This was very good as it included four
containers that had fallen in trees.

The report of Jed team Giles continued:

> ...the heads of the different maquis of Finistere started to
> come in to our HQ....So many men came in that we got to
> repeating our lecture on Reception Committees in our sleep.
> During this period we organized, and sent off to London, the
> following grounds [for supplying dropping]: Poire, Cerise,
> Framboise, Orange, Abricot, Raisin, Amande. All of them
> were served. On July 12th we were visited by the FFI chief of
> Finistere, Lieutenant Colonel Berthaud...we had to shoot one
> of the men in his car, who was a known Gestapo agent. We
> decided, in view of this, and several other indiscreet actions of
> Berthaud's, to have as indirect a liaison as possible with him.

The trouble about the French resistance was that it was indiscreet—and often dangerously and criminally so. As Ben Cow-
burn, an SOE agent who spent more time in France than almost
any other agent, reported afterwards, "Security in France was nil,
and 95 per cent of the people arrested, were caught simply because
their friends had been incapable of keeping their mouths shut."
One of the French leaders who could be trusted was the indomita-
ble Le Manchot, the one-armed man, who was the commander of
the Battalion of Heaven, the French *paras* who came just after
midnight on D-Day to help the Bretons form an army amid the
strange, prehistoric dolmens on the moors. The Germans put a
million marks on his head, dead or alive, and arrested every one-
armed man in Brittany in the hope of scooping him up. There is
this record of a Joan-Eleanor phone conversation between Le

Manchot, hiding in the shadow of a menhir, and an intelligence officer in a bomber overhead:

> *Fleuriot:* What type of MG do you want?
> *Le Manchot:* Heavy ones, Brownings. Send any stuff you can, and biscuits.
> *Fleuriot:* 890 containers have been dropped in the past three nights. How many did you receive?
> *Le Manchot:* About 100 received.
> *Fleuriot:* Do you want more jeeps? If so, must have glider DZ.
> *Le Manchot:* Yes. DZ will be present one.
> *Fleuriot:* Can you raise more maquis if arms available?
> *Le Manchot:* Always.
> *Fleuriot:* Are you employing Russians? What are their approx numbers?
> *Le Manchot:* Rather sleepy at the moment. One thousand.
> *Fleuriot:* Pilots report too many lights on your DZ. These lights must be controlled as they lead to inaccurate dropping.
> *Le Manchot:* You tell your pilots.... [sentence unfinished]. Has one the intention of using forces in a full-scale operation? If so, it must be soon.
> *Fleuriot:* You will be advised. Goodnight, commandant.
> *Le Manchot:* [No reply.]

Here, in this short conversation, conducted by fitful moonlight as night fighters prowled amongst the clouds and German cavalrymen beat the bush of the moors, was the world of the clandestine in capsule. As for the Germans, they were deeply worried, as a Radio Paris broadcast showed. The announcer warned to beware of the flood of agents pouring into Brittany. These agents were

> provocateurs...who, though outwardly polite and expressing love for our country, may be members of the [British] Intelligence Service....We all remember Colonel Lawrence [of Arabia]. Who knows but that this man Lawrence, who was reputed to have been killed in a motor-cycle accident, is still wandering about the world. In any case, a large number of lesser Lawrences have descended...like a plague of locusts.

Jed team Giles further reported:

> One evening as we listened to the BBC and checked off our messages we heard "Fifi a une bouche en cerise"—a message which we had been expecting for a long time. But it continued—

Fifi recevra la visite de neuf amis ce cois [sic]. So one of us had to go [to the DZ], and in a car, it was much too far to walk. Captain Lebel went in the end, and we received Jed teams Horace and Hilary, as well as three French parachutist officers —Equation, Egalité and Equivalence. So now all five [Jed] teams were working in Finistère. We were joined about this time by a Canadian pilot, Flight Lieutenant Brown, who had been shot down over Brest, and was wandering through Brittany. [It was all like getting onto or off a bus.]

While at Lennon we finally organized the medical service which was to save so many lives during the operations to come.... During the whole of this period we were organizing arms drops on an ever-increasing scale. How we managed to get them all over without German interference I shall never understand.

The sheer flatness of Giles' prose is startling. Only a trained clandestine, only a man who had been playing the game for a very long time, only a man who understood men and danger, could have written such mundane words. There was none of the lyricism of Lawrence, none of the majesty of St. Exupery. Yet it was a murderous game played out in a queerly Celtic world of Breton moors, pollarded oaks, the *patrons* and *pardons,* the legends of Merlin and Viviane, Tristan and Iseult, the Grail, the town of Ys. Colin Ogden-Smith had been murdered and the Germans had found in his pockets a map marked with the DZs—Pêche, Poire, Pomme, Framboise, Amande, Raisin, Orange, Ananas, Groseille, Cerise, Prunelle, Mandarine, Noix. Marienne had been caught and murdered by the 2nd Paras, and the Sicherheitsidenst was now trying to play wireless games with his one-time pad. Jed team Horace had infiltrated Brest, hidden in wine casks on the back of an old gazogene truck; Jed team George had managed to get down to the Loire, hidden under wire cages of chickens, and they were ridden with fleas and chicken droppings. Jed team Frederick had seen two agents, a man and a woman, daggered and shot respectively when it was discovered that they were German CI agents. At Samwest redoubt, built up on the Breton moors from England and supplied by air, two German paratroop officers stopped at the kitchen of a farmhouse to ask the way: the answer one of them got was "five slugs in the belly." Meunier was dead—his rucksack, laden with grenades and *plastique,* exploded when it hit the ground hard. Botella's thigh was broken, Litzler was mortally wounded in the chest, the Germans put Ruelle and Tanjin into a farmhouse, set fire to the thatch, and burned them alive. Le Manchot was missing.

Chenaille was hiding on the moors. Squadron Leader Smith was
hiding in a charcoal pit. Carre was killed at Cruguel. Jordan lost
his wireless set and ciphers—leaving London wide open to a wireless game.

Giles directed that *iron discipline* be enforced. Nobody was to go
to farmhouses to ask for food without permission. Men must
march on the verge and not on the road. Silence and disaction were
to be enforced until the *ratissage*—literally rat-hunt, the clandestine's jargon for a man-hunt—was over. Don't carry detonators in
the same rucksack as the *plastique*. Never hesitate to march that
extra mile to avoid a village about which you have no information.
It's better to sleep in a ditch than to be wakened in bed at four in
the morning by the Gestapo. Only ask help of the peasants; avoid
refugees like the plague. Avoid letting yourself be seen, let alone
spoken to by children, who always talk. These peasants never trust
even their own children for this sort of work. Pay well for what you
take from farms. Never talk politics. Don't hesitate to change into
plain clothes to carry out a task if it offers advantages. If you are
captured you are shot however you are dressed. Beware of cider—
it is stronger than you think—and still more of Calvados, also
called *la goutte* or *le fort*. It will often be put before you, but you
must remember how much you need to keep your head clear. Find
boots and shoes; when on the march sabots are tiring—and noisy.

This was the stuff of clandestinity in Brittany as Jed team Giles
was forced on to the run ever higher and deeper into the wild
moorlands around Chateauneuf. Some of the maquisards began to
drop out as the straw soles they had tied to their feet as makeshift
shoes began to fall apart. Back in England, a storesman was making up a container for Frederick, who had called urgently for army
boots. The quartermaster had misunderstood the three-letter code
for boots and so, mystified, the storesman was filling the container
with sanitary towels. Jed team Giles' report went on:

Hunted. That morning we learned that German paratroopers
had arrived at Lennon, and were searching the whole area. We
put out posts in position to observe the Pleyben-Chateauneuf
road, where the first signs of German concentration against our
new position would be visible. That afternoon we learned that
five men from our maquis who were passing near Lennon on a
mission to get food, had been captured by the *Feldgendarmerie*.
One of them was a radio operator, who had been working with
Sgt. Tack.... As we crossed the canal we saw many more flares
ahead of us—the Boche seemed to be holding the whole line of
the canal. Just after we crossed the bridge we heard machine

gun and rifle fire behind us. We made a forced march for two miles and then sat down to rest. . . . The men dropped off behind us one by one, and when we arrived at about 0700 hours there were only 8 of us left. The others had been unable to stand the pace, and had hidden in barns along the road. This incident shows the defects of these troops. They had no physical stamina, and once separated from their real leaders, they disintegrated.

As Knox and team Giles went on the run from hamlet to hamlet, General Omar N. Bradley, commanding the U.S. First Army in Normandy, prepared his divisions and corps for the mighty breakout operation that would liberate most of western Europe. The army struck out of the dawn mist on 26 July 1944, behind one of the greatest rolling artillery barrages of the war. The *feldgrau* fought like demons; but soon the German commander-in-chief was reporting to Hilter that his front was *"eine Riesensauerei"*—one hell of a mess. Bradley's plan began to take shape: his armor was to seize the charming old town of Avranches at the junction of the Norman and Breton peninsulas. One part of the army was then to turn east towards Le Mans while another was to turn west towards and take the great port of Brest. Brest would then be used as the port of entry for the divisions coming in from the United States for the march to Berlin. The key to the movement of the army towards Brest was the great viaduct at Morlaix. This was in the hands of Le Manchot's Battalion of Heaven. But if the German paratroopers succeeded in retaking and blowing it, the American armor would be stranded on the wrong side of a deep, wide river gorge. Jed team Giles and their companies of maquisards had a part to play in preventing the 2nd Para from getting to the bridge. Knox had succeeded in re-forming and re-disciplining his maquis, and now—in the last days of July 1944—it consisted of about 2,000 armed and fairly dependable men. But first they had to get rid of the source of their trouble, the German observer post on the roof of the Chateau de Trévarez.

Our position, and all the surrounding countryside, was dominated by the Chateau de Trévarez, which was occupied by a German garrison, who maintained an observation service from the roof. In view of the German concentration [of paratroopers, the maquisards' sworn enemies] we could not overlook the possibility that we might be forced to move by day, and in that event we would be watched from the chateau. We therefore asked London to bombard it. On the 30th of July, early in the morning, it was dive-bombed by three RAF planes. We learned afterwards that the whole population of Chateauneuf had run out of church to watch the proceedings. The chief of the *Feldgendarmerie* of Chateauneuf, Albert Ehrharot, had promised the citizens that there would be a surprise for them before Sunday. He hadn't expected this one. The whole population was jubilant. The Germans had put on a huge party the night before, and had been caught, quite literally, with their pants down. The number of dead was kept a closely-guarded secret, but when we occupied the chateau ten days later, there were still quite a lot of them under the ruins. We could smell them. On July 31st in view of renewed German activity in the areas we moved again, this time back to our old haunts, west of Laz, to the village of Plessis.

General George S. Patton, commanding the U.S. Third Army, often directing traffic himself, managed to get seven divisions across the two-lane bridge at Pontaubault in six days. The weather turned hot and dry—tanker's weather. One division shot across the moors and took Rennes, thereby cutting Brittany off from the rest of France. Now General Robert W. Grow, commanding the U.S. 6th Armored Division, received orders to run the 200 miles to Brest and take the port. The two main roads—the one through Morlaix and the Rennes-Brest highway—were partly under Jed, maquis or Special Air Service (SAS) control. All bridges were guarded by counter-scorching missions—missions to prevent the Germans from blowing these important structures to slow the American advance. London had poured Jeds and SAS parties into the peninsula: Samwest, Dingson, Lost, Grog, Horace, Hilary, Felix, Giles, Gilbert, Francis, Gerald, Guy, Gavin, Wash. Some 30,000 Bretons were armed, another 50,000 carried grenades or acted as couriers and guides. All waited for the London order to rise and strike—Le chapeau de Napoléon, est-il toujours à Perros-Guirec?

Plessis. This was to be the HQ from which we carried on the attack on the 2nd Parachutists Division. We did not leave it, until central Finisterre was liberated from the Boche. Our first move was to carry out a reconnaissance in the grounds of the chateau—in the course of which seventeen Germans were killed. The Germans evacuated the ruins the next day. On 2 August we received a message from Capt. Lezachmeur telling us of the death of Major Ogden-Smith. We sent a message to London cancelling all his grounds, since the Germans had found papers on his body. Meanwhile our arms drops continued. From Plessis we organised the drops on Groseille, Noisette,

Noix, Ananas, Prune, Mandarine, Fraise, Ananas. Ground Ananas was almost in our backyard—we had two battalions around it, and we intended to fight instead of moving if we were attacked. We had one drop on it on 1 August, and, since we expected four planes, we prepared fires, for the reception. On this particular occasion, many of the local peasants had asked to be allowed to come to the *parachutage*. To their surprise, and ours, the *parachutage* took the form of a strafing attack by a JU 88, armed with four cannon. We could not get the fires out in time, and the German plane was able to make two runs. Luckily, there were no casualties.

The German 2nd Paras began moving towards the Morlaix viaduct between 31 July and 2 August. As Knox was debating whether to come out into the open and attack—something he had been forbidden to do until he got the Chapeau signal from London—one of the great moments occurred in modern French history. Preceded by the SAS iodoform *Lillibulero*—a piece of music played by the BBC to warn the field that an SAS message was about to be broadcast—there came the electrifying signal from London. *"Le ... chapeau ... de ... Napoleon ... est-il ... toujours ... a ... Perros-Guirec? Je vous dit encore, Le-Chap-eau-de-Napoléon,est-il-toujours-à-Perros-Guirec?"* It was the signal for which the entire Allied secret apparatus in France had waited for five years. It was the signal for a national insurrection to begin in Brittany—the first major rural insurrection since the Chouans rose against the Bonapartists at the end of the French Revolution. Knox was ready.

On August 2nd we learned that the *Zwerte Fallschirnjager* [sic] Division was on the move from its base in the Chateaulin area eastward along the road to Carhaix. They were on foot, on bicycles and in horse-drawn carts. We were very much tempted to attack them, but this would have been contrary to our orders. But that afternoon we heard the message we had so long been waiting for—and the attack on the 2nd Paratroop Division began. We had seven companies in position along the main road, and they were immediately given orders to begin harassing attacks on the 2nd Division. In order to get instructions to the companies north of the road, we had to send armed groups in cars to rush across, firing and throwing grenades. Most of them got across, but in one of the expeditions, the young brother of Legal was killed. The head of the division was already in Carhaix, and in order to prevent any more of them getting through we destroyed the bridge near Laneblau. This was accompanied by a large-scale ambush which forced the Germans to leave the road and strike into the countryside. After two days of attack all along the road, the division turned back, concentrating in villages between Pleyben and Chateaulin. The advance guard stayed in Carhaix.

Now came the retribution.

In the course of these attacks a considerable number of prisoners was taken. Captain Knox together with Legal interrogated them. They were all from the 2nd Paratroop Division, and all of them Hitlerites to a man. They admitted to the atrocities they had committed, refused to believe the Americans had taken Rennes, refused to discuss the Hitler regime, and refused to explain why they had French jewellery, money and identity cards on them. They were all very young (one of the worst was only 17) and they were all subsequently shot by [the maquisards]. Even if we had wished to prevent this shooting, we would have been powerless—these men had burned farms and farmers with their wives and children all the way along the road.

Three days later, the first jeeps carrying American and British intelligence teams arrived at Knox's headquarters. The Shermans followed. The bridge was held at Morlaix, and the march on Brest was not stopped. It had been a brave and masterful minor action. The guerrilla war was not yet over, any more than was the main battle. But Knox and his maquisards—men trained, formed and armed by SOE/SO—had won. Knox stayed with his maquis for another month or so, cleaning out stay-behinds and snipers, and then received orders to return to London. As they loaded their jeep, Legal's *Groupes Mobiles d'Attaque* marched up. They formed ranks around the jeep and, in the ragged manner of partisans the world over, presented arms. Then Legal, the Communist, stepped forward and, quite forgetting that Knox was an American, delivered a little speech:

We regret that it was not possible to do more and do better. The lack of matériel, a certain amount of incohesion and some petty political rivalries were our handicap. Nevertheless it was with great joy that we acclaimed [you as] the first parachutists [to come to our area] and we tried to give of our very best in assisting [you] to hunt the common enemy, "the Boches." We can never thank you sufficiently for what you have done for us and the liberation of our country. Furthermore, we regret deeply that certain untoward incidents cause a shadow on those happy days. No doubt they will be smoothed out in the near future. That is our most fervent desire, the desire of our Frenchmen of the "resistance" who are your comrades of days gone by as well as of the future. To His Britannic Majesty, to you Sir, and to your proud warriors who were our liberators and our comrades, I and my fellow Frenchmen of the Resistance send our sincere thanks and best wishes for the good fortune and prosperity of your country—which we consider, a little, our own.

But perhaps Legal was not so wrong in forgetting that Knox was American. The one matter of enduring importance was that, for once in their history, the Anglo-Saxons stood up and fought together almost as a single nation. It was therefore inevitable that they should win. And Jed team Giles, in miniature, was the history of OSS, MI-6 and SOE.

The editor is grateful to Dr. Andor Klay, who was Donovan's aide, and Dr. B.M.W. Knox, who was a Jedburgh and then the leader of a special mission to the partisans in Italy, for their advice and cooperation in the preparation of this work. I am also grateful to William H. Cunliffe and John E. Taylor, of Modern Military Records, National Archives, Washington, D.C., for their guidance concerning OSS documents. The publishers are indebted to Brigadier General Robert Gaynor, an expert on military decorations and insignia, Angus McLean Thuermer of the Central Intelligence Agency, and Charles B. MacDonald, of the Center for Military History, Washington, D.C., for their cooperation in regard to the art work. Thanks must also be accorded J.W. Ewing, the U.S. Army staff curator, and his assistant, Norman M. Carey, Jr., for their help regarding the Goering regalia which appears on the cover of this volume.

WASHINGTON, D.C.   ANTHONY CAVE BROWN
May 1976

A NOTE BY KERMIT ROOSEVELT

This Report of the operations of the Office of Strategic Services has been prepared at the request of Admiral William D. Leahy on the behalf of the Joint Chiefs of Staff.

Admiral Leahy's memorandum dated 26 July 1946 observed that there was in existence "no comprehensive official war record of the operations of the Office of Strategic Services in the field of intelligence research and coordination, clandestine intelligence procurement, counter-espionage, sabotage, guerrilla warfare and psychological para-military operations." During the existence of OSS preparation of a comprehensive history had been begun. To complete it upon the scale at which it started would have required a large staff and many years, and the project was discontinued upon the liquidation of OSS in October 1945. Accordingly, it was directed that a small staff be assigned in the Strategic Services Unit to prepare an official war record within the space of approximately six months.

The terms of this assignment automatically placed certain limitations upon the nature of the Report. It could not be a detailed account of every project undertaken, every operation mounted or every administrative change made by OSS. Rather, it must present a selection of typical or especially significant operations and activities through which might be given an accurate general picture of the work of the organization.

In making such a selection there was danger that, by inclusion of a high percentage of spectacularly successful operations and the neglect of many less interesting or less successful operations, a false picture would be given. We have sought to avoid this danger as far as possible by a critical commentary which places the operations described in the context of the whole, and by the selection of a certain number of operations which indicate the failures made by OSS.

Selection, then, was governed by two principles: (1) that continuing security interests be not endangered, and (2) that the incident be sufficiently important in itself or as an illustration of the nature of OSS activities to warrant its inclusion.

The Director of OSS and certain individuals who played an important personal role in the establishment of the Office of the Coordinator of Information (the predecessor of OSS), are mentioned by name [in the early part of the Report]. Otherwise, names have not been used in this Report. It is recognized that the inclusion of names would have added a certain interest to the text. Other considerations were felt to outweigh this advantage. First was the matter of length; it would have been difficult to draw the line at which anonymity should prevail. Time and space would have been occupied which, in view of the limitations upon both, did not seem justified in an official classified report. There were also problems of security to be considered. Finally, it was felt that objectivity in tone would be better attained by the elimination of personalities wherever possible.

This Report recounts the genesis and development of a new organization performing functions which were in many cases foreign to American thought and experience, even to American instinct. The purpose of COI-OSS as originally conceived was to conduct propaganda, collect and analyze intelligence, and, in the event of war, wage unorthodox warfare in support of the armed forces. Such unorthodox warfare would include not only propaganda and intelligence but also sabotage, morale and physical subversion, guerrilla activities and development and support of underground and resistance groups.

War came five months after the new organization had been established. This naturally produced a change of emphasis resulting from the urgency of military needs. The necessarily slow development of deep cover penetration which characterizes classic peacetime intelligence methods had to yield to rapid procurement of intelligence of immediate use to the armed forces. Infiltration of the enemy homeland by individual saboteurs which might never succeed (particularly in view of the haste in which they would have had to be planned) was obviously less important to theater commanders than support of resistance groups already operating in areas where the Allies were soon to land.

The coming of war also impressed upon responsible officials the need for a counter-espionage service to perform a task the nature and scope of which were new to American history.

Propaganda, too, is subject to different urgencies once war has begun. Propaganda of ideas, in which truth should be the weapon and conversion the objective, must make room for "black" propaganda which, through judicious mixture of rumor and deception with truth as a bait, fosters disunity and confusion to support military operations. Half a year after Pearl Harbor the original propaganda function of COI was removed; the adjustment of the early concept of the COI-OSS task to this change was a difficult one.

Even apart from its field operations, OSS was a peculiarly complex and many-sided organization. The modifications and adaptations which were necessary to meet the varying circumstances of war—both in theaters of operation and at the political center where strategy was decided—complicate the problem of simplified exposition. [Deletion]

The [early] section [of this Report] takes up first, as a separate unit, the account of COI as an executive agency, and of the events leading to its dissolution. Thereafter, the establishment of OSS and its development under the JCS is described. The conflict and complications which attended the definition of its functions and the general acceptance of its status form the main topic of this section. The process of definition was affected by both external and internal factors, resulting in the establishment of functional branches and the welding of these branches into an effective whole.

Once the Washington organization had become established and accepted, its role was largely that of servicing its overseas bases and its Washington "customers." These apparently separate tasks were actually closely related. OSS could not service such authorities as the White House, the Joint Chiefs of Staff, State, War and Navy Departments, unless its outposts had strong support from the highest U.S. authorities in the field—theater commands or embassies. Such support in turn depended to a great extent upon recognition in Washington of the value of OSS services. [Deletion]

The most extensive intelligence networks were set up in France and Italy. Partisan forces in both countries, supplied in large measure by OSS, and assisted by OSS personnel, inflicted serious losses upon the Germans and diverted forces which would otherwise have been used against the Allied armies.

The pressing requirements of theater commands for intelligence from areas of imminent military operations and support to resistance groups in those areas meant that it was not until the Allies approached the German borders that direct penetration of Germany was undertaken by OSS or British services on any appreciable scale.

The basic reason for the lack of a greater number of OSS agents operating in Germany, was the refusal of the British to permit American agents in late 1942 and early 1943 to be sent from England to that area. This is understandable. British intelligence was concerned with the protection of the home front. It had perfected its counter-espionage organization so that Nazi agents had great difficulty in penetrating its security. Officials did not wish to risk the possible infiltration of agents dropped into Germany from

England, who, through capture or by initial purpose might disclose information to the enemy.

A few OSS representatives in strategic centers conducted indirect penetrations of Germany and produced some of the most valuable intelligence of the war.

In many cases the theoretical conception of OSS methods of operation was altered by the exigencies of the situation and the requirements of military strategy. Other operations, however, could have served as models of the original conception. Outstanding examples of intelligence, sabotage and guerrilla activities supported the landings in Normandy and Southern France. The exploitation of source "Wood" by OSS/Bern provided a classic example of indirect penetration of an enemy country—except that it might be rejected as too good to be true.

OSS was often assisted in the development of its own techniques by experienced British agencies. This was especially important in the field of counter-espionage, where OSS was given full information on British operations, and access to techniques and records built up through years of observation and research. [Deletion]

The written sources, reports and administrative records upon which this Report has been based, are assembled for the most part in the History Project Files which are in the OSS Archives. Bibliographic notes supporting individual sections of the Report will be found in the same files. In addition to the written records consulted, a number of former key personnel of OSS were interviewed in an effort to keep to a minimum errors resulting from time and personnel limitations. General Donovan was consulted on all phases of the preparation of this Report, and his comments were of invaluable assistance.

Under my general supervision, principal responsibility [for various parts of the Report] was assumed by Mr. Wayne Nelson, Mr. John C. L. Hulley, Mr. Edmond L. Taylor, and Mr. S. Peter Karlow. [Deletion]

Drafts for certain specialized activities were prepared by several former members of OSS, [including Dr. John Waldron and Mr. Samuel Halpern. Among others of assistance are Miss Delia T. Pleasants, Miss Mary Louise Olsson, Miss Maryette A. Coxe, Miss Barbara Bronson, Major Jane M. Tanner, WAC, and Captain Emily L. Shek, WAC].

Among the former members of OSS who served as consultants for varying periods of time were: Messrs. Walter Lord, Edward J. Michelson, William A. Underwood, Richard de Roussy de Sales, Colonel William R. Peers, and Lt. Colonel William C. Wilkinson, Jr.

[Deletion] Special mention should be made of the high caliber of clerical work and the devotion to duty of Mrs. Gladys J. Lane and Miss Charlene Olsson.

KERMIT ROOSEVELT
Chief, History Project

The Secret War Report of The OSS

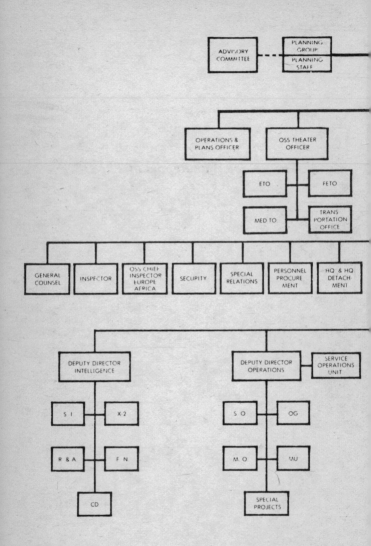

ADVISORY COMMITTEE

PLANNING GROUP

PLANNING STAFF

OPERATIONS & PLANS OFFICER

OSS THEATER OFFICER

ETO

FETO

MED TO

TRANS PORTATION OFFICE

GENERAL COUNSEL

INSPECTOR

OSS CHIEF INSPECTOR EUROPE AFRICA

SECURITY

SPECIAL RELATIONS

PERSONNEL PROCURE MENT

HQ & HQ DETACH MENT

DEPUTY DIRECTOR INTELLIGENCE

S I

X 2

R & A

F N

CD

DEPUTY DIRECTOR OPERATIONS

SERVICE OPERATIONS UNIT

S O

OG

M O

MU

SPECIAL PROJECTS

26 MAY 1944

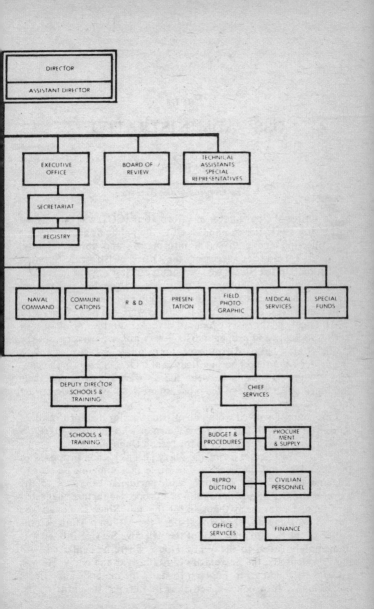

Part I

OSS—ADMINISTRATIVE

CHAPTER 1

The Origins of the Service

The Office of Coordinator of Information (COI) was established on 11 July 1941. It was announced to the public as an agency for the collection and analysis of information and data. Actually, through COI and its successor, the Office of Strategic Services (OSS), the United States was beginning its first organized venture into the fields of espionage, propaganda, subversion and related activities under the aegis of a centralized intelligence agency.

In themselves, these various functions were not new. Every war in American history has produced diverse examples of the use of spies, saboteurs and propagandists. Every major power, except the United States, has used espionage, for example, in peace as well as in war, for centuries. The significance of COI/OSS was in the concept of the relationship between these varied activities and their combined effect as one of the most potent weapons in modern warfare.

This concept evolved from two missions performed for President Roosevelt in 1940 and 1941 by the man who guided COI/OSS throughout its existence—William Joseph Donovan.

In July 1940 Secretary of the Navy [Frank] Knox proposed to the President and the Secretary of State that someone be sent to England to study the situation, with particular reference to the work of the German fifth column in Europe. He further suggested his friend, Donovan, as the man for this job. Since Donovan was then in Washington, appearing before the Military Affairs Committee of the Senate on behalf of the Selective Service Bill, he was immediately called to the White House where he conferred with the President and the Secretaries of State, War and Navy. He was asked if he would go to England to study the methods and effects of German's fifth column activities in Europe. In addition, the

President wished him to observe how the British were standing up at a time when their fortunes were at their lowest ebb and they faced Germany alone. Donovan agreed to undertake the mission, and other departments of the Government asked him to obtain specific information on various other subjects.

In his varied career Donovan had been uniformly successful as college athlete, lawyer and public official. As a soldier, he had established one of the most distinguished records of World War I. He had observed the beginnings of Fascist aggression in Ethiopia in 1935 and the Axis testing ground of Spain in 1936. His wide range of knowledge and experience eminently fitted him for the broad mission of inquiry and appraisal which the President desired.

Donovan departed for England in mid-July 1940. Though he was there for only a few weeks, the relationships which he established with British leaders were to be of great significance to the future agency. There he became convinced that the British would hold out; that America must help, at least in the matter of supplies; and that fifth column activity had become a factor of major importance in modern warfare. These convictions served to strengthen British confidence in him, and he was initiated into the mysteries of the British organizations which dealt with secret intelligence and the various elements of unorthodox warfare.

He returned to America on 4 August 1940 and immediately reported to his friend, Secretary Knox. A few days later he reported to the President. Thereafter, the British sent to America in response to Donovan's requests a series of reports on various phases of British experience in the new war.

The results of his investigations on the subject of fifth column activities were turned over to Edgar A. Mowrer, veteran Chicago Daily News correspondent, who wrote a series of articles on the subject which appeared under the joint signatures of Donovan and Mowrer. Secretary Knox wrote an introduction for these articles and they were disseminated throughout the world by the three leading American news agencies and widely distributed in pamphlet form. It was at the instance of the President that Donovan's name was associated with these articles.

In November 1940, President Roosevelt called Donovan to Washington once more, and asked him if he would undertake a mission to make a strategic appreciation from an economic, political and military standpoint of the Mediterranean area. He accepted with alacrity, for one of the concrete ideas which had developed in his mind was the importance of the Mediterranean in World War II. [Donovan felt that many people were prone to think of the

Mediterranean as an East-West channel for shipping. He believed
it should be thought of primarily as a no-man's-land between
Europe and Africa, two great forces, or potential forces, facing
each other from the North and South. Germany controlled, either
directly or indirectly, most of the northern "battle line" of this
front on the Continent of Europe. It was imperative in Donovan's
view for the British—or the British and the Americans—to control
the southern front along the Mediterranean shore of Africa. (Footnote)]

In August 1940 he had stressed particularly the necessity of
some kind of agreement with the French in order to secure American interests in Northwest Africa. In discussing the mission, the
President suggested that Donovan find occasion en route to see
General [Maxime]Weygand [governor of French North Africa]
and to discuss the question. However, Donovan proposed that it
would be better for him to proceed to southeastern Europe and the
Eastern Mediterranean first; he felt that he would be in a better
position to confer with Weygand after such an opportunity to
study the situation. He therefore suggested that Mr. Robert D.
Murphy initiate the discussions. [As a result of Donovan's attempts to stiffen resistance in the Balkans, the French, under German pressure, refused to permit him to enter French territory and
he was therefore unable to see General Weygand. (Footnote)]

Donovan departed on 6 December 1940 for England. During the
succeeding three and a half months, he visited Gibraltar, Malta,
Egypt, Greece, Bulgaria, Yugoslavia, Turkey, Cyprus, Palestine,
Iraq, Spain and Portugal. On 18 March 1941, he returned to the
United States. On the following day, again accompanied by Secretary Knox, he made the first of a series of calls at the White House
to report to the President.

He stressed three major points: First, the gravity of the shipping
problem; second, the dangers and opportunities which the situation
in French Northwest Africa represented for the United States; and
third, the extraordinary importance of psychological and political
elements in the war and the necessity of making the most of these
elements in planning and executing national policies.

Both on this mission and his earlier mission in 1940, Donovan
had studied the manner in which the Germans were exploiting the
psychological and political elements. They were making the fullest
use of threats and promises, of subversion and sabotage, and of
special intelligence. They sowed dissension, confusion and despair
among their victims and aggravated any lack of faith and hope.

Yet, Donovan reported, neither America nor Britain was fighting this new and important type of war on more than the smallest

scale. Their defenses against political and psychological warfare were feeble, and even such gestures as were made toward carrying the fight to the enemy were pitifully inadequate. Preparation in the field of irregular and unorthodox warfare was as important as orthodox military preparedness—Donovan urged upon the President the necessity for action.

There was another situation which had impressed itself upon Donovan. On each of his two missions he had been asked on all sides to secure information. Information was pouring into Washington from many sources in that critical period. But it was fragmentary, and it was not humanly possible for the men who were responsible for formulating policy to assimilate the growing mass of material. In London he had found that there existed a central committee [Joint Intelligence Committee—JIC] where much information was analyzed and available. However, the procedure was cumbersome and ineffective, and there was no central depot where all the information on a given subject was collected, analyzed and available in digestible form.

The greatest victim of the situation in Washington was the President himself. In the summer of 1941 he appointed a committee of Cabinet members, consisting of [Henry L.] Stimson [Secretary of War], Knox and [Robert H.] Jackson [later the Supreme Court Justice], to consider the intelligence problem generally and recommend a plan of action. The committee consulted with Donovan and he expounded to it his concept of an over-all intelligence agency with propaganda and subversive attributes. The committee's report to the President recommended the establishment of such an organization.

In early June, therefore, the President asked Donovan to make specific proposals for the implementation of his ideas for psychological warfare and the development of an intelligence program. Donovan prepared and submitted to the White House on 10 June 1941 a paper entitled "Memorandum of Establishment of Service of Strategic Information."

In this memorandum Donovan set forth the relation of information to strategic planning in total warfare. He pointed out the inadequacy of the intelligence set-up then existing and stated: "It is essential that we set up a central enemy intelligence organization which would itself collect either directly or through existing departments of the government, at home and abroad, pertinent information." Such information and data should be analyzed and interpreted by applying to it the experience of "specialized trained research officials in the relative scientific fields (including technological, economic, financial and psychological scholars)."

"But there is another element in modern warfare," he continued, "and that is the psychological attack against the moral and spiritual defenses of a nation. In this attack the most powerful weapon is radio." In this type of warfare, "perfection can be realized only by planning, and planning is dependent upon accurate information."

The elements of physical subversion which mad been included in the recommendations to the Cabinet committee, were not specifically set forth.

The President accepted these proposals as a basis for action and directed that an appropriate order be drafted. The order, however, was not to be specific as to the functions proposed for the new agency; both the President and Donovan agreed that, in the delicate situation then existing, it would be preferable to have no precise definition appear. On 25 June 1941 an order was drafted which would establish the agency as the Office of Coordinator of Strategic Information. This order was designed to be issued by the President in his capacity as Commander-in-Chief of the armed forces and its entire tone was military in nature.

The 25 June draft was circulated among State, War and Navy Departments at Donovan's request. It met particularly vigorous opposition from the Army and Navy on the ground that the new agency might usurp some of their functions. Therefore, it was decided to establish COI as a part of the Executive Office of the President.

*   *   *

[The Office of Strategic Services was created out of, and replaced, the COI in June 1942, partly to end the interminable rows that had marked the birth of COI. The State Department, the Office of War Information, the Military Intelligence Service (MIS), and the Joint Chiefs of Staff (JCS), all demonstrated hostility to the newborn intelligence service. The MIS of George V. Strong tried to strangle it at birth, largely because of one of Donovan's "capers"—trainee-agents acting under orders burgled a factory producing top secret equipment and "stole" the most secret of blue prints. Strong was considerably embarrassed by the attack, since his service was responsible for the security of the plant. He had never liked Donovan, and this action resulted in an emnity which did not dissolve until OSS itself was liquidated.

[There was a long gap between the formation of OSS and the issuance of its charter. The reason was that the intellectuals in and around OSS were arguing with the Joint War Plans Committee on a definition of what psychological warfare was, and who should direct it in the name of the United States of America. The definition was agreed upon and it read that psychological warfare

> ...is the coordination and use of all means, including moral and physical, by which the end is to be attained—other than those of recognized military operations, but including the psychological exploitation of the result of those recognized military actions—which tend to destroy the will of the enemy to achieve victory and to damage his political or economic capacity to do so; which tend to deprive the enemy of the support, assistance or sympathy of his allies or associates or of neutrals, or to prevent his acquisition of such support, assistance or sympathy; or which tend to create, maintain, or increase the will to victory of our own people and allies and to acquire, maintain, or increase the support, assistance and sympathy of neutrals.

[It was not a very good definition: Winston Churchill had a better, shorter definition. Psychological warfare, he said, was an instrument that left the enemy baffled as well as beaten.

[This orgy of words to describe a relatively simple concept was very typical of the complicated bureaucracy in which OSS was expected to fight some of the world's best intelligence services, the *Sicherheitsdienst* of the Nazi party and the *Abwehr* of the German General Staff. This bureaucratic embrace is best left to the Joint Chiefs:

> All plans for projects to be undertaken by the Office of Strategic Services will be submitted to the Joint U.S. Chiefs of Staff through the Joint Psychological Warfare Committee for approval. The Joint Psychological Warfare Committee will refer such papers as it deems necessary to the Joint Staff Planners (JSP) prior to submission to the Joint U.S. Chiefs of Staff. The Joint Psychological Warfare Committee will take final action on all internal administrative plans pertaining to the Office of Strategic Services which do not involve military or naval personnel or military or naval equipment.

[The mind boggles at such a bureaucratic snarl on the eve of Torch, the great landing by American and British forces in French North Africa in November of 1942. It did not last long because it could not—there was a very clever, powerful and determined enemy to fight. And so it was that on 23 December 1942 the question of psychological warfare, which in the end would make few perceptible contributions to victory, was ironed out: its function was given to OSS, as General Donovan had intended all along—and had taken nearly two priceless years to get. As the War Report stated:

> ...OSS was designated as the agency of the JCS charged (outside the Western Hemisphere), in general, with "the planning, development, coordination and execution of the military program for psychological warfare," and with "the compilation of such political, psychological, sociological and economic information as may be required by military operations." The propaganda aspects of such plans were limited to recommendations to the JCS which was responsible for securing the cooperation of OWI. OSS was given authority to operate in the fields of sabotage, espionage and counter-espionage in enemy-occupied or controlled territory, guerrilla warfare, underground groups in enemy-occupied or controlled territory and foreign nationality groups in the United States. It provided for a Planning Group to be "set up in the Office of Strategic Services" consisting of one member from State, two appointed by the Chief of Staff, two by the Commander-in-Chief U.S. Fleet and Chief of Naval Operations, and four members, including the Chairman, appointed by the Director of OSS. It stipulated that OSS psychological warfare plans be submitted to the JCS through the JSP. In the field of intelligence it placed OSS on a par with MIS and ONI.

[In a letter to Donovan written on the same day this directive was issued, 23 December 1942, General Marshall, the venerated Chief of Staff of the United States Army, deprecated all the fuss and bother with the words:

> I regret that after voluntarily coming under the jurisdiction of the Joint Chiefs of Staff your organization has not had smoother sailing. Nevertheless, it has rendered invaluable service, particularly with reference to the North African Campaign. I am hopeful that the new Office of Strategic Services' directive will eliminate most, if not all, of your difficulties.

[The vast expenditure of toil by lawyers and administrators was wasted in the end, for in practice the OSS became a tool of theater commanders such as General MacArthur, General Eisenhower, General Wilson and Admiral the Lord Louis Mountbatten, to do with OSS what they wanted—or, as occasionally happened, to refuse to avail themselves of the organization's services at all. As the War Report puts it:

The real decision as to what any agency would be able to accomplish on the field was being removed from Washington.... Regardless of whether [OSS] was under civil or military control jurisdictionally in Washington, it was obvious that any activities it performed in the theaters would be subject to military direction.

[In the meantime, General Donovan had been getting on with forming the operational branches of his organization. An early activity was counterespionage in enemy-occupied or controlled territory. It had always been recognized that the development of a secret intelligence organization would necessitate the performance of counterintelligence activities for its protection. However, through the close relations which obtained between the British Security Coordination—the cover name for the headquarters of the British intelligence service branch in New York—and OSS, the British made an offer which created an unusually advantageous opportunity for the United States, through the medium of OSS, to develop an organization in the wider field of counterespionage.]

* * *

The British [the War Report continues] had built up over many years a highly coordinated net of security services which had by long experience been pointed to a high degree of efficiency and world-wide coverage. Prior to 7 December 1941, they were exchanging some counter-espionage information with G-2, ONI, FBI and COI/OSS. After the outbreak of war, however, the British became disturbed about giving such information to several uncoordinated agencies which lacked carefully-trained specialists concerned exclusively with counter-espionage techniques. Therefore, they suggested that all counter-espionage material be channeled through a single agency, and offered to make available to such an agency the body of counter-espionage records which they had accumulated.

Following negotiations in London in the winter of 1942-43 between OSS and the British security services, a Counter-Intelligence Division [this Division was to receive all counter-espionage information sent by the British, except that relating to espionage in the Western Hemisphere, for which FBI continued independent liaison (footnote)] was established within SI on 1 March 1943. Included in the agreements made with the British in London were arrangements for the transfer to America of duplicates of the large body of counterespionage records which the British had accumulated. The United States thus gained in a very short time the fruits of years of counter-espionage activity. The Counter-Intelligence Division sent a small staff to London to arrange for the transmittal of the files.

It soon became evident that, by working in close collaboration with the British, knowledge could be acquired and personnel trained in the highly intricate techniques of counter-espionage manipulation and the control of enemy agents through which knowledge could be gained of the enemy's plans and intentions and the enemy could be deceived as to one's own.

With the unique opportunity thus offered to create in a short time a counter-espionage organization and to engage in such activity on a wide scale, proposals were made that the Counter-Intelligence Division of SI be given separate branch status. Therefore, on 15 June 1943, the Division became the Counter-Espionage Branch (X-2), one of the three major branches of the Intelligence Service.

[This was an extremely important start for the infant intelligence service; and it was concluded with great harmony with the British —the British wanted things from the United States. But if anybody thought that OSS was out of its procedural difficulties, they were wrong. No sooner was X-2 established than the old problem of psychological warfare emerged to trouble Donovan and his executive again. The intellectuals around Robert Sherwood and Elmer Davis decided they wanted a new definition, in order to define the frontier between OSS and OWI operations—everybody was empire-building in those days. Psywar became "Strategic Services Operations," and the Joint Chiefs defined Strategic Services to be:

...all measures (except those pertaining to the Federal program of radio, press, publication and related foreign propaganda activity involving the dissemination of information) taken to enforce our will upon the enemy by means other than military action, as may be applied in support of actual or planned military operations or in furtherance of the war effort.

[The War Report noted this latest development with satisfaction, stating:

Thus, after some twenty-seven months as COI and OSS, the agency had definitive authorization and sufficient scope to develop maximum efficiency. By that time it was accepted as a valid and valuable auxiliary to military operations.

[With less agony, more important branches of OSS had been formed. S(pecial) O(perations) existed to engage in sabotage and support of resistance movements in occupied countries. The O(perational) G(roups) were forming in order to be able to place harassing bands of highly-trained, bilingual guerrillas behind the lines. M(orale) O(perations) existed to engage in the world-wide dissemination of "black" propaganda and other forms of morale subversion, especially political and diplomatic warfare. M(aritime) U(nits) was forming to engage in maritime infiltration, development of maritime warfare devices and maritime sabotage operations. The S(ecret) I(ntelligence) service, which had been started with British assistance in 1941, now existed as an agency of growing power and efficiency. All this was noted with considerable satisfaction in the War Report, which observed that:

> . . . OSS/Washington had achieved its major purpose. The organization which it had established was not only functioning but authorized to function. The justification for the long struggle would rest with those whom it sent to the field.

[There were to be some bitter disappointments, some terrible blunders, some awful disasters before the first triumph emerged. There were also to be some problems of complexity and acrimony to be settled with the godfather of OSS, the British intelligence and special operations services. On this issue, the War Report would state:

> External relations in the various theaters created numerous problems, many of which evolved from the local situation and from the nature of a particular theater establishment. There was, however, one difficulty which was common to most theaters. This difficulty revolved around the firm premise which Donovan had enunciated from the beginning, namely, that the secret intelligence organization of OSS should be free and independent. The reasons for this independence had often been stated. In fact, as Donovan noted in his memorandum of 17 September 1943 to Major General W. B. Smith, the committee of Cabinet members, which met in Washington in the summer of 1941 [to discuss the formation of COI], had stressed the point of independence in secret intelligence. After conferring with Donovan, that committee had stated that the requirements for a long-range strategic intelligence service with subversive attributes made it mandatory:
>
> . . . that the intelligence services of one nation should be kept independent from that of any other nation, each with its own agents, communications, and transportation—for the following reasons:

a. *Security.* The disclosure of one will not necessarily involve damage to another.

b. *Verification.* If networks are truly separate, it is improbable that information, simultaneously received from the two chains, springs from a single source.

c. *Control.* The effectiveness of intelligence work is dependent upon permanence—at least in so far as it is not subject to the power of another to terminate it. The danger that its operation may be terminated by the act of another means subordination.

The independence of SI was subject to question in widely separated areas. With regard to the British, the question was raised in London at an early date. In NATO [North African Theater of Operations] it was necessary to negotiate constantly during 1943 to secure transportation and documents which would allow SI to operate in France and Italy from the Algiers base without being dependent upon the British. In NATO, also, it was necessary to preserve independence with regard to the French intelligence services in connection with operations into France. In Cairo, while METO [Middle East Theater of Operations] was a theater under British command, the independence of intelligence operations—particularly those directed toward the Balkans—came into constant question.

[The OSS did not last very long. Its life span was less than three years. But it did achieve a great deal, and it provided the framework for the peacetime intelligence service which the United States would need to guard its security in the long, complicated and bitter moral and diplomatic struggle with the Soviet Union.]

*   *   *

The progress of Allied armies in Europe during the fall of 1944 [the Report resumes] resulted in a decrease of resistance group requirements for materiel and supply, and there was a sharp drop in shipments. In addition to changes in supply requirements, as the emphasis began to shift to the Far East, there was also a decrease in the numbers of personnel required for the European war. While the actual termination of hostilities in Europe was not to occur for some six months, the defeat of Germany was clearly in prospect.

Donovan had never lost sight of the fact that, while OSS was in one sense a wartime expedient, it was also an experiment of vital significance to determination of the question of a peacetime intelligence structure for the United States. His own thinking on the matter, which led to the establishment of COI in 1941, had been bùttressed by some three years' actual experience which the organization had accumulated by the fall of 1944.

On 31 October 1944, President Roosevelt asked Donovan to submit his views on the organization of an intelligence service for the post-war period. Donovan replied in a memorandum of 18 November, with which he submitted a proposal for a central intelligence service. In his memorandum, Donovan proposed the liquidation of OSS once the wartime necessity for the organization had ceased. However, he was anxious to preserve its intelligence functions in some form for permanent peacetime use. In essence, this involved returning to the original COI concept of a central authority, reporting directly to the President, which could collect and analyze the mass of intelligence material required for the planning and implementation of national policy and strategy. In his memorandum, Donovan stated:

> In the early days of the war, when the demands upon intelligence services were mainly in and for military operations, the OSS was placed under the direction of the JCS.
>
> Once our enemies are defeated the demand will be equally pressing for information that will aid us in solving the problems of peace.
>
> This will require two things:
>
> 1. That intelligence control be returned to the supervision of the President.
>
> 2. The establishment of a central authority reporting directly to you, with responsibility to frame intelligence objectives and to collect and coordinate the intelligence material required by the Executive Branch in planning and carrying out national policy and strategy.
>
> I attach in the form of a draft directive the means by which I think this could be realized without difficulty or loss of time. You will note that coordination and centralization are placed at the policy level but operational intelligence (that pertaining primarily to Department action) remains within the existing agencies concerned. The creation of a central authority thus would not conflict with or limit necessary intelligence functions within the Army, Navy, Department of State and other agencies.
>
> In accordance with your wish, this is set up as a permanent long-range plan. But you may want to consider whether this (or part of it) should be done now, by executive or legislative action. There are common-sense reasons why you may desire to lay the keel of the ship at once.
>
> The immediate revision and coordination of our present in-

telligence system would effect substantial economies and aid in the more efficient and speedy termination of the war.

Information important to the national defense, being gathered now by certain Departments and agencies, is not being used to full advantage in the war. Coordination at the strategy level would prevent waste, and avoid the present confusion that leads to waste and unnecessary duplication.

Though in the midst of war, we are also in a period of transition which, before we are aware, will take us into the tumult of rehabilitation. An adequate and orderly intelligence system will contribute to informed decisions.

We have now in the Government the trained and specialized personnel needed for the task. This talent should not be dispersed.

However, immediate action was not taken. The Ardennes offensive in December proved that the European war would take longer than had been anticipated in the fall and that defeat of the German armies in France would not insure an internal collapse in Germany.

December 1944 marked the maximum expansion of OSS. The agency employed some 13,000 personnel, approximately 5,500 of which were in the United States and the remainder overseas. Personnel and supply requirements of OSS in the European theaters had been sufficiently built up and, with the exception of supplying personnel qualified to work on Germany itself and preparing for the post-hostilities phase, the organization could devote the major part of its operations in 1945 to problems in the Far East.

By the middle of 1944, OSS had seven principal bases in the Far East—at Chungking and Kunming in China; and at Kandy, New Delhi, Calcutta and Nazira in India. After October 1944, when the CBI Theater was split into the India-Burma Theater and the China Theater, OSS reorganized its detachments. The new China Theater Commander made OSS responsible for all clandestine activities (except Chinese) in China. The organization in China, following some two years of effort, thus achieved the basis for effective operation: integrated forces and independent control.

In the Pacific Ocean theaters, OSS as a whole was never active. Admiral Nimitz originally rejected a plan for psychological warfare in the Pacific Theater. Similarly, OSS was never fully active in the Southwest Pacific Theater. In the spring of 1945, General MacArthur approved the dispatch of personnel and equipment for JAVAMAN, a secret weapon developed by the Special Projects Branch. However, the Japanese war ended before the mission reached the field.

The most spectacular OSS activity in the Far East was Detachment 101, the nucleus of which had arrived in India in the early summer of 1942. This Detachment carried on effective guerrilla and intelligence operations in Burma. In this respect, its work was only paralleled by the activity of OSS/China in the last months of the war. In Burma, OSS became the principal and ultimately, the only U.S. ground force in combat; in China, OSS guerrilla activity was important not only in support of the Chinese armies in the field but also in developing offensive action by them.

The work of OSS in collaborating with the Siamese was a unique example of the possibilities of a secret organization. In this instance, the Siamese Government, officially under Japanese domination, became in effect a resistance group working for OSS. Such an operation could not have been carried out by an agency having official status. Through the Siamese, OSS effected indirect penetration of Japan proper.

By 1945, OSS had at last established itself in the Far East. The process had been a slow one, due not only to complicating factors of race, culture and geography, as well as political considerations, but to the fact that Allied war priorities were on Europe. The work of OSS in the Far East developed differently from that in Europe. Paramilitary operations were paramount; secret intelligence operations were often combined with other types of operation; and, in general, there was less branch-consciousness than in Europe. However, the principle of strategic services proved itself. By VJ-Day OSS had received a degree of support in the Far Eastern theaters on the Asiatic Continent which was an effective indication of the extent of its contribution.

The mechanics of liquidating an organization such as OSS, which operated on a worldwide basis, were complicated. There were demands from almost all theaters and by various State Department missions that certain of the agency's functions be continued. However, responsible officials were not agreed upon the form of organization which should be set up in peacetime. It was imperative in Donovan's view, as it was in the view of many others, that the intelligence functions of OSS should be preserved in such form as to be projected into peacetime as a service to the interests of national policy and security.

On 25 August 1945, Donovan informed the Director of the Bureau of the Budget that OSS was, in effect, working under a liquidation budget. He stated that, within the restrictions of that budget, OSS was in the process of terminating many operational activities and reducing the remaining parts to a size consistent with obligations then current in the Far East, in occupied Germany and Austria and in the maintenance of missions in the Middle East and on the Asiatic and European continents. He further stated that OSS had established a liquidating committee to provide for the gradual elimination of OSS services in line with the orderly reduction of personnel. He estimated that the effectiveness of OSS as a war agency would end as of 1 January, or at the latest 1 February 1946, at which time he anticipated that liquidation would be completed.

In this letter, however, Donovan urged the necessity of a centralized peacetime intelligence structure. He stated that, upon the completion of liquidation,

> ...I wish to return to private life. Therefore, in considering the disposition to be made of the assets created by OSS, I speak as a private citizen concerned with the future of his country.
>
> In our Government today there is no permanent agency to take over the functions which OSS will have then ceased to perform. These functions while carried on as incident to the war are in reality essential in the effective discharge by this nation of its responsibilities in the organization and maintenance of the peace.
>
> Since last November, I have pointed out the immediate necessity of setting up such an agency to take over the valuable assets created by OSS. Among these assets was the establishment for the first time in our nation's history of a foreign secret intelligence service which reported information as seen through American eyes. As an integral and inseparable part of this service there is a group of specialists to analyze and evaluate the material for presentation to those who determine national policy.
>
> It is not easy to set up a modern intelligence system. It is more difficult to do so in time of peace than in time of war.
>
> It is important therefore that it be done before the War Agency has disappeared so that profit may be made of its experience and "know how" in deciding how the new agency may best be conducted.
>
> I have already submitted a plan for the establishment of a centralized system. However, the discussion of that proposal indicated the need of an agreement upon certain fundamental principles before a detailed plan is formulated. If those concerned could agree upon the principles within which such a system should be established, acceptance of a common plan would be more easily achieved.

To the above letter, Donovan attached a statement of principles which should govern the establishment of a centralized foreign intelligence system, based upon the experience of OSS and a first-hand study of the intelligence system of other nations. The statement of principles began with the assertion that the formulation of national policy is "influenced and determined by knowledge (or ignorance) of the aims, capabilities, intentions and policies of other nations." It continued that all major powers except the United States had maintained permanent world-wide intelligence services long prior to World War II and that the United States, prior to the war, had no foreign secret intelligence service. Further, the United States never had and did not then have a coordinated intelligence system. The statement noted that the difficulties and dangers of the situation were generally recognized.

The first of the principles stated that each department of the Government should have its own intelligence bureau for collecting and purchasing the informational material necessary to its functions. However, since secret intelligence covered all fields and, because of the possible embarrassment of duplication and resultant confusion, no department should be permitted to engage in that field but should call upon the central agency for such service in appropriate cases.

As its second major point, the statement set forth the fact that there should be established a national central foreign intelligence agency which should have authority:

A. To serve all Departments of the Government.

B. To procure and obtain political, economic, psychological, sociological, military and other information which may bear upon the national interest and which has been collected by the different Governmental Departments or agencies.

C. To collect when necessary supplemental information either at its own instance or at the request of any Governmental Department by open or secret means from other and various sources.

D. To integrate, analyze, process and disseminate, to authorized Governmental agencies and officials, intelligence in the form of strategic interpretive studies.

The third principle was that the central agency should be prohibited from carrying on clandestine activities within the United States and should be forbidden to exercise any police functions arising either within the country or in foreign areas.

The fourth principle stated that, since the nature of its functions required official status, the agency should be independent of any department of the Government, "since it is obliged to serve all and must be free of the natural bias of an operating department." Therefore, it should be under a deputy appointed by the President and should be administered under Presidential direction. The statement of principles further set forth the need of a board, on which the Secretaries of State, War, Navy and Treasury should be represented, which would determine policy for the intelligence agency.

As the sole organization having secret intelligence functions, it should be authorized, "in the foreign field only, to carry on services such as espionage, counter-espionage and those special operations (including morale and psychological) designed to anticipate and counter any attempted penetration and subversion" of national security by foreign powers.

Succeeding principles provided that the central agency should have an independent budget directly granted by Congress, and that it should be authorized to have its own system of codes and should be furnished by other departments of the Government with such facilities as were proper and necessary for the performance of its duties. In addition, the central service should include among its personnel staff specialists, professionally trained in the analysis of information and possessing linguistic, regional or functional competence, in order to coordinate, analyze and evaluate information, to make special intelligence reports and to provide guidance for collecting branches of the agency.

In conclusion, the principles stated that, in time of war or unlimited national emergency, all programs of such an agency in areas of actual or projected military operations should be coordinated with military plans and should be subject to the approval of the JCS or, in the event of consolidation of the armed services, the supreme commander.

The future of intelligence in the United States was subject to intensive consideration at many levels in the late summer and fall of 1945. The weakness of the United States in this respect prior to World War II was generally admitted and it was obvious that the United States and its leaders could not permit a repetition of the pre-war situation. The letter to the Director of the Bureau of the Budget and the principles which it enclosed were widely circulated to key officials in Washington, including the President. With the agency in process of liquidation, there was once again a recognition of the value of various of its components. That the functions which were assembled in OSS, diverse though they appeared superficially, actually were related and could achieve their maximum effectiveness only in combination, however, was not generally accepted. In transmitting to Judge Samuel Rosenman a copy of the letter to the Budget and the attached principles, Donovan stated:

> I understand that there has been talk of attempting to allocate different segments of the organization to different departments. This would be an absurd and unsatisfactory thing to do. The organization was set up as an entity, every function supporting and supplementing the other.
>
> It's time for us to grow up, Sam, and realize that the new responsibilities we have assumed require an adequate intelligence system.
>
> Increasingly, the President will see the need and I hope a new agency will be set up to take over a very useful legacy.

There had been at least two crises in which the continued existence of COI/OSS came into serious question. The first, in the spring of 1942, resulted in loss of the function of open propaganda. At the same time, however, the agency was placed under the jurisdiction of the JCS, which was the only status permitting it to achieve its maximum wartime effectiveness. The second arose in the fall of 1942, when there was a definite move to strip the agency of some of its most valuable components and weaken the remainder to the extent that it could not possibly have fulfilled its original concept. In the late summer of 1945 the continued existence of the agency was not at issue. Donovan himself had recommended its liquidation almost a year before. It was not for the continuance of the agency that he was concerned, but rather the preservation of intelligence assets which had a manifest significance for the future.

The impending liquidation of OSS created grave problems in the field. Activities were being carried on in the immediate post-hostilities period, both in Europe and the Far East, as well as elsewhere, which were valuable and necessary. But the Government had not established the machinery to take over these essential functions in a gradual and orderly manner. It seemed probable that it would be necessary to drop the ends of activities which might be valuable in the future and, should a new organization later be established, attempt to find them, pick them up and piece them together. It was against the potential loss of these assets, to say nothing of the dispersion of personnel experienced in a field in which qualified people were rare, that Donovan sought to guard.

By the fall of 1945, COI/OSS had operated as a secret organization for some four years and three months. The fact of its existence had been known, but few were aware of the nature and the extent of its activities. In the late summer and early fall of 1945, the agency was de-briefing and releasing large numbers of personnel. Stories began to appear in periodicals and in the press regarding OSS.

This raised a serious problem of security. There were certain activities of OSS which could be made known following the end of hostilities. However, there were others which the possibility of a continued peacetime organization made subject to security restrictions.

It was apparent that some publicity was inevitable following the war. If it were uncontrolled, however, existing and future activities might be jeopardized. Donovan therefore decided to reveal the general nature of OSS activities and make known certain of its accomplishments. In addition, he established within OSS machinery for the formal review and clearance of stories prior to publication.

The public thus learned of the way in which OSS had assisted the preparation of target areas for large-scale military invasions in Europe, such as *TORCH* and *ANVIL*, and of the intelligence, SO and resistance work performed for *OVERLORD*. It learned of the supply and assistance to resistance groups in Italy. It learned of the exploits of Detachment 101 in Burma. The fact that the Government of Siam was, in effect, a resistance group working in collaboration with OSS was revealed. The part that OSS/Bern played in Operation SUNRISE, involving the surrender of some 2,000,000 German troops in North Italy, was also made known.

Less newsworthy, perhaps, but nonetheless important, was the development of the organization which made these exploits possible as well as making possible other activities the existence of which could not be mentioned publicly: The establishment of the first world-wide United States espionage and counter-espionage systems; the complex nature of the research and analysis function and the influence which it had exercised upon the whole field of American intelligence; the development of the arts of "black" propaganda and morale subversion; and the theory and practice of physical subversion which had evolved into SO and OG.

More important, the public did not realize, and it is quite possible that some of the initiated did not comprehend fully, the significance and potential value to America of developing the doctrine of unorthodox warfare; in providing a foundation for the American practice of espionage and counter-espionage which could be projected into the future; in providing a basis of experience for the various aspects of morale and physical subversion which could be used in the future should a war crisis arise; and in promulgating the principle of a central intelligence agency.

On 20 September 1945, Executive Order No. 9620 terminated OSS as of 1 October. R&A, Presentation and FN were transferred to the Department of State; the remainder of the agency was transferred to the Department of War.

In a letter of 20 September 1945, informing Donovan of the issuance of the Executive Order, President Truman stated, in part:

> I want to take this occasion to thank you for the capable leadership you have brought to a vital wartime activity in your capacity as Director of Strategic Services. You may well find satisfaction in the achievements of the Office and take pride in your own contribution to them. These are in themselves large rewards. Great additional reward for your efforts should lie in the knowledge that the peacetime intelligence services of the Government are being erected on the foundation of the facilities and resources mobilized through the Office of Strategic Services during the war.

[The parting of the ways was very, very cool.]

CHAPTER 2

The Structure of the OSS

[The structure of OSS was less complicated than it seemed on the charts. There was Donovan's office, the offices of the Assistant Directors, Special Assistants and Representatives, the office of the Executive Officer, and the Secretariat. The Registry maintained the files, the Theater Officers kept a watchful but benevolent eye on the four areas into which OSS divided the world. But there was one office that had much influence: OSS was formed by lawyers and therefore lawyers dominated much of the superstructure. In a world of illegalities the General Counsel sat supremely powerful, trying, so far as was possible, to keep the game honest, to keep OSS out of trouble.]

*　　　*　　　*

General Counsel. The General Counsel [the War Report states] was responsible for professional supervision of the myriad legal problems attendant upon OSS activities, particularly in respect to clandestine intelligence operations. He was charged with the preparation and review of all contracts, leases or legal obligations entered into by any branch or individual in OSS prior to commitment on behalf of the organization or the Government. In addition, legal advice and direction in matters of law relative to any phase of OSS operations were supplied by the General Counsel's Office upon request.

Problems of cover and security complicated the work of the General Counsel. His office frequently acted as legal advisor to OSS agent personnel while in training or in the field. [In the summer and fall of 1944, for example, the office represented an undercover agent, at that time active in a theater of war, in a divorce suit. (footnote)]

The General Counsel gave constant attention to problems of the Special Funds Branch, advising and assisting in the determination of financial procedures with respect to unvouchered funds [secret moneys from the Emergency Fund for which no accounting was needed] in order to insure proper and accurate accounting for expenditures. As the activities of Special Funds ramified, the General

Counsel assigned a representative who devoted his entire time to Special Funds matters.

Cover corporations were established for a variety of purposes and functions, ranging from radio monitoring and trading and shipping agencies to publishing firms for overseas newspapers. The majority of such corporations were located in the New York area. [While the use of the corporate form was successful in giving anonymity to specific activities, the use of corporations for more than a short term or for limited purposes had certain disadvantages. The extensive legal and paper work incident to corporate organization and reporting in some cases entailed more work in maintaining the cover than in carrying out the activities for which the corporation was established.

[Corporations, even though established for cover purposes, were recognized as bona fide government companies, under a Treasury ruling issued at the time of the liquidation of OSS. Employees of such corporations received credit toward government service longevity. (footnote)]

The General Counsel coordinated all OSS liquidation procedures, both in the United States and overseas. Contracts with individuals and corporations, leases and other legal commitments were terminated, and procedures were established for the settlement of claims for casualties, death benefits and losses. Items which had been requisitioned all over the world, from caiques in the Mediterranean to elephants in Asia, were returned to their owners.

All information procured by OSS relevant to war crimes, both against OSS agents and personnel and against other Americans and the Allies, was centralized in the General Counsel's Office. In the summer of 1945, a special *War Crimes Section* was established by the General Counsel. It was subsequently transferred to Justice Jackson's staff at Nuremberg. [Deletion]

* * *

[The purely administrative departments apart, the next two offices directly concerned with maintaining clandestines in the field were the Special Relations Office and the Transportation Office.]

* * *

Special Relations Office. Special Relations was the OSS unit which established liaison with agencies and departments of the Government and with embassies, legations and missions of foreign governments located in Washington. It was responsible only for the establishment of the initial contacts, whereafter working liaison was maintained by the respective branches.

The principal responsibility of Special Relations was the conduct of relations with the State Department in connection with agents and operatives under State cover in various overseas posts. This entailed many problems, not only in establishing the cover securely but in setting up the procedures necessary to maintain cover once the agent was in the field.

Arrangements for passports and visas were preliminary to the agent's dispatch. Such routine matters as arranging for innoculations, with due regard to the security factors involved, and myriad other details required discreet and specialized handling.

It was necessary to establish means of paying the agent through the State Department in the field in such fashion that he would appear to be a regular employee of the Department. To accomplish this, a revolving fund was established with the State Department from which disbursements could be made in accordance with instructions given through Special Relations.

Special Relations was also responsible for the proper handling by OSS of pouch privileges granted by State Department. Pouch communications, between agents in the field and their desks in Washington, were channeled through Special Relations, which had to certify the propriety of the content and check the physical dispatch of the material so that the agent's cover would not be violated.

Special Relations established a *Transportation Office*, which was responsible for the shipment of OSS personnel and supplies overseas. Complex liaisons were necessary, particularly with the State Department and with the sea and air transport authorities of the Army and Navy, to cope with such varied OSS requirements as arranging for an agent to travel under cover to a neutral country, dispatching supplies for resistance groups or routing operations specialists or researchers to specific assignments in the theaters.

It was originally thought that the Transportation Office would be concerned principally with transporting agents to friendly or neutral territory. It therefore recruited a staff experienced in civilian travel agencies. The increasing concentration of OSS overseas activity in military theaters led to complications, however. It was found that the civilian experience of the staff was of little avail in adapting State, War and Navy procedures to OSS requirements.

The newness of OSS was, of course, basic to such difficulties. It was necessary to rely on the cooperation of military and State Department officials accustomed to rigid procedures and unfamiliar with the peculiar needs and problems of OSS which required flexibility. The unusual degree of security required in a secret organization necessitates elaborate safeguards in the most routine matters. The seemingly elaborate precautions necessary to protect secret operations cannot be explained; they must be accepted.

Otherwise, the quality of secrecy is destroyed and the operation rendered valueless. This was not always understood by the officials with whom Transportation had to deal. On the other hand, understanding of the requirements of other agencies and departments was not always present on the part of OSS, as was indicated on occasion by unrealistic demands of the individual branches for involved transportation arrangements on short notice. [Deletion]

Board of Review. The Board of Review was established in the spring of 1944. Its functions were to "advise the Director with respect to the formulation of policies for, and the direction of, all OSS finances both in Washington and in the field." In addition, the Board was to "study, review and make recommendations with respect to: (1) All financial controls, records and accountings; (2) all proposed expenditures of unvouchered OSS funds requiring the approval of the Director or Assistant Director; (3) such other matters pertaining to OSS finances as the Director may approve." The Board was composed of three members, assisted by the General Counsel.

All financial matters requring the attention or approval of Donovan were first examined by the Board, which gathered full details and factual data to support its recommendations to Donovan. Matters submitted to the Board included funds for new projects, missions or bases; agent, property or liability claims; and any expenditures not specifically authorized or provided for. Policy was established on rates of pay from excepted or unvouchered funds, as well as living and quarters allowances, both in the United States and overseas.

In 1944, Boards of Review were established at the various OSS theater headquarters in order to advise the Strategic Services Officers on matters of financial policy. In addition to their basic duties, these Boards frequently undertook claims investigations and other assignments as directed.

Expenditures of both vouchered and unvouchered funds came under the Board's jurisdiction, and the Board was responsible for the determination of whether vouchered or unvouchered funds should be used for specific projects or operations. [Deletion]

The Planning Group was set up in OSS to act as a JCS medium to insure that strategic services operations would be coordinated with military operations. It was therefore charged with responsibility for supervising and coordinating the planning and execution of the military program for psychological warfare. [Deletion]

The Security Office was responsible for the establishment and maintenance of "such protective measures as shall be necessary or advisable in order to safeguard and make secure the OSS, its operations, members, property and records, and the areas, offices and buildings which it occupies or uses." It was also responsible for the security of all OSS installations in the United States and overseas. [Deletion]

Special security provisions were made for the employment of individuals on operational assignments, yet segregated in such a manner as would not expose them to knowledge of the organization as a whole. Such cases ranged from newly-arrived European refugees employed in particular research capacities to Japanese or Japanese-Americans obtained from internment or relocation centers.

The nature of OSS activities made it vitally important for the agency to protect itself against the employment of persons of dubious allegiance or affiliated with potentially anti-American elements. Numerous applicants, both of American and foreign nationality, were rejected for employment after investigation revealed connections with business firms or organizations of known pro-Nazi interests. In other cases, rejections occurred when careful checks revealed doubtful loyalty through past activities with the Communist Party or showed connections with questionable or possibly subversive organizations.

TECHNICAL BRANCHES

Communications. The importance of communications to secret activities cannot be over-stated. It is the efficiency of the communications system which makes possible rapid intelligence procurement and dissemination. In the development of special devices for clandestine transmission and reception, communications performs a vital service to agent and guerrilla operations. Through the procurement and carefully directed use of codes and ciphers, it preserves the secrecy of information and activities. Consequently, security is of the utmost importance in the field of communications.

Although communications is a servicing function, it is so highly technical in nature that the use of most communications equipment must be controlled by technical experts; the misuse of a secret radio, a code or a cipher in one localized instance may result in a breach of security jeopardizing operations in other areas. Therefore, control must be exercised by communications personnel, who are not only technically proficient but understand the unique problems and demands which arise out of the nature of secret activities.

A small, inadequately staffed Code and Cable section and a Message Center had been established by COI. Lack of clearly defined functions, research and development facilities, central administration and personnel became apparent early when the principal branches outlined their specific communications requirements. Many of them would need technical assistance, message centers, traffic offices and specialized telephonic, radio and electronic equipment for field-to-base, ship-to-shore and aircraft-to-ground communications. Particularly pressing was the need for new devices which would be efficient and would provide the maximum degree of physical security behind enemy lines. In view of the fact that no Federal departments or agencies then extant could provide OSS with these requirements, Donovan asked the JCS to approve the establishment of a Communications Branch.

His proposal, submitted 9 September 1942, explained to a special committee of the JCS that the basic requirement for OSS communications was a system capable of achieving rapid and secret communication with OSS agents in the field. Specially trained field agents would be equipped with newly developed portable sending and receiving sets. Fixed and mobile base stations would be set up in secure areas in the field to receive agent traffic and relay instructions from headquarters to agents. In addition, these base stations would maintain wireless and cable communications between each other and with OSS headquarters in Washington and the theaters via Army, Navy and commercial facilities.

Donovan's proposal was still being studied on 22 September when he issued an order combining all OSS signal and traffic facilities in the new Communications Branch. [Deletion]

Recruiting and Training. In October 1942 the Communications Branch was made responsible for all OSS communications training. [Deletion]

Communications worked out a curriculum, the principal element of which was a ten-week course covering code practice, cryptography, security and procedure. Trainees were given sufficient radio theory and maintenance experience to care properly for their equipment and to make repairs. The course culminated in a field program carried out under conditions simulating those which were likely to be encountered in the field. [Deletion]

This Section found itself competing with the Army, Navy and commercial agencies for manpower. Its object was: (1) To recruit enough civilians to staff the training schools; (2) to provide civilian operator-technicians for overseas assignment as instructors and as construction-maintenance men; (3) to recruit officers and enlisted men to be trained for overseas duty; and (4) to commission directly into the Army, Navy or Marine Corps certain highly qualified technicians who could be assigned to the Communications Branch immediately for active duty abroad. Despite the tremendous demand by the armed forces for radio and electronics personnel, the recruiting program was successful. Advertisements, carefully worded to preserve security, were placed in metropolitan newspapers. Members of the Enlisted Reserve Corps of the Army Signal Corps were approached and interviewed. Communications Branch personnel called on likely prospects directly. The newspaper advertisements alone accounted for 300 volunteers between March and May 1943. All candidates were carefully screened according to temperament and personality, as well as technical ability, the highest priority being placed on volunteers with extensive background experience in communications work, both commercial and amateur. Candidates lacking such qualifications, but considered capable of being trained rapidly and effectively, also were considered. Less than half of those interviewed were accepted. [Deletion]

Research and Development Division and Plant and Engineering Division. Research and development was necessary in order to solve communications problems involving physical and electronic characteristics unique in the light of ordinary commercial and military requirements. [Deletion] The problems dealt with by the Division were, in general, of three types: (1) Those submitted by the Plant and Engineering Division of the Communications Branch, which related primarily to radio equipment for the important task of agent traffic, and secondarily to audio and radio equipment for intelligence and "homing" operations; (2) problems submitted by other OSS branches, relating to communications equipment and/or devices for specific operations (such equipment, in addition to radio, also made use of sound and light—both visible and invisible systems); and (3) anticipatory development work initiated by the Division to utilize newly discovered techniques for solving either existing problems or problems which could confidently be expected to arise as enemy counter-measures made existing equipment inadequate.

In November 1942 the Research and Development Division acquired a small laboratory for communications research. As a result, the Division could provide technical information which commercial laboratories and commercial manufacturers, under war pressure, were slow in making available. The laboratory did not include a model shop with a store of extra components for rapid assembly of equipment. Consequently, the Division was compelled throughout the war to spend much time in locating materials and manufacturers and in developing a procurement staff for gathering such logistical information. [Deletion]

The Division engaged in elaborate liaison and cooperative staff work. At its inception it drew on the long experience of British

SOE [Special Operations Executive] in the highly specialized field of clandestine communications. SOE was extremely cooperative, with the result that a complete interchange of information, models and operational reports was achieved. The Division, in turn, helped SOE by locating in the United States equipment needed by the latter organization and by furnishing instruction concerning the utilization of such equipment. [Deletion]

One of the first models of radio apparatus which the Communications Branch undertook to develop was a lightweight portable radio station suitable for clandestine activities. Development work on this problem led to the production of the Strategic Services Transmitter-Receiver, commonly known as the SSTR-1.

An early model, designed prior to the establishment of the Communications Branch, failed to perform satisfactorily when delivered for testing. The model operated from 220 or 110-volt AC or DC commercial power, consuming considerably more electric current than was considered necessary; also the antenna tuning circuit was inadequate for agent operation. The early set was adopted for use only a stopgap pending the development of a better unit.

An entirely new transmitter was therefore designed. It employed a single tube and a coupling network suitable for various types of antenna, which its predecessor lacked. The new transmitter was combined with the receiver of the original model and housed in a metal container. Meanwhile, research to develop a better receiver continued. In its final phase of development, the SSTR-1 consisted of new transmitter and receiver units housed in splashproof cans 9¾ inches long, 4 inches wide and 3½ inches high. The accompanying power supply unit was 5¾ inches wide. The three units could be enclosed in a single small suitcase or, if necessary, in three small packages. In operation, this "suitcase" radio proved satisfactory and efficient. [The SSTR-1 became the standard OSS radio for clandestine operation in enemy and enemy-occupied territory. It was widely known as the "suitcase radio," since the most effective camouflage was found to be a valise manufactured in the particular area of operation. Suitcases of foreign origin were procured from refugees and by combing second-hand shops. (footnote)] Certain refinements were made, such as a rotary tuning coil and a thermocouple battery charger (SSP-3). The battery charger burned solid fuels and produced six to nine watts of energy for charging six-volt batteries in areas where wood, charcoal or other fuels were available. When field operations indicated that a gasoline-powered generator would be desirable, a lightweight unit (SSP-8) was developed.

Although the SSTR-1 was the standard radio sender-receiver for all branches in the field, a portable chest radio transmitter with a range of one to five miles was developed for SO. This set, known as the SSTR-3, operated on the 40-megacycle band and was the outgrowth of a project initiated prior to the establishment of the Communications Branch. In the same category was the SSTR-5, a portable CW transmitter-receiver so small that it was housed, complete with batteries, in a case 8x10x2 inches. The unit included a self-contained 50-foot antenna.

Possibly the most spectacular development produced by the Communications Branch was the OSS air-to-ground (Joan-Eleanor), a combination of the SSTR-6 and SSTC-502. This unit included a magnetic wire recorder installed in aircraft to record ultra-high frequency voice transmissions between plane and ground. The equipment was successfully used both in ETO and the Far East.

Problems arising out of experience in the field prompted the development of the SST-102 crystal oscillator to enable an operator to calibrate his SSTR-1 receiver. The unit measured 4x2x2 inches complete with batteries. A wire-tapping and amplifier unit of extremely small dimensions (SSAA-401) was developed, which was unique in that telephone communications could be intercepted without physically tapping telephone lines. In addition, a small microphone was devised which could pick up conversations in distant rooms.

The SSLD-321 and SSLV-322 were a three-cornered mirror reflector and a night-landing headset, respectively, to be used in locating parachute pinpoints on which personnel and/or supplies could be dropped. The reflector on the ground returned a beam of light sent from a headset in the plane, the return beam being visible only to the plane. [This apparatus was based on the principle that three plane mirror surfaces placed at right angles to one another will reflect light back in a direct line to its source, the light being visible only to someone in a position along such a direct line. (footnote)]

For flares, demolition charges and signals, the SSR-204 radio switch was developed. Capable of detonation within a span of 72 hours, the switch could be controlled from a plane at any time during its operating life for the purpose of setting off flares, demolitions or signals. The development was particularly useful for pinpointing bombing objectives and for delayed demolitions work. [Deletion]

Message Center. Under COI, the Message Center was at first controlled by the Liaison Office, and subsequently by the Registry Section. When the Communications Branch was organized in September 1942, the Center acquired guidance as to operational and policy matters, its primary responsibility being the sending and receiving of all official outgoing and incoming telegrams and cables and the performance of all attendant functions incidental to these duties.

Beginning with three clerks in December 1941, the Center grew to include a maximum of 130 employees in Washington and 400 in the field by late 1945. Originally, all clerks were required to perform enciphering, paraphrasing, typing, logging, teletypewriting and other duties. As the establishment expanded, the separate functions of the Center were divided into the Code Room, the Paraphrasing and Distribution Section, the Teletype Section and Typing Room. In addition, a Maintenance Section was formed to maintain cryptographic and other mechanical devices used by the Message Center; and a Cryptographic Security Section checked traffic for cryptographic insecurities, devised new cipher systems, and instructed Message Center employees in the intricacies of these systems. A Personnel Section was given authority over both military and civilian employees.

For transmission facilities the Message Center originally relied on commercial circuits, messages being filed on a per-word basis. Circuits were installed to provide direct lines between the Message Center and the Washington offices of Western Union, Postal Telegraph and RCA. Early in 1943, OSS found that Army transmission facilities provided the agency with excellent service. By April the Army network was handling so much OSS traffic that a TWX teletype circuit was installed between the Message Center and the Army Signal Center, obviating the need for couriers. Beginning in early 1944, Navy radio facilities also proved useful for transmissions to some Far East stations. From the start, in October 1941, the facilities of the Department of State were used to transmit messages in OSS cipher to and from field agents who were under diplomatic cover.

The most noteworthy commercial communications line utilized by OSS was a Western Union cable between Washington and London. Use of this channel was limited considerably in 1942 since it was shared by a number of government agencies. In the following year, Western Union introduced a system known as Varioplex, which permitted 12 subscribers to use a cable channel virtually simultaneously. The agency continued to use the company's Washington-London facilities and in 1944 OSS introduced new high-speed enciphering and deciphering devices on the circuit which made possible a series of secret conferences in high-grade cipher. These devices functioned so rapidly that conferences by cable could be held almost as rapidly as by transatlantic telephone.

From 1943 until the end of the war, OSS in Washington was in communication by radio-telephone several nights weekly with its representative in Bern. On the following mornings, appropriate OSS branches received recordings of the conversations.

New cipher systems were introduced periodically in order to replace those which had become outdated or to tighten security. In addition, procedures were instituted to step up the processing of messages. Early in 1945, the Communications Branch maintained message centers not only in Washington but in some 25 major locations in fifteen countries. The Washington Center alone handled about 500,000 code groups monthly. The total for all OSS message centers throughout the world during April 1945 was 60,500 messages comprising some 5,868,000 code groups.

Physically separated from the rest of OSS due to the unusual requirements of cryptographic security, the members of the Message Center were not always well informed concerning the operations of the various branches of the organization and some confusion developed as to how individual cables should be distributed. In an effort to solve the situation, the Secretariat, which received copies of all incoming and outgoing cables, prepared a distribution list to cover all "routine" cables. Messages not regarded as routine were sent to the Secretariat, which determined their distribution. Inasmuch as approximately half the cables could be considered routine, the other half had to be submitted to the Secretariat for distribution. [Deletion]

The needs of OSS with regard to communications were unprecedented. The Communications Branch required the highest degree of technical knowledge, research and development. It produced special equipment and devices vital to the successful prosecution of espionage and special operations, and trained radio operators to facilitate those operations. It secured and protected codes and ciphers to maintain the secrecy of operations. The Branch regulated traffic between Washington and field bases and between Washington and agents in neutral territories who could make use of diplomatic and commercial channels for communication by OSS cipher. Washington also supervised lateral communications between major field bases. The Washington headquarters was further under constant pressure to send highly-qualified personnel and ever-increasing amounts of special and standard equipment overseas.

One of the most important tasks of the Branch, however, was to indoctrinate its personnel with an understanding of the specialized needs of OSS. It was not enough that Communications members be technically proficient. They had to be able to adapt their expert knowledge to the demands of OSS activities. The capacity for improvisation was one of the greatest assets of the Branch. This was, of course, vital in the development of new devices. It was further important in the training of agent personnel for the operating branches. [Deletion]

RESEARCH AND DEVELOPMENT—(R&D)

This was specifically responsible for the development of special weapons and equipment necessary to subversive warfare; the provision of the myriad items necessary to support agent cover; the camouflage of personal accessories or devices to facilitate special operations; and the collection and dissemination of information on all types of equipment, developed within or without the agency, which would be of use in OSS activities. [Deletion]

Just as the activities of OSS were unique, so research and development on devices, equipment and cover details necessary to support those activities was a distinct and unusual problem. While certain branches, such as OG, could rely to some extent upon standard military weapons, the undercover activities of SO and SI required the development of specialized devices and cover details. [Deletion]

In order to secure necessary laboratory facilities to carry out its work, an arrangement was made in the fall of 1942 with the National Defense Research Committee (NDRC) by which the latter agreed to create a unit for the exclusive purpose of developing weapons and devices for OSS. The unit, designated Division 19— Special Weapons, was supplemented by the establishment of the Maryland Research Laboratory (MRL) to perform the laboratory work. Subsequently, when MRL's facilities became over-taxed, temporary arrangements were made with certain universities and laboratories for work on specific projects. Thus R&D was able to draw on the skills, techniques and facilities of the leading scientists and laboratories of the United States. [Deletion]

Special Devices, Weapons and Equipment. It would be impossible in the space available to list all the gadgets developed either originally by R&D or improved after the procurement of the original idea or model from the British. However, certain items may be noted to indicate the nature of the work.

Basic to the performance of sabotage was a time delay device which would allow the agent to put an explosive or incendiary charge in position and permit a period of time before detonation, to give him a chance to escape. Among such devices produced by

R&D was the pocket incendiary which, by virtue of its size, combined the two essential features of compactness and camouflage potential. This incendiary device was capable of starting more than nine fires simultaneously at a given time after being placed in position.

Among the explosive charges developed was the "limpet." This was a charge which could be placed on the side of a ship below the water line and which would detonate after a period of time delay adjustable to the situation. It could be used from small craft operating clandestinely or by underwater swimmers. The first "limpets" were of a magnet type, held to the side of the ship by six extremely powerful, small horseshoe magnets. Field experience later demonstrated the necessity for some other method of attachment, since in certain cases, barnacles on the hulls prevented the "limpets" from sticking. R&D therefore developed the "Pin-Up Girl"—a hardened steel nail driven into the plates of the ship by an explosive cartridge.

In some cases it was possible to use standardized equipment by the development of special parts which would adapt it to OSS operations. Among these were silenced weapons and silencers to be attached to standard weapons. The silenced .22 calibre pistol developed by R&D was a clip-fed automatic pistol with a special silenced barrel, the clip holding ten rounds of high-speed, long-range ammunition. It was designed for use in stealthy attacks to eliminate sentries or other enemy personnel without causing widespread alarm. In addition to the silencing feature, no muzzle flash was visible, even in darkness.

R&D also developed a silenced barrel for the .45 calibre M-3 sub-machine gun. It was impossible to achieve total elimination of noise in an automatic weapon such as the M-3, but, whereas a previous silencer had reduced the noise by 50%, R&D was able to effect a 90% reduction. In the case of the M-3, all that was necessary was to unscrew the old barrel and replace it with the R&D product; therefore, only the silenced barrel required transportation to the field. The silenced M-3 was used successfully by OSS and was also used by the Marine Corps.

Among the very unusual requests received by R&D was one from the Far East. This was for an explosive that could be camouflaged as flour. It was desired that the end product be capable of mixing with water to form a "dough" which could be baked into "biscuits or loaves of bread." It was further specified that the "bread" so baked should be edible. It was thought that such "flour" could be transported through the Japanese lines by the Chinese with safety and could be kept in a peasant's home without arousing suspicion. The request was fulfilled, the resultant product being designated "Aunt Jemima." [The only test that was not conclusively met in laboratory trials in America was that of edibility. When this "flour" was sent to the Far East, it was later learned that three Chinese cooks who had baked biscuits from the material ate some of the biscuits contrary to orders. The field reports indicated that no ill effects were observed. (footnote)]

Field experience, even in late stages of the war, indicated the need for improvement in sabotage techniques. A request came from ETO that R&D re-examine methods for derailing trains. Tests disclosed that the British "one-meter" technique (the placing of two ¾-pound charges of plastic explosive on the side of a train rail one meter apart) did not result in major derailment. In fact, the use of that method resulted in 50% failures. R&D evolved a system of placing charges beneath the rail so as not only to remove about eight feet of the rail, but at the same time create a crater beneath the gap into which the engine would fall. This method was forwarded to agents operating in ETO, where subsequent results showed a margin of only 10% failures.

A somewhat different type of sabotage was envisioned in the "Caccolube," or "Turtle Egg." This was designed to effect sabotage on gasoline engines. It was a small packet of abrasive material which, when placed in the oil intake pipe of a gasoline engine, would cause seizure of the bearings and disruption of the pistons and connecting rods some hours later.

It was found that contaminants, such as sand, popularly believed to be highly efficacious for the sabotage of vehicles, were practially non-effective. The common contaminants for gasoline, such as sugar, were also found to be ineffective, in addition to being scarce in occupied territory. R&D developed the "Firefly." This was a small three-ounce gadget which, when placed in the gasoline tank of a vehicle, would, between 1½ and 10 hours later, cause an explosion that would rip out the bottom of the tank and set fire to the gasoline. Reports from the field later indicated that it was determined to be effective in 85% of the operations in which it was used.

R&D received a joint request from SI and Communications in early 1945 to develop a submersible raft, powered by sail or by a small electric motor, which could be transported in a submarine. The request specified that the raft should be capable of carrying 400 pounds of dead weight, including the entire radio apparatus needed by the agent. The radio apparatus obviously had to be carried in dry storage. After an agent had gone ashore from a submarine on this raft, he should be able to submerge the raft in twenty-five feet of sea water and leave it until such time as he had

established the fact that he was relatively secure in the position
chosen for landing. It was required that the raft surface itself and
re-submerge at least eight times from a depth of twenty-five feet in
order that the agent might be able to use his radio or obtain new
supplies, and between those times submerge it for concealment
purposes. In essence, R&D had been asked to produce what was
practically a midget submarine. This requisition was fulfilled in approximately four months.

Agent Authentication. The production of the various documents, clothes and accessories, as well as all the other minutiae
necessary to enable an agent to maintain cover, was the responsibility of the Documentation, Camouflage and Special Assistants
Divisions.

An engraving shop was established in Washington for the production of various types of European and Far Eastern documents.
Identity cards, work permits, chauffeurs' licenses, etc., were metic-
ulously prepared with appropriate regard for the enormous
amount of detail necessary to provide the authenticity upon which
the agent's life might depend. Through OG's, the French Maquis
was supplied with all necessary documents for travel and activity in
Germany, France, Belgium and the Netherlands. CD was, of
course, responsible for securing the intelligence necessary to the
production of agent documentation, but R&D also secured a great
deal of information from other sources and from its own personnel
in the field. In fact, R&D and CD personnel worked together in
many theaters on questions of documentation and camouflage,
e.g., in London, where a joint office was set up. Such details as the
size of type, kind of paper and ink used, methods of watermarking,
etc., were of vital importance.

The work of camouflage included not only methods of disguising
various types of explosive and other devices (for example, the
preparation of plastic explosives in the shape and appearance of
lumps of coal, stones normal to a given locality, or manure), but
the outfitting of an agent for travel in a given enemy or neutral territory. The enormity of such a task is indicated when it is realized
that each agent had to be equipped with clothing sewn exactly as it
would have been sewn if it were made in the local area for which he
was destined; his eyeglasses, dental work, toothbrush, razor, brief
case, travelling bag, shoes, and every item of wearing apparel or
accessory had to be microscopically accurate. Upon such details
the life of the agent and, consequently, the success of his mission
might depend.

The Camouflage Division also produced specialized devices to
be used as inanimate letter drops. At first, several letter drops were

made in the form of old pieces of wood, such as a small part of a branch from the limb of a tree. The wood was split and a metal container inserted in such fashion that the wood could be replaced and present an innocent appearance to any observer. It was soon discovered that the cardinal principle in producing inanimate letter drops was that the subject of disguise be neither edible nor burnable. In such cases it is liable to be used by some casual passer-by. Thereafter, letter drops were made in many other forms, such as stones, old tin cans of various localities, etc. Such letter drops could be placed in position by agents (e.g., at a pre-arranged distance from a given kilometer marker on a European road) and provide a two-way channel of communication for intelligence, such as map overlays, which was unsuitable for transmission by radio.

Other items produced, in this case by the Special Assistants Division, to support the agent in his operations were "K," "L" and "TD" tablets. The "K" tablet was designed to insure that the person to whom it was to be administered would be knocked out for a reasonable period of time, and the "TD" tablet was designed to insure that the subject would respond favorably to interrogation. The "L" tablet was to produce death rapidly. "L" tablets were carried by agents as a precautionary measure, to be self-administered in the event of capture in order to preclude the possibility of revealing information under the strain of interrogation and torture. [Deletion]

Another significant technical development was the so-called "spy camera," which could take a full-view picture from any position. It required no focussing—nothing more than general aiming at the object. The working model was completed on 3 November 1943, and Eastman Kodak produced the finished product. It was generally acknowledged to be the finest espionage camera in existence from the standpoint of simplicity in operation and design. [Deletion]

RESEARCH AND ANALYSIS—(R&A)

The functions of R&A were so broad and complex as to resist precise definition. Basically, the concept of the Branch grew out of realization that the intelligence set-up of the United States was inadequate to cope with the demands of modern war. Consequently, as related in the account of the Branch under COI, there were marshalled to the over-all intelligence effort sources previously untapped and skills previously unused. Though not new in themselves, they constituted an innovation when combined and applied to the field of intelligence. [Deletion]

Four principal divisions were created, regional in responsibility but with functional subdivisions. They were designated Europe-Africa, Far East, USSR and Latin America, each comprising Economic, Political and Geographic Subdivisions. [Deletion]

R&A operated in an intelligence area previously little developed by the United States—the complex field of economic, political and geographic relationships. The collection of great stores of source material and the analytic employment of such material furnished a rounded background of intelligence, primarily employed for military operations but holding manifold peacetime possibilities for the strengthening of America's knowledge of foreign affairs, and contributing to the future security of the United States.

With the dissolution of OSS on 30 September 1945, R&A was transferred intact to the State Department. [Deletion]

SECRET INTELLIGENCE—(SI)

The object of secret intelligence activity is to obtain by secret means information which cannot otherwise be secured and which is not elsewhere available. Such information is vital in the determination of strategy or the formulation of policy. Through the quality of secrecy, its possessor gains the benefit of surprise on the offense; and on the defense the opposition is deprived of this invaluable asset. An effective secret intelligence organization is one which not only can obtain such information at random, but can secure it when needed. It thus becomes a vital national asset gaining value through permanence.

The continuing effectiveness of a secret intelligence organization depends upon the secrecy of its methods. That secrecy is in constant jeopardy. For example, the very action in which secret information is used may perforce reveal pre-knowledge. Consequently, the organization must eliminate evidence of method (e.g., source) upon dissemination, and must constantly strive for originality in technique.

It is axiomatic, therefore, that there are no formulae for the successful accomplishment of espionage. Repetition of pattern in operations is one of the surest ways of inviting detection. A secret intelligence organization cannot become standardized in operations or procedures; it must always be in process of development. The situations which it exploits for intelligence may demand the colorless at one moment, the bizarre at the next. The challenge to judgment and ingenuity is constant.

SI was thus a process rather than a system. From the smallest one-man outpost with an operating military unit, to the bases in neutral territory and the Washington headquarters, it sought always to adapt old methods and develop new ones. [Deletion]

Geographic Desks. The Geographic Desks were grouped [Deletion] in four divisions: Europe, Africa, Middle East and Far East. Under OSS, as under COI, these Desks were the operating sections and initiated SI activities. [Deletion]

In the principal neutral countries on the perimeter of the Axis, e.g., Sweden and Spain, X-2 was the sole OSS activity authorized, but sizable SI missions were stationed there for the purpose of penetrating enemy or enemy-occupied territory. A special case was Switzerland, where a few SI operatives had been placed in the first ten months of 1942. The country was completely encircled from the time of the German occupation of Vichy France in November 1942 until September 1944. This isolation made it impossible to dispatch additional personnel and also created difficult problems of communications and supply. Nevertheless, the intelligence which SI procured from Switzerland throughout the war was outstanding.

Therefore, in the case of those Desks servicing agents in neutral countries the job was more than one of supply and personnel. The search for suitable cover occupations and qualified people was continuous. SI representation in Spain at its peak consisted of some fifty agents. Since these agents were engaged in directing the activities of more than a thousand sub-agents in France, Madrid became in effect a field base. The same was true of Scandinavia, where OSS representation reached a total of approximately fifty in late 1944. In Stockholm, however, SO and MO also carried on activities directed toward enemy and enemy-occupied territory. [Deletion]

Many Americans of French or Italian descent were recruited in 1942 to serve as undercover agents in France and Italy. The demand for personnel in field bases and outposts in various military theaters made it necessary to divert most of these recruits to operational staffs there, however. In any event, the requirements of effective cover made it more practicable in most instances to recruit locally in territories such as Africa (and later in Sicily, Corsica, Sardinia and southern Italy, as those regions were occupied by the Allies) agents who had recent residence in the target areas, and correspondingly greater facilities for cover. Consequently, the Americans recruited in 1942 and trained in the United States became SI operations officers at such bases as Algiers, London and Cairo. [Deletion]

Personnel problems were particularly complex and troublesome. The need for additional personnel in the field was constant; the number of individuals with the requisite skills, experience, language, specialized knowledge and aptitudes for SI was small. When a suitable recruit for field staff was found, the time required to secure his services and dispatch him was extensive. If he were in the Army, it would require five weeks for security check, two weeks for transfer, three weeks for minimum schooling and, on the average, two weeks in transit. All this, of course, was exclusive of any time spent in waiting for military transportation.

There were many cases where the lack of commission allotments handicapped recruiting and caused a poor morale situation. For example, a recruit of exceptional qualifications might be secured, inducted into the Army as an enlisted man and sent overseas with the promise of a commission. In many instances it was impracticable for such a man to operate in civilian clothes in the field, and in uniform his usefulness was considerably curtailed by his enlisted rank. This often resulted in particular knowledges of language and target area being applied in the field merely to barter activities or the direction of foreign motor pool employees. The Desks were constantly struggling to get commissions for such personnel. This problem, which was also encountered by other branches and sections, was particularly acute in the case of SI. [Deletion]

As emphasis was increasingly placed upon personnel for military theaters, the type of personnel desired for SI also changed. Whereas the Desks sending operatives to neutral countries were bound by few, if any, restrictions as to age or physical condition, those dispatching personnel to theaters of operation naturally sought younger people in good physical condition. Therefore, while the principal officials of SI were civilian, recruiting efforts were increasingly directed toward the various branches of military service.

There was a constant and fundamental conflict in attempts to impose a military approach on secret intelligence problems, which was particularly apparent in the matter of personnel. The military approach to recruiting, training and replacement is on a unit basis; mass movement and mass operations require standardization. The opposite is the case in the field of secret intelligence, where it is imperative that personnel be recruited and trained and operate on an individual and voluntary basis. The unorthodox is the norm. No force of discipline can extract that exercise of ingenuity, judgment and energy which the work itself requires. The subject requires some emphasis, since it arises out of the unique nature of secret intelligence activity and lack of understanding of such basic differences breeds ineffectiveness. [Deletion]

Reporting Board. In 1943 the Board established a system of grading the reports of various agents, which resulted in average evaluations. Thus an agent would be rated on the basis of the intelligence he produced; such ratings would be raised or lowered, as the quality of the intelligence indicated. In this fashion the Desks were kept informed of the calibre of the work performed by their agents and networks. The system had the further effect of assisting evaluation; a startling or improbable report from an agent whose work had gained a "B" rating would immediately attract attention and careful analysis. [Deletion] [This activity was all-important because it was one of the few ways to establish whether a man was that most dangerous animal—a turncoat, or double-agent. Thus an agent who sent in too much good data might be as suspect as the agent who sent in too little—both might be under enemy control and especially in the former case, might have been purchased by the enemy for some long-range game.]

[The OSS was a prolific agency from the start. For example:] During 1943, 32,499 reports were disseminated by the Board, each report averaging five items of intelligence.

On 4 January 1944, the Chief of SI directed that increased emphasis should be placed on quality of intelligence rather than on quantity. However, the activity of OSS in 1944 was so great that, despite the strictest elimination of every piece of duplication and of all antiquated and inconsequential reports, the Board by 24 November had processed 54,862 reports representing approximately 500,000 items of intelligence.

Labor Section. The Labor Section was a functional unit established within SI to enlist the support of labor in all countries, chiefly for purposes of intelligence, but also for sabotage and subversion.

Little had been done to invoke labor's cooperation in securing the organized resistance of European labor undergrounds during the first few months after Pearl Harbor. [Deletion]

In view of the traditional distrust which existed between labor and official government agencies throughout the world, it was obvious that the type of personnel selected would largely determine the success of the venture. Men who knew labor problems, and who understood and respected the points of view of labor and its leaders—who had or could inspire their confidence—were essential to the work. At the same time, rivalries among various factions in the field of trade unionism made it impractical to staff the Section with men from the unions themselves. These factors were paramount in the selection of personnel. The Chief of the Section was a practicing attorney in Chicago who had specialized in civil liberties and labor cases and had acted as counsel for many important unions. He established the Section in New York and sought to

recruit for it men who were thoroughly familiar with labor questions but who were not identified with any particular labor element
or point of view. The staff soon included a former chief trial ex-
aminer for NLRB, a lawyer of some experience in the Department
of Interior and in NLRB, and another who had served in FHA,
SEC, NLRB, and had been counsel for the La Follette Senate
Committee which had investigated anti-labor practices. [Deletion]

Field operations were, as in other sections of SI, most important. The first field office was established in London in the fall of
1942. The national federations of labor of six occupied countries
had set up new headquarters there, as had the secretariats of five
international federations of crafts and industries. In addition, London was the outlet for European refugees and headquarters for the
many governments-in-exile. The labor organizations of neutral
countries also maintained representatives there.

When the Chief of the Labor Section first proceeded to London
in September 1942 to make preliminary arrangements, he found
that the British authorities were cooperating only tentatively with
continental labor in the prosecution of the war. Only one man, a
protege of Ernest Bevin, was working full time on labor questions.
Ostensibly, he was an advisor to PWE on labor questions; actually
he was doing secret intelligence work for SOE in this field. He was
enthusiastic about the prospect of an OSS Labor Section office in
London and endorsed the plans for cooperation with the continental labor underground. He was convinced that if the American
Government acted in this field the British would follow suit—
which they did.

Additional field offices were soon established, in North Africa
and Stockholm in early 1943, and in Cairo later that year. At its
peak, the Labor Section had field offices in London, North Africa,
Bern, Stockholm, Cairo, Bari, Naples, Istanbul, Buenos Aires and
Santiago de Chile. The latter two offices (working on a limited
basis, and in cooperation with the FBI) served as outposts for the
Ship Observer Project.

The Ship Observer Unit (SOU) was created in December 1942
"to secure strategic information about military, naval, economic
and political conditions in enemy, occupied and neutral territories
through seamen, seamen's organizations, ship operators, and other
maritime channels." A secondary function was to obtain facilities
for transporting agents under the guise or cover of seamen or ship's
officers. In addition, the SOU was to recruit agents from among
neutral merchant fleets.

SOU was established in offices at 42 Broadway, New York, in
December 1942. While its operations centered there, a subsidiary

office was later opened in Philadelphia and for a time SOU had a
representative in New Orleans. Representatives in Buenos Aires
and Santiago de Chile were also maintained.

SOU secured the cooperation and support of practically all
American and neutral maritime unions. In addition, the War Shipping Administration lent valuable assistance, principally by advising SOU of the movements of ships whose officers and crews
might be expected to have valuable information, and by transporting agents to theaters of operation.

Hundreds of seamen of the merchant marines of many nations
were interviewed. Stewards and radio operators proved to be the
most useful, but crew members of every other category, as well as
ship's officers, were of value. Approximately one hundred men on
neutral ships and approximately one thousand on American vessels
were enlisted as regular informants. Hundreds of others contributed occasionally to the SOU's growing fund of information.

These men told little to representatives of the Army, Navy and
FBI who interrogated them on arrival. They distrusted armies and
navies in general almost as much as they distrusted police. Besides,
official interrogations were often conducted with inadequate staff
and through interpreters. But they talked to SOU representatives—over coffee or rum—in a waterfront saloon, a seamen's
restaurant or a union hall. The SOU representatives were more
nearly their kind of people, were vouched for by others whom they
trusted, and spoke their language—both literally and figuratively.
[Deletion]

Most of the information procured by the seamen dealt with harbor and beach defenses and other military and naval installations.
However, information was also forthcoming on political attitudes,
economics and other factors. In addition, X-2 information was
secured on the Nazi sympathies and activities of individuals.

SOU obtained four types of material: (1) Oral descriptions supplemented in some cases by notes on the spot, which were made into written reports. (2) Maps, in some cases sketch maps of key
areas and installations drawn by the seamen themselves, and in
others standard maps provided by SOU, on which the seamen
marked the locations of significant features. (3) Photographs taken
by seamen. (In some cases SOU provided the men with cameras
and equipment; sometimes the men furnished their own. Among
others, photographs were obtained of harbor defenses and other installations at Marseille and of both shores of the Straits of Mes-
sina.) (4) Foreign publications, among the most useful of which
were underground newspapers and periodicals.

In addition to those who were recruited, briefed and sent out from the United States, labor representatives abroad enlisted the cooperation of seamen in infiltrating agents into enemy and enemy-occupied territory.

A second project operating in the United States was the Office of European Labor Research (OELR). OELR was established on 15 August 1942 in offices at 11 West 42nd Street, New York City. It was a semi-autonomous private agency, having no ostensible connection with the Government and working for the Labor Section on a contract basis. Its staff was composed of German and Austrian emigre labor leaders, who acted as private citizens and not as government officials or employees.

The purpose of OELR was to collect information on the European labor situation, related economic problems and the status of resistance; to introduce Labor Section officers and field representatives to foreign labor leaders and vouch for their good faith; and to assist the Labor Section in finding qualified agent recruits of foreign origin.

The OELR produced some 200 short reports and more than eighty large studies. In addition to its work for the Labor Section, it prepared in 1943 five special reports on various French labor questions at the request of [United Nations Relief and Rehabilitation Administration, more widely known as UNRRA, an agency established to help the war-ravaged nations get back on their feet]. Its more comprehensive surveys included labor manuals for France, Austria, Belgium, the Netherlands and Germany, and "Who's Who" listings of labor in Axis and Axis-occupied countries. These surveys were continuing studies, maintained on a current basis.

Most important were OELR's introductions. Almost every representative of the Labor Section, and a good many representatives of other OSS units, profited at one time or another by OELR introductions to international labor leaders. [Deletion]

It is worthy of note that the first OSS agent in Germany was infiltrated by the Labor Section.

The Labor Section was a successful experiment in secret intelligence. It was an experiment, because seldom in either peace or war have organized labor and an undercover government agency cooperated more closely, or more confidently. It was another example of applying to the field of intelligence careful choice of personnel and knowledge of delicate human factors which sometimes hinder cooperation, however great the desire on both sides.

The accomplishments of the Labor Section have significance for the future. The value of labor's contribution to secret intelligence and unorthodox warfare should be recognized and developed promptly.

Technical Section. The Technical Section was established on or about 1 May 1943 to assist in reviewing and screening technical reports and to cooperate with translators to insure technical accuracy. In addition, it assisted R&D, Communications and Special Projects, and cooperated with other agencies and departments of the Government and armed services on technical matters. It was of particular value in preparing "indicators" which were sent to agents in the field to facilitate recognition of installations, equipment and devices and their proper designations in finished reports.

The work of the office grew rapidly to such an extent that the Army, Navy, and especially the Air Force, regularly sent representatives to the Technical Section's office to obtain quickly at first-hand late information. The collection of information regarding research areas and development of V-1 and V-2 weapons was particularly instrumental in increased defensive activity. The Section reviewed as many as 5,500 technical reports per month, screened them and disseminated the important ones to appropriate officials.

The Technical Section was the instigator, and cooperated with R&A, in preparing and sending abroad for the Army and for OSS special operational use, certain condensed technical and design information on road and rail bridges and water aqueducts in Italy, France, the Low Countries, Yugoslavia and Germany. Such detailed information on design, spans, strength, etc., was particularly valuable in showing points vulnerable to sabotage. Such information also was useful to the armed forces in making quick repairs. [Deletion]

SI maintained liaison with the undercover agencies of other United Nations governments both in America and abroad. Much information was procured through these services, with the relation becoming active collaboration in certain localized instances, such as the *Sussex* plan [see below] and the Labor Section's VARLIN [see below] project. [In this context, "United Nations governments" is used as the official term for the Allied governments in the war against Germany and Japan, not as governments represented at the Manhattan headquarters which, of course, did not exist at this time. Churchill's term for the UN governments was the Grand Alliance.] [Deletion]

COUNTER-ESPIONAGE—X-2

Counter-espionage is a distinct and independent intelligence function. It embraces not only the protection of the intelligence in-

terests of the government it serves, but, by control and manipulation of the intelligence operations of other nations, it performs a
dynamic function in discerning their plans and intentions, as well
as in deceiving them. An effective counter-espionage organization
is therefore an intelligence instrument of vital importance to national security.

The development of a secret intelligence organization makes
protective counter-intelligence inevitable. However, to confine
such activity to its protective aspects would be to eschew the development of the affirmative phases of counter-espionage which give
it its unique and distinct value.

A counter-espionage organization usually develops slowly. Basic
to it is the vast body of records which is the key to its operations
and which normally takes years to accumulate. A second requirement, however, no less vital, is skilled personnel familiar with the
intricate techniques by which the intelligence efforts of other nations may be controlled and directed.

The United States lacked these basic factors. At the outbreak of
the war its counter-intelligence activities were performed by several agencies and departments of the Government and the armed
forces, principally FBI, G-2 [U.S. Army intelligence] and ONI
[Office of Naval Intelligence]. Fortunately, the domestic security
problem, most important at that time, was efficiently handled by
the FBI, which kept itself alerted to threats from beyond United
States borders by liaison with Allied security services, chiefly those
of the British. With respect to areas outside the Western Hemisphere, however, the United States had virtually no security protection. Also, the divisions of interest of the various American organizations concerned with counter-intelligence and the limitations
upon their several missions had resulted in incomplete and duplica-
tive records, which were scattered and uncoordinated. [The editor
can attest from personal experience to the dismaying confusion of
the U.S. Army and Navy intelligence and attaches' reports. They
were presented to the U.S. National Archives in a state that suggested they had never been filed at all.] The lack of complete past
and current records of enemy espionage organizations, their personnel and activities, made the effective prosecution of counter-
espionage seem impossible.

The development by COI/OSS of a secret intelligence organization to operate outside the Western Hemisphere made it obvious
that it would be necessary to establish a security organization for
its protection. It is, of course, inevitable that a secret intelligence
agent in a foreign area will attempt to acquaint himself with the intelligence activities and undercover personnel of other nations

operating in the same area. This, however, provides only localized and uncoordinated knowledge. Furthermore, it does not take advantage of the affirmative possibilities inherent in the possession of such knowledge, if it is coordinated with related data and supported by an efficient centralized organization.

It was widely recognized that centralization was the key to counter-espionage. This may be said to be true of secret intelligence generally. When it became apparent in early 1942 that SI would have to set up some form of security organization, the question of centralization was raised. By midsummer, the subject had been discussed by COI/OSS, not only with other agencies and departments of the Government, but with the British Security Coordination. [BSC, the New York branch offices of the British secret services, which had their headquarters in London throughout the war, contrary to the statements of William Stevenson in his 1976 book *A Man Called Intrepid*]. Such discussions stimulated the move to establish a CI Division [counter-intelligence] in SI.

The British had been sharing with COI, G-2, FBI, ONI and other interested agencies certain counter-espionage information. Experience gained in unravelling Axis espionage and sabotage organizations had developed a high degree of efficiency in the coordinated net of security services which the British had long maintained. In addition, they had built up over many years one of the essential instruments for CE work [counter-espionage CE, offensive counter-intelligence branch. See section entitled Field Operations in this chapter]—a comprehensive and current registry on hostile and suspected persons and on their organizations and relationships. Nothing remotely like it on overseas CE intelligence was available to American agencies. Nor could such a body of records be produced except after decades of extensive operations. Therefore, the British were particularly anxious that the handling of the information which they made available to the American services should be consonant with the highly specialized CE techniques they had evolved. This demanded carefully trained specialists, solely concerned with CE material. In addition, America's entry into the war complicated the problem of disseminating CE material to loosely coordinated United States agencies. [The British security services' registry was in fact a good deal less well organized than the Americans realized, especially in the early part of the war. A counter-intelligence failure to spot the German naval intelligence agent Albert Oertel—a man who came to England in 1927 as a sleeper, became a naturalized Englishman, and established his cover as a jeweler and watchmaker near the great British naval base at Scapa Flow—resulted in the loss in October 1939, a month

after the outbreak of the German war, of the British battleship
Royal Oak. Working against charts supplied by Oertel, which
showed there were no torpedo nets around *Royal Oak's* moorings,
a U-boat crept into the fjord and sank the battleship in what was
regarded as an impregnable anchorage. This disaster was followed
by a greater and even more serious one. MI-5's registry, stored in
the London prison called Wormwood Scrubs, was set on fire by a
German bomb in 1940. Without this registry, MI-5 was, for the
time being, neutralized.

[Neither did Colonel Sir Vernon Kell, the World War I spymaster, redeem his service's reputation after the Scapa Flow incident
with an intelligent recruiting policy. Bruce Page and his collaborators in *The Philby Conspiracy* have recorded how Kell stated
that his policy was to recruit girls of good breeding with good legs.
MI-5 headquarters thus swarmed with debby girls who worked in
what Page *et al.* described as "the atmosphere of dormitory feast
hysteria." The files in the registry were "voluminous but quite
meaningless," one of Page *et al.'s* informants stated. As another
revealed: "We would be asked for the card on someone or other.
You would spend hours plodding patiently through card after card
and finally discover it said: 'Once signed a petition against book
censorship.' Kell was fired by Churchill, and in came such brilliant
and dangerous (to the German services) officials as Dick Gold-
smith White and Guy Liddell. However, throughout this period the
files of the Special Branch at Scotland Yard, the executive arm of
the security services, remained as intact, comprehensive and efficient, and saved MI-5's bacon from time to time when suspicious
foreigners were found slipping into the islands from the Continent
after Dunkirk. In the end, the security services redeemed themselves and emerged triumphantly with either the German services
in control or destroyed.]

In August 1942, therefore, representations were made by the
British which strongly suggested an arrangement between the British and American agencies that would provide a more restricted
and secure channel for the handling of CE information. If such an
arrangement were concluded, the British indicated that they would
be willing to make available all the CE information in their possession. The significance of this offer to the development by the
United States of a counter-espionage organization cannot be over-
stated. The United States was given the opportunity of gaining in a
short period extensive CE records which represented the fruits of
many decades of counter-espionage experience. Furthermore, the
British offered to train American personnel in the techniques essential to the proper use of those records and the prosecution of CE

operations.

The proposed arrangement envisioned the establishment of a civilian CE organization within OSS—in short, an American entity similar to MI-6(V) and MI-5, the British services for overseas and home security respectively, both of which were civilian services only nominally under military control. Following preliminary discussions in the United States, Donovan designated one of his special assistants to proceed to London in November 1942, where he worked out with the British arrangements whereby a small liaison unit of the projected CE organization would be stationed in London. Procedure for transmission of the CE material to the United States also resulted from these discussions.

At that time it was intended that the new CE unit to be established within OSS should become the exclusive link between British and American CE services. FBI, however, had long maintained a close and cordial liaison with the British security services, particularly MI-5, in the interests of American security in the Western Hemisphere. It was therefore agreed that FBI, in view of its jurisdiction over CE in the Western Hemisphere, would continue its independent liaison with the British services in so far as exchange of CE information relating to that area was concerned.

Definitive arrangements having been concluded, a Counter-Intelligence Division within the SI Branch of OSS was established [on] 1 March 1943. Arrangements were made to send four officers and four secretaries to London [under Norman Holmes Pearson, Robert Blum and Hubert Will] for the sole purpose of preparing the British CE material for transmission through British channels to the United States. This group arrived in London by the end of March. The American offices of the Division were established in the OSS headquarters in New York City, which adjoined the offices of the British Security Coordination. CE material from overseas and from Washington was received through the British in New York and was indexed and carded by the CI Division there. The New York office served as headquarters for the new Division for some six months. [Deletion] On 15 June [Donovan received authority] to create the Counter-Espionage Branch (X-2) of the Intelligence Service of OSS.

X-2 was therefore free to develop the possibilities of CE in the protection of the security of American intelligence activities abroad, as well as the protection of national interests in foreign areas. In addition, the Branch was in a position to take advantage of long British experience and knowledge of the techniques of manipulating enemy agents, and therefore to enter the intricate field of CE operations.

The London office of X-2 soon became, and remained for the
duration of hostilities, the base for the control of CE operations in
Europe. The broad liaison established in London diminished the
significance of the relations with the British in New York. Further,
the arrangements for carding and processing of incoming material
in New York, useful while the American carders were in the tutorial stage and needed the help of their British colleagues, became
awkward when that stage had passed. [Deletion] Therefore, in September 1943, the research work in New York was discontinued.
[By this time, British Security Control in New York had lost much
of its early importance and the locus of British CI/CE operations
centered at Allied Supreme Headquarters in London. Most CI/CE
operations were based at MI-6 headquarters in Broadway, near
Parliament Square, and Leconfield House in St. James's,
London.]

By September 1943, X-2 was therefore in a position to address
itself to the job of developing a major security organization in the
remaining period of the war.

Registry. One of the main coordinating CE instruments is the
body of records—of foreign, enemy or potential enemy personnel,
organizations, relationships, activities, known plans—kept by the
registry section. In a certain sense, the organization exists to produce its files of current, tested, readily available information, and
to apply them to the protection of national interests. It is, therefore, at once an end and means of all CE activities, being the focal
point at which all lines of such activities meet. It thus provides the
basis for the coordination which is essential. The files provide leads
for the field, which in turn produces material for the growing accumulation of data in the files. The CE registry may supply data
useful in illuminating decisions on the application of national policy in certain areas, or for the light it can throw on the problems
met by CE workers in the field. No positive intelligence collecting
agency can operate safely for long without the protection CE files
can afford to its agents.

CE cases may take years to mature. [A case in point is the *Royal
Oak* affair, see above, where a German agent submerged in Scotland in 1927 and surfaced 12 years later to provide the information
that led to the sinking of the *Royal Oak*.] Items in the files that
have every appearance of being dead can suddenly become of primary importance. Thus, it is known that enemy organizations will
normally plant as many "sleeper" agents as they can to be alerted
and used at a later date. It is well in all cases to go on the old CE
axiom: "Once an agent, always an agent—for someone." Such individuals may not be important in themselves, but they will in due

time be visited by and call attention to more significant figures.

The assembling of CE records is usually a long and expensive business. The European intelligence services—because of the geographical, industrial, military and political situation of their states vis-a-vis their neighbor states—have been forced to recognize the significance of security information. They never go out of business, and they regard the money laid out for keeping up their files as money well spent. CE operations cannot be mounted quickly and still be made to yield useful returns.

Liaison with other government agencies and the intelligence services of friendly governments—and, on occasion, those of unfriendly ones—provides a valuable source of CE information. This is particularly true in time of crisis or of war when mutual interests can be served by exchange of information. Thus the X-2 liaison in Washington with FBI, G-2, ONI, State Department, Office of Censorship, Treasury Department, FEA and OWI, was carefully maintained throughout the war. The reports passed on by other branches of OSS also added valuable material to the files. The richest sources, however, were those opened to the Branch by the British, and, in varying degrees, by other Allied services.

Like control of the enemy's pouched messages, the interception, when possible, of his telephoned, telegraphed or wireless messages provided positive and security intelligence of the highest value. A CE organization inevitably secures—especially in wartime from captured agents—information very useful to the cryptographic departments of its government; in turn, such relevant information as those departments pass on is used to protect the security of national interests. Interchange of mutual services apart, there is normally in all major intelligence systems a close tie, based on security considerations, between the overseas CE organization and the departments that work on codes. [Deletion]

The Branch Chief was able to announce in September 1945 that X-2 had received a total of more than 80,000 documents and reports and 10,000 cables, yielding a card file of some 400,000 entries. [Deletion]

Liaison With Other Agencies. One of the chief activities of X-2/Washington was the transmission of CE information to other user agencies and for that reason the Liaison Section was one of its busiest units. [Deletion]

In the year before the German collapse more than 3,000 reports were disseminated to Washington agencies. Of these, 682 went to the Office of Censorship, 410 to FBI, 977 to G-2, 480 to State, and 125 to ONI. In addition to such disseminations, X-2 made available to FBI a list of titles of approximately 5,000 documents of an intelligence nature from its records. The liaison with FBI was concerned largely with the exchange of information on the overseas background of persons of interest to the Bureau; with intelligence regarding enemy agents who might operate in the United States, as well as on enemy schools and training centers abroad in which agents were especially prepared for work in the United States; and with the coordination of policies and arrangements for the handling of certain double agents prior to their departure from Europe for the United States.

Special Units. A Watch List Unit was set up in July 1943 to collect for dissemination to the United States Office of Censorship, British Imperial Censorship and French Censorship all CE information derived by X-2 from the communications of known or suspected agents. The Unit listed all names of such agents, and their cover addresses, letter boxes or mail drops, so that enemy communications could be intercepted and surveyed. It was possible for the Unit to pass on to the censorship offices with which it cooperated studies not only on persons and organizations but also on methods of secret communication. In turn, it received like information from those offices.

An Insurance Unit was established when X-2 headquarters were in New York and its work was directed from there throughout the existence of the Branch. Its function was the detection of enemy intelligence activities operated through insurance cover. As its work progressed, it evolved into an X-2-SI unit, with its most profitable investigations those of a secret intelligence nature. Never a large unit—it was staffed by six officers who were insurance experts—it did impressive work. For example, its London office secured, after other American intelligence investigators had failed, information valuable to the military, naval and, especially, air commands, with regard to the Far East, as well as Europe. The procurement of such information illustrated once more the intelligence principle that the richest intelligence on an area frequently can be gathered at a point outside that area. [Deletion]

An X-2 Art Looting Investigation Unit was established in the second half of 1944, when it became apparent that the Germans intended to carry on with plans for subversive action after the cessation of hostilities, and were making arrangements for a supply of funds during the post-hostilities period. It was known that various sorts of treasure, in the form of items of small bulk but great value (jewels, paintings, objets d'art), which could be converted into money, had been stolen or otherwise acquired and were being stored at various places in Europe. The Allies appointed the Roberts Commission and the McMillan Commission to advise the

United States War Department and the British War Office, respectively, on questions involved in returning such objects to their rightful owners. X-2 was primarily interested in the people who would attempt to dispose of works of art of this kind, as a source of information on current and future activities and plans of the enemy. The staff of the Art Looting Investigation Unit, which was related to the commissions mentioned above, worked under the direction of the London office.

OSS Field Security. The rapid growth of CE files, resulting from Washington and London liaison and from field operations, made it possible by early summer of 1944 for X-2 to be increasingly useful to OSS field security at a time when SI and other OSS operations ramified on the European Continent. Pursuant to a directive from Donovan, X-2 took over the CE investigation of a large number of new categories of OSS personnel. In July 1944, 677 names were vetted [Vetting is the process of checking all available CE files to ascertain whether the individual in question has ever been reported to have unfavorable or potentially dangerous associations. (footnote)]; in August, 1,167. Field stations of American agencies, other than OSS, had recourse to X-2 files for the vetting of employees, especially in enemy territory under American control, as did foreign offices of the State Department in connection with visa applications and arrangements for the entry of members of foreign missions to the United States. Such work was performed under the supervision of an X-2 Vetting Officer. [Deletion]

Field Operations. The principal function of CE was to penetrate the enemy's or potential enemy's closely guarded undercover intelligence services in order to discover his intelligence objectives. Knowing the enemy's aims, it was the further function of CE to neutralize his intelligence efforts or control and direct them to its own purposes.

One of the principal methods by which this was accomplished was the manipulation of double agents, that is to say, captured agents who would be persuaded to continue their activities for the enemy, ostensibly in good faith but actually at the direction of X-2. [X-2 obtained its name and its modus operandi from the XX-Committee, a British MI-5 organization whose Roman numerals meant the double-cross. The British parent organization was headed by a clever Seaforth Highlander, Colonel T. A. Robertson, a man whom Ladislas Farago in *The Game of the Foxes* describes as "a remarkably brainy Scot in his twenties, strikingly handsome with devastating charm, imaginative and enterprising." On Robertson's staff was an Oxford don, J. C. Masterman, who became the historian of the XX-Committee. In theory, and for a long time in practice, all these deception organizations worked under the ultimate control of Colonel John Henry Bevan, a leading London stockbroker who was quite unknown to the general public. With Colonel Sir Ronald Wingate, a former high-ranking Indian civil servant, and Dennis Wheatley, the London novelist, as his principal assistants, the London Controlling Section was formed at Churchill's war headquarters at Storey's Gate, just off Parliament Square. Especially for the invasions of North Africa, Sicily, Italy and Normandy, the LCS coordinated all deception activity throughout the world. This activity had, by 1944, become a large industry; and X-2, which commanded some of the best brains in the United States, was a component of that industry.] Various forms of pressure were brought to bear upon such agents, depending upon the particular situation. Generally, however, the motivations of self-interest and self-preservation were sufficient. A second standardized form of double agent operation would be the case of an agent recruited by X-2 and infiltrated into enemy territory to induce the enemy to employ him as an agent and return him to Allied territory.

In both of the above basic types of double agent operations, there were varying benefits from the standpoint of intelligence. The controlled agent could call for supplies or money. His reports to the enemy could attract replies which revealed not only actual or projected enemy intelligence activities, but enemy intentions of greater magnitude. Further, such a controlled agent could serve as a magnet to draw other enemy agents into the CE-controlled network.

Such operations naturally required the utmost delicacy in the handling. The two basic types of operation mentioned above were subject to an infinity of variations and adaptations, depending upon the particular circumstances. On occasion, operations involving controlled agents became extremely complicated. The enemy, of course, engaged in the same types of activity. Thus, an enemy agent might be infiltrated into Allied territory to seek employment as an agent. His objective would be to return to enemy territory, ostensibly working for an Allied service, but actually operating for the enemy. Such an agent might be tripled, if his real purpose were discovered when he sought employment with the Allies.

Another variation would be a captured agent who might agree to be doubled, that is, to continue ostensibly operating his radio or other channel of communication for the enemy while under Allied control. If the enemy realized that such an agent had been "turned," he might try to feed the Allies deceptive material in the form of questionnaires. However, if it were realized that the enemy was aware of Allied control, the agent might be quadrupled in an intricate operation of deception and counter-deception. On occasion, the operation might become too complicated, whereupon it would be dropped.

One of the principal uses of double agents was to feed the enemy such seemingly good information from a given area that he would feel no need of sending additional agents to the region. In this fashion, X-2 could gain complete control of the intelligence which the enemy received from a particular area.

There were infinite variations in methods of manipulating agents. They depended solely upon imagination, ingenuity and judgment. The value of success in such operations was, of course, great. Control of the enemy's intelligence instruments provided an important channel of deception; examination of the enemy's intelligence questionnaires to agents gave an indication of what he wished to know, and thereby provided a basis for deducing his plans and intentions.

A primary principle was not to induce open defections on the part of enemy agents. If the enemy were aware that one of his agents had defected to the Allies, not only was an important channel of deception and a source of information closed, but the enemy would be inclined to send other, and perhaps more successful, agents to the region in question.

The actual operations of X-2 were, of course, carried out in the field. It was the function of the Washington headquarters to receive and preserve in usable form the fruits of field operations. The Washington Registry, however, made many field operations possible. The central Registry, in which was collected all available data concerning enemy intelligence organizations, agents and subagents, as well as organizational and individual relationships, provided the coordinating instrument which was vital to success in counter-espionage. Those files did not lose their value at the conclusion of a given operation, or of a war. Individuals or relationships which have seemed dormant for a long period may become active again and provide the key to detection of widespread intelligence activities.

The uncoordinated fragments of enemy subversive personality lists, which had existed in June 1943 when the Branch was established, had by 1945 grown to a registry of some 400,000 carded names. These records, together with those of FBI, provided a foundation for American security intelligence.

By October 1945, when OSS was liquidated, X-2/Washington had become the headquarters for a widespread net of overseas stations, with a total of some 650 personnel. London was operational headquarters for North Africa, Western Europe, the Balkans and the Middle East, with missions in France, Belgium, Italy, Germany, Austria, Switzerland, Sweden, Spain and Portugal; Rumania, Bulgaria, Hungary; Greece, Turkey, Syria, Egypt. CE work in India, Burma, Ceylon and China had been organized around headquarters in New Delhi, Myitkyina, Kandy, Kunming and Shanghai, each of which reported directly to Washington.

In addition to the valuable files of CE intelligence kept current by these stations and the reports resulting from liaison, X-2 had developed two other major elements of an effective CE organization: A pool of trained and experienced personnel and a net of relationships, principally in the form of basic agreements and operating contracts, with Allied counter-espionage services at home and abroad.

Virtually all of the X-2 staff had received extensive CE operational training and experience in cooperation with Allied specialists in such work, both in the United States and overseas. The high success of a number of exclusively conducted X-2 operations in the field indicates the degree to which the staff of the Branch benefited from this experience.

In the two years and four months of its existence, X-2 worked out firm agreements with FBI, G-2 and the Department of State. In London, the basic operating agreement that was negotiated in 1943 with MI-6(V) was supplemented by a scarcely less important agreement with MI-5 in early 1944. [Section V of MI-6, the counter-espionage branch of the British Secret Intelligence Service. Kim Philby, the Soviet spy, was chief of the Iberian subsection of this branch and intrigued to take over the entire section, apparently unsuccessfully. One of his American assistants was Melvin Purvis, the FBI agent who killed Dillinger. Philby eventually became chief of the Soviet section of V, where he was able to render his Russian masters important services.] X-2 thus gained full access to the experience and extensive files of both the external and internal British CE services. Similar working agreements were concluded with the French services. Liaison contacts were established with the competent services in liberated countries, notably Belgium, Holland, Denmark and Norway. [Deletion]

Starting at a late date, X-2 developed a CE organization for wartime service which could take its place among the major security services of the world. No small part of the credit for making this achievement possible was due to the records and experience made available by the British. In the course of exploiting that opportunity for wartime purposes, the United States assembled the elements of an effective CE service.

FOREIGN NATIONALITIES—(FN)

Following the establishment of OSS in June 1942, some question was raised as to whether FN should continue as an OSS activity or be transferred to the Department of State. [Deletion] Effective evidence that the State Department because of its official status was not in a position to do the work was secured early in July. At that time FN obtained from a Czechoslovak official information on a secret treaty concluded in July 1941 between the Czechoslovak Government-in-Exile and the USSR. The State Department had known of this development by rumor only, since its officers were forbidden to make the necessary approaches to get information.

The JCS decided that FN functions belonged in OSS, and the reorganization which followed 23 December 1942 fixed the position of the Branch as part of the Intelligence Service. FN's assignment was defined as "Contact with foreign nationality groups in the United States to aid in the collection of essential information for the execution of psychological warfare operations in consultation with the State Department." [Deletion]

In early 1943, the FN staff had reached a total of approximately fifty regular employees and one hundred volunteers—a total which it maintained throughout the OSS period. Activities of the volunteer readers, located at twenty universities throughout the country, were directed from Princeton. In addition to the offices at New York and Washington, field representatives were established in Pittsburgh and San Francisco.

By the end of 1944, there were additional field representatives in Boston, Seattle, Chicago, Cleveland, Detroit, and two cities in Wisconsin. Pittsburgh, an important center for many foreign nationality groups, supplied particularly valuable information. The field to be covered varied not only geographically but in character. For this reason approaches varied. In at least one case, the field representative worked under cover but the more practicable arrangement was to operate as the representative of a government agency, naming OSS if necessary, who acted as a channel to the Government for the desires of foreign nationality groups. The success of field representatives depended substantially on their ability to overcome the predilection of a given contact to regard them as "government spies." At the same time, they had to present the subject with an attractive proposition and continue contacts with maximum discretion.

FN's main sources of information were the press summaries, reports on public meetings and situation reports. The general press summaries supplied by the Special Defense Unit of the Department of Justice were discontinued in November 1943 along with the Unit itself, and FN began to rely heavily for this type of information upon the Overseas News Agency, a commercial service to which it subscribed early in 1943. The State Department wished FN to continue at least some of the services supplied by the Department of Justice. It was arranged therefore that, in addition to the political analyses of its volunteer readers, FN would supply State with information on new developments in that part of the foreign language press not covered by the Department. This was accomplished by supplementing the work of the volunteers and the Overseas News Agency with scanning in the Chancery Division itself. [Deletion]

The situation reports, obtained through personal contact and observation, were interpretive reports on activities and trends in foreign nationality groups. They were prepared by field representatives or other members of the regular staff, by the volunteer reporters or readers, and by specialists in the foreign nationality field hired on a temporary basis.

Liaison with other agencies supplied FN with additional information. The Office of Censorship watched the mail of certain individuals, and the FCC monitored specific broadcasts as requested by FN. Appropriate Canadian and British officials, principally the British Security Coordination in New York, supplied information on Canadian groups. The CIAA and State Department diplomatic missions supplied information on Latin American groups. Additional contributors to FN's total information were SI, R&A and the Foreign Agents Registration Section of the Department of Justice.

The information received from these various sources was analyzed, briefed and indexed in the Chancery Division at Washington, and used as the basis for reports prepared for distribution by FN analysts. These reports were issued in categories which the Branch set up. The most substantial of FN's disseminations were the *Reports*, intended to deal with large situations in a comprehensive way. The first of these was issued on 13 February 1942.

Bulletins followed, the first being circulated on 11 September 1942. They were designed to keep readers posted on recent developments in a given foreign nationality area and to treat generally subjects not of sufficient significance to warrant Report status.

The next category was a series of *Specials*, beginning in April 1943. These dealt with matters particularly secret or controversial, or closely related to the formulation of policy. They were prepared by the Branch Chief, usually in the form of memoranda to the

Director of OSS and the Secretary of State, and distribution was extremely limited. Often they included reports of interviews with such important figures as Count Sforza, Don Luigi Sturzo, Jacques Maritain, Archduke Otto of Hapsburg, Tibor Eckhardt, Eduard Benes, Milan Hodza, and many others.

A series of *News Notes* was inaugurated on 28 August 1944 to call attention to "spot news." These were generally obtained from press items, emphasizing unusual news not mentioned elsewhere or significant changes in editorial opinion. The first information of the startling reversal of Communist policy in the United States in 1945 was disseminated in May 1945 in the News Notes. [Deletion]

On 16 March 1945 the Chief of FN resigned and was made a Special Consultant to the Director. Before he left the Branch he prepared, under date of 15 February 1945, an appraisal of FN's work up to 31 December 1944. This appeared in booklet form entitled "The Study of Foreign Political Developments in the United States, A New Field of Political Intelligence." It stated that the FN yield of intelligence had developed to cover three main subjects: (1) Reflection in the United States of situations abroad and foreshadowing here of possible developments abroad; (2) diplomatically unrecognized movements and dissident agitation; and (3) the American democratic process—pressures at Washington touching points in international relations. The first subject, the wartime focus of FN activity, would probably recede in importance with the opening of more direct means of obtaining foreign political intelligence in the post-hostilities period. However, the other two categories of FN information would still be a necessary aid in the formulation of foreign policy. It would be essential to have contact with movements-in-opposition which might some day become governments. Even apart from the possibility of their ultimate success, these movements affected the relations of the United States with foreign powers. Nationality group pressures were becoming increasingly articulate, which made it incumbent upon the Government to know exactly the nature of the pressures, who originated them and why. [Deletion]

The new Chief of FN brought up the question of establishing FN work in the Oriental field in the spring of 1945. Up to that time FN had consistently side-stepped proposals to this effect, maintaining that the Orient was removed from the study of normal politics, and that clandestine and subversive activities were for the FBI or other agencies. The new Chief, however, secured approval to set up an Oriental section and drafted a budget proposal in May. Request was made at the same time for funds to allow expansion of FN activity in anticipation of an increased need for material on the

German-American community. However, the OSS budget for 1945 obliged FN to begin in July an over-all reduction in force and to become by September a skeleton staff operating in New York.

During August the activities of the field representatives were terminated and the permanent staff in Washington and New York was cut from 47 to fourteen. The office moved to New York on 1 September, and the volume of reports—61 in July—dropped to 22 in August and nine in September. On 28 September FN was transferred to R&A, and on 30 September moved with R&A to the State Department.

Throughout its existence FN kept the State Department and other customers supplied with a valuable and substantial body of intelligence totalling, as of 24 September 1945, 247 Reports, 399 Bulletins, 271 Meeting Reports, 152 News Notes, and 126 Specials. In addition, 350 individual memoranda had been sent to various State Department officers. Incoming reports, totalling 18,082, were excerpted, indexed and filed for ready reference. Such reports covered 20,350 individuals, 3,550 organizations and 2,053 publications.

FN proved that through study of foreign nationality groups in America it was possible to obtain indications of future European developments. For example, it deduced that the new Czechoslovakia would have to be recognized on a basis of much wider local autonomy, it foresaw the problems of the restored Greek Government, and it discerned the great issues affecting Poland and her neighbors.

FN's contribution was not confined to the field of political intelligence. It made an incidental contribution to the democratic process. In fulfilling its function as intelligence reporter, FN became automatically a channel to policy-makers of the thinking, particularly with respect to foreign policy, of foreign nationality groups.

CENSORSHIP AND DOCUMENTS—(CD)

Censorship Division. [Deletion] There were five types of material which OSS received from the Office of Censorship, namely, postal intercepts, cable intercepts, telephone summaries, Censorship Reports and Travelers' Censorship Interrogation Reports.

During the period when CD was handling intercepts, considerable progress was made in demonstrating to other branches the value of the material contained therein, and advances were also made in clarifying the requirements of OSS to the Office of Censorship. Moreover, trips to various censorship centers including San Juan, Puerto Rico, Trinidad, Bermuda, and the New York Prisoner of War Station, and a trip during which arrangements were made to examine the mail being brought back on the Gripsholm, did much to expand the value of the material received.

Document Intelligence Division. Although R&D had been counterfeiting documents for agents entering neutral and enemy countries at the request of the dispatching branches since late 1942, no immediate attempt was made to collect and catalogue the background information for such work.

In the fall of 1943 it was found desirable to centralize the collection of personal documents and related intelligence for the use of those branches which required false documents as authentication for agents.

After some discussion it was decided that, in order to avoid duplicating R&D activities, CD would concern itself only with the collection, evaluation and distribution of documents and related intelligence; R&D would continue to handle the actual manufacture. At first it had been thought that CD would undertake the preparation of cover stories, and, working from these, provide all clothing and other accessories necessary to substantiate them. However, since the operating branches already had cover experts, they continued to fabricate the original cover story. CD would then provide the document or equipment intelligence necessary to authenticate the agent's cover.

In order to expand the collection of documents as far as possible, liaison was established with the Documents Section and the Prisoner of War Branch of G-2, as well as the Division of Travellers' Censorship of the Office of Censorship, all of which provided valuable material. The Survey of Foreign Experts and SI also supplied additional material.

From the first it was realized that Washington would be primarily a storehouse and servicing unit for the overseas units of the Branch.

When CD first sent representatives overseas, OSS was largely dependent for documentation on the British in ETO and on the French in NATO. Within a year and a half, however, the OSS had become independent in this respect and approximately 900 agents were authenticated by CD in ETO and NATO. [Deletion]

In the reorganization of January 1943, the post of Deputy Director—Psychological Warfare Operations (PWO) was established to supervise and direct the activities of the two operations branches: SO and MO. [Deletion]

SPECIAL OPERATIONS—(SO)

The purpose of SO was to effect physical subversion of the enemy. As defined [officially], its functions included sabotage operations in enemy and enemy-occupied countries, and support and supply of resistance groups in those countries.

The nature of such work and the increasing portion of the world which came under the jurisdiction of military theaters of operation made it imperative that SO activities be almost exclusively under the control of the various theater commanders. Consequently, the job of SO/Washington was a servicing one in the main. Its staff personnel in Washington numbered only approximately 45 at the peak of activity in 1944. These servicing functions were principally in the fields of recruiting, training and supply. Over-all planning was accomplished in Washington, but its effectiveness was handicapped by the operational control of theater commands and the constantly changing situation in the field. [Deletion]

Unlike secret intelligence, where independence of the American organization was both desirable and necessary, it was recognized at the outset that independence in special operations was impractical and would lead to confusion and chaos. Therefore, it was essential to work out some sort of firm arrangement with British SOE for the necessary world-wide collaboration.

Negotiations by Donovan and [P. Reston] Goodfellow [a Brooklyn newspaper publisher and deputy director of operations] for OSS and Sir Charles Hambro [the London merchant banker who was head of the British service from May 1942 until September 1943] for SOE were in progress in London when COI became OSS in June 1942. They resulted in the SO/SOE agreement of 26 June. The agreement, which set forth the basic elements of cooperation in every theater of war, was based upon the general principle that Americans would control areas specifically designated as spheres of American influence, while SOE would control special operations in areas dominated by the British. India, East Africa, the Balkans and the Middle East were to be the province of SOE, with American liaison and assistance. SO was to control special operations in China, Manchuria, Korea, Australia, the Atlantic islands and Finland.

Several vital areas were subject to special consideration. It was agreed that Western Europe, where SOE was already operating, would continue under its supervision. However, American units were to begin operations on the Continent under general SOE control, preserving the independence of separate unit command. Special procedures were also established for North Africa, including Spanish Morocco. This area was regarded as predominantly an American sphere of operations and the Chief of SO in North Africa was to coordinate the activities of SO and SOE. (Gibraltar, however, was an exception to this arrangement since it was to remain outside the sphere of the American SO mission in North Africa.) West Africa was to have an American mission working through the British SOE office there.

In the matter of resources and supplies, it was agreed that there should be interchange of personnel and plans to effect the greatest possible economy and cooperation. The agreement provided that each organization should finance its own operations. For security reasons, however, and because of the practical impossibility of separating accounts in dual operations, records were to be kept of the destination of all material issued but there would be no payments or financial obligations as between SO and SOE or their respective governments. The agreement also confirmed arrangements for training American recruits in SOE schools in England and Canada. [Deletion]

By December 1942 several SO activities in the field had begun to bear fruit, and it became easier to impress upon military authorities the value of SO. The work of SO personnel in North Africa in connection with *TORCH* was of demonstrable aid. [Deletion]

Regardless of the attitude of the authorities in Washington, the essential point was to convince the respective theater commanders that SO would be of benefit to their operations. To this end, the Chief of SO, who became Deputy Director—PWO, made an extensive tour of METO, NATO and ETO in the winter of 1942-43. His primary purpose was to promote acceptance of SO and OG [Operational Groups, see below], as well as other OSS services. Success in this mission was reflected in the requests for SO from these theaters and the definite arrangements to establish SO personnel in the principal OSS field bases which were made at that time.

The first operations, such as *TORCH*, had been carried out by recruiting and training small groups of capable men and putting them in the field, with only a directive as to the general objects of their mission. In the case of [Deletion] *TORCH*, it was to prepare for the invasion of North Africa, subject to operational directives worked out, for the most part, in London. Supplies for *TORCH* were borrowed from the British. [Deletion] Such arrangements placed emphasis on the leadership and ability to improvise of the individuals concerned. It is a tribute to them that these early missions were so eminently successful, and the subsequent opportunities of OSS in the SO field may be attributed in no small measure to their efforts. [Deletion]

Recruiting. One of the major functions of SO/Washington was recruiting. [Deletion] Five OSS officers conducted a recruiting trip in May, during which they visited Camp Mackall, Fort Bragg and Fort Benning, seeking various types of Italian-speaking officers and men for both OG's and SO. Recruits were required to speak fluent Italian, and be willing to participate in dangerous sabotage operations (not always in uniform). They had to be of such calibre that they could absorb training in intelligence work as well as sabotage technique. The tour resulted in the selection for SO of some 50 recruits out of 4,000 applicants. A subsequent recruiting visit to Camp Forrest in Tennessee produced the additional 25 needed to fill the quota specified by General Eisenhower. [Deletion]

In mid-1943, METO requested some hundreds of personnel for Yugoslavia, Albania and Greece. Recruiting in connection with this request was particularly difficult since many potential recruits among the appropriate groups in America were subject to doubts as to their ultimate political allegiances, and traditional divisions along national, tribal and religious lines further complicated the matter.

Experience in the field indicated eventually that, rather than using agents of foreign descent, it was often better to use men who were obviously Americans as organizers to work with resistance groups in certain enemy-occupied territories, such as Yugoslavia and Greece. Such personnel were found to be less susceptible to participation in factional differences inside the country than those with local ties. In addition, the prestige of being obviously a representative of the United States had a certain symbolic value during the war. This did not mean that the recruits sought were less difficult to find, for personnel with the requisite degree of tact, intelligence and good sense, in addition to the requirements of courage and daring implicit in all SO work, were extremely scarce.

One of the most important recruiting jobs was that for Western European operations, which became particularly intense in 1943-44. Possible recruits for France and the Low Countries existed in greater numbers than for some territories having less cultural affiliations with the United States. The pool of French-speaking officers at Fort Benning was an excellent source and, with the cooperation of the War Department, a number of suitable men were interviewed, screened and trained. Prospects from such French-speaking centers as New Orleans and New York City were canvassed on numerous recruiting trips. SO files contained a long list of French personalities in America. From this list men who could meet the exacting standards set up for French agents were chosen. In this connection the problem of adequate commissions was particularly acute. It was difficult to secure appropriate rank for many mature men who were available and had unusually good qualifications for agent work. In the case of many agents, who volunteered out of deep-seated patriotism and desire to assist the war effort, only second lieutenancies were available when field grades were merited.

Recruiting [of the] JEDBURGH [personnel] was a separate task. These special teams consisted of one American or British officer, one French officer, and one American, British or French enlisted W/T operator. Their job was to organize resistance groups. [Deletion] The SO recruiting objective was 44 officers for staff, 50 officers fluent in French for team leaders, and 50 enlisted men for W/T. [Deletion] The Communications Branch accccepted responsibility for W/T training; OG's assisted in finding and training officer leaders; the British detailed a skilled training officer from SOE in Canada to temporary duty with OSS to aid in the training program. By 2 November 1943, 59 officers were in training and ready for shipment to England, where further specialized training was to be given. By the end of December the requisite 94 officers and 50 enlisted men had been dispatched. [Deletion]

After the recruits had been trained in the United States and dispatched to London, they were subjected to further screening and training. Only 46% passed the final tests and were accepted for actual operations; yet this percentage was far higher than that achieved by the British. JEDBURGH recruiting was discontinued after D-Day in Normandy.

The task of SO/Washington in preparation for Allied invasion of the Continent was not confined to JEDBURGH and agent personnel. Demands for additional staff, training and services personnel were continuous. [Deletion]

In the development of the JEDBURGH and SO program, men from all walks of life had a part. Imaginative planning and recruiting was necessary in order to find volunteers with a wide enough range of talents and aptitudes to learn the techniques of parachutage, bridge blowing, radio, lock-picking, booby traps and forging.

The experience of SO confirmed the fact that physical subversion had important psychological implications. It does more than merely destroy or kill—it surrounds the enemy with an atmosphere of insecurity and fear. As Donovan once stated, it keeps the enemy "looking over his shoulder."

MORALE OPERATIONS ("Black" Propaganda)—(MO)

Among the many distinctions drawn between aspects of propaganda (or political) warfare is that between "white" and "black." The former is actually or apparently objective, admits its source, and conforms to the policies of the government for which it speaks. The latter is subversive by every possible device, disguises its source, and is disowned by the government using it.

"Black" propaganda was always an essential part of Donovan's program for psychological warfare. "Persuasion, penetration and intimidation," Donovan felt, "are the modern counterpart of sapping and mining in the siege warfare of former days." In his view, "white" and "black" propaganda warfare should be conducted in accordance with a single coordinated program under the over-all direction of the military. FIS successfully fought against the idea of military supervision in the spring of 1942, and the result was the assignment of foreign propaganda to OWI when that agency was established in June. After the reorganization it was Donovan's intention that MO be conducted and directed as a part of SO. However, British inter-agency conflicts made such a set-up impracticable. PWE, which conducted both "black" and "white" operations, was under the direction of the Foreign Office. SOE, of which SO was the American counterpart, was responsible to the Ministry of Economic Warfare. PWE balked at working not only with SOE but with any foreign unit closely associated with SOE. "Black" propaganda and sabotage, therefore, had to be separate in OSS in order to avoid involvement in British internal controversy. [Deletion]

In April 1943 the Chief of the Branch gave the following list of unmistakably "black" operations:

> Contacts with underground movements...bribery and subsidies, blackmail, counterfeiting of currency, ration cards, passports, personal papers of enemy prisoners or dead, rumor, abduction, chain letters, poisoning (distribution of and instructions on how to use toy gadgets and tricks), assassination by suggestion or agents, illness and epidemics by suggestion or agents, and diverse manipulations such as black market in neutral countries, etc. [Deletion]

On 27 October 1943 the JCS charged MO with the "execution of all forms of morale subversion by divers means including: False rumors, 'freedom stations,' false leaflets and false documents, the organization and support of fifth column activities by grants, trained personnel and supplies and the use of agents, all for the purpose of creating confusion, division and undermining the morale of the enemy." [Deletion]

[One of the earliest "black" operations was called the Orleman- ski Affair.] In April 1944 an obscure Roman Catholic priest from Springfield, Mass., went to Russia and secured an interview with Stalin. He returned to the United States with assurances of Stalin's friendly intentions toward Poland. German propaganda was ex- ploiting the "Bolshevik Menace" extensively, particularly among Catholics. The MO line suggested in the "black" directive was that Orlemanski's trip, assertedly made with the knowledge and ap- proval of the Vatican, proved beyond all doubt the close collabo- ration between the Western Allies and Russia and foreshadowed a rapprochement between Moscow and the Holy See. Radio Paris, under German control, was forced to deny this rumor, which served to give it still wider circulation.

ETO/MedTO. [Deletion] In the summer and fall of 1944, the campaign by OSS against Hitler was an example of particularly ef- fective teamwork in the execution of "white" and "black" opera- tions. At OWI's request, the MO directive of 20 June stated, "It is important that you commit Hitler to deliver a speech on August 3rd, anniversary of the founding of the SA, so that 'white' may later explain his non-appearance." Hitler had not spoken or ap- peared in public for some time, Germany was suffering reverses, and the rumors were designed to convince the Germans that Ger- many's plight was indeed hopeless. An attempt was made on Hitler's life on 20 July while the rumor campaign was in progress. The attempted assassination gave MO unexpected opportunities. The "black" directive instructed the field to play up in every way the rumor that Hitler had really been killed. The previously- rumored speech of 3 August was used to strengthen this supposi- tion. Later, the theme that Hitler was dead was abandoned, and Hitler's continued silence was explained by alleging a growing schism within the Nazi Party (Himmler would not allow Hitler to speak), Hitler's flight by submarine to Argentina or Japan, and, fi- nally, the proposal that Hitler was actually insane.

These rumors, launched or encouraged by "black" methods, were picked up by Allied broadcasting stations, which gave them increased circulation by speculating on their veracity. MO/Cairo planted stories implicating [Franz] Von Papen [German ambas- sador to Turkey] and other Germans in Turkey in the anti-Hitler plot. MO/Rome, through the SAUERKRAUT operations, infil- trated German POW's to plant subversive material, and the German commander in Italy, [Field Marshal Albert] Kesselring, was forced to deny authorship of an "official proclamation" posted by these agents in his name.

Finally, Hitler was again "committed" to speak on 9 November [anniversary of the Munich beerhall putsch. (footnote)] and his failure to do so resulted in a frenzy of speculation in the Allied and neutral press. Rumors and counter-rumors about Hitler's illness or death continued until they were largely dispelled by his speech on 1 January 1945. Even then, the possibility was put forth that the speech was either a recording or had been delivered by a "double."

Other ETO/MedTO projects to which the Plans and Production Section made substantial contributions were Das Neue Deutschland, the SIOUX mission in Stockholm, and MUZAC.

Das Neue Deutschland (DND) purported to be the organ of an underground German peace party. Its contents were conceived as though such a party, liberal and religious in character, actually existed in Germany, and in such fashion that a genuine party might crystallize around the DND program. One of its goals was to make more palatable to Germans the "unconditional surrender" formula of the Allies, an object which could not be achieved by "white" propaganda.

This undertaking, first reported by the Chief of MO in the Mediterranean in April 1944, was warmly received by OWI and the State Department, although certain possible dangers in it were perceived. For one thing, reports of such a movement might strengthen in Allied countries the position of proponents of a "soft peace" for Germany, and MO's creature might take on a dangerous life of its own. In July, an Editorial Board of OWI, State Department and OSS membership was established as the strategy board for "black" propaganda against Germany. One of its main tasks was the direction of policy for DND. However, even before this Board met, MO/MedTO had already published one edition of the paper, and distributed it to reception committees in France and the Balkans with instructions for its dissemination to German troops. Later, Washington contributed not only guidance on the paper's editorial policy but considerable "copy."

The major contribution made by MO/Washington to the SIOUX mission in Stockholm was in connection with the "Harvard Project." This was a weekly news letter (July 1944-April 1945), purporting to be prepared by German interests in Sweden for the information of businessmen within the Reich. It had limited circulation, and was intended to subvert a small but influential group which, by tradition, social status, financial investments and pre-war international connections, would be especially susceptible to MO's designs.

Copy for the "*Harvard* Project" was prepared weekly by an editor in Washington. The publication, named *Handel und Wandel*, sought to impress upon German businessmen the damage to their interests resulting from Nazi policy and leadership. It stressed the effectiveness of Allied industrial efforts and the willingness of Allied businessmen to work with German businessmen once the Nazis were out of the way.

One issue reported that Himmler was organizing secret groups of saboteurs in all industrial plants to make sure that the official "scorched earth" policy would be ruthlessly carried out. *Handel und Wandel* urged plant owners to protect their property by forming their own counter-groups. It argued also that the dominant radical wing of the Nazi Party was making a deal with the Russians in order to maintain its power. The obvious remedy was a sound German capitalism which the Allies could support.

Copy for the "*Harvard* Project" was cleared with the State Department, and the fact that such delicate material should be allowed out of MO/Washington was an indication that "black" propaganda had become an accepted weapon in psychological warfare and that confidence in MO was increasing.

MO/Washington also contributed to the "MUZAC Project," which constituted MO/London's participation in the operations of "Soldatensender West." This was a powerful radio station run by the British which posed as a German station relaying entertainment and news to the Wehrmacht. It became a joint Anglo-American undertaking, with MO providing the entertainment features which, during the last year of the war, commanded a steadily growing audience of German troops. American popular music (all of it known as "jazz" in Europe) was the mainstay of "Soldatensender West." German lyrics were written for American tunes, and sung by artists of German or Central European origin. Some of this work was performed in England, but most of it was done by recording in New York. A dummy corporation was organized to handle the business matters involved, such as hiring orchestras, studios, performers, negotiating with the musicians' union, etc. A small MO staff made translations and supervised production. From July 1944 until April 1945, 312 recordings were made, many by celebrities such as Marlene Dietrich, the Metropolitan Opera Star, Grete Stueckgold, and various night club entertainers.

The German lyrics, composed by a former writer for the Austrian stage, were of high quality. Many of them had no propaganda content whatsoever, but were intended solely to attract and hold listeners. Others had a nostalgic appeal designed to promote war-weariness and defection. Still others were hard-hitting satirical songs attacking Nazi leaders or relating the discomforts and dangers of army life.

In addition to the straight musical programs, there were three fifteen-minute variety shows in the best tradition of the "political cabaret" so well liked in Europe. The "MUZAC Project," which kept the Wehrmacht listening to Allied propaganda for ten crucial months, was one of MO's most proficient and worthwhile achievements. [Deletion]

MO's efforts to disrupt, confuse and divide the enemy through "black" techniques had been made in the face of serious handicaps. Among these were failure to coordinate "black" and "white" operations; confusion and controversy over MO's functions; a late start, which made it difficult to secure first-class personnel and necessary equipment; and lack of confidence in MO, which was often justified by the circumstances, on the part of other OSS operating branches.

Nevertheless, by the time hostilities ended the principle of morale operations had come to be appreciated by other military and political agencies. MO had demonstrated its value against both Germany and Japan. Perhaps the greatest contribution of MO was that it brought to the attention of American authorities a weapon which the United States had not theretofore systematically and effectively employed. It drew attention, also, in time of peace, to the advantages of a specialized type of intelligence—information on the morale, social cleavages and underlying worries of foreign peoples.

OPERATIONAL GROUPS—(OG)

OG's were authorized by the JCS directive of 23 December 1942 which provided that OSS should organize operational nuclei to be used in enemy and enemy-occupied territory. The OG's were highly trained foreign language-speaking soldiers, skilled in methods of sabotage and small arms, and trained parachutists, designed to be used in small groups behind enemy lines to harass the enemy. [Deletion]

The first definite request for OG's developed out of the approval by AFHQ of JCS 170 [deletion], which set forth the objectives of OSS in the Western Mediterranean. The request, as it applied to OG's, involved four to eight operational groups to be used as organizers, fomenters and operational nuclei in areas adjacent to North Africa. When the War Department was requested to assign officers and men for OG operations in NATO, G-1 inquired whether tables of organization would also be submitted for other theaters. OSS replied in the affirmative, and the War Department granted the OG's approximately 540 slots.

The OG Branch was established 13 May 1943. [Deletion] Following the initial allotment to OG, a recruiting program was immediately undertaken. It was thought that the best qualified men would be found in line outfits, and for this reason the first OG's were secured from infantry and engineer units. Radio operators were secured from the Signal Corps; trained medical technicians from the Medical Corps. Knowledge of foreign language was essential.

Prospective recruits were usually interviewed in groups made up of individuals who met the two basic requirements of physical qualifications and linguistic ability in order to judge whether they were otherwise suitable. They were given the opportunity to volunteer for "hazardous duty behind enemy lines." Such groups were then advised that interested individuals would be granted personal interviews. In the interests of security, operational plans were not divulged, yet enough was told so that the recruit understood what he might expect. Only men giving evidence of a real desire for such duty were chosen. It was found that approximately ten percent of those initially interviewed in groups subsequently volunteered.

The basic unit of organization was originally conceived to be a group composed of four officers and thirty enlisted men. Each such group was to be commanded by a captain and a first lieutenant, and divided into two sections of sixteen men; each section was subdivided into two squads.

In actual experience, units used in the field varied from a liaison team of one officer and two enlisted men (T/Sgt. and radio operator) to units slightly larger than the group. For the NATO-based French operations, the section, commanded by a captain rather than a lieutenant, was the basic unit.

On 27 November 1944 the Operational Group Command was activated as a separate military unit within OSS. [Deletion] This was the result of several factors which indicated the wisdom of separating the OG's as far as possible from OSS administratively. One such consideration was experience in the field indicating that OG's were likely, despite the fact that they operated exclusively in uniform, to be treated without regard to the Geneva Convention when captured. It was felt that for their protection in the event of capture every effort should be made to eliminate the possibility of connection with OSS. Another consideration was the fact that the OG's were exclusively military, and the quasi-military administration of OSS caused some confusion. OSS continued throughout, however, to maintain coordinated operational control.

Since all OG's were recruited from the Army, it could be assumed that they had completed basic training. As a result, OG training was specialized in nature, with particular emphasis on physical conditioning. Courses were conducted by men who had themselves volunteered for OG duty and were therefore combat soldiers in the United States on a temporary basis. This policy served as an incentive to instructors and pupils alike. Courses were designed to make all OG's proficient in demolitions; small arms (both of American and foreign make); scouting, patrolling and reconnaissance; first-aid; unit security measures; living off the land; knife and hand-to-hand fighting; camouflage, map reading and compass; and equipment and methods of operation of airborne and seaborne raids. A large percentage of the tactical exercises were conducted at night. Operational training included mountain operations, parachutage, amphibious operations, skiing and mountain climbing, light artillery, radio operation, and advance espionage tactics. Aggressiveness of spirit and willingness to close with the enemy were stressed.

The OG's recruited for Italian operations were designated Company A, those for France Company B, and those for the Balkans Company C. An additional unit, not designated by a company symbol, consisted of OG's to be used in Norway.

In April 1943 recruiting parties toured Army camps to secure personnel for the groups intended for operations in Italy. Approximately 200 volunteers, of whom nineteen were officers, were selected. [Deletion]

In July and August 1943 recruiting for French OG's was in progress. The first group consisted of thirteen officers and 83 enlisted men. As part of their tactical training they took part in the combined airborne troop carrier maneuvers in North Carolina in December 1943. They were dispatched in January and arrived in NATO in February.

Six additional groups, two Italian and four French, were formed in the winter of 1943 and 1944 and departed in March 1944 to augment Companies A and B in NATO. One German group was formed in the spring of 1944 and arrived in North Africa in July, where it was attached to Company A.

The first OG's for Yugoslavia left the United States on 24 October 1943; others left on 24 January. The Yugoslav OG's comprised fifteen officers and 110 enlisted men.

A Greek OG unit was formed at the request of the Greek Government-in-Exile. In the summer of 1943 an OSS recruiting team visited Camp Carson, Colorado, seeking personnel with Greek language qualifications. So many of the 122nd Infantry Battalion (Sep.) volunteered for this duty that its Commanding Officer offered the entire Battalion. Negotiations with the War Department were undertaken to secure approval of this unusual step, and in September 1943 the requisite authority was granted. The Battalion was assessed by the OSS recruiting team, and officers and men were given a second opportunity to volunteer. Almost all reaffirmed their desire to become OG's. Of the Battalion, 17 officers and 205 enlisted men were chosen and trained in units of approximately 25 men each. A total of 172 enlisted men and 18 officers was dispatched to Cairo in early 1944.

As a result of discussions held in early 1943 in London between the Deputy Director—PWO and officials of the Norwegian Government-in-Exile, and subsequent discussions with the Norwegian Military Attache in America in the spring of that year, it was decided to recruit qualified officers and enlisted men from the 99th Infantry Battalion (Sep.), an all-Norwegian United States Army unit stationed at Camp Hale, Colorado. In July 1943, 10 officers and 69 enlisted men volunteered and were transferred to OSS. In the succeeding five months this group went through intensive specialized training and was dispatched in December 1943. [Deletion]

In August 1944 the OG's became known as the 2671st Special Reconnaissance Battalion, Separate (Prov.). At that time the OG's numbered some 1,100.

After the collapse of Germany in the spring of 1945, OG's who had participated in operations against the Axis were returned to America and processed for transfer to the Far East. This involved reassessment and additional training.

The actual record of OG operations is a matter for the theater accounts. The OG's were not Rangers, an idea which Donovan had sponsored in early 1942. However, they did partake of the nature of commandoes and of Rangers in some aspects of their operations. The distinction was simply that, while Donovan saw the Rangers as operating in front of the enemy, the OG's fitted into the pattern of OSS activities behind the enemy lines. All of the OG's saw action. [Deletion]

MARITIME UNIT—(MU)

The Maritime Unit evolved from SA/G training activities begun at Area D in April 1942 which were designed to educate SO and SI agents in techniques of clandestine infiltration by sea. The importance of maritime activities became clearer as Allied forces reached striking distance of the enemy, whereupon the number of

MU personnel increased and the Branch developed in status and function. [(Training) Area D was near Washington.]

MU was established as a Branch under the Deputy Director. It had four principal functions: (1) Infiltration of agents for other branches by sea; (2) supply of resistance groups and others by sea; (3) execution of maritime sabotage; and (4) development of special equipment and devices to effectuate the foregoing.

The first maritime training activities were begun with personnel allotted by the United States Navy under the direction of an experienced British naval officer who had been loaned to COI in February 1942. The area selected presented certain obstacles to small boat maneuvers: Lack of surf and beach conditions comparable to those existing in theaters of operation, together with pollution of Potomac River water. However, the area afforded good security, and, in view of this advantage and its proximity to Washington headquarters, a lease was executed. A small cabin cruiser was procured for use in night exercises to represent a submarine or surface vessel from which the operatives would land by rubber boat or other small craft.

The first class, consisting of eighteen students from SI and SO, began training on 4 August 1942. The training schedule was designed to fit them to effect clandestine entry by sea, and also to engage personally or through sub-agents in sabotage of cargoes, dock facilities, warehouses, etc. Simple seamanship, elementary navigation and small boat handling, particularly folboat, rubber boat and raft, were also studied. Other equipment, such as kayaks and canoes, was gradually obtained. Equipment was, however, rudimentary compared to that which was later developed. Nevertheless, this training was valuable in the field since the latest equipment was not always available in areas of actual operations and improvisation was often necessary. Throughout 1942 maritime activities were confined to training and had no separate identity. [Deletion]

In the meantime, the Section was performing research on new equipment, notably an inflatable surfboard and a collapsible eight-man kayak which could be taken apart easily and used from a submarine. In addition, a new two-man kayak was developed. The latter caused such favorable comment that the British immediately ordered 275 of them for shipment to various parts of the world.

Underwater swimming groups developed out of plans for such a unit approved by Donovan on 18 February 1943. The first group was placed in training at Annapolis on 24 May, becoming familiar with such devices as the Lambertsen Unit (an underwater breathing apparatus which permits a man to remain beneath the surface for as long as an hour or more). Subsequently, the group [trained] in small boats, limpets, navigation, etc. The polluted water at Area D prevented effective swimming training and the men were later sent to Silver Springs, Florida, for further training and research in underwater breathing devices. [Deletion]

The Maritime Unit was instrumental in the development of undersea breathing apparatus, a compass which could operate under water and which would resist the effect of magnetic limpets, luminous and water-proof watches, and depth gauges. An electrically powered inflated surfboard capable of carrying two men (total weight-carrying capacity 1,800 pounds) was also developed. It had a speed of five knots and a maximum cruising range of fifteen miles. The silent electric motor and the low silhouette made it particularly effective for approaching ships at anchor without detection, and it could also be used for clandestine landing of operatives.

MU collaborated with the Navy in experiments conducted in Guantanamo Bay, Cuba, designed to test the effectiveness of harbor defenses, such as submarine, anti-torpedo and various other types of underwater nets. In these tests the lengthy training showed commendable results, because the swimmers were able to circumvent the net defenses in each instance. An additional point of value was proof that the Navy sound-detection gear did not reveal the presence of underwater swimmers.

MU also experimented with midget submarines; while the experiments never got beyond the model stage during the war, their results should be valuable to any future efforts in this field.

The field histories recount the numerous instances in which clandestine maritime operations were used to infiltrate agents. This method of infiltration was particularly effective from Corsica toward North Italy and southern France, from bases in the Aegean Islands and southern Italy toward Greece, Albania and Yugoslavia, and in the Far East. The success of the maritime supply (caique) service operated by MU in the Eastern Mediterranean was another achievement. Underwater swimming groups were effective in the Pacific towards the close of the war.

The full possibilities of maritime sabotage were never realized, however. In the latter stages of the North Italian campaign, the San Marco Battalion (Italian) was used to good effect, but, in general, the United States was slow to realize the possibilities of this form of attack. America was, therefore, far behind both its enemies and its Allies in this respect. The Japanese used midget submarines in the attack on Pearl Harbor. The British had not been slow to develop these instruments, and the attack of two-man submarines upon the Tirpitz is well known. Perhaps the most effective, and certainly the most impressive, operations in maritime sabotage were conducted by the Italians. Their exploits in destroying shipping in Gibraltar and Algiers in 1942-43 were particularly successful. [Deletion]

Despite its late start, MU was able to demonstrate the effectiveness of clandestine maritime entry and attack and to develop new and valuable special maritime devices and equipment.

SPECIAL PROJECTS OFFICE

The Special Projects Office was established on 31 December 1943 to "carry out special assignments and missions as approved by the Director." It was, therefore, responsible for operational purposes directly to Donovan. [Deletion]

The Office grew out of the MACGREGOR Project which was started under SO in the summer of 1943. MACGREGOR, with Donovan's approval and the active support of the Secretary of the Navy, had for its purpose the subversion of a portion of the Italian fleet. However, the capitulation of Italy in the late summer of 1943, while the Project was in progress with a mission overseas, obviated the necessity for continuing with the original plan.

When Donovan arrived in NATO in September 1943, he secured Italian clearance for MACGREGOR to pursue the results of certain Italian experiments on secret weapons, particularly glider bombs. [The dramatic and effective use of the glider bomb by the Germans during the landings at Salerno made this subject of prime interest to Allied intelligence. (footnote)] Accordingly, MACGREGOR made contact with an Italian vice-admiral and an Italian scientist who specialized in the field of electronics, and transported them to the United States. At the same time, some personnel remained in NATO to search the ruins of the Torpedo Works at Baia in an effort to salvage a barge loaded with secret and experimental weapons which the Italians had sunk in Naples harbor. When the equipment had been salvaged and certain important Italian engineers and technicians had been contacted and dispatched to the United States, the Secretary of the Navy issued a priority making an LST available to carry the salvaged material directly to America.

The equipment included, in either model or descriptive form, magnetic torpedo pistols, new guided torpedoes, winged aerial bombs, and a three-man assault submarine. The Italians and the equipment were turned over to Naval Ordnance experts at the United States Naval Torpedo Station at Newport, Rhode Island. The Navy later stated that the results of this operation had saved one year's work on the part of the Research and Technical Sections of the Torpedo Station. [Deletion]

Although the Branch was not limited as to the nature of the projects to be handled, the great interest in secret weapons in late 1943 and early 1944, together with the results achieved by MACGREGOR in this field, determined its focus of interest. Of the projects which were undertaken by the Branch, SIMMONS and JAVAMAN merit particular interest.

The SIMMONS Project began in April 1944. Its purpose was to secure intelligence data on secret weapons, particularly the HS-293, a new guided radio missile which had been developed by the Germans in late 1943. Special Projects had compiled some information on the subject in the form of photographs and information based on pictures taken by a scientist who happened to be on the Island of Bornholm in September 1943, when the Germans launched (presumably from Peenemunde) a radio-controlled missile against the Island. He was later captured by the Germans, but the British had the pictures and the technical data which he had compiled subsequent to the attack. This information was forwarded to the United States in December.

In April 1944 SIMMONS became active, following the receipt of intelligence which indicated that a factory in Portes des Valence was being used by the Germans as a storehouse for HS-293's. Special Projects enlisted the cooperation of the Air Force and the French Resistance in planning an operation to secure physical possession of an HS-293 receiver and/or transmitter. The MAAF supplied twelve planes to bomb the factory; following the attack members of the resistance, disguised as firemen, were to search the debris for specimens of the missile. This was one of the first plans for coordinated resistance ground-air bombing operations. The operation was first laid on for the night of 10-11 May. It failed when a storm prevented the attacking planes from reaching the target area, although a diversionary raid was made on schedule and the Maquis arrived on time. Another operation was thereupon scheduled for a month later, the night of 9-10 June. However, two days after D-Day, all German troops in the Portes des Valence area were moved out, together with the HS-293's.

Following the abortive Portes des Valence operation, a Special Projects representative went to Cairo to discover what intelligence was available there with regard to secret weapons. While he was in Cairo, contact was established with a German officer who was willing to deal with OSS in regard to the radio control mechanism of the HS-293. The equipment in question was from an Me-109 grounded in Greece. It was forwarded to the Air Corps, which subsequently requested that SIMMONS expand its operations in connection with secret weapons generally.

In the SIMMONS Project, the Branch had been concerned with procuring high priority technical intelligence. However [deletion] its attention soon turned toward the field of actual operations. The JAVAMAN Project, which had been under consideration as early as the spring of 1944, provided the opportunity.

JAVAMAN was a missile craft [Air-sea rescue boats, appropriately modified, were the foundation for JAVAMAN craft. (footnote)] designed to effect the sabotage of enemy vessels and installations which, because of tight protection by inner and outer harbor defenses, could only be attacked by using operational deception. Disguised as an ordinary craft normal to the area of operations, JAVAMAN would operate by remote control radio from an aircraft and be aimed by the use of television. [The first use of TV for military purposes].

Experimentation and development were in progress throughout the late spring of 1944. A test was made in August. In this test the cooperation of the Air Forces, begun during SIMMONS, was continued. They made available to Special Projects a 5,000-ton, 300-foot derelict for the experiment, which took place on 11 August 1944 in the Gulf of Mexico. Representatives of the JCS, the Navy, the Air Forces and OSS were present at the maneuvers. In these tests, a JAVAMAN craft, containing high explosives, under remote control from a plane which aimed the missile by the use of television, was completely successful in sinking the target vessel.

Consequently, at the end of September JAVAMAN was declared ready for operational use in ETO. Maneuvers and operational runs continued during the period of waiting, pending Theater Commander approval. By March 1945, this approval was not forthcoming and Special Projects turned to another theater to find operational employment for JAVAMAN.

In May 1945 General MacArthur requested and approved appropriate air priority for Special Projects personnel to proceed to his Theater to discuss the possibilities of JAVAMAN there. Personnel was dispatched and, as a result of the discussions, General MacArthur on 21 June approved the dispatch to his Theater of a JAVAMAN mission with appropriate equipment.

By mid-July, the first group of [air-rescue boats] was ready for shipment to the Pacific on tankers allotted by the Army Transportation Corps. The sudden end of hostilities in the Pacific on 17 August obviated the possibility of using JAVAMAN in actual operations against the enemy. Contracts were cancelled, work was stopped and liquidation begun. [Deletion]

SCHOOLS AND TRAINING—(S&T)

The problem of training personnel for the varied activities of OSS was a complex one, in some respects as unusual as the activities themselves. There was no precedent in America for such an undertaking and it was necessary at first to piece together various fragments of seemingly relevant knowledge from other agencies of the Government, to borrow instructional techniques from the British, and to adapt certain technical aspects of orthodox military training to the probable conditions under which guerrilla units and resistance organizers might operate.

The initial task was to establish training facilities and programs which would produce spies, saboteurs and guerrillas. By 1943 the problem was complicated by the necessity of preparing "black" propagandists and counter-espionage experts. In addition, it was necessary to train the staff members who would direct from field or Washington headquarters the activities of agents and operatives, and also to train in the fundamentals of OSS those who would perform more routine tasks, so that they would understand the unusual security requirements upon which the lives of agents and the success of operations depended. Consequently, S&T was called upon to establish training curricula to prepare a wide variety of personnel for the unorthodox and unprecedented activities in which OSS engaged.

The complexity of the over-all training program was added to by the fact that, with the exception of certain types of paramilitary training, all training had to be as highly individualized as possible. Ideally, the training of spies, saboteurs, "black" propagandists and counter-espionage experts should probably be on a completely individual, i. e., tutorial, basis. However, in a situation of war, with the heavy demands from the field for large numbers of staff members, agents and operatives which the rapid expansion of OSS dictated, it was necessary to establish training by classes.

There were two separate categories of training initially established under COI in 1942. One was designed to prepare agents for espionage, principally under conditions prevailing in neutral territories. The other was designed to prepare personnel for various forms of sabotage and to establish simultaneously a program and physical facilities which could be adapted to the training of guerrilla units when authorization therefor should be secured.

As the progress of the war transformed most of the areas of interest in the world into either Allied military theaters or enemy and enemy-occupied territory, the numbers of agents which could or should be sent to neutral territories diminished in relation to those destined for military theaters or actual infiltration into enemy or occupied regions. Therefore, the cover technique and the method of infiltration of the spy became essentially the same as that of the saboteur in most cases. The entry of the spy into a neutral country was illegal in intent but not in method, and his cover was predicated upon authentic documents. In enemy or enemy-occupied territory, however, he was, like the saboteur, dependent upon forged credentials and such unlawful modes of entry as the parachute, the rubber boat, or a surreptitious crossing of battle lines.

It thus became evident shortly after the establishment of OSS that training for all OSS branches should be centralized and the various types of training subdivided within one branch, so that trainees could secure more readily any type of training pertinent to their missions.

The first move in this direction was the establishment in September 1942 of a Training Directorate. [Deletion]

There were few in America experienced in the activities in which OSS was engaged, and it was necessary to school the instructors themselves. Even this was difficult, however, since the functions of the various branches of OSS were actually being defined and developed by experience in the field, so that clear-cut direction from the operating branches in this early period was lacking. During 1943 S&T was forced to lean heavily on the British for assistance, both by sending potential instructors to British schools and by borrowing instructors from the British for varying periods of time. [Deletion]

Training. The principles of undercover training derived primarily from espionage techniques. However, they were also applicable to the work of saboteurs who might infiltrate enemy or enemy-occupied territory to operate under cover, to "black" propagandists who might similarly be engaged in infiltration operations and to counterespionage staff members who had to be thoroughly familiar with the techniques of enemy espionage which it would be their purpose to circumvent and turn to advantage.

In this field, cover was synonymous with security. Upon the effectiveness of an agent's cover depended the success of his activities. It was recognized that there were several types of cover. In neutral territory, an agent might be semi-overt, that is to say, he would be ostensibly in a diplomatic or other government post, his connection with the United States Government being obvious. In some such instances, the fact that the individual was engaged in intelligence activities might be well known, which would attract disaffected political elements or individuals who, for various motivations, were willing to give information. However, even in such semi-overt activities, the cover in a given operation had to remain strictly inviolate. In other words, secrecy had to be maintained as to connection with OSS and as to how intelligence operations were executed.

A more complicated type of cover in neutral countries would be that of ostensibly engaging in a business or profession. In such cases the cover requirements were more rigid, since knowledge of the fact that the individual was engaged in intelligence work was not to be revealed. However, such cover was generally predicated upon an occupation with which the agent was familiar, and his presence in the area would be supported by authentic credentials. In most such cases, the problem was to find an occupation for the agent which would allow him freedom of time and movement to carry on his clandestine activities without jeopardizing his cover.

Perhaps the most rigid type of cover was that of the agent infiltrated illegally into enemy or enemy-occupied territory. In such cases, cover was quite often supported by documents, forged at least in part, and the identity assumed by the agent was often completely false. The agent would take up an occupation, compatible with the identity he assumed, in which the same qualification was present as in the case of neutral countries, namely, freedom of time and movement to carry on surreptitious activity.

A variation of cover in enemy or enemy-occupied territory was that which was only partly false, that is to say, someone who had previously engaged in the cover occupation in the assigned area and who had all or most of the requisite documents necessary to support his presence in the area. However, there would necessarily be a period of absence which had to be covered by falsification.

The matter of cover was basic to practically all of the activities in which OSS engaged. Staff members, operations officers and intelligence officers, who were to deal with agents and would on occasion recruit and direct agent activities in the field, had to understand cover and the techniques necessary to preserve it. Needless to say, those who were actually to act as undercover agents, whether in neutral, enemy or enemy-occupied territory, had even more necessity for such knowledge.

Therefore, all OSS training, with the exception of that for OG units, stressed from the beginning the importance of maintaining cover. An informal civilian atmosphere prevailed at the intelligence schools and the students were forbidden to disclose their real identities and lived under assumed names. At the same time they were instructed to attempt to pierce the cover of their fellow students. It was sought to create, under a relaxed surface, an atmosphere of tension which would characterize real activities in the field. In the SO schools, as in the Communications areas, students wore fatigue uniforms without designation of rank. While these schools were run along more military lines, the identities of the students were not revealed and the preservation of cover was equally stressed.

Intensive interrogation exercises of various types were carried on in attempts to force the student to break his assumed identity. In each of these the student was made familiar with the various techniques of interrogation and the importance of the most minute detail in his cover preparations was stressed. The entire atmosphere at all training establishments was designed to prepare the trainees psychologically for the fact that the life of an agent is a constant and continuing gamble with detection.

If the agent were to accomplish anything, however, it would be necessary for him to take action, and every action taken would create another vulnerable point in his cover. Most agents were to operate primarily as organizers. Their object would be to organize chains of sub-agents to perform the actual espionage, sabotage or dissemination of "black" propaganda. Therefore, a great deal of attention was given to methods of agent organization. The primary purpose of such methods was to insulate the main agent from the possible consequences of detection of any part of the various activities carried out under his direction.

One of the prime factors was the use of cut-outs—an intermediary who would handle all actual dealings with sub-agents for the principal agent. In the event of a "blow," arrangements would be made for the cut-out to go underground or leave the area, whereupon the remnants of a given chain could be re-activated by a new cut-out. In this fashion, sub-agents would not know the identity of the principal agent, and would therefore be unable to implicate him. A principal agent might use any number of cut-outs, depending upon the situation in the area in which he was operating at a given time. Modifications and adaptations of the cut-out principle might also be devised.

Another expression of the principle of insulation was the cell system. While subject to numerous variations, its basis was organization of a chain of small units of sub-agents. One member of each unit would know one member of the group above, and another member of the same unit would be the only one who would know the identity of a member of the unit below. In a chain of this nature, a "blow" would result generally in the loss of only one group, and at most three, before the possibility of further detection could be blocked off.

Communications, other than technical, were also basic to agent activity. All students were familiarized with various cipher and code systems and were apprised of their inherent weaknesses. It was, of course, basic that no cipher or code system could be used through technical facilities provided by the Communications Branch unless formally authorized. However, it was recognized that certain low-grade ciphers and home-made codes might be employed for local communications with sub-agents in a given area, where detection by the enemy would not jeopardize other operations. The technique of writing "innocent text" letters, i.e., seemingly ordinary letters which concealed a previously enciphered message, was also practiced.

The precautions necessary to the establishment of "safe houses" were also explained. A "safe house" (one where the people were friendly and willing to take the risk of harboring an agent or sub-agent) might be necessary to assist the concealment or escape of a sub-agent, or, on occasion, the principal agent himself. As it developed in the field, chains of "safe houses" were often useful in facilitating the escape of wanted individuals who possessed experience or knowledge potentially valuable to the Allies. Also, chains of "safe houses" frequently constituted a route to safety for escaped prisoners of war. The use of "safe houses" to receive newly infiltrated agents and shelter them until they could make arrangements to establish themselves in their cover occupations was of primary importance in enemy and enemy-occupied territory.

Letter drops were necessary to agent communication. Such letter drops might be animate or inanimate. A news dealer or tobacconist might be used to receive and pass messages. A designated tree, or an empty tin can placed at a pre-arranged spot in relation to a given kilometer marker on a European road, might be used. It was possible to use an inanimate letter drop for the actual transportation of intelligence reports over great distances. For example, agents might place intelligence material at a designated spot on a railroad car or locomotive. Such material would be removed by confederates in another city and forwarded.

The above subjects were not taught so that the trainees would learn them by rote. They were given merely as principles and examples of what had been done. The students were constantly made aware that variations and adaptations, as well as entirely new techniques, must be developed by them. All instruction was designed to sharpen the student's ingenuity, and to impress upon him the necessity for exercising the utmost judgment in calculating the risks inherent in a given activity.

The study of cover and security and the techniques of agent or-

ganization and communication was fundamental to all activities of
OSS. Basic courses also included Intelligence Objectives and Re-
porting, Small Arms, Sabotage, Demolitions and Close Combat.
[This was the system of unarmed combat developed by Major
Fairbairn, whom the British lent to OSS as an instructor in 1942.]
In addition, rudimentary training in counter-espionage and the
various techniques of "black" propaganda was added, as those
functions became integral parts of OSS activities.

The basic course included two separate undercover field problems in the course of which students were dispatched to various
cities. Such problems required that each student prepare a cover
story, with appropriate cover credentials, and attempt to penetrate
an industrial establishment in such cities as Baltimore, Philadelphia or Pittsburgh. While such practice operations could not involve the element of actual danger which would be met in the field,
they gave the students an opportunity to test in practice some of
the theories which had been given them in the courses, and were
valuable as a means of psychological conditioning for actual
operations. [A by-product of these field problems was that by reporting security weaknesses in defense plants, OSS was able to
contribute indirectly to the improvement of security practices in
various industries. (footnote)] Field problems, which comprised
simulated night sabotage attacks, compass runs and various tests
of observation and reporting, were also carried out in the course of
basic training.

The period covered by basic training was only three weeks, and,
since it was so short, was necessarily intensive. Students were kept
hard at work from dawn until late at night and were given no
breaks for weekends or holidays. This intensity had not only the effect of teaching the most in the shortest possible time, but also, by
the pressure which it exerted, eliminated some of the lazy or incompetent.

The final night of basic training was ostensibly a party, with
refreshments freely available. In actuality, this farewell "party"—
in an atmosphere which fostered the feeling in the students that
they were not under pressure and could relax after the arduous
training program—provided an excellent opportunity for final
judgment. A thorough evaluation of each student was prepared by
the instructors and submitted to Washington headquarters upon
the conclusion of each course.

The basic training was not intended to produce finished OSS operatives, but to be preliminary to more advance courses for those
who would specialize in some particular activity, and to provide
those who were to go overseas in staff positions with a general un-

derstanding of the problems inherent in OSS operations.

A second type of training was SO basic training. This was designed to fit SO men for their missions, and was quite often given to such personnel subsequent to OSS basic training. The emphasis was upon physical conditioning, survival in the field and knowledge of sabotage devices. The course was three weeks in duration.

Subjects given during SO basic training included Field Craft, Demolitions, Map Reading, Weapons, Morse Code and Close Combat. Students were taught how to make basic types of demolitions charges for the sabotage of industrial establishments, rail lines, bridges, etc. They were instructed in the use of small arms for most rapid and effective day and night firing. They were further instructed in methods of sabotage by abrasives, contaminants, "slow-downs," etc.

The course included field problems comprising night map and compass runs, various types of reconnaissance and the placing of demolition charges on dummy targets.

The atmosphere of the SO schools was military in nature. As stated above, trainees wore no designations of rank and preserved cover identities throughout the course.

MO personnel usually took OSS basic training first. Thereafter, they received advanced MO training in such subjects as propaganda fundamentals, propaganda writing and radio propaganda. Emphasis was chiefly upon "black" propaganda, including such subversive techniques as poison-pen letters, rumors, etc.

For X-2 personnel, basic OSS training was also considered preliminary to advanced courses which went into the more detailed aspects of the enemy intelligence services and also into the techniques of manipulating and controlling double agents, as well as the specialized X-2 personality report.

OG training was originally set up by SO instructors who worked out a program which consisted, in effect, of longer and more elaborate courses of physical toughening, weapons training, close combat, map reading, and the like. OSS basic training was not considered essential to OG's. Their training was distinguished from that of SO in that they were to operate as uniformed troops in well-organized and disciplined units, rather than as individuals or small teams.

When MU was established, maritime training became the responsibility of that Branch, but S&T remained in charge of administration. Originally, maritime training was a specialized aspect of SO training and included small boat infiltration operations and the elementary techniques of maritime sabotage. In the early period it was one of the advanced courses for trainees who had been given SO basic training. Following the establishment of MU, specialized maritime schools were set up, and the training was extended to include various advanced forms of maritime sabotage, underwater demolitions, beach reconnaissance and the use of the new and specialized devices which MU developed.

Another type of training for which S&T was only administratively responsible was communications. There were two categories of trainees at the communications areas—those intended for base station duty overseas and those who would enter enemy territory either as SO or SI agents. The general atmosphere of the communications schools was military. In the case of prospective base station operators, there was no concealment of rank or true identity. Student agents, however, preserved cover identities and bore no indication of rank.

In communications training for clandestine radio operation, the emphasis was not upon the speed of transmission, but rather its accuracy. Student agents generally were not required to be proficient in Morse code beyond a speed of 18 words per minute. It was realized that, in transmitting under conditions where the base station operator could not "break" the agent, accuracy was the prime consideration. Agent radio operators were given instruction in radio theory and in maintenance of their sets, with emphasis upon the improvisation which might be necessary in enemy or enemy-occupied territory, where replacement parts would be difficult to obtain. Two of the most difficult problems facing the clandestine radio operator were power supply and concealment of his antenna. Field problems, in which the prospective agent was required to set up a radio clandestinely and make contact with the "base" (school), were carried out over distances up to 200 miles.

In communications training, also, it was sought to impress upon the agent the necessity for the exercise of ingenuity in carrying on his operations. The period of training for an agent radio operator was normally some 10 weeks.

[A cardinal principle of agent radio operation was that the agent might interrupt base transmission at any time when the exigencies of his situation demanded it, whereas the base station (which could not know the conditions of emergency under which the agent was sending) might under no circumstances interrupt the agent.

[One of the developments to camouflage antennae was the concealment of antenna wire in the form of a clothes line. Students were encouraged to use their ingenuity to the utmost. On one occasion, a student on a field problem managed to make contact with the school over a short range of 75 miles by using the springs of a bed as an antenna. (footnote)]

Therefore, the complete training of a secret agent required 16 weeks—3 weeks for OSS intelligence training, 3 weeks for SO basic training and 10 weeks for communications training. At the conclusion of such period, the prospective agent was familiar with undercover intelligence practices, the arts of sabotage, the elements of field craft and the procedures and techniques of clandestine radio operation.

Certain other branches gave their overseas personnel various types of training prior to dispatch. R&A personnel for the most part required no training which was included among S&T curricula. However, certain R&A personnel were given OSS basic training prior to departure for overseas assignments. Prior to dispatch for overseas missions, most Special Funds officers received OSS basic training and most Field Photographic personnel went through the SO basic course.

There was never any consistent policy with regard to S&T indoctrination or orientation for all OSS personnel. Many people were sent overseas without any particular training because it was assumed that they would be engaged in purely servicing functions. In some instances where the exigencies of the situation in the field made it necessary for such personnel to be transferred to more active duties, the lack of training constituted a handicap.

One other type of training played an important role in many OSS operations overseas. In the early days of COI, a small parachute school had been established. The staff of this school was sent to North Africa in late 1942 to establish parachute training facilities there. Arrangements were made with the Army in order that OSS personnel requiring parachute training in the United States might receive it at Fort Benning. Those who were sent overseas without parachute training, and whose missions required such training, received it at the OSS school in North Africa or at British schools in England.

One additional responsibility of S&T was to set up courses to fulfill Army requirements that all enlisted men receive basic military training before going overseas. The necessity for this developed out of the fact that many OSS civilians were drafted and reassigned to the agency prior to departure for overseas assignments. By considerable streamlining and intensive work, S&T compressed the elements of basic military training into a 4-week course.

Assessment. In the summer and fall of 1943, the rapid expansion of OSS [deletion] resulted in an intense recruiting drive by all branches which taxed to the utmost the capacity of the training areas. There was naturally a percentage of recruits who were either unfit to receive training for various reasons or psychologically unsuited for operations overseas. In addition, instruction was handicapped because the poorer students established the pace of the class. There were security risks in releasing students who "washed out" during training, since they received at least some knowledge of the secret operations and methods of the organization. The risk in sending overseas personnel who might not be emotionally fit for field activity was even greater.

In the fall of 1943, therefore, it was proposed that a holding area be established, at which no actual training would be given but which would serve to screen prospective trainees as to their physical, mental and emotional capabilities for their intended assignments. Before this proposal could be put into effect, reports were received that the British SOE had established a program of psychological evaluation for the potential agents. The merits of this idea seemed so obvious that members of S&T proceeded to evolve, independently of the British, a plan of psychological assessment. The OSS plan proved to be remarkably similar to that of SOE.

Several prominent psychologists and psychiatrists were called to Washington to implement the program. A country estate (Station S) in Fairfax, Virginia, was leased. In January 1944, Station S opened as the first OSS assessment school. The program called for a three and a half day period of tests and problems designed to evaluate the potential trainee from the standpoint of emotional stability, mentality, personality, aptitude, etc. Initially, the assessment program was considered in the nature of an experiment, and its facilities were offered to OSS branches on an optional basis. The results of the first three months proved so impressive, however, that in March 1944 Donovan ordered that all OSS personnel destined for overseas assignments be assessed before departure from the United States. [Deletion]

Assessment had two primary objectives: (1) To analyze the personality of the candidate in order to determine his ability to withstand the rigors of war; and (2) to make some estimate as to the type of activity for which he was best suited, and, incidentally, whether he could perform the job for which he was intended.

[Assessment reports were for OSS use only. They were kept separate from personnel files and were not available to the subject, or to the scrutiny of persons outside of OSS. They were ordered destroyed at the time of the liquidation of OSS. (footnote)]

By April 1944, Station S rated all candidates in terms of twenty major qualifications. These included motivation, initiative, resourcefulness, inference, discretion and leadership; an additional category—job fitness—was added later. [Deletion]

During the course all candidates wore Army fatigue uniforms

without indication of rank. Immediately upon arrival, each candidate was subjected to routine paper and pencil intelligence tests which provided a general index of his intellectual capabilities and aptitudes.

A variety of tests were evolved which were designed to produce not only material for a psychological analysis of the candidate but also a job analysis, namely what he could do best and whether he was capable of performing the task for which he was employed.

However, no test produced one type of evidence only. For example, a candidate would be required to transport a 150-pound case, presumably of ammunition, to the top of a nine-foot wall. He would be provided with two ladders, a block and tackle, several planks and a hand truck. He would be given six minutes to complete the job. Obviously the results of a test such as this demonstrated a variety of things about the candidate, including physical strength, ingenuity, presence of mind, etc. The same was true of a test which involved supervising and directing two assistants in setting up a complicated frame construction in ten minutes. The assistants, who were actually junior members of the assessment staff, were directed to make things as difficult as possible for the candidate, while professing every desire to assist him. This type of test indicated the candidate's ability to withstand frustration, to persevere, to think clearly, etc. The results of such tests as these were on the whole general in nature.

More precise tests undertook to discover the candidate's ability to memorize maps, faces, terrain, etc. In one test, two sets of slides were used. Each slide of the first set had on it a man's photograph, his name, age, occupation and place of residence. The second set consisted only of the photographs. The candidate would be shown the first set of slides in groups of four, each slide being exposed for twenty seconds. After each group, the corresponding slides of the second set were shown for thirty seconds in random order. During the showing of the second set of slides, the student was asked to write down all that he could recall of the information appearing on the first slide. Aptitude of this nature was more essential to an intelligence agent than a saboteur and pronounced skill in the test was considered an indication that the candidate might have additional capabilities which would make him a worth-while intelligence officer or agent.

Other tests, designed to indicate a candidate's specific aptitudes, involved assignments to process propaganda material (MO), and ability to instruct and speak extemporaneously before a group (which was useful in determining the potentialities of prospective instructors). Additional tests were devised to indicate aptitudes for other OSS activities.

The clinical interview played a decisive role in the assessment of a candidate. This was a personal conference of varying length between the candidate and a staff member designated as mentor for him. The interview was designed to bring together by conversational and interrogational techniques all the data on the candidate which had been acquired in paper tests, by observation, etc. Following the interview, the results of the various tests and the opinions of the interviewer were compared. In addition, the observations of other staff members were also considered. On occasion, the interview evaluation conflicted with the cumulative indications provided by the tests. This raised a question as to the validity of the tests vis-a-vis the clinical interview. On the whole, it was the interview which carried more weight. Actually, there was seldom conflict of this nature, and the fact that it arose in certain exceptional cases did not destroy the validity of the original concept, which was that clinical data is stronger when supported by situational data but is not invalidated by an occasional discrepancy.

The assessment program was most effective in providing a psychological evaluation of the candidate. It was less effective in determining the candidate's suitability for a particular job. There were many reasons for the latter. For one thing, no member of the assessment staff, at least until very near the close of the war, had actual field experience with OSS and, with the wide latitude necessarily given to theater units to divert personnel from their original assignments to other activities, it was difficult to secure from the branches precise job descriptions. Furthermore, even when a reasonably precise job description could be provided, there was no assurance that the candidate would not be transferred in the field to another assignment.

From January 1944 to July 1945 the OSS assessment schools screened 5,300 candidates for the European theaters. On the West Coast, Station WS handled 210 candidates. [Deletion] The assessment program certainly succeeded in screening out the 15% to 20% who were obviously unfit. However, it is impossible to ascertain with any exactitude whether the courses could have been so designed as to be more effective.

The effort to assess an individuals's total personality had never before been attempted in the United States. The psychologists and psychiatrists who handled the program for OSS later used the techniques developed under the stress of war to establish programs for the Veterans Administration and several leading universities, in addition to giving the benefit of their experience to various departments of the Government. It seems obvious that the OSS assessment program established a precedent and accumulated experience which will in the future facilitate effective personnel selection in many fields.

Training Areas. In June of 1942 only four schools were in actual operation. These were RTU-11 (the "Farm") and Areas A, B and C.

The "Farm" was located in Maryland about 20 miles from Washington. It was used for both elementary and advanced intelligence training until basic training began at Area E, whereupon it became the advanced, or finishing, intelligence school.

Area A, which comprised approximately 5,000 acres of heavily wooded terrain near Quantico, Virginia, was subdivided into four separate schools, designated A-2, A-3, A-4 and A-5. Area A-4 was used primarily for basic SO training.

Area B, comprising some 9,000 acres of mountainous wooded terrain in the Catoctin area in Maryland, was used primarily for paramilitary training.

Area C was located on wooded terrain adjacent to Area A, and was used for communications training.

In mid-November 1942 Area E, located in Maryland some 30 miles north of Baltimore, was opened. It was somewhat similar to the "Farm," consisting of three country houses, and became the principal school for OSS basic training.

Area D, located on the Potomac River near Quantico, was activated in March 1943 to conduct training in maritime activities.

Area F was acquired in April 1943. It was located at the Congressional Country Club on the outskirts of Washington, and was used primarily for the training of OG's. Toward the close of the war, when large numbers of personnel were returning from European theaters for de-briefing or transfer to the Far East, Area F became a holding area and was used for de-briefing and reassessment.

In October 1943, Area M, a former Signal Corps camp (Mac-Dowell) in Indiana, was acquired and used for communications training

In January 1944, Station S, a country estate at Fairfax, Virginia, was acquired to provide facilities for the assessment program. In a short time, Area S proved inadequate to handle the large numbers of candidates, and a house was acquired in Washington (Station W) where a shorter assessment program was established for clerical and services personnel.

In mid-1944, a West Coast assessment program was established at the Capistrano Beach Club in San Clemente, California.

After mid-1944, most training was performed on the West

Coast, and the schools in the east were gradually closed. By VE-Day, the eastern establishments were being used mainly as holding areas, in which personnel could be de-briefed or screened for possible use in the Far East.

The need for exceptionally qualified people in the Far East led to the establishment of courses under university auspices. Georgetown University made available facilities for a two-week course on the economic and political backgrounds of Far Eastern countries. In January 1945, arrangements were made with the University of Pennsylvania to train specially selected students in the Japanese and Korean languages. This was a six month course which included, in addition to language instruction, a comprehensive survey of the sociological, political and economic problems of the Far East.

Overseas Training. Until the middle of 1944, S&T/Washington had practically no authority over training programs conducted in various theaters. It was called upon for instructors, and made available the material used in training in the United States.

Late in 1942 several instructors were dispatched to NATO, where they took part in the Tunisian campaign. After the fall of Tunis, training schools were established in NATO for Italian and French agents. North Africa soon proved to be a fertile area for recruiting and an excellent base for infiltration operations. When parachute training became necessary, the staff of a parachute training school which had been set up under COI in the United States was dispatched to NATO in early 1943. In the following two years over 2,500 male and female agents were given parachute training. Included in this total were agents trained for the British and French services, as well as for OSS. When parachute infiltration into southern France and Italy was virtually completed, the parachute school was moved to China where it achieved a notable record in the training of American and Chinese commando groups for parachute operations. [Deletion]

In addition to providing personnel for overseas training, S&T/Washington also developed a considerable research staff to see that the proper training aids, lecture materials, etc. were dispatched to all overseas training establishments. In turn, S&T/Washington received from overseas some of its most beneficial training material in the form of reports of agent operation.

From the first day of January 1944 to July 1945, the assessment schools evaluated and/or screened 5,300 candidates. Basic Espionage Schools graduated over 1,800 trained personnel as operatives in gathering, analyzing and disseminating information. The Paramilitary Schools, concerned with the training of sabotage men, trained a total of 1,027. The "Farm," specializing in advanced intelligence training, graduated from May 1942 to December 1944 over 800 men and women.

The above figures cover only those trained for European operations and, furthermore, do not take into account specialized groups, over which S&T had divided or little control, such as Communications, OG, MU, etc. From the beginning of training on the West Coast until its conclusion, close to 1,000 personnel were given basic OSS training, approximately 250 advanced SO training and 200 advanced SI training; 210 were assessed on the West Coast, where approximately 100 were given advance MO training. These are, of course, over-all figures, and give only a general indication of the scope of the program.

The rapid expansion of OSS, both in numbers of personnel and in function, presented a challenge to the training program. There was another challenge which cannot be so clearly delineated by the use of statistics. It grew out of the fact that only a small portion of OSS operations consisted of subjects that could be taught by concrete example, e.g., the use of demolitions materials, small arms, codes and ciphers. The precise situation which any agent or agent team would encounter in the field could not be foreseen. Therefore, the major goal was psychological—to develop in the student-agent an attitude of mind which would respond to an emergency in accordance with the exigencies of the particular situation. Examples were cited and principles discussed, not for the purpose of learning them by rote, but so that the student could use them as a springboard for his own ingenuity.

Field problems, likewise, were not used so that the student-agent, be he spy, saboteur or guerrilla, would learn to react according to habit; they were in no sense rehearsals. Rather, they were designed, as was the general atmosphere at the schools, to provoke an undercurrent of tension and nervous pressure beneath a relaxed surface. Even in such technical fields as demolitions, only the fundamentals could be taught—the successful execution of sabotage would require the ingenious application of such principles in the context of a given situation in the field.

Thus, the OSS training program was never static, but was constantly being developed, refined and improved in the light of experience from its inception in 1942 until the liquidation of the agency on 1 October 1945. [Deletion]

Part II

OSS—OPERATIONS

CHAPTER 3

North Africa

North Africa was the testing ground for OSS. Initiated in January 1942, the first large-scale COI/OSS operation involved placing agents in an area where British services had been excluded, to gather intelligence, prepare sabotage units in the event of German invasion and prevail on military and other groups to support an Allied landing. Success was important, both in Washington for the future of the agency, and in the field as a demonstration to the theater commands (on whom OSS depended for facilities, transportation and other services) of its potentialities in support of the more orthodox forms of warfare. The operation was carried out by only ten Americans working under State Department cover in North Africa. [Deletion]

[The American agents were struck immediately by the attitude of British secret agents in the field; their reception was a good deal less cordial than that afforded their seniors when they arrived in London. R. Harris Smith, the former CIA research and analysis officer, would record in his unofficial history of OSS that the MI-6 station chief at Tangier was a man who would "sell his country, his soul, or his mother for a peseta" and that he was so "violently jealous of the Americans" that "he allegedly plotted to poison his own assistant, a British major, for being 'too straightforward' with Donovan's officers." The second major difficulty was encountered in the attitude of some of the French administrators in North Africa; they came to believe that the American agents were encouraging anti-colonial movements, a suspicion that was not wholly unfounded. As for the Germans and Italians, they treated these first agents of the world's newest intelligence service with undisguised contempt.]

OPERATION TORCH

The Vice-Consuls. In February 1941 an economic pact was concluded by the State Department with General Maxime Weygand,
the Commander of Vichy French forces in North Africa. To supplement the agreement, twelve U.S. vice-consuls were added to
U.S. representation in North Africa for the purpose of checking on
the distribution of U.S. cotton, sugar, tea and petroleum to be
allocated. They were to have access to ports to observe incoming
American shipments and the distribution of goods when they arrived, and to check all outgoing ships carrying goods similar to
those imported, in order to prevent their acquisition by the Axis.

The twelve control officers were selected by G-2 and ONI, in cooperation with State Department. Ostensibly vice-consuls, they
were briefed for intelligence activities. When military and naval
undercover intelligence outside the Western Hemisphere was taken
over by the new Coordinator of Information in the fall of 1941,
COI dispatched a chief agent [Colonel William Eddy, former head
of the English department of the American University in Cairo] to
set up a head office in the international port of Tangier. [Excision]

The subversive job in North Africa was divided between himself
and Robert D. Murphy of State. While Murphy would handle the
political negotiations with French leaders, COI would direct the
secret aspects of intelligence, subversion and resistance. These involved, in addition to the actual collection of intelligence, disseminating propaganda designed to minimize French support of the
Axis, obtaining the cooperation of French military groups and organizing units for sabotage and armed coup-de-main resistance to
counteract the quasi-fascist organizations, S.O.L. and P.P.F. [Ser-
vice d'Ordre Legionnaire (a veterans' organization) and Parti Po-
pulaire Francais. (footnote)]

[Robert D. Murphy, of whom De Gaulle would write: "Skillful
and determined, long familiar with the best society and apparently
inclined to believe that France consisted of the people he dined
with in town." The Germans were more complimentary: "Tall,
slim, good-looking, polyglot, a man of the world, cultured, fond of
social life, an excellent conversationalist, easy-mannered, able to
deal with any situation, making an excellent impression.... He is a
man of ideas far above the average from a European point of view,
and certainly an extraordinary type for an American." State evidently thought as did the Germans; he became U.S. representative
to the Allied military government in occupied Germany, ambassador to Belgium and Japan, Under-Secretary of State, president

of Corning Glass International, and a member of the Foreign Intelligence Advisory Committee.]

The British shelling of the French navy at Mers el Kebir and Dakar in July 1940 had closed French North Africa to open British activity. All British nationals were banned from the area and their diplomatic and intelligence representation evacuated to a perimeter position in the international city of Tangier overlooking the Straits of Gibraltar. Concomitant with this diplomatic break was the psychological severance that was to handicap seriously British relations with patriotic Frenchmen until the end of the war. The incident put the as yet non-belligerent Americans in a favorable position for subversive experimentation. They were able to assist the British Intelligence Services and borrow special equipment without having to rival these more experienced institutions. Intelligence in North Africa, preparatory to the landings, became a COI/OSS responsibility.

Clandestine Radio Stations. Of the twelve vice-consuls, two each were operating in offices at Tunis, Oran and Algiers, and the remainder at Casablanca. The new COI chief immediately began the process of setting up a coordinated intelligence and special operations system, designed to meet the alternate possibilities of German or Allied invasion. Choosing six of the control officers and a regular State Department vice-consul of ten-years' standing, who had shown themselves most resourceful in organizing and working with agents, he appointed definite tasks of an intelligence and operational nature. He directed that all intelligence reports be channeled through Tangier for appropriate dissemination, instead of being dispatched direct to Washington from the various consulates.

An intrinsic part of Donovan's plan for North Africa had been the establishment of rapid communications in such fashion that they could continue to operate in the event of a diplomatic break with the Vichy Government. COI's first and most pressing problem, therefore, was to establish—rapidly, in view of the continuing possibility of diplomatic rupture or military action by either the Germans or the Allies—a clandestine radio network for the ports where the control officers were operating.

Frenchmen with some knowledge of radio were recruited by the vice-consuls, sent secretly to Gibraltar to be drilled by the British, and returned to await the arrival of enough equipment to set up permanent field stations. The Casablanca office was the first to obtain both a wireless set and an operator with which to begin, in March 1942, a daily schedule to MIDWAY, the base station in Tangier. The location was a wine-press overlooking the airfield.

Agent sets and parts were smuggled in from the British supplies in Gibraltar. By July wireless stations similar to the one in Casablanca (LINCOLN) had been clandestinely set up in Algiers (YANKEE), Tunis (PILGRIM) and Oran (FRANKLIN), and were regularly contacting Tangier or Gibraltar. [The chief radio operator for the Division of Oran also worked the OSS station there. His position offered excellent concealment, for he was able to keep the radio set broken down in his office, assembling it only for transmission and reception. (footnote)].

The necessity for secrecy on extra-curricular activities led to a degree of misunderstanding on the part of the career members of the State Department, who frequently had cause to wonder about the movements of these food control officers. With the help of Murphy, and, later, the COI/OSS chief in the area, together with the precautions and stratagems of the men themselves, the invasion plan was never revealed to other U.S. representatives, even during the extremely active weeks directly preceding the Allied landing in November 1942.

Chains of Informants. Present in the main cities of North Africa, under the terms of the German treaty with a defeated France, were the Italian and German Armistice Commissions. These consisted of economists, military experts and agents gathering intelligence under cover of obtaining foodstuffs and minerals for the German war effort. The presence of these Axis officials helped to stiffen the Vichy-sponsored collaborationist government in North Africa and was a serious obstacle to the Americans in building up their own system.

Pearl Harbor and the official U.S. entry into the war in December 1941 brought about severe restrictions for Americans in North Africa and reprisals to Frenchmen seen associating with them. Americans were denied free access to docks, airfields and other strategic installations, while Gestapo agents in the German Armistice Commission, who had maintained a hands-off policy with regard to the Americans, now began to apply political and strong-arm pressure to oust them. Intelligence continued nevertheless to be supplied through well-placed sub-agents.

Even before the arrival of the American control officers, opposition to Axis rule in North Africa was being organized by Frenchmen themselves. These groups were especially active in Algiers and Tunis where they had established contacts with U.S. State Department representatives and with British SIS via radio to Tangier. Upon the advent of the vice-consuls, more and more Frenchmen, as well as Allied sympathizers of other nationalities who had escaped to North Africa, put themselves in the service of the Ameri-

cans and their sub-agents. The head of a French youth movement,
a police commissioner, officers in the French intelligence service
(Deuxieme Bureau), an aviation workshops manager, a garage
owner with widespread Moroccan contacts, a wealthy French industrialist [Jacques Lemaigre-Dubreuil, a vegetable oil millionaire
and right-winger who played both sides at once during the pre-
Torch period], a host of French army officers, including many in
high positions, Royalists, Communists, Jesuits, Arabs, Jews, de
Gaullists and anti-de Gaullists worked with COI/OSS for the
common purpose of helping to restore France as an independent
power.

The threat of a German thrust through Spain to North Africa
before, during and after the Allied landing was of constant concern
to the planners of Operation *TORCH*. To help prepare for this
contingency, two COI agents, trained in sabotage and other subversive techniques and with first-hand knowledge of French and
Spanish Morocco, arrived in April and May 1942 to work in and
around Tangier.

Their task was to build within the heterogeneous native population of these Axis-infested areas pro-American intelligence and
resistance groups. Since the menace to American security from
this vulnerable flank was to continue until the Germans surrendered Tunisia on 8 May 1943, the groundwork laid by these men
and the contacts made were to prove as important after the Allied
landings as before. [Excision]

In the U.S. Legation at Tangier, the new COI recruits set themselves up as dispensers of U.S. information, assisting with public
relations disseminations and distributing other forms of printed
propaganda. They made, almost immediately, key intelligence
contacts among the main streams of Moroccan society. "Strings,"
the leader of the most powerful religious brotherhood in northern
Morocco, and "Tassels," one of the most influential undercover
tribal leaders in Er Rif [the hilly coastal region transversing central
Spanish Morocco and extending into French Morocco—(footnote)] were put in touch with COI by one of its English-speaking
Moslem agents, and financed by State Department and COI funds.
Leaders of the diverse nationalist groups (elements of the Moroccan Nationalist Party), were also used, but to lesser advantage.
The last were politically active intellectuals constantly under the
surveillance of the French secret police, and therefore of little value
for undercover work.

Members of the "Strings" group numbered tens of thousands of
Moors from every walk of life, ready to obey unquestioningly the
will of their divine leader. "Strings' " reports to COI came from

caids and sheiks, holy men who penetrated the areas forbidden by the French authorities to the general populace, and from farmers and shepherds who relayed pertinent items of intelligence in comparative anonymity.

The Riffs under "Tassels," on the other hand, were Berber adventurers, willing to carry out any job regardless of the danger involved, and highly adept at avoiding detection by Spanish or French police. These men knew how to handle arms and conduct guerrilla warfare in difficult terrain. [The Atlas Mountain tribes of Morocco were the greatest obstacle to French conquest of Morocco. Marshal Petain required ten months and a force of 150,000 men and 30 batteries of 65 mm mountain guns to put down the Abd-el-Krim insurrection of 1925-26. (footnote)]

COI handled both groups with caution, letting neither know of the other's cooperation. Secret meetings were held at regular intervals with "Tassels" and "Strings," or their leg-men, at frequently changed rendezvous. Here were reported at length detailed combat intelligence—Spanish battle order, troop movements, fortifications, etc.—and significant political events. Appropriate information was turned over by COI to G-2, ONI, the State Department and the British.

Individuals having natural occupational covers were also recruited as COI agents. A fisherman was able to report the exact locations of Spanish troops between Sidi Kassem and Cap Spartel, and turned in intelligence on Spanish AA guns overlooking the Straits and the movements of German submarines operating out of caves in the same vicinity. A sherif notified COI of secret fortifications in the Tetuan-Ceuta area. An Arab tribesman helped to explode the report of an enemy airport at Tammanrot.

Aside from the organizational phases of COI planning and intelligence in Morocco, the Tangier agents personally accomplished several on-the-spot services. Using State Department vehicles, they made frequent trips through the Spanish Zone to confirm specific items of reported intelligence or to make first-hand observations for the benefit of the Army and Navy. On one of these trips they checked on alleged Spanish airfields which were a matter of concern to American intelligence and the British, and were able to report definitely that these consisted of nothing but a few antiaircraft batteries. On another, they clocked the road from Tangier to Melilla and noted all possible targets for demolition or air attack. This road, extending along the coastal length of the Spanish Zone, was one which U.S. armies would have to use in the event of military operations in the area.

Two agents, secured by a COI representative at Casablanca [Excision] supplied the Americans with decoded copies of all German Armistice Commission and Spanish Consulate cables passing through that office. An agent employed in the ticket office at the Casablanca airport reported Axis arrivals and departures, while [Excision] contributed official figures on plane stocks and the plans of all airfields, including secondary ones, and their defenses, down to safety channels and recognition signals.

To supplement the detailed strategic reports on ports and other facilities already submitted to the Army, Navy and Air Force, OSS agents reported new defense measures or increased preparations in the ports, and followed the activities and methods of the Armistice Commissions. Movements of all ships and cargoes in and out of North African ports were noted. On the basis of this information, the RAF struck repeatedly at enemy planes and ships, to prevent vital supplies from going to the Germans.

By the time of U.S. entry into the war, the vice-consuls had established reliable chains of informants in each of the major North African ports and were transmitting intelligence of long-range and tactical value to Algiers and Washington via diplomatic pouch and cable. In the first category were many sketches and overlays of port installations (sent in answer to specific Army and Navy questionnaires) and information on the disposition of the French fleet, in particular on the presence of the 35,000 ton battleship "Jean Bart" in Casablanca harbor. Examples of short-range intelligence were reports on shipments of crude rubber, iron ore and cobalt. These were, on different occasions, diminished in supply or denied exportation altogether as a result of the observations of native agents, translated into acts of sabotage or effective political pressure by the control consuls.

Sabotage Groups. To meet a possible German attack, the Riff and Moslem groups were directed by COI in laying definite plans for organized revolt, for the reception of Allied sea- and air-borne troops, the delivery of guns and the cutting off of roads and garrisons. A system of signals was laid on, arranging for [80,000] Riffs to [revolt] and seize key positions. "Strings" was prepared to conceal the COI organizers should the Germans surprise them at Tangier, and to hide friendly Europeans for them. [Excision]

In Casablanca, the COI men divided their labors. While one narrowed his attention to the increasing demands of the new communications system, another concentrated on developing teams for special operational missions, such as the demolition of a bridge, the seizure and protection of a power house or signal station, or the detonation of mines. One group was given training in protecting rail installations and blocking the lines to prevent reinforcements of Axis troops from the Arab centers of Fez, Meknes and Marrakech. Another group of twelve Frenchmen was recruited to lead ten-man strong-arm squads to kidnap the members of the German Armistice Commission on [Torch] D-Day. [This plot was stopped, along with a number of other OSS-planned maneuvers, when the French military group under directions from Algiers superseded civilians in the crucial hours before the invasion. (footnote)]

Agents in the offices of [the Axis-controlled] Radio Maroc (Rabat) prepared to cut off the power and establish a secret studio from which to broadcast emergency signals without the knowledge of the Axis. The Chief of S.O.L. in Morocco was personally contacted by a COI agent, and won over to the U.S. viewpoint to the extent of dissolving his fascist organization altogether. Similar preparations were being made in the other ports where landings might be attempted. In Oran, combat groups totalled more than 2,500 men. [These groups were organized in cells. The men involved knew only their own leader, each leader knew no other but the ringleader, and the ringleader himself knew only the leaders of the various teams. (footnote)]

Since the Allied landing, first expected in May, was indefinitely postponed, the problem of maintaining the morale of the groups developed. Practice maneuvers were begun, but arms were difficult to obtain, and British SOE again offered invaluable assistance. It agreed to make available to the Americans supplies from its arsenal at Gibraltar, and a series of subterfuges was undertaken to get this equipment into North Africa. Sten guns, .45 pistols, ammunition, flares, explosives and other needed items were loaded in British diplomatic pouches in Gibraltar and shipped across on a Portuguese tugboat to the British Legation at Tangier. Here they were shifted to the U.S. Legation where they were reloaded into U.S. Navy or State Department pouches and smuggled through the Spanish Zone to Casablanca. Any Allied official might be asked to double as courier to deliver these items to the resistance groups in Algiers, Oran and Tunis. The vice-consuls, travelling to Tangier for conferences, frequently acted in this capacity.

Hand grenades, a forbidden article in the British pouch, were obtained from a Riff leader who had access to a large supply left over from the Spanish Civil War. Grenades were smuggled over the Spanish Moroccan border on mule pack, disguised as contraband tea and sugar, to a COI agent who carted them to safety. These grenade-passing operations were conducted without detection, despite a large German reward offered for the name of the men responsible for their distribution.

Propaganda. In order to counteract derogatory and false reports about American military preparedness by the Axis-controlled Radio Maroc in Rabat, a COI vice-consul undertook, in January 1942, an extensive propaganda tour of Morocco, using a French interpreter popular among Moroccans.

A series of photographs of U.S. war materials being produced in factories, loaded on ships, etc., was shown to Frenchmen and natives in cities and outlying areas throughout French Morocco, including, in spite of the French Resident-General's warnings not to trespass, French military zones. French officers were impressed. Admiring Arab chieftains, notorious for their habit of playing the winning side, carried the reports via the grapevine to the German-controlled Arab center of Fez. Shortly afterwards COI agents were warned by the United States consul at Casablanca, as a result of pressure from the German Armistice Commission, to restrict their Arab contacts.

The hostile attitude displayed by Germans and collaborationists toward the Americans in North Africa became more pronounced with the rise to power of Laval in France in the spring of 1942. COI's program of influencing as many of the French and natives of North Africa as possible to favor the Allies was approached with greater caution, but nevertheless continued.

One outstanding performance was a free Arabic translation of President Roosevelt's Flag Day or "Four Freedoms" speech. The message was mailed all over the Spanish Zone (with some copies going accidentally to the French Zone) and broadcast several times over the Vichy-controlled Rabat radio station. It did more than anything else up to that time to assure the Moroccans of U.S. friendship and, at the same time, unfortunately convinced them that liberation from colonial status was near at hand. Other propaganda produced by the COI representatives included attacks on General Nogues (the Vichy Resident-General in Morocco) and complaints about black market conditions in Tangier.

Preparations for D-Day. Allied sympathizers in North Africa who were in danger, and persons capable of giving technical assistance to the invasion planners in Washington and London, were secretly exfiltrated with COI help. This was usually accomplished by shipping them at night aboard Portuguese schooners plying between Casablanca and Lisbon, or on British boats going from Tangier to Gibraltar. The chief pilot of Port Lyautey was thus secured, when a request was received from Washington for a guide who knew the harbor. He was cached in the baggage compartment of a COI agent's car going to Tangier, and sent to Washington via Gibraltar. The pilot's services with the incoming fleet on D-Day were recognized with a Silver Star and the Navy Cross.

During the summer of 1942, three COI vice-consuls who had helped organize intelligence and resistance at Casablanca, Oran and Algiers respectively, left to confer with military planners. They were personally to report to the invading Task Force on preparations for resistance in each of those ports and economic, geographic and political data obtained during their assignment to North Africa.

On 22 October 1942 General Mark Clark was secretly landed on the Cherchell beach (75 miles from Algiers) to meet with Ambassador Murphy and French military and naval leaders in a villa secured through an OSS/Oran agent. Here some of the final details of *TORCH* were revealed and plans coordinated. Cooperation of the French Army in North Africa was confirmed at this time, although, for security reasons, the Allied High Command did not divulge to any but the American undercover agents in North Africa the actual date and places of landing. [The French were held throughout the war to be fundamentally insecure. Therefore they were not entrusted with any major Allied secret. As one OSS officer would record of the days in North Africa before Torch: "You put three Frenchmen and a bottle of whiskey in the same room. Then all you do is to sit back and take mental notes until the bottle is finished. With the emptying of their bottle their supply of information will be as clean as their bottles."] In preparation for the secret arrival of General Giraud from Gibraltar on D-Day, French military commanders were appointed at each port to lead armed resistance in support of the Allied landing. [General Henri Giraud, a leading French army officer, escaped from a German prison with the help of MI-6 and was now waiting at Gibraltar to come to French North Africa and persuade the French colonial army to assist rather than resist the U.S. army when it landed.]

Rumors hinting at an Allied invasion at any number of possible points had been rife for some time. Both sides originated and encouraged these: the Axis in order to smoke out denials; the Allies for the purpose of misleading German opposition. COI agents spread the word that Americans would land at Dakar. Information later received by OSS agents working at Axis-controlled Radio Maroc and from an agent in the Spanish officers' mess at Tangier, revealed that the Axis governments did not suspect landings at any place except Dakar, and that the Germans were, in fact, planning an invasion of their own at a somewhat later date than that chosen for *TORCH*. As a result of deliberately spread stories about Malta, the Germans were so convinced of a British decision to rush at all costs a food convoy to that starving island that they completely misinterpreted the move of 150 Allied ships through the Straits of

Gibraltar on D-Day.

Final arrangements were made at each of the ports and beaches where Allied landings were to take place. Although the cooperation of French Army leaders was assured, the Allies expected the Navy to resist strongly. Persuasion of some, but not all, French naval battery commanders to withhold resistance was effected without revealing when the invasion would come. Strong-arm squads were appointed to guard all important public buildings and to make arrests if the order not to resist were ignored. Others were instructed to cut telegraph and telephone lines and to obstruct public utilities generally. Still others were to go just before H-Hour to detonate mines on roads and beaches which the Allies would have to use. Groups were assigned to beachheads and landing and parachute fields, with flares to signal in troops. Guides and interpreters were briefed with passwords to meet them and aid their ingress. An OSS/Oran representative, trained by the Army Signal Corps in the use of the secret "Rebecca" radio beacon device, led an armed group charged with the reception of paratroopers on the plain between La Senia and Tafaroui airports.

Headquarters at Tangier were shifted, five days before the invasion, to Gibraltar to coordinate all North Africa activity with AFHQ plans. OSS agents coded and decoded all secret messages between AFHQ and the North African stations, including, besides intelligence reports, all instructions from Eisenhower to Murphy and arrangements for the flight and reception of General Giraud. The signal to alert groups for action was to come to OSS communication operators as a BBC announcement: "Robert Arrive." General Giraud was scheduled, upon arrival at Algiers, to broadcast publicly the announcement of French entry into the war on the side of the Allies.

Cover for the heightened activity just before 8 November was provided by various means. One OSS man sent out invitations for a party to be given on a date shortly after that set for the landings. Another made arrangements for a trip to the country on the designated weekend. Since none of the French military or resistance groups knew exactly when the attack would occur, they could not reveal the plans by unnatural excitement or suspicious behavior. Many of the civilian resistance volunteers were actually absent from their posts at the time of the invasion, because they had not expected anything to happen so soon and had left for weekend vacations.

For varying reasons, including French defections and lack of American authorization to carry them out, several of the resistance and sabotage plans were not accomplished. [The French Resident-General of Morocco was not arrested by a subordinate as planned. The French military leader in charge of resistance at Oran turned traitor at the last minute. (This development was reported by OSS radio station FRANKLIN, but the message appears to have been garbled.) American troops arrived in Algiers too late to relieve the resistance group which had seized control there, and Admiral Darlan waited three days to issue a "cease fire" order. (footnote)] Many were. OSS furthermore brought intelligence to the landing forces throughout the operation. The large-scale deception plan was also effective. Some 107,000 Allied troops went ashore over a stretch of almost 2,000 miles of North African coast while seven squadrons of Sicily-based Luftwaffe fruitlessly circled the Mediterranean opposite Cap Bon, 300 miles to the east, to bomb a "Malta-bound" convoy.

U.S. troops were met on many beaches by friendly guides. On the previous night, an OSS/Oran agent had removed the caps from demolition charges in the tunnel connecting Mers el Kebir with Oran. The tunnel was vital to Allied movement and it was estimated that it would have required three montts to rebuild.

In the absence of either a Spanish or German alarm, resistance to the Allies consisted of a determined but short-lived opposition of a surprised French navy and scattered military troops. Allied Army, Navy and Air officers with the invasion fleet received until the last minute of H-Hour, and beyond, detailed information on what to expect (with the exception of the sudden defection of the Oran resistance leader) at every landing point. They had maps and diagrams of airport locations and measurements, and of port dimensions and facilities. They knew the disposition of the French fleet, the batteries actually being manned, and the number of planes on every airfield, with the amount of aviation gas available at each. They were aware of conditions of wind, weather and tide and they had the expert advice of guides who knew the harbors intimately. Before and after the landings, they were advised, by OSS representatives who accompanied them, on terrain, locations of French headquarters and of German Armistice Commission offices, and the officials on whom they could rely for assistance in the administration of civil affairs.

The techniques developed during *TORCH* for informing invasion commanders of last-minute conditions up to the moment of arrival represented a new kind of efficiency in warfare. The established value of OSS subsequently helped the new organization to gain support in both Washington and the theaters of military operations. [Deletion]

TUNISIA

With the Armistice that was signed on 11 November 1942, control of French North Africa west of German-occupied Tunisia passed to [Eisenhower] and intelligence activities became the responsibility of the Counter-Intelligence Corps and G-2. OSS headquarters moved from Gibraltar to Algiers, where control was transferred from the State Department to Allied Force Headquarters (AFHQ).

Recognition of the OSS contribution to Operation *TORCH* and confidence in the ability of the new organization to attain strategic and tactical goals through irregular operations was given expression in General Clark's request, in early 1943, for an OSS contingent with the Fifth Army at Oujda to further the work of counterintelligence and sabotage built up for *TORCH* in Morocco.

Although operations into the Continent were uppermost in the minds of those making plans for the Algiers base, it was recognized that activity would have to be continued against German-occupied Tunisia on the east and a hostile Spanish Morocco on the west. Meanwhile, British SOE had reentered North Africa in force, with the *Brandon* and *Massingham* missions, the first for operations in Tunisia, the second for infiltration of agents into Europe.

OSS/Algiers improvised with what littte personnel, transportation and supplies were available and cooperated with French and British services. Agents in Tangier and Casablanca, continuing intelligence channels and Moroccan contacts built up during *TORCH*, worked closely with Army counter-intelligence and G-2. An Algiers radio operator with *TORCH* experience began organizing a clandestine mission to Corsica, and, in order to learn the techniques of SO and guerrilla operations, OSS representatives accompanied the British SOE mission already active in Tunisia.

Brandon was the British SOE mission appointed to work with the British First Army and the American divisions attempting to oust the Germans from Tunisia. Agents were to infiltrate enemy lines for demolition and sabotage of enemy communications and transportation, and to gather tactical intelligence for G-3. With German troops concentrated around Tunis and Bizerte, the first, or northern, phase of *Brandon* consisted in the holding of the northern flank of the Allied line by SOE alone, against some 500 Italian troops. The second, or southern, phase began when German troops moved through the Kasserine Pass. So far as SOE and OSS were concerned, this phase involved front-line tactical intelligence.

Participation in this British operation constituted the first OSS experience in sabotage and combat intelligence teams in front areas and behind enemy lines. That the jobs actually done by the handful of OSS men who joined in the SOE Tunisian campaign were not typical of future activity was perhaps due as much to the exigencies of the battle situation as to the misunderstanding of their function by the British and American Army officers whom they served. Their activity was not that of an intelligence service, but consisted in effect of reconnaissance patrolling and in one case of holding a small sector of the front.

Five advance outposts were established by SOE for the northern phase of *Brandon*. Each was under the command of a British officer, with a few French junior officers, and manned by anti-fascist French and Spanish recruits from concentration camps, the [French army] and elsewhere. Few of these had military training; most were badly undernourished if not actually unfit for combat.

Radio communications were maintained between each of the bases, an advanced holding base, the main base at Guelma and with 5th Corps Hq. of the British First Army.

As OSS representative was dispatched to visit the outposts and acquaint himself with the way in which each performed intelligence and demolition work from its strategic position in no-man's land. As it worked out, he spent most of his time at the northernmost post, Cap Serrat, and was in charge of the group there during the absence of the British commander. This lighthouse post, located on the Mediterranean coast, was the best organized of the five, its British commander being the only one in *Brandon* with SOE training and experience.

During his assignment at Cap Serrat, the OSS observer performed three types of operational tasks—defensive, observational and offensive. Defensive operations included manning the lighthouse semaphore, the bridge over the Ziatine River and the beach. The OSS representative supervised the setting of booby traps, signal wires, rockets, etc., to warn of enemy approach. Observational activities consisted in scanning the surrounding countryside at the semaphore, in sending out patrols for information and in using Arab watchers and informers to advise of enemy movements. Offensive operations, owing to the small size of the garrison and the poor physical condition and morale of its men, were limited to several mining expeditions. These amounted to little, as the Italians were less active in the area than the German Messerschmitts, which regularly raided the few passable roads and made movement overland dangerous.

In addition to liaison duties, the OSS man was put in charge of work with the Arabs, involving interviews with hostages and prisoners for intelligence information. Allied relations with the Arabs were not of the best in Tunisia, mostly as a result of the open hostility that existed between Arabs and French. The Americans were associated with the latter, and not even the distribution of cotton, tea and sugar served to turn more than a very small percentage of the Tunisian Arabs to Allied assistance. A hostage system was employed:

> We found that when we entered a distant village where loyalty was wavering, we could take the eldest son of the most important man and hold him in the lighthouse pending his father's arrival. The old man inevitably came, with gifts, demanding his son. He was sent back to get good information of enemy positions, and when he came the second time his son was released, if the information was satisfactory.... This use of hostages was our chief source of intelligence aside from the work of our own patrols.

Only one demolition job is known to have been successfully carried out from Cap Serrat. Two Arabs who had supplied intelligence on Italian positions, supply dumps, etc., were trained by the OSS representative in railroad demolitions and sent to blow the Tindja-Ferryville railroad at Mateur. They infiltrated enemy lines on a mule, with explosives sewn in the pack-saddle. An OSS agent, who later visited the area, reported that the mission had been accomplished successfully.

Late in January 1943, seven OSS operatives came briefly to Guelma and trained forty released Spanish internees, at Mahouna, for the southern phase of *Brandon*. At least four of the OSS men were veterans of the Spanish Civil War, and although veteran leaders of guerrilla groups, they were given, prior to leaving America, the rating of Army sergeants. This low rating only served to weaken their position as special operatives and made it difficult to assign them to anything besides routine patrol and demolition tasks at the front.

All but one of the seven OSS men who instructed at Mahouna were assigned to the SOE unit at Sbeitla under a British major responsible to G-3, II Corps at Tebessa. The remaining agent went to the *Brandon* holding area to coordinate G-2 and *Brandon* intelligence and later to help as liaison with an observation post on Hill 609. In an area where attack by superior German panzer divisions was imminent, the OSS men at Sbeitla were assigned by G-2 and G-3 officers to reconnaissance patrols. They were given orders to destroy tanks with Mills and Petard hand grenades. Two

OSS men were wounded and had to be withdrawn as the result of such a mission. Two others were captured on patrol duty after one of them had been wounded by unsuspected enemy artillery. An OSS Marine officer and one of the sergeants were wounded by a mine while accompanying an advance reconnaissance unit looking for snipers; both were retired to hospitals in Algiers. Another OSS Marine observer volunteered to lead a combat patrol group and was wounded in the course of destroying a German machine-gun nest single-handed. With the OSS contingent thus depleted, it was recalled to Algiers on 22 March 1943.

That these men, many of them experts in the clandestine techniques of guerrilla warfare, should be used for infantry work had not been anticipated. Such use, though justifiable in an emergency, was inevitably wasteful of talented and trained men. However, despite the difficulties and disappointments encountered by *Brandon* personnel, the losses were less severe than they might have been. This problem—the degree of combat work to be undertaken by OSS—was later worked out in Italy and France.

OUJDA BASE OPERATIONS

After the landings of 8 November 1942, the important job of protecting the western defenses of North Africa fell to the American occupation army. Danger from within and without threatened the Allied supply line between Casablanca and the Tunisian battlefront: In Spanish Morocco and in Spain proper, Axis intelligence services trained agents for sabotage and espionage against Allied transport and communications; in Allied-occupied French Morocco and Algeria, pro-Vichy French officials and Falangist Spaniards openly menaced the security of Allied military and intelligence operations; in Tunisia, highly paid and heavily propagandized Arabs actively aided the German troops.

The army, thinly spread as it was, was further hampered by two conditions over which it had no control. Overt entrance into Spanish territory was prohibited by diplomatic and military agreement. Pro-Axis officials in French territories could not be ousted due to political considerations. Covert counter-intelligence and the arming of native groups were thus the Allies' sole defenses. This job was to be an OSS concern while it remained in North Africa, not only until the fall of Tunis, but through most of the war, as a result of the threat represented by Franco Spain.

The networks of agents in Spanish and French Morocco, developed for the *TORCH* operation, were put to immediate use. An OSS representative in Casablanca introduced to the local CIC officer his most valuable agent in Morocco, a former member of the French Services de Renseignements (SR), who had built up an effective intelligence chain. Through his efficient handling of native sub-agents and access to friendly French organizations and officials, the agent was able to uncover a number of Axis spy rings in the border region and to effect the arrest, through French authorities, of Frenchmen illegally attempting to return to France through the Spanish Zone. In addition, this agent helped CIC establish intelligence contacts of its own in key Moroccan cities.

In Tangier, an SI representative set up a border patrol and increased the intelligence output of the "Strings" chain. "Tassels"' Riffs, restless with inaction, and Moorish Nationalists, disappointed by U.S. failure to occupy the Spanish Zone, were kept carefully in hand by the Tangier agent, pending possible combat activity.

General Clark came to Morocco in December 1942 to begin training his Fifth Army for operations against the Continent. To meet the possibility of attack from Spain, the *BACKBONE* plan was prepared, to send American armored columns northward into Spanish Morocco in the event of a German advance. To tie in their organized Moslems and Riffs with *BACKBONE*, two OSS/Tangier men went to Oujda in February to confer with G-2, Fifth Army Headquarters. General Clark and G-2 officers were quick to see the advantages of using COI/OSS chains. Liaison, first established in Casablanca, was continued.

SO/SOE plans involving the "Strings-Tassels" subversive groups were laid on, with the Army agreeing to pay all operational expenses. Arms were withheld from the Tunisia battlefront for native use.

Aside from these precautions against the threat of actual military attack, General Clark's major concern was with political intelligence. This was necessitated by the extremely doubtful loyalties of persons in high position in the French territories, as well as the insecurity represented by Fascist persuasions among the French, Spanish and Arab populations. General Clark needed to know: (1) Military preparations by the Axis in Spain; (2) information about Axis intelligence services and sabotage schools; and (3) Vichy officials, "New Order" French, and Arabs undermining Allied security in North Africa.

Impressed with the assistance given CIC by OSS agents, General Clark arranged to have an OSS contingent [led by Donald Downes, former ONI and MI-6 agent, by profession a schoolteacher in Massachusetts] attached to his G-2 branch. The OSS representatives were to maintain their undercover contacts in close collaboration with CIC, G-2, SOE and as many French organizations as possible. One OSS agent was to cover the Spanish Zone from Tangier, another remained at Oujda for liaison and work along the southern and eastern borders of Spanish Morocco. Two Frenchmen who had worked closely with OSS before and after *TORCH* were attached to the Oujda base as liaison officers. This was the first time that an OSS unit was attached to an American army at the specific request of its commander.

Through the French liaison agents, OSS established close relationships with the most important administrative officials in Oujda and elsewhere, including the local heads of the Police and of the French Deuxieme Bureau and key personnel in the Bureau des Affaires Indigenes. With their cooperation, French civil and military officials discovered by underground channels to be illegally working for the Axis, were removed from office. For example, the commander of the Fez garrison, an active Axis collaborator, was ousted.

German and Italian espionage schools at Tetuan in Spanish Morocco were penetrated. OSS-controlled agents were smuggled across the border to enlist in these schools on different occasions. A German-Swiss agent, obtained through the French Services, succeeded in entering the German service. He came back with German questionnaires on the American Army and on Casablanca harbor, and returned to Spanish Morocco a week later with answers deceptively filled in by Allied intelligence officers. The Italian school was penetrated by an Italian-born agent who was smuggled across the border with a radio. He was able to report to OSS/Oujda 86 enemy saboteurs crossing the border to destroy railway lines and gasoline and ammunition dumps. Most of the 86 were caught.

A German spy ring which had been suspected of operating in the vicinity of Oran was uncovered. Several agents, sent from Oujda to try to discover enemy agents and methods, found that Riffian Arabs were carrying documents between the Spanish Consul at Oran and the German Consul at Melilla. This chain of agents and Arab couriers was revealed by buying out a member of the Spanish Consulate.

Once informed of such illegal crossings, OSS/Oujda passed on descriptions of the agents to the French Goums [battalions of local, mostly Berber, militia, commanded by French officers. (footnote)] deployed along the border. The Goum guards turned over all couriers and documents thus caught to French military authorities cooperating with the Allies. The Americans would have preferred to use Arabs, who were natives of the border region, for the seizure of Axis agents, since they were less apt to arouse the suspicions of the enemy. The French, however, with whom cooperation was essential for purposes of arrest, discouraged all American-Arab contacts and insisted on using their own troops. The border, as a result, remained porous in many places.

Clandestine contact with the Arabs was continued by OSS nevertheless, and, when large numbers of German escapees from Tunisia began streaming through, the French did cooperate with the Oujda Detachment in establishing Arab networks and offering rewards to natives for the capture of Germans. Many of the Spanish and Arab shelterers of such prisoners were arrested by the French, when an OSS agent disguised himself as a German escapee and reported names and addresses of those who aided his egress toward the Spanish Zone.

The relative ease with which many of these penetrations were effected by Allied agents revealed weaknesses in an otherwise impressive Axis network. Neither this weakness nor the ejection of the Germans from Tunisia were enough, however, to make the area secure. It was common knowledge that, in violation of Franco's diplomatic assurances, Spain was giving every possible subrosa help to German and Italian subversive operations based on Spanish Morocco and directed against the security of the Allies in North Africa and the Fifth Army in particular.

In discussions between G-2, Fifth Army and OSS/Algiers in May 1943, it was decided to attempt more extensive over-the-border work to get highly important information directly from Spanish Morocco and Spain. During the summer of 1943 a clandestine route was established overland to the hub of Axis military and intelligence activity, Melilla, and agents infiltrated with radios into Malaga to obtain intelligence on the Spanish mainland.

To instruct Spaniards as intelligence agents for these new infiltrations, a training camp was established near Oujda by OSS, at the request of G-2, Fifth Army and with army equipment and funds. At this camp, on a mountain-top twenty miles from the nearest village, OSS veterans of the *Brandon* mission [including Downes] trained 35 men recruited from the Spanish Republican underground. From the Oujda camp, the trainees were sent to the OSS base at Algiers to learn secret wireless communication at the newly-formed OSS radio school.

The first agents were sent without radios to Melilla, to report via courier on developments at the espionage schools and military bases in the vicinity. Secret overland transportation for these infiltrations was arranged through a few Arab chieftains who volunteered their services and those of their relatives. OSS agents disguised as Arab natives were smuggled over the border and escorted

through the Spanish Zone. Once established in key spots from
which to observe German, Italian and Spanish activities first-hand,
the agents sent back bi-weekly reports by couriers who were escorted in a like manner. Of the men who took advantage of this "underground railroad" none were lost; of those who attempted the
trip alone, approximately fifty percent were captured.

Through this bi-weekly reporting system, from well-trained and
strategically placed agents around Melilla, came intelligence of
specific importance to the Fifth Army. A closer and more regular
check than had before been possible was maintained on Spanish
battle order, Spanish cooperation with the Axis, German personnel movements and German contacts with the Arabs.

In July 1943, the first BANANA operation was launched from
Oujda to obtain intelligence in Spain. Four trained Spanish agents
and a Spanish operator were smuggled to Tangier via the Arab underground route and deposited at Malaga, Spain. [Excision]. Radio communications started within seven days, and reports on
Spanish defenses and other military information of interest to
Fifth Army were received by OSS/Oujda. These messages were
translated and turned over to G-2, with copies going to OSS/Al-
giers for AFHQ as well. Five more men entered Spain on 23 September and joined the first group.

Unfortunately, several errors were made in the BANANA
operations:

(1) The agents were Communists, recruited through the "popular front" Union Democratica Espanol [U.D.E.] in Mexico and
North Africa;

(2) They carried in neutral territory U.S. Army materiel, including grenades, submachine guns, ammunition and SSTR-1 radio
sets, all with U.S. markings and serial numbers;

(3) The area was already covered, to the knowledge of the commanding officer of OSS/Oujda, by OSS/Spain, in fact by four
American and better than fifty Spanish agents, who had turned in
bi-weekly reports giving detailed plans of all fortifications of the
south Spanish coast, plans of all airfields and complete order of
battle information.

The agents were eventually captured by the Spanish police both
in Malaga and Melilla. Communist code-books were reportedly
discovered on them [possibly these were planted by the Spanish police. (footnote)] as well as the code-books for communication with
Oujda. After suitable "processing" by the Spanish police, the men
revealed the details of their American training in Oujda, the use of
the SSTR-1's and like information, all of which was presumably
passed on to German intelligence. They also gave away some of

their leftist comrades, resulting in a widespread clean-up by the [Franco] government with 261 arrests and 22 executions. A confidential brief was prepared by the Spanish police stating that the United States was backing the Communist movement in Spain. Since this was a neutral country with which the United States was maintaining friendly relations, it did not look well for American arms to be received by Communist elements there.

In this case the blame fell squarely on [a high official of the OSS in the Mediterranean]. He was subsequently released. He had been warned that the recruits from the U.D.E. were unreliable and he was personally aware of the existence of SI in Spain. He never checked with OSS/Washington to obtain approval for the infiltration.

The U.S. Ambassador in Spain [Carlton Hayes, former Columbia University professor of history, who refused to permit OSS agents to collect intelligence in Spanish territory] covered the OSS error, denying any U.S. implication in the operation. However, BANANA nearly ended OSS activity in Spain and through Spain into southern France. It was the largest OSS blunder of the war, and could only partly be excused by the youth of the U.S. espionage agency.

Despite the embarrassment to OSS in general, and to OSS/Spain and Ambassador Hayes in particular, OSS/Oujda had carried out General Clark's requests to his satisfaction. The weak supply line stretching east to the Tunisian battlefront had required active organization, intelligence and counter-intelligence to protect it from Axis activities in and around Spanish Morocco. Collaborators in the local French Government were ousted, German agents were caught in large numbers and military developments in Spanish Morocco and Spain were reported. The record in itself proved exceedingly useful in obtaining authorization for OSS activity in Italy.

On 9 September 1943 the OSS/Fifth Army Detachment left North Africa to accompany the landings at Salerno. Oujda was closed, and local OSS offices in Tangier, Oran, Casablanca and Tunis carried on the work of counter-intelligence until the end of the war.

CHAPTER 4

The Secondary Neutral Countries

EIRE

A German invasion of Eire was feared to be imminent in 1940, and through 1941 and 1942 the threat remained serious. The Irish Government would allow no Allied forces in the country, necessitating the continued presence of a large Anglo-American contingent in North Ireland, prepared to enter Eire to repel the Germans before they could fully establish themselves on the southern coast. Local military support for the Germans was, furthermore, to be expected from the underground Irish Republican Army (I.R.A.), some of whose members were actively working for the Nazis. [While Anglo-Irish political relations were, at best, cool throughout the war, there is some evidence that there was a "secret treaty" between the U.S./U.K. military command and the Irish army by which the three would have cooperated to eject the Germans if they invaded.]

On 23 December 1941 the first COI representative left for Dublin on a two-month "Special Temporary Mission to the Minister of Ireland." [Excision] He reported on the poor condition of Irish defenses and on the location of a Nazi spy center at Tralee. There he enlisted a local cattle inspector to communicate directly with the U.S. Military Attache in Dublin on local German activities.

In London, British intelligence services proved hesitant in turning over to the United States their intelligence on Ireland. It was hoped, however, that the Irish would be more willing to cooperate with Americans than they had with their British "big brothers." Accordingly, three OSS agents were dispatched.

One of these, the chief agent, worked from the U.S. Legation. [Excision] Two others went in under private cover, arriving in September 1942 and May 1943, respectively, but were shortly removed at the request of the U.S. Minister who stated that they made him "uneasy." The chief agent, "Hurst," meanwhile remained, despite the disapproval of the Minister, sending in reports on shipping to and from Eire, on Irish politics (the activities of the I.R.A. in particular), on German propaganda, on government attitudes and methods and on Irish radio direction-finding equipment. A quantity of counter-espionage material was also procured. Situation reports and censorship summaries received from the Washington base helped him in the analysis and collection of this information.

"Hurst's" major accomplishment was his official liaison with the Eire Government itself. [Excision] "Hurst's" main difficulties were with the American Minister. Although he submitted all intelligence to the Minister and took no step vis-a-vis the Irish without prior approval from him, personality difficulties arose, and in November 1942 the Minister cabled the State Department recommending severance of connection with OSS because the Eire Government might resent the latter's activities. This denial of Eire's clear cooperation was apparently ignored, other difficulties were ironed out and "Hurst" continued his work. His position as open, high-echelon OSS representative in neutral Eire was fruitful. Although he built up nothing in the way of undercover agent networks, his liaison with the Irish secret police and foreign services produced substantial results in intelligence.

[Curiously, and significantly, the official historian does not discuss the involvement of the Irish government with the Vatican in 1942, the Vessel Project. In that year, Msgr. Giovanni Battista Montini, the Under Secretary of State for Current Affairs at the Vatican, and later to reign as Pope Paul VI, was in contact with Earl Brennan, chief of OSS/SI in Washington. Representatives at Tokyo of the Holy See were obtaining intelligence about bombing targets in Tokyo. Did the OSS wish to receive this intelligence? The OSS accepted, the intelligence was relayed by the Holy See from Tokyo to the Irish embassy in Rome. With the knowledge and approval of the Irish prime minister, Eamon de Valera, this dangerous and volatile material was collected by an OSS/London SI officer, Ricardo Mazzerini, who became sales manager in Europe, Africa and the Middle East of Hilton International in Rome, and was then sent in special naval cipher to Washington. Thence it went out to the U.S. Air Forces in the Pacific, which employed the intelligence as part of the operational file for the firebombing of Tokyo. This was an unheard-of abuse of diplomatic and religious immunity on the part of the Holy See and its representatives in Tokyo and, with Hitler ever watchful for an excuse to occupy or obliterate the Vatican, one that invited savage retaliation by the Axis powers. As surprising—and a reflection upon the OSS's sense of discretion—was the fact that information about the Vessel Project became known after the war. It can be surmised safely that many people—perhaps thousands—lost their lives in Tokyo through this type of espionage, to say nothing of the damage to Japanese industrial potential wrought by the bombing attacks.]

With D-Day in Normandy, Eire lost the significance of a potential military zone. "Hurst" turned over his official contacts to a London X-2 representative who made occasional trips to Dublin, and continuous OSS operation in Eire was concluded by July 1944.

SPAIN AND PORTUGAL

From America's entry into the war until the fall of Tunis in the spring of 1943, the possibility of a German occupation of Spain (with or without the consent of the Franco Government) represented a major strategic danger to the Allies. The danger was especially acute during the months immediately following the North African landings, when the extended supply lines across French North Africa to the Tunisian front offered an obvious and inviting target for an Axis striking force. That this danger was far from imaginary was adequately demonstrated by the discovery, after the liberation of France, of some 150 tons of German military maps of Spain, printed in 1941 and 1942, and stored since 1942 within a hundred miles of the Franco-Spanish border. Persistent rumors reached Washington of Hispano-German cooperation, extending considerably beyond accepted definitions of "non-belligerency", then the ostensible policy of the Spanish government.

The early intelligence assignments of OSS/Spain, largely shared by OSS/Portugal, were threefold: (1) The securing of all information, military, political and economic, about a possible Nazi coup or invasion; (2) the securing of intelligence regarding Spanish aid, economic and otherwise, to the Axis, to the end that such assistance might be exposed or blocked; and (3) the amassing of the sort of background material which would be vital to the Allies if the Iberian Peninsula became a battlefield (including the recruiting of agents who could be counted on in such an eventuality).

Consolidation of the Allied position in the Mediterranean meant that Spain gradually lost its military interest. The major attention of SI became centered on France, with X-2, aided by SI agents, concentrating on counter-espionage and counter-smuggling activity, defecting many enemy agents and stopping secret transactions in such war materials as tungsten.

The task was made more difficult by the German control of Spain, although the venality of many Spanish officials rendered control something less than fully effective. Himmler's office had reorganized the Spanish police system in 1940. The head of the Spanish police was on the German pay roll, as were many of his subordinates. Numbers of Nazi police and intelligence personnel had been there since the beginning of the Spanish Civil War. Himmler's control combined with the high-level influence of the Abwehr [the German foreign military intelligence service under Rear Admiral Wilhelm Canaris], covered every section of Spanish intelligence and counter-intelligence. Portugal, on the other hand, had the laxest of controls. Lisbon, as one of the important terminals of traffic to and from the United States, South America and Africa, was a nest of spies and informants at work for all the belligerents.

SI. In April 1942 the first two SI agents arrived in Lisbon and Madrid under State Department cover. As oil attaches they were to allocate half their time to observing the use of fuel supplied to Spain by the Allied governments, meanwhile giving the remainder to secret intelligence. By October 1944, twenty agents had been sent in under private cover [excision] and fifty-two under State Department cover. [Several of the agents under private cover were seconded from their jobs with the Standard Oil Company. The first OSS/Lisbon station chief, Colonel Robert Solborg, the Polish-born former U.S. military attache in Paris who had served in the Czar's army in World War I and became an executive with Armco Steel in the U.S., was dismissed from command by Donovan personally, for meddling dangerously in the snake pit of French North African politics. The first OSS station chief in Madrid was Donald Steele, a Chicago businessman who had served in the North Russian Expeditionary Force at Murmansk and Archangel in 1919. There he fought the Lenin-Trotsky Red Army. His successor was H. G. Thomas, an executive in the perfume industry—he became chairman of the board of Chanel. His Madrid team included a *pied-noir* from Algiers who had been with the U.S. Narcotics Bureau, and a one-time physical training instructor with the YMCA in Shanghai. Among the activities of the OSS that annoyed and worried U.S. Ambassador Carlton Hayes were those of agent Frank Schoonmaker, an author of travel guides, who was caught by Spanish police passing OSS funds to French clandestines. Schoonmaker spent six months in a Spanish jail—a rigorous experience which he never forgot—before Hayes managed to have him released and expelled to Algiers.]

[Deletion] The diplomatic pouch and OSS courier constituted the chief method of intercommunication for the U.S. agents. Occasionally the interconsular phones were used for coded messages, or the regular long-distance lines for American double-talk. From Madrid, intelligence was pouched to Washington, with priority information being transmitted from a secret radio station. [Excision]

Communicating via these various lines were some forty chains, averaging twenty agents each. These were paralleled in Portugal by a netword of over 250 agents and sub-agents. [The majority of the agents under private cover were compelled to travel by the nature of their ostensible activities, and had no fixed base. There were more or less fixed agents in or around Malaga (2 to 3), Teneriffe (Canaries), Seville (2 to 3), Palma (Mallorca), Lisbon (a staff), Madrid (a staff), Horta (Azores), Bilbao, Barcelona (3 to 5), Valencia, San Sebastian, Vigo and Coruna (2). (Footnote)]

Under a broad general directive from the Joint Chiefs of Staff, OSS in Spain and Portugal carried out its three major assignments. Irrefutable evidences of military cooperation between Spain and Germany were secured, including the use of Spanish military airfields by Axis planes, the supplying of German submarines, sabotage operations in Gibraltar harbor carried out by Italo-Spanish teams, the forced recruiting of Spanish technical personnel for service in Germany and the maintenance of the "Blue Division" on the Russian front after its official recall. Fully documented reports on all these subjects were forwarded by Washington, with digests cabled in OSS cipher through the Embassy.

On the subject of economic cooperation between MADRID AND Berlin, OSS/Spain was able to report even more fully. Detailed and accurate copies of the bills of lading or manifests covering all merchandise shipped to France, whether by rail or sea, were received and transmitted weekly, including everything from orange juice, rice, wheat, barley and olive oil (at a time when Spain was starving) to steel rails from Sagunto, quicksilver from Almaden and tungsten ore from Galicia. Equally complete intelligence was secured concerning the flagrant cooperation given the Germans in matters of espionage and counter-espionage by Spanish officials of all grades. [The Abwehr station chief, Gustav Leissner, working under business cover—the Excelsior Import and Export Company, traders in lead, zinc, cork and mercury—had great influence with Franco, with the Spanish Security Service, and with the Foreign Ministry. Through the latter he could read all Spanish diplomatic reports from London and consular stations in England. The same privileged contact was enjoyed by the Abwehr's rival in foreign intelligence, the Sicherheitsdienst of Brigadefuhrer SS Walter Schellenburg. What is mysterious about American fears that the Spaniards would join forces with Hitler was that Washington should have known after the end of 1940—if only through Ultra—that Franco had decided he would not join the Axis and fight the Western powers.] OSS material in such fields was frequently used by the Ambassador in his reports, and the ONI gave a high rating to naval intelligence from Madrid.

It was, however in the third of its three assignments that the record of OSS/Spain was particularly outstanding. A country almost as large as France, concerning which the available information of MID was both antiquated and extremely limited, was covered in eight months with remarkable thoroughness. In preparation for possible military operations in Spain, detailed road reports were prepared, with photographs of the more important bridges, grades and curves; these were rated by [U.S. military intelligence] as the best road reports submitted on Spain and covered virtually every military or strategic highway in eastern and southern Spain. Complete descriptions, with plans and in many cases photographs, of all major Spanish airfields were sent in, and permanent watchers at most of these airfields, who reported weekly on all traffic and other activities, were made part of the OSS organization. A separate and detailed report (in many cases with samples of sand, in most cases with photographs, and in all cases with maps) was prepared for every possible landing beach on the Spanish coast. Over 1,000 maps of France and the Iberian Peninsula taxed the facilities of the diplomatic pouch. About eighty percent of these were to the scale of 1:50,000; many were originals prepared by agents, while others were maps not known by MID to be in existence. Among them were revised plans of important cities and towns, aerial photographs, hydrographic maps, sketches and a few highly secret military fortification plans. Finally, charts of possible bombing targets were prepared and checked, including a partly documented report on gasoline and oil supplies.

After the North African landings, hundreds and eventually thousands of patriotic Frenchmen found means of crossing clandestinely into Spain, in the hope of joining the Allied forces in North Africa. Many of these were persons of great potential usefulness to the Allied cause—high ranking officers, SR personnel with recent intelligence of German activities, technical specialists or badly-needed fighter pilots. OSS/Spain, in order to facilitate their clandestine departure for African ports, set up safe houses in Barcelona and Madrid, and purchased three small sailing vessels [feluccas], which ostensibly carried cargo between Barcelona and Cadiz or Huelva. Some twenty selected Frenchmen went aboard each ship and were transferred to British patrol boats off Gibraltar.

The [feluccas] were in poor condition when purchased, and frequently breakdowns interfered with their schedule. The crews, unquestionably loyal, had no notion of security and there is reason to believe that the Spanish Police was aware of the existence of this service within two months of its inception. [Donald Downes, recovered from the wounds of the Oudja affair, was behind part of this disastrous scheme and was conniving with the Spanish exiles to overthrow Franco. After Banana's early success, Downes and his masters had broadened the intelligence attack on Spanish territory to include Cadiz, Cartagena and Huelva. At a time when rumors were strong that OSS "eager beavers" were developing plans to overthrow Portuguese authority in the Azores, and that OSS/Spain was collaborating secretly with left-wing Spanish naval officers to take over the Armada, this was dangerous business which Franco could not ignore. His police raided the rendezvous at Malaga between Downes' agents and the local Communist-republicans, there was a fire fight, and Downes' agents were all killed or captured. The Franco police also captured considerable evidence—submachine-guns, grenades, *plastique*—to show that the U.S. Army had supplied the weapons. Contrary to the official report, some of the captured agents named names under torture. They mentioned two—Downes and Arthur Goldberg, who was a high officer of OSS in Washington. Goldberg later became U.S. Secretary of Labor, Justice of the Supreme Court, ambassador to the United Nations, and unsuccessful Democratic candidate for the governorship of New York. Goldberg was hauled over the coals in Washington and almost fired, and Downes would have been dismissed but for the fact that his services were needed by Eisenhower for the invasion of Sicily and Italy in 1943. State and Hayes clamped down on OSS activities in Spain.] It nevertheless permitted the evacuation to North Africa of the most seriously compromised Spanish agent of OSS (who had stolen the plans of the fortifications on the Balearic Islands), and later of his equally endangered wife and daughter. The two "directors" of the "shipping company" were eventually arrested and imprisoned. So far as is known, they gave no damaging information to the Spanish police or the Falange.

In Madrid and Lisbon, close relations with the representatives of various Allied and enemy governments produced useful intelligence. Liaison with the Hungarian Minister provided coverage of Hungarian political developments. The diplomatic courier offered communication to Hungary itself. The Polish Exile Government representation offered reports from its returning agents, dropped by plane from London into Poland to make their way back across France and over the Pyrenees. Friendship with the Rumanian Charge d'Affaires in Lisbon brought a prediction a month ahead of time of the overthrow of the pro-German Antonescu regime, which was within a week of the exact date. Members of both the Swiss and Swedish Legations were helpful, particularly in passing on counter-espionage material. Often, in response to OSS requests, they would go directly to German representatives to obtain desired information. [Kermit Roosevelt neglects to mention the close contact that existed between the OSS and the German ambassador at Lisbon, Baron Oswald Hoyningen-Huene, an anti-Hitlerite whose embassy became a clearing house for German military secrets going to London and Washington. These included data about the missile plant and test range of Peenemünde, which was obliterated by the Royal Air Force in 1943, ten days after a German passed the information to Allied intelligence services with contacts at Huene's embassy.]

Continued SI work in Spain was, however, hampered by State Department representation there. Agents under private cover were producing most of the intelligence. The first OSS Chief of Mission [Steele] to arrive in Madrid was recalled to Washington at the request of the Ambassador. [He later went to Portugal where he worked under State Department cover. (footnote)]

Members of the Madrid Embassy objected to OSS activities in general, feeling that they themselves were competent to cover developments in Spain. OSS salaries and allowances, often incorrectly understood, caused considerable envy, as did consular ranks of OSS officers (granted by the Department of State), especially when the OSS officials showed lack of training in consular practice. OSS supplies (which were used for bartering), OSS cars and OSS entertainment (of potentially useful persons) all contributed to the general irritation of Embassy personnel. The latter made little effort to conceal from Spanish officials the real activities of OSS representatives. As early as December 1942 an agent leaving Washington was told, "Good luck, you'll probably have more trouble keeping under cover from Americans than from the Gestapo."

The Ambassador considered espionage against a "friendly" country to be "un-American." He stated that OSS activities were jeopardizing his efforts to maintain close bonds between Spain and the United States (although other nations, enemy and Allied, with whom Spain was friendly, depended on large intelligence services). Several OSS sub-agents and two Americans were arrested between June and September 1943, the latter two for black market financial transactions in the purchase of European currencies for OSS operations. This was felt by the Ambassador to be proof that OSS activities endangered relations with Franco. OSS argued, on the other hand, that Spain no longer represented a military threat, and that a certain percentage of embarrassments in espionage must be expected.

Hayes requested the complete withdrawal of OSS from the whole Iberian Peninsula; and, although this request was not granted, he was able, in November 1943, to gain certain concessions, principally that SI/Spain "will cover only such intelligence as may be requested or agreed to by the Ambassador and the Military and Naval Attaches, or be required by the Joint Chiefs of Staff with the concurrence of the State Department."

Hayes also insisted on censoring all incoming and outgoing OSS messages. His job, as he saw it, was to maintain normal relations with the Franco government (even after the military threat had passed), and he wished to see that no other U.S. activities got out of line from that policy; that, above all, no "embarrassments" arise from the activities of any of the members of his official family. He insisted on "abstention from contracts and arrangements that might adversely affect the Chancery and our Consulates," and accordingly ruled that the Embassy must approve all agents hired (within the categories settled in the terms of the agreement) and all contracts and operational plans.

His actions, in effect, made him an accomplice to OSS undercover activity and put him in just that "embarrassing" position which he wished to avoid.

In addition, Hayes, through his censors, the Counselor and First Secretary of Embassy, prohibited any reports on Spain itself or tending to discredit the Spanish Government.

The Spanish Desk/SI in Washington made further efforts to locate private covers for agents, but could find few more than those already in use. Trade with Spain had been cut to a minimum, with the result that there was little excuse for a U.S. citizen to come to the country on business. Nearly all American residents had, furthermore, been evacuated at the outbreak of the war in 1939. OSS activity was continued, mainly by those free agents under private rather than State cover.

In October 1944 a branch of the AQUITAINE mission was established with headquarters at Toulouse, under OSS/Paris direction, to infiltrate agents over the Pyrenees. Under cover of debriefing old agent chains, one of the organizers of the pre-liberation chains into France contacted these agents and sent them back to Spain. Through Spaniards operating across the border, a check was kept on Spanish battle order in the area. Acquaintances in Basque circles produced a steady flow of information on the extent of Spanish aid to the beleaguered German garrisons along the French west coast. Considerable political intelligence was also gathered on Spanish Republican activities in the area. Interviews were conducted with officials of the refugee government. Through certain other contacts, intelligence was obtained on the secreting of German economic assets in Spain.

In Portugal and Spain tungsten smuggling was successfully traced and stopped. Contraband traffic had begun after the Allied governments exacted agreements from the Portuguese and Spanish governments to curtail sales to the Germans of this vital metal. The extensive OSS organization in northern Portugal and Spain had for some time been keeping accurate check on all shipments out of the Peninsula, and had been able to prevent smuggling of tin and other minerals. In the case of tungsten, the arrest of a large ring of smugglers in Portugal, involving Army officers and customs officials, was accomplished. In Spain, OSS intelligence made it possible for a British submarine to sink a German ship loading at a secret port near Bilboa. This action blocked the only sea outlet used for Axis tungsten smuggling. [The "Wolfram Campaign"— undertaken to deny tungsten to the Germans—was one of the most bitter economic warfare campaigns of the war, and Hayes was constantly aghast at OSS/BEW operations in Iberia to blow up or flood mines supplying the Germans with this vital metal. It was especially important to the Germans, who required it to make tough, heat-resistant steel for high-speed cutting tools, armor plate, and armor-piercing ammunition. More than 95% of Europe's wolfram was located in Iberia, and such was the frantic bidding for wolfram by England and America on the one hand and the Axis powers on the other, that in Portugal the price per ton shot up from $1,144 in August 1940 to nearly $20,000 in October 1941.]

X-2. X-2 representation arrived in Lisbon in November 1943. During the negotiations of the same month, Ambassador Hayes had agreed to the establishment of X-2 offices in Spain. In the following year these were set up in Madrid, Barcelona, Bilbao and San Sebastian, all under State cover.

During the first year of X-2 operation, the Branch was principally dependent on SI for contacts and personality data. Both SI and the British provided the material with which X-2 built up its basic files. SI contacts with various Spanish and enemy officials were turned over to X-2, as were many of the "tailing gangs" and other watchers.

The new X-2 stations served to coordinate counter-intelligence activities of the Embassy and other U.S. representatives in Spain and Portugal with the central registry in London, and to vet U.S. employees and visa applicants. Hampered by ambassadorial restriction, X-2 still performed successfully the penetration of German organizations in southwest France, the surveillance of enemy agent traffic between France and Spain, and the identification and eventual deportation of German undercover personnel and French collaborators who had fled to Spain in some numbers.

German reorganization of the Spanish Police apparently produced corruption and corruptibility on a large scale. The Spanish control officer at one of the most important points of entry into Spain from France reported, for a price, the comings and goings of important German agents and their missions. Inasmuch as these agents carried letters of identification to him, his coverage was thorough.

The Barcelona station kept a close surveillance of enemy agent traffic over the Pyrenees and controlled a number of double-agents who worked between Spain and France. None of this activity involved more than the usual local counter-espionage aims of (1) obtaining information about enemy personalities in Spain, and (2) rigging traps for enemy agents in France. The work of these double-agents supported the exploitation of enemy agent chains by the SCI (Special Counter-Intelligence) units in southwest France, and provided useful information on the kind of data that the Germans were seeking on France. A network of advantageously placed informants, originally set up by SI, covered arrivals and departures not only at frontier points, but also at airports and at all hotels in the main cities.

By the time of the German collapse in May 1945, most of the German undercover agents in Spain had been identified, while their courier and other chains into northern Europe had been penetrated and placed under surveillance. The gaps in Allied data were filled in by defecting Germans who came in growing numbers to the American consulates. The liquidation of those services was furthered by a joint [Excision] list of German intelligence and subversion officers and agents, passed to the Spanish Foreign Office with a request for their deportation to Germany and France.

By VE-Day, X-2 files (largely based on British and SI reports) identified nearly 3,000 enemy agents, some 600 suspects, and more than 400 officials of enemy undercover services. Of those agents and officials, 45 were under X-2 control. A number of well-placed members of the Spanish Police and of the Servicio de Informacion Militar had early been converted to a cooperative attitude by SI, and more were won over by X-2. These and other sources helped to uncover forty-six commercial firms in Spain being used by the enemy as cover for espionage purposes. Interrogations of enemy officials and agents, after the collapse of Germany, indicated that the control of the northern border, maintained in cooperation with SCI of southern France, was highly successful.

X-2 files in Lisbon contained identifications of 1,900 enemy agents, 200 enemy officials and 350 suspect agents. Of these, seven were defected and twenty controlled. Through representations to the Portuguese Government, 75 more were confined and 50 expelled.

One of the more interesting cases was a double-agent originally hired by SI/Portugal. This was Jean Charles Alexandre, alias Alendorf (real name probably Gessman or Gasman), reputed to be one of the most successful international intelligence wholesalers in Europe.

An Austrian, Alexandre had worked in Austria for the French Deuxieme Bureau as a double-agent in the German Abwehr. After the Anschluss the Germans learned this fact, but nevertheless used him later in Portugal. In 1939 he was sent to Portugal by the French and remained there after the fall of France, allying himself with the British and with the Czechoslovak Intelligence Service, which the British were controlling for operations into France. His official position was that of second-in-command of the Czech station. During this time the whole of the Czech network was blown to the Germans. Fritz Cramer, head of the counter-espionage department of the Abwehr in Lisbon, later stated that Alexandre was responsible for this betrayal.

The British, however, had learned this and quickly eased him out of service. Little more could be done about him at this point except to issue a general warning to Allied circles, since the British did not wish to burn the source of their information, and since Alexandre had close connections with the Chief of the Secret Police. He parried all sorts of attractive offers for excursions to Allied territory—where he could have been interrogated and broken.

Nevertheless, Alexandre was almost immediately taken on by SI and set up by them as an important agent. He made adroit use of his new sponsorship to enhance his value to the Germans and to counter the effect of the British brush-off. He worked for SI from 1942 until mid-1943, introducing a group of agents who were used by SI. Others insinuated themselves on the SI pay roll by proffering their services under Alexandre's tutelage, without revealing that they were working for him.

The X-2 officer in Lisbon was able to put the full weight of the evidence against Alexandre, largely based on British reports, before SI and to convince them of his dangerous character. An investigation of all SI agents in Portugal was instigated, and, although no proof was found that Alexandre had actually sold his new information to the Germans, a purge of his agents was achieved. The man himself was safe in Portugal, but he was driven temporarily into semi-retirement. [Later he was discovered in an Allied intelligence agency working under another name. (footnote)]

On the other hand, X-2 operated dozens of successful double-agents against the Germans. The Spanish border control officer has already been cited. The covert defection in the spring of 1945 of Fritz Cramer, Chief of Abwehr III (Counter-Espionage Department) in Lisbon, was especially rewarding. Cramer was in possession of all information on German personnel and operations in Portugal, and informed on German intelligence matters in Germany and elsewhere. [Deletion] [But for all the excellence of their work in Iberia, one disaster would forever be recalled whenever OSS's name was mentioned in connection with Lisbon. In a fit of zealousness, a group of young OSS officers, without referring the project to Washington, burgled the Japanese embassy at Lisbon and stole the Japanese military cipher. The Japanese discovered the theft and changed the system. What OSS did not know was that the Signals Intelligence Service of the U.S. Army had been reading this cipher for some time, and it had become a vital—if not decisive—source of intelligence in the war in the Pacific. The U.S. Joint Chiefs of Staff exploded with anger, and heads rolled. Mercifully, the new system was quickly broken through the Ultra/Magic service of the Central Bureau at General MacArthur's headquarters, and this triumph of cryptanalysis returned to the U.S. the intelligence it needed to kill Yamamoto, to destroy the Japanese fleet at Midway, and to sink almost the entire Japanese mercantile marine.]

Following the liberation of France, OSS chains through the Pyrenees were terminated. Meanwhile the Germans began to set up their own networks; X-2 in Barcelona succeeded shortly in penetrating this new organization and in locating the agents for apprehension by French authorities.

After the collapse of Germany, all the premises that had been occupied by agencies of that government were placed under the control of the U.S., British and French diplomatic missions. German passport and citizenship records revealed that naturalization in Spain had been used as a device by local Germans to avoid repatriation, and that these arrangements had been facilitated by Spanish officials. These and other sources indicated a post-war organization in Spain. The leaders were to be chosen from Germans who had escaped repatriation, the sub-agents from members of the Falange and the Blue Division. The organization counted on a slackening in Allied counter-measures as a result of conflicting political and economic interests. Funds were available in the form of money and valuables on deposit in Spain. In the summer of 1945,

X-2 accomplished the penetration of both German and Japanese espionage rings in Madrid, although no action could be taken.

To trace the flight of Axis funds from Europe into and through Spain and Portugal, OSS collaborated with State Department personnel in "Safe Haven" investigations. [The State Department "Safe Haven" program, to uncover the movement of assets out of enemy countries, was assisted by OSS throughout Europe. (footnote)] In Portugal, a secret arrangement was made to give OSS access to information on enemy safe deposit boxes in all but four banks (covered by the British); a list of all boxes was obtained, together with specific information requested on any individual or business account. Contacts of the AQUITAINE mission in Toulouse gave additional information.

Since November 1943, by ambassadorial restriction, OSS had been limited, inside Spain itself, to counter-espionage and counter-smuggling. It had carried out these assignments successfully. In September 1945, SI/Spain was withdrawn, according to over-all State Department policy, and X-2 remained.

CHAPTER 5

Africa and The Middle East

AFRICA

During the first year of United States participation in World War II, Axis invasion of the whole African Continent was considered a distinct possibility. At bases in West Africa, German forces would threaten the lightly-defended Brazilian coast. Prior to the North African landings, the U.S. Army had planned, but did not execute, a small operation to invade the Cape Verde Islands. A British naval attempt to seize the port of Dakar had failed.

In the event that Africa became a battleground, every kind of military, naval, economic, political and psychological intelligence would be needed. State Department coverage was small; consulates were few and far between. In Angola, for instance, there had been no consular representation since 1925.

One agent had been dispatched by COI in February 1942. In April, an Africa Desk was organized in Washington, and its first agent left for Africa in that month. By the end of the war, posts had been established in Tangier, the Canary Islands, the Cape Verde Islands, French West Africa, Portuguese Guinea, Liberia, French Equatorial Africa, British East Africa, the Belgian Congo, Angola, the Union of South Africa, Mozambique, Ethiopia and French Somaliland. Finally, when the 2677th Regiment OSS (Prov.), Algiers moved to Italy, its posts at Casablanca, Morocco, Oran, Algeria and Tunis were transferred to the Africa Desk/SI and a similar post was set up at Algiers.

Certain special characteristics of the African Continent made the job of penetration and securing intelligence peculiarly difficult:

(a) Suitable agents who had had any previous residence or experience in Africa were scarce;

(b) The severity of the climate, and the resultant effect upon their health, made many of those who might otherwise have served unavailable;

(c) The problems of communication and transportation were so difficult of solution that preoccupation with them considerably hampered agent operations;

(d) The total number of white inhabitants on the entire Continent was so small (only 600,000 excluding French North Africa and the Union of South Africa), that it was next to impossible to infiltrate agents under effective cover. Every new arrival was suspect from the start. [Not always was this the fault of the agent; naivete—sometimes dangerous naivete—at headquarters was occasionally the basic reason why cover was quickly detected. Such a case involved the first OSS attempt to put an agent into the Canary Islands. A Donovan aide disclosed that no commercial steamships called at the islands during wartime. "No matter! Buy a ship," he was told. One was bought for a million dollars or so. Only after the purchase was made was it realized that it would not be the most secret way to plant an undercover agent to have a special steamship land him.]

[Excision] SI/Africa first pursued the policy of selecting agents from persons who had already resided in the target areas. The policy was eventually abandoned when experience showed that such individuals were scarce and often not those most suited for intelligence work. Many agents thus chosen involved themselves too much in their previous activities; for example, one anthropologist spent his six-month tour of duty acquiring apes, caring for them when they fell ill and eventually catching their disease himself.

[The countries covered by OSS/Africa included:]

Tunisia (French	3 men
Algeria (French)	7 men
Tangier (International)	7 men
Spanish Morocco	1 man
French Morocco	16 men
Canary Islands (Spanish)	1 man
Cape Verde Islands (Portuguese)	2 men
French West Africa	4 men
Portuguese Guinea	1 man
Liberia	7 men
French Equatorial Africa	1 man
British West Africa	18 men
Belgian Congo	4 men
Angola (Portuguese)	8 men
The Union of South Africa	5 men
Mozambique (Portuguese)	5 men
Ethiopia	2 men
French Somaliland	1 man

[Egypt and the Sudan were covered by OSS/Cairo. (footnote)]

Since the lack of transcontinental communication obviated the possibility of establishing a main base in Africa itself from which the work throughout the Continent could be supervised, Washington directed all agents. Casablanca served as an advance base for stations and agents in North Africa only. Accra served as an advance base for agents in West Africa only, and was the one overt mission set up south of the Sahara. All other installations there were covert or semi-covert.

It was possible to a certain extent to cooperate with British intelligence and certain elements of French Intelligence. [Excision] An agreement between British SOE and OSS/SO prohibited U.S. undercover operations in British territory, but in return the British agreed to supply information from their own sources.

From the British services came basic topographic intelligence on the surrounding territory, French battle order in West Africa, regular reports on pro-Axis activities and on the political and economic developments in Frech West Africa. Notable contributions were the British files on Angola and the Cape Verde Islands. They included biographical data on government personalities together with data on airfields, terrain, military installations, resources, trade and shipping and Axis activity. Liaison with the U.S. Theater authorities in Africa, and in particular with G-2, provided supplies and pouch and wire service.

Most of the agents placed in Africa during the first year of operation were intended as defensive stay-behind agents, whose mission was to undertake sabotage and intelligence activities in the event that Axis forces should occupy Africa. An SO team of five was dispatched in August 1942 to Nigeria, [Excision] with the mission of cooperating with SOE in setting up intelligence chains in the area and preparing for defensive action should it become necessary.

The turning point came with the Allied landings in November 1942, when most of Africa became a field for counter-intelligence. An agreement between the X-2 and SI Branches in July 1943 provided for the joint briefing of agents dispatched by the Africa Desk/SI and for the joint use of intelligence transmitted. In late 1943, a plan was formulated to turn over the SI operations in North Africa to the SI Desk/Washington, but, with the exception of the Tangier station, this plan was not put into effect until October 1944.

After the landings in 1942, a greater need was felt for Allied coverage of East and South Africa, in order to aid the discovery of Axis submarine refuelling, Axis diamond smuggling and Axis shipping intelligence. In particular this last enemy activity was causing high losses on the sea lanes outside Gibraltar, off the Cape of Good Hope and in the waters about Madagascar.

The success of all missions depended largely upon the degree of cooperation from State Department representatives. Unfortunately, most of the Foreign Service officers had not been properly briefed, and whether or not they contributed to or hampered the activities of OSS agents depended upon each individual's understanding of the situation and the extent to which Foreign Service and OSS representatives got along personally. [Deletion]

Investigation of Diamond Smuggling. Germany's supply of industrial diamonds came, throughout the war, almost entirely from South and Central Africa by illegal channels.

[Germany had no domestic supply of industrial diamonds. The Germans took extraordinary measures to secure them for jewel bearings in aircraft instruments, for drawing the finest wires, for use as abrasives in grinding precision instruments, especially in her missile program. As a result, industrial diamonds worth less than $1 a carat on the London market were fetching between $30 and $60 a carat in Tangier. In one diamond-smuggling operation traced by the Blockade Division of the U.S. Foreign Economic Administration, a pocketful of stones changed hands five times: first at 58 cents a carat, second at $1.56, third at $2.60, fourth at $11.70, and the Nazi agent who took final delivery paid $26 a carat.]

The U.S. Foreign Economic Administration became interested in attempting to block this clandestine supply line, and in the summer of 1943 the FEA representative in Angola asked OSS/Accra to assist in the investigation of the traffic. OSS and FEA investigations were successful, but action against enemy agents engaged in diamond smuggling was blocked by the action of both the British Ministry of Economic Warfare and by the U.S. Consul-General in the Congo.

Offers by both FEA and OSS representatives to cooperate with British MEW were rebuffed. On 9 October the OSS office was informed that London had no interest in the problem. A further inspection of the diamond fields in Angola by FEA, and in the Congo by OSS, brought a sudden reversal in the British attitude. Before the end of the same month, British investigators had been sent to the diamond fields. In November 1943, MEW issued a study showing that German stocks of industrial diamonds were down to an eight-month supply and that smuggling was the only possible source of replenishment. The British then approached the Americans, and agreements were concluded between OSS and SOE, and between FEA and MEW, to pursue the diamond investigation jointly.

Despite continuing MEW opposition, OSS agents established: (1) That, through contracts and ownership of purchasing and distributing channels, the DeBeers Syndicate controlled ninety-five percent of the world diamond market; (2) that three out of five members of the Diamond Committee of MEW represented the DeBeers interests; and (3) that for all practical purposes the Diamond Control Committee of MEW was controlled by the Syndicate. A report from the Chief of OSS/Accra stated:

> We have now come to the conclusion (a) that our assistance was requested in this program primarily so that the Diamond Trading Corporation might discover how much we actually knew of the ramifications of the DeBeers world monopoly, and (b) that the OSS/Accra recommendations for a Security Committee were sabotaged, not by the British Government, but by the representatives of the Diamond Trading Corporation, Ltd. London, through their domination of the Diamond Committee of MEW.

Further OSS/SOE investigation uncovered enemy smuggling channels through the Gold Coast, Mozambique, Angola, Cairo, the Belgian Congo and the Union of South Africa. Operators were named. A crisis arose when OSS agent "Teton" traced a smuggling chain to the Chief of Police at Leopoldville, capital of the Belgian Congo. "Teton," [Excision] had established excellent contacts during an official tour of the Congo to register all American males of draft age. Available information indicated that the major source of leakage to Germany was the Forminiere mines in the Congo, and through his various contacts "Teton" discovered evidence that a full year's supply of diamonds had reached Germany from Forminiere through Red Cross parcels. He also uncovered an important secondary channel through Bulawayo in Southern Rhodesia.

In April 1943, SOE apprised OSS/Accra that MEW, London required more complete evidence before it could take official action against the enemy smuggling traffic, and OSS directed "Teton" to attempt the purchase of diamonds through illicit channels. "Teton" chose a pro-Allied Belgian to make the purchases for him and supplied him the funds. The Belgian was shortly thereafter arrested by the Belgian police, and a subsequent raid on "Teton's" house showed that "Teton" had in fact traced the smuggling to the Police Chief himself. Charges that "Teton" was engaged in "questionable activities" were then carried to the Governor General of the Congo, who referred them to the U.S. Consul-General. The latter knew of "Teton's" activities but merely asked the Governor General whether he considered him persona non grata. The Governor had only to nod an affirmative, and the OSS agent was forced to leave.

An OSS/SOE conference in Accra in February 1944 recommended the establishment of an advisory commission on diamond security, which met with a counter-proposal from MEW to conduct a survey of security measures employed in the Congo mines, bu two experts, one a diamond mining engineer, the other a diamond security expert, both to be named by Sir Ernest Oppenheimer, Chairman of DeBeers. Thus the responsibility for security would have been turned over entirely to the industry, except that this plan also was dropped and eventually SOE worked out a program, which, though well planned, was unable to cope with the Syndicate's control of the industry and its dealings with the enemy.

Angola. In Angola complete information on the Benguela railroad, the only transcontinental line in Africa, was obtained, and plans were laid to blow the three most important bridges, should Marshal Rommel take North Africa. Observation of the coast line uncovered one spot where Nazi submarines were being supplied from the shore, and, on representations from British SOE, with which OSS cooperated closely, the Governor General agreed to remove suspect individuals and close the area to all foreigners.

South Africa. In the Union of South Africa one OSS agent, cooperating with an OWI representative, uncovered evidence of pro-Axis activities on the part of the Ossewa Brandwag. This widespread local Fascist organization was strong enough to prevent Marshal Smuts from taking serious repressive action. By the fall of 1943, however, U.S. and British espionage services had accumulated sufficient evidence so that the British Foreign Office might approach General Smuts in London and thereby enable him to take action against the Ossewa Brandwag. It was learned later that the report, submitted by the OSS agent, on an interview with the Ossewa Brandwag leader, had played an important part in the South African cabinet decision to adopt a firm policy against that organization.

Mozambique. The most outstanding counter-espionage operation undertaken by representatives of SI/Africa took place in the Portuguese colony of Mozambique, and was carried out by OSS agent "Ebert."

Leopold Wertz, German vice-consul in Lourenco Marques, assisted by Campini, the Italian Consul General, and Manna, Director of the Stefani News Agency, operated a large espionage and sabotage ring in Mozambique and South Africa, gathering, in particular, shipping information, and actively spreading Nazi propaganda. "Ebert" arrived in December 1942 and, within a year, had acquired fairly complete data on the espionage chain. He sent to Washington a chart of the German and Italian intelligence organizations in Portugese East Africa with backgrounds, photographs and descriptions of approximately 100 individuals conducting espionage activities for the Axis. Through wireless, couriers and the use of advertisements in Union newspapers, these agents were transmitting shipping news from Angola and South Africa to Lourenco Marques, whence it was sent directly to Berlin over the Marconi Radio Station, for relay to submarines.

"Ebert" worked jointly with British SIS and SOE on a plan to break up the entire ring.

[The principal British agent involved in this operation was Malcolm Muggeridge, the British journalist, author, broadcaster and lay preacher. He was sent to Mozambique by Kim Philby, the head of the SIS section involved, and Muggeridge's assignment was to destroy the Abwehr agent's credibility at Berlin by feeding him—and inducing him to transmit to Berlin—false information. While the operation was successful, Muggeridge was withdrawn. "Ebert" became the joint OSS/SIS station chief.]

Operations were occasionally hampered by the rivalry between the two British organizations, but they were nearly blown by various indignant cables sent to the State Department by the Consul-General, who did not sympathize with the irregular activities of the American and British intelligence agencies. Nevertheless, action was taken against the Axis agents, and the first to be removed from effective operation was the number three man. [Excision] A renegade Greek journalist employed by the Germans was removed to Kenya in August, and in October, through pressure on the Portuguese authorities, a Union national, in charge of shipping intelligence for the Germans, was deported to the same place.

Several Italians were induced to break with the Mussolini Government and form the nucleus of a local Free Italy Movement which was directed by OSS agent "Ebert." Members of the Free Italy Movement demonstrated before the Italian Consulate and the Stefani News Agency in Lourenco Marques, threw a bomb into the former, propagandized their fellow nationals and gave information to OSS on the Italian intelligence system.

"Ebert" took over actual control of the U.S./British operations in 1944, when the SIS chief was recalled to London, and he then directed his activities principally toward the ousting of German agents through legal means. A member of the German espionage organization,"Dram," joined him and helped to tap telephones, steal papers and persuade other Germans to break with the German Consulate. Sufficient evidence was obtained against the Germans so that Vice-Consul Wertz and four of his assistants were forced to leave Mozambique, and the German Consulate was closed by the Portuguese authorities.

In addition to his work against the German and Italian espionage chains, "Ebert" was able to send in reports on Portuguese battle order in Mozambique, with descriptions of every major airfield and sketches drawn to scale from aerial photographs, plus a considerable amount of economic and political intelligence. [Excision]

The North African Stations. The first SI/Africa agent in North Africa was sent to Tangier to take over from the chief of the OSS unit of Operation TORCH. Representatives at this station continued the activity already initiated against official and unofficial Axis agents operating in the International and Spanish Zones of Morocco. They were able to identify all of the German, Italian and Japanese agents in the two Zones and, eventually, to submit such evidence against them as to require the Spanish High Commissioner to demand the withdrawal of their consular representatives and order the arrest of local collaborators.

Through their network of some fifty informants, they were able to report on German submarine activity near the Straits of Gibraltar. This intelligence, passed on to the American Naval Command at Casablanca, resulted in at least two sinkings. They uncovered to the Spanish High Commisioner a clandestine shipping, observation and submarine directing station operated in the town of Ceuta by German and Spanish nationals, and personally participated in the official capture of the radio equipment, codes and personnel. Their counter-intelligence activity resulted in the expulsion by diplomatic means of a total of thirty-eight enemy agents.

[This operation caused considerable embarrassment to all concerned. Bruce Page, David Leitch and Phillip Knightley would recount in *The Philby Conspiracy* (Doubleday, New York, 1968, p.149) that "The SIS men in Tangier wanted to keep an eye on German submarine movements...and so they hired a Spanish marquis who had advertised himself as a suitable agent, furnished him with money, and sent him to the town for a month. The marquis, a man of taste, established himself at an excellent hotel, and, being a homosexual, amused himself copiously with the local boyhood. On the day before the deadline after a number of cables of reminder, he suddenly produced a fat wad of information about submarine sightings in the most circumstantial detail. The SIS dispatched this with great excitement to Naval Intelligence in Britain, where sadly it was found to correspond with no single item of information already known, and to include quantities of U-boats whose numbers were plainly fictional."] [Deletion]

MIDDLE EAST

OSS was organized in the Middle East, as in Eire, Spain and Africa, during the defense period against German advance. In the spring of 1942, Axis armies in North Africa and Southeastern Europe threatened a gigantic pincer movement around the Eastern Mediterranean. Preparations had to be made against possible German success.

Two COI representatives arrived in Cairo in April 1942 with the following general directive:

(1) To gather geographical-military, naval and economic intelligence in preparation for invasion;

(2) To conduct counter-intelligence;

(3) To collect political and economic information not available to official State Department sources; and

(4) To organize a stay-behind agent network, for future operation behind the advancing Axis lines.

A base was established at Cairo to direct SI, counter-intelligence and R&A activities in Syria, Lebanon, Palestine, Transjordan, Iraq, Saudi Arabia, Iran, Afghanistan and Turkey.

Exchange of information was early arranged with the British Inter-Service Liaison Department [ISLD], and this SIS subsection made unusual concessions. On the understanding that OSS would forward them to Washington for U.S. officials only, ISLD agreed to turn over all its intelligence reports from the Middle East and southeastern Europe.

[There was little simple about the Anglo-American relationship in Cairo. Cairo, as Harold Macmillan—later Prime Minister of Great Britain, then a high political and diplomatic official in the Mediterranean-Middle East—noted in his memoir, *The Blast of War* (p. 122), was "suspect" by the Americans. It was "somehow connected in their minds with Imperialism, Kipling and all that." When the first OSS official (a former advertising director for United Fruit) arrived, he was received icily by SOE. An SOE officer confessed later that "Our people in Cairo frankly wished to keep any similar American organization out of the theater altogether, or if this was not practicable, to keep it under strict control.... This attitude was unfortunate because it naturally made the Americans suspicious and even eager to conceal their plans from us." Another British secret officer would record that "Nobody who did not experience it, can possibly imagine the atmosphere of jealousy, suspicion and intrigue which embittered the relations between the various secret and semi-secret departments in Cairo....It was not quite Hobbes' war of every man against every man. But certainly every secret organization seemed to be set against every other secret organization." Nor did the conduct of the early Americans assure good relations. More than one person lost his position.]

[Excision] [Deletion] Shortly after [the arrival in Egypt of an X-2 agent who feared that his corporate cover would be blown], auditors (British)

....developed closer contact with our office and for one reason or another made frequent and long visits, often doing some of the detailed auditing with the excuse that they would have that much less work to do at the time of final audit. This practice permitted them to check our company bank books periodically and thereby incidentally keep abreast of my withdrawals. I am strongly of the opinion that this firm had more than a mere business interest in their close contact with our office during my stay. In the same general sphere, it may be well to mention my company's banks, all of whom were advised that I was given authority to draw considerable sums of money. These banks called me and seemed to manifest a great interest in whether or not I would utilize the authority granted me.

Communications proved to be a weakness. Once the German threat to the area ceased, the British were interested in maintaining control. If OSS wished to plant long-term agents unknown to the British, radio sets were not feasible. State Department pouch, on the other hand, was extremely slow, that from Teheran to Cairo often taking from two to three weeks. State cover was permitted in only a few locations. In others, OSS agents had to blow their activities, because of the necessity of entering State Department offices directly, in order to deliver reports and cables for transmittal. Agents located at points away from State offices had almost no method of communication, since transportation facilities were inadequate. For instance, the only recourse open to an agent at Dhahran, Arabia, was to take the trip all the way to Cairo to deliver his reports.

By September 1944, SI/Cairo had infiltrated agents into the following Middle Eastern countries:

[Egypt, Lebanon, Syria, Palestine, Transjordan, Iraq, Saudi

Arabia, Afghanistan. Largely because the British and French did not want American agents "buzzing about" in the Near East—and because the German nets had been destroyed—the OSS effort in the theater in general must be considered a waste of time and money. However, some valuable work against the Russians was done. By far the most important Middle East country was Turkey.

[At first the State Department refused to permit American agents to work against Turkey, although it did permit Turkey to be used as a base of operations into the Balkans. X-2 was, however, allowed to operate within Turkey against the Germans. Toulmin was retained as regional controller, a post, doubtless, he wished later he had passed onto somebody else. X-2 and SI were, in fact, disastrously infiltrated by German agents and by pro-Nazi officers of the Turkish Security Service, Eminyet, and Toulmin was compelled to replace the first station chief, a Chicago banker, with Frank Wisner, a Wall Street lawyer, who became chief of the CIA's Office of Policy Coordination, Deputy Director of Plans, and station chief at London before his breakdown and suicide in 1965. Under Wisner, SI operations into the Balkans were effective —perhaps even more effective than England's.] [Deletion]

Twenty-nine undercover agents had been placed in the Middle East, and in all but two countries (Afghanistan and Arabia) intelligence coverage was good. As the war moved away, reports shifted from a strictly military-geographical interest to more general political and economic information. Over 500 sub-agents helped turn in, by June 1945, more than 5,000 reports. [Deletion]

Lebanon and Syria (Ten agents: seven SI and three X-2). During the war, the French remained in control of these countries and it was dangerous for natives to travel with secret material in their possession. As a result, only two of the agents were successful in building up local chains.

Agent "Stallion," who established the first of these, had arrived in the winter of 1942. In the summer of 1943, he obtained a bona fide position with an American commercial company, a job which enabled him to travel through the area maintaining contact with his sub-sources. In December 1943, he was able to hire another OSS agent as his business assistant, and between them they operated the old chain, set up a second one, bringing the total of known sub-sources to sixty, and continued transmitting intelligence obtained by themselves. They uncovered the contact system between natives in Syria and Italian submarines operating in the Mediterranean. Sub-sources provided considerable material on smuggling and espionage activities. In 1945 "Stallion" also produced valuable intelligence on pro-Russian factions within the Armenian community and on French economic activities used to promote the French position in Lebanon, tracing the latter down to its operational center, a commercial company used as cover.

Two other agents also worked together, one a businessman, the other a female clerk in a U.S. war agency. The latter did the code work for both of them, while each sent in valuable reports on industrial installations, economic and political developments, the Syrian and Lebanese press, etc. Harbor plans of several Syrian ports were eagerly received by MID.

"Squirrel" arrived as Military Observer in Damascus in April 1944. There he developed a chain of about one hundred witting and unwitting informants, including six paid agents. He submitted thorough regional studies on the Druze and Jezireh territories. Most of his reports dealt with political and military developments, for which he maintained particularly good relations with British and Syrian military circles. In May 1945, during the time of the French shelling of Damascus, he received commendation from the American Charge d'Affaires at the Damascus Legation for his cool and competent coverage of the incident.

"Carat," an X-2 agent, arrived in Beirut in early 1944 as Cultural Attache of the Legation. He was assisted by an Army Public Relations Officer, also in Beirut, and by other representatives in Damascus and Aleppo. There was, however, practically no enemy espionage activity in the area. British and French services during their three years' occupation had cleaned up the remnants of the enemy systems, and the realistic Arabs had long since given up their Nazi affiliations. The X-2 agents built up files on local politicians and political movements, propagandists, potential agents and members of the British and French Intelligence Services. Studies of the growth of Russian activity in the area were of particular interest as were those on the development of the Syrian National Party. Thorough reports covered the unrest in the Alawite territory of Syria, discovering a French hand in the disturbances. "Carat's" political intelligence was well received by the U.S. Minister, who forwarded many of his reports directly to the State Department.

Palestine-Transjordan (Six agents: five SI, one X-2). Several travelling agents briefly visited this British-controlled area, but only two set up long-term chains. These two were associated with Jewish and Arab political circles, respectively, with the result that Cairo/SI received intelligence from both of the conflicting groups.

Iraq (Four SI agents). British control of Iraq insured adequate military and counter-espionage coverage. However, road reports, strategic terrain analyses and coverage of the Kurd Movement were rated by MIS as excellent work.

Two agents, "Bunny" and "Buffalo," worked as a team. "Buffalo" was a commercial dealer in U.S. goods, representing also several specific firms. His cover was not successful, however, because trade regulations, priorities and a shortage of dollar exchange in Iraq prohibited any quantity of trade. "Bunny" was [Excision] hired by the Iraqi Government. [Excision] His contacts were excellent. He knew the Prime Minister and various other high government officials, and provided OSS/Cairo with a running commentary on political developments.

In April 1944 a neutral diplomat, on his way out of Germany, gave "Bunny" a detailed report on the results of the Allied bombings of Berlin. He mentioned the Berliner attitude of doing the day's work between 2 and 5 p.m., when Allied bombers never came over. Specific commendation from the highest military authorities and from the White House rewarded this information, which was one of the first such reports to come out of the Reich. Bombing of Berlin between 2 and 5 p.m. commenced.

"Bunny" and "Buffalo" maintained close relations with the American Minister and with British Security Intelligence. They assisted the latter in uncovering and breaking several Nazi spy rings. "Buffalo" personally interrogated one agent who, after 23 hours, finally broke. The exchange of information, arranged as a result of these successes, provided OSS with future counter-intelligence files.

Saudi Arabia (Two SI agents). Intelligence in this country was unsuccessful. Communication difficulties proved insoluble for the only two agents who could be recruited in the country; from their location, the U.S. Legation at Jiddah was almost inaccessible. One agent did bring in several reports on trips to Cairo.

Iran (Eight SI agents). The initial OSS purpose in Iran was to collect military-geographical information in preparation for a possible German advance through the Caucasus. A two-man team began operations early in the war, one of the men arriving in the autumn of 1941 (operating under COI), the other late in 1942. Each had previously lived in the country, engaged in research, and this activity was continued as cover. The reports were more of a scholarly than of a current intelligence nature, but the material submitted on roads, economic conditions, and popular sentiment, the press reviews, biographical compilations and analyses of Soviet and British policy in Iran formed valuable basic intelligence.

As Axis success turned to defeat, the emphasis shifted to political and economic intelligence. Two men, trained in Washington, were given commissions with the Persian Gulf Command, by arrangement between its commanding general and OSS/Cairo. The plan was to gather intelligence on Russian internal affairs by developing agent networks among the Polish refugees in Azerbaijan. The two agents failed in their admittedly difficult task and turned to economic reporting plus a running analysis of the Russian program in Iran.

However, of two other Americans working for the Iranian Government, one acquired a particularly good sub-source in Azerbaijan. This man built up a chain and provided reports on all phases of Russian activity in the area, including military unit locations, activities of the leftist Tudeh Party, and similar intelligence. He was the only Anglo-American source of information in the area. [Deletion] [Excision]

In Turkey, by early 1944 British services had the situation well in hand. Most of the key German agents had long since been identified, and many were giving themselves up for Allied exfiltration and internment. During the first days of January 1944, the British arranged the defection of Erich Vermehren, number two man of the Abwehr in Turkey. Three more Abwehr defections in the first week of February, those of Mr. and Mrs. Kleczkowski, and of Willi Hamburger, had been accepted (without authority) by two OWI men, who subsequently asked X-2 to take over.

Normally, a counter-espionage organization prefers in such circumstances to persuade defectors to maintain their positions and work under control. Removing them notifies the enemy of the penetration and merely invites a fresh and better disciplined set of officials and agents into the area. The whole process must be repeated of identifying, surveying and penetrating the new organization.

In this case, however, Vermehren, Hamburger and the Kleczkowskis were suspected by the Germans and had been ordered home. It was decided to take them to Syria for the valuable counter-intelligence material to be gained from interrogation. [The Russians requested the opportunity also to interrogate the Kleczkowskis. OSS stated that this was impossible but agreed to give them a prepared questionnaire and return the answers. The offer was accepted by the Russians whose questionnaire provided OSS with incidental indications of past Russian intelligence activities and clues to their intentions. (footnote)] The effect on the Abwehr in Turkey was demoralizing. The chief was recalled in disgrace, and a complete reorganization attempted, with the Sicherheitsdienst (SD) making a bid to dominate. Double-agents under British/X-2 control reported developments among the Germans, principally that of the discouragement of Pfeiffer, the new chief. The operation appeared to be a highly successful and profitable one—

and, considered alone, was so.

However, the advantage given to the SD (one of Himmler's secret Nazi organizations) over the Abwehr (the old-line, partially anti-Nazi foreign secret service) was a blow to OSS/Bern operations. Penetration of the Abwehr on a high level was bringing Bern valuable intelligence, notably inside reports on all the preparations for the anti-Hitler coup of 20 July 1944. The disorganization of the Abwehr in Turkey gave Himmler an opportunity to push forward his Sicherheitsdienst, as part of a campaign to establish Nazi supremacy over the Wehrmacht. The suspicion and investigations following the defections caused some of Bern's sources to dry up temporarily.

X-2/Washington subsequently issued an order forbidding further defections from the Abwehr. The real lesson, however, was the necessity for centralization of all penetration operations. Lacking an adequate and efficient central control, British and OSS counter-espionage encouraged the Abwehr defections. [It may be noted that Himmler's advantage was short-lived. The next defection was that of Nellie Kapp, who had been in the employment of Moyzisch, the head of Himmler's SD in Turkey. Then Moyzisch began to collaborate with the Ankara Committee, the joint U.K.-U.S. intelligence bureau in Turkey. What was especially interesting about these two defections was that both revealed information that cast suspicion upon Cicero, the famous butler who was burgling the secrets of the British embassy in Turkey. Cicero was then brought under control in the interests of Fortitude, the cover plan for the invasion at Normandy. At the same time, as is shown in my *Bodyguard of Lies*, these defections, by labyrinthine circumstances, almost destroyed the XX-Committee (the British organization in England for controlling German agents) by "blowing" one key agent, Tricycle, and his Lisbon contact, Artist. Artist was murdered by the SD.]

In collaboration with the British, X-2 continued the job, principally of protecting U.S. agencies in the area (since the British, according to agreement, handled all double-agents). The two services identified some 1,500 agents, and of these after Allied representations to the Turkish Government, about 800 were neutralized:

Confined	750 (approximately)
Extradited	25
Defected	9
Controlled	14

Among others, a German agent was uncovered working in OWI.

OSS/Istanbul had had some difficulty with OWI personnel. Many of the newspaper reporters seemed to take an unpatriotic delight in hunting out, through their American connections, OSS personnel and proclaiming them as "spies" and "super-sleuths." The actual threat of spies seemed humorous to these Americans. Therefore, when an old and trusted employee, Yumni Reshid, was accused by X-2 of working for the Germans, OWI personnel ridiculed the possibility. Under interrogation, he made a full confession.

The discovery of a German group of some thirty agents, trained for the penetration of OSS and other U.S. agencies, revealed an interesting line of attack on the Allied intelligence system in the Middle East. Four of its officials voluntarily offered information through which the project was neutralized.

CHAPTER 6

Corsica, Sardinia, Sicily, Italian Mainland

CORSICA

The first OSS secret agent team inside enemy-occupied Europe was successfully infiltrated one month after the Allied landings in North Africa. Established north of Ajaccio, Corsica, the team's clandestine radio station, PEARL HARBOR, sent its first message to Algiers on 25 December 1942, and continued almost daily contact until May 1943. Through direct liaison with the Corsican Maquis, the team reported extensively German and Italian order of battle on the island. The intelligence was relayed to AFHQ.

[OSS agent] "Tommy" was on friendly terms with the chiefs of the French Deuxieme Bureau in Algiers, and through it he obtained an officer to lead a four-man team and to direct intelligence from Corsica. Through its offices, too, he obtained the permission of Admiral Darlan and General Giraud to use the submarine "Casabianca." [The 1,600-ton "Casabianca," latest type of submarine in the French Navy, had just escaped from Toulon to Algiers with its commander and full crew aboard. (footnote)] AFHQ and the British Admiralty, in charge of the harbor, also gave approval for the mission, and essential equipment was furnished to ready the submarine. [The codename was Pearl Harbor.]

To work under the intelligence officer provided by Deuxieme Bureau, "Tommy" recruited his Corsican radio assistant as operator for the mission and two other Corsicans as assistant operator and liaison agent, respectively. The submarine commander was to help "Tommy" pick the most suitable point for the group to land along the Corsican coast, and await "Tommy's" return after the landing. With three wireless sets, a million French francs and several thousand Italian lire, food, supplies and false documents, the five OSS men headed for Corsica on 11 December 1942.

The technique employed by l'Herminier, commander of the "Casabianca," for finding a landing site and putting agents ashore, became standard for subsequent missions. Upon first reaching the target area, he made a daylight periscope reconnaissance until a suitable landing point was found—in this case, a beach at the foot of the Bay of Chioni. He then submerged and held the submarine on the bottom until after dark. This required detailed knowledge of the underwater terrain and conditions in the Mediterranean and great skill in maneuvering and handling the submarine. Shortly after midnight on the night of 14 December, the "Casabianca" resurfaced—barely out of water, to avoid being sighted by Italian patrols—and moved to within a mile off shore. Two crew members, armed with Sten guns, landed the agents and their equipment by dinghy. The submarine returned to its original position and remained submerged for thirty hours, when a second boatload of supplies was to be taken in and "Tommy" brought back.

On this second trip, the dinghy capsized. The two crew members, stranded, remained with the agents for two months. [A subsequent submarine operation in February evacuated the two sailors and delivered the first U.S.-dispatched arms and ammunition to reach a European underground movement. (footnote)] "Tommy" himself returned to the submarine after a perilous hour-and-a-half swim.

Although, of necessity, no preparations for the arrival of the agents had been made in Corsica itself, they were welcomed by friendly local inhabitants and aided in the unloading of supplies. From 24 December until the capture of the PEARL HARBOR station by occupation troops five months later, the four-man combination of intelligence leader, liaison man and radio operators worked with a growing number of agents to obtain and transmit information from enemy-occupied Corsica, and to establish a resistance nucleus for use in the event of future landing operations.

They found that the Italians (25,000 as of 8 December) had occupied the Island of Corsica without meeting resistance (the result of orders from Vichy), and that, although stationed in strength at beaches on the east and west coasts, they had not penetrated to the interior except on main highways and railroads. The two brigades of the French Army in Corsica had been demobilized, and the French general placed in "residence surveillee." Italian morale was low, since the population was universally hostile to the Fascist invaders, and the Corsican gendarmes used by them were noncooperative. For example, when the gendarmes were ordered to collect all firearms, they passed among inhabitants recommending that they hide their arms and only turn over those which were unserviceable. The inhabitants were, on the other hand, anxious to assist the OSS agents, and freely furnished information from villages and out-of-the-way places.

Security, on the other hand, was practically non-existent. Insularity, widespread inter-family connections and a united hatred of the occupying forces, meant that the Corsicans took little care to guard their speech from possible traitors in their midst. That PEARL HARBOR operated for as long as it did without enemy discovery was proof of Corsican solidarity and Italian weakness. In the summer of 1943, the chief radio operator was captured, tortured and killed. No more was heard from the other members of the team. During its period of operation, PEARL HARBOR dispatched 202 messages. Although the first OSS unit in enemy-occupied Europe, it had been considered by AFHQ a model for battle order reporting.

OSS, having as yet only slow procedures for issuing decorations, was forced simply to pay the operator's mother in recognition of her son's services. The importance of decorations and agent psychology in general was something OSS had already learned, but for which it had not yet been able to develop satisfactory arrangements with the Theater Command.

On the night of 8 September 1943, when the Italian surrender was announced, French Maquis groups rose in all parts of the Island of Corsica and seized control of towns and installations. A radio appeal was broadcast to Allied authorities in North Africa, urgently asking assistance against the Germans, who were moving onto the Island in strength from Sardinia. French headquarters in North Africa hastily prepared the Battaillon de Choc and several units of Moroccan and Algerian colonial troops, as a skeleton Expeditionary Force to aid in the liberation of the Island. AFHQ requested OSS to supply troops as a token Allied force to accompany the French.

Donovan selected one Operational Group (OG) of two officers and thirty men to carry out the mission, accompanied by a demolitions instructor for the Maquis and a small group of SI officers and trained Corsican agents from the SI/France Desk. The OSS group left Algiers with the French troops on French cruisers and destroyers, and arrived in Ajaccio on 17 September. A second group followed shortly to set up an advanced base for maritime penetration of Italy and France.

Corsica was now occupied by 80,000 Italians and a small German garrison consisting principally of radar observation and other air force technical crews. Upon the Italian collapse, the Germans decided to evacuate their forces in Sardinia, overland as far as possible, to avoid Allied air attack. Ignoring their recent Italian allies, the Germans began to move from Sardinia to Corsica, up the level east coast of that Island and across to Elba and the Italian mainland.

The size of the Allied Expeditionary Force limited it to harassing operations. The Maquis groups had been supplied with guns and ammunition from SOE and OSS by ship, submarine and plane. However, the insular Corsicans found it difficult to turn their attention from their traditional enemy, the Italians, toward the Germans who were relatively unknown to them. Furthermore, the French officers of the Expeditionary Force tended to deprecate and antagonize the leaders of the Maquis. [Deletion]

The OG moved northward with the French Goumiers to attack the east coast road, just south of Bastia. Bazookas were inoperative because of a shortage of fresh batteries. A three-man OG team, on an advance patrol to place mines and harass a German armored column, was killed by cross-fire ahead of the most advanced French positions.

The last German units were evacuated from Bastia on the morning of 4 October. That same day an advance group of OSS officers entered the town with OG's and the first French troops. A variety of recent data on the German army was collected as well as newly manufactured items of abandoned equipment. Much recent and otherwise unavailable information on continental France was secured and sent back to Algiers for analysis. [Deletion]

SARDINIA

On 29 June 1942, SI/Italy dispatched its first team, consisting of a W/T operator and four enlisted men, to penetrate Sardinia. The PT carrying the agents, escorted by two other PT's, drew in close to the coast of northwestern Sardinia on the night of 30 June. The agents rowed themselves and their equipment ashore in a rubber boat, which was attached by a line to the PT so that it could be pulled back after the agents had landed.

Rough seas had disturbed navigation. Since no conducting officer rowed in with the agents, the fact that the landing was not made exactly at the selected pinpoint did not become apparent to those on the PT. On shore, the agents, who were in uniform, did not find their bearings until the next day and were quickly captured by Italian sentries. They were not turned over to the Germans but were forced to play back their radio under control of Italian intelligence officers. In their first message, however, they covertly informed Algiers, by their prearranged danger signal, that they were captured and operating under duress. Security had been preserved, but the operation itself was a failure.

After the Italian surrender on 8 September 1943, reports reached AFHQ that the Germans had decided to evacuate Sardinia. AFHQ requested OSS to reconnoiter the Island, report on the situation and, if possible, win over, or arrange for the surrender of, the Italian garrison. Donovan appointed three SO and OG officers to the task.

[The OSS team was commanded by Colonel Serge Obolensky, an officer of the former Imperial Russian Army. For political reasons, Obolensky preferred New York to his native country after the revolution. Active in the hotel business and with an Astor for his wife, he enjoyed the highest society status. He would become vice-president of Hilton International. He had come to Donovan's attention through his efforts in translating a secretly-acquired copy of Mao Tse-tung's guerrilla warfare manual.]

Accompanied by a British radio operator, the team was parachuted in uniform near Cagliari on the night of 12 September, where it found that southern Sardinia was already free of Germans. Bearing letters from General Eisenhower and from the newly-established Badoglio headquarters, the team contacted the Italian commander on the Island, who placed himself at its disposal. [Marshal Pietro Badoglio, former Chief of the Italian General Staff, headed the Italian government that succeeded Benito Mussolini when the Italian dictator was deposed in a palace revolution which led to Italy's surrender on 8 September 1943. Mussolini fled and continued to resist the Allies.] Communications were immediately established with AFHQ and reception arranged for General Theodore Roosevelt's occupation forces. The OSS team, that had been held for a month as prisoners by the Italians, was released unharmed, and its radio equipment returned intact.

SICILY

Corsica and Sardinia were of minor AFHQ interest compared to Sicily [where one American and one British army landed under the Supreme Command of General Eisenhower on 9/10 July 1943]. Although OSS had one team ready for dispatch to that Island early in June, AFHQ clearance was cancelled at the last minute for fear that agents entering at so late a date might alert coastal defenses.

During the campaign itself, OSS attempted line-crossings for intelligence and sabotage but was largely unsuccessful, although the task appointed and procedures developed represented a step forward from the errors of the Tunisian campaign. One OSS agent went ashore on D-Day, 11 July 1943. This was "Sorel," who had been dispatched from Washington to act independently of OSS/Algiers. [Excision] He accompanied the first wave of the 3rd Division ashore. Speaking fluent Italian, he interrogated prisoners on the spot, obtained information on camouflaged enemy gun emplacements that were pinning down the landing forces, and himself led a charge on a pillbox and an Italian command post. From there he maintained a deceptive phone contact with Italian rear headquarters, denying the need for reinforcements in "his sector."

Donovan also went ashore on D-Day, and subsequently directed the main OSS unit for Sicily of two officers and eight enlisted men, who landed on D-plus-4. [This of course was madness. Donovan also went ashore on D-Day in Normandy. One wonders—as did the heads of SIS/SOE—what would have happened had Donovan been captured, as was always possible. He knew all about the British as well as the American intelligence services, and especially about the atomic bomb and Ultra. This rash behavior on the part of senior OSS officials was one of the root causes of the intense suspicion with which the British secret services were now coming to regard their American comrades-in-arms. The loss of the SO chief in a frontline escapade in Sicily (see below) illustrates the great dangers in this type of bravado.]

It was quickly found that agent personnel recruited and trained in the United States for secret intelligence work could not be used on short-range tactical or combat intelligence missions. In contrast, selected natives, recruited, trained and briefed on the spot, had not only natural cover for line-crossing but also an intimate knowledge of the terrain.

[The Sicilian OSS project was initiated by Earl Brennan, a former State Department consular official, Republican member of the New Hampshire legislature, and in 1943 chief of SI/Washington. While on U.S. diplomatic business in Canada, he had encountered the chiefs of the Italian Mafia, who had been banished from Italy by Mussolini.

[In March 1943, Brennan recruited Max Corvo, a U.S. Army private of Sicilian descent, into the OSS, and in turn Corvo recruited twelve Sicilian-Americans as field agents, and two young lawyers, Victor Anfuso (later a Justice of the New York Supreme Court and Democratic congressman from Brooklyn) and Vincent Scamporino, who had been at Boston University, as organizers. The OSS team was delayed in its departure from the United States because of allegations that one of them had engaged in alleged Communist-subversive actions in the United States. This was not proven, and the group departed.

[Meanwhile, Murray Gurfein, then an assistant New York district attorney, later a Federal judge in New York, negotiated a deal with Lucky Luciano, the New York Mafia leader, then in prison, that would enable the Mafia in Sicily to engage in clandestine—

and especially espionage—operations in support of the Sicilian invasion. While this was not strictly speaking an OSS operation—ONI was behind it and its main object was to use the Mafia-controlled dock unions in the United States to report German intelligence and sabotage operations—the OSS in Sicily did benefit. In return, on the very day World War II in Europe ended, a petition for executive clemency for Luciano was sent to Governor Thomas E. Dewey of New York. In jail for crimes concerning prostitution, Luciano was said to have "cooperated with high military authorities. He is rendering a definite service to the war effort." His efforts, said a representative of ONI, appearing on Luciano's behalf, "had helped shorten the war in Sicily and Italy." The Governor approved the appeal and Luciano was deported from the United States.

[Corvo's group landed in Sicily in July, but at all times—despite the Luciano deal—the project suffered from lack of personnel: there were insufficient Italian-American volunteers who were, as one OSS agent put it, prepared to "take a shot at their relatives." Nevertheless, the Corvo group behaved well, and did much brave and valuable service.] [Deletion]

In late July the chief of SO/Sicily arrived and laid plans for sabotage operations behind the lines. [Deletion] On 1 August, after several projects proved abortive due to the rapid Allied advance, the SO chief organized a team and personally led it towards enemy lines in the north-central sector in the mountainous region above Mistretta.

The team, consisting of three enlisted men, one radio operator and two native guides, headed towards an Italian unit whose morale had been reported at a low ebb. While crossing a stream past the main enemy positions, the radio man was seriously wounded on a land mine, which exploded and gave away the team's position to a German patrol.

The team members ahead and behind regained Allied lines; the SO chief and one enlisted man, also wounded, remained with the radio operator and were captured; the Germans left the radio man as mortally wounded. After two days, the latter succeeded in attracting a native's attention and was recovered by advance American units. The enlisted man managed to escape, after killing the German officer who was guarding him, and returned to American lines to report his observations. The SO chief was not heard from again, although several penetrations, both of agents and native sub-agents, were attempted in order to try to recover him. Having just come from the United States with extensive information on OSS plans and organization, he should not, in the interest of security, have undertaken to lead a mission into enemy territory. [Deletion]

SI/Italy, meanwhile, established a base at Palermo and sent several small missions with occupying forces to the smaller Italian islands of Stromboli, Lipari, Ventotene, San Stefano and Ponza. Many of these were penal colonies where SI interrogated (and in some cases recruited) Mussolini's political prisoners, and collected enemy documents, equipment and codes.

In Sicily OSS had acquired little experience in behind-the-lines work in support of ground armies. Most of the staff had become involved in occupation and political work. The failures, both on Sardinia and in Sicily itself, were principally those of SI/Italy, a unit whose activities were later sharply curtailed by Donovan.

SI/Italy began from bases in Palermo and South Italy to attempt long-range agent operations and to establish political contacts. However, a new unit, including an experienced French intelligence officer, was formed to accompany Fifth Army on the campaign in Italy itself, while a third set of operations (SI and OG) were initiated from Corsica.

ITALIAN MAINLAND

Prior to the Salerno landing [which occurred on 9 September 1943], OSS had participated in no extensive military campaigns. In both Tunisia and Sicily there had been insufficient time to develop its functions in support of ground armies. Furthermore, there were no OSS agents or informant chains yet established on the Italian mainland from North African bases. Initial contacts with Italian resistance elements had been made by the SI/Italy section in Sicily, but these were not as well developed as the active liaison between the OSS staff in Switzerland and the Italian patriot movements in the north.

The OSS position in the Theater was inevitably that of a new agency about whose functions and relative position neither its own members, nor those to whom it was immediately responsible, were sure. [Deletion]

For OSS it was important to land at a beachhead at least with army headquarters, principally: (1) To exploit the early confusion of landing, for the infiltration of agents through enemy lines; (2) to contact friendly resistance groups for information and as an immediate source of reliable recruits; (3) to recruit [informants and labor] from among overrun civilians or military casuals; and (4) to detect potentially dangerous overrun enemy agents or sympathizers. In Italy this importance was heightened by uncertainty over the extent of the effect of Italy's collapse on the German position in southern Europe.

In both the Sicilian and the subsequent Italian invasion, the absence of a clear directive from AFHQ to the army concerned made it necessary for OSS to sell itself directly to the field commander at the beachhead, by commitments of tactical and combat intelligence, and by undertaking or improvising any other services possible in direct support of immediate military operations. In this respect, the OSS unit at Fifth Army Headquarters in North Africa was fortunate in gaining the active support of General Clark, and landed on D-Day both at Salerno and Anzio. Special Detachment (OSS), Fifth Army could thus, through the long Italian campaign, develop for the first time the functions and techniques of an OSS unit supporting ground armies.

[So far, OSS achievements in no way compared with those of the British. But the organization was established, it did have the support of the U.S. Joint Chiefs of Staff and, to a lesser degree, that of their tutors, the British secret services. It had shown itself remarkably quick to learn—although the "eager beavers" had caused terrible distress and casualties among friends and supporters through ill-considered or rash action. Now, on the eve of the Salerno landings, however, the record began to improve.

[Donald Downes, now much more sober and professional, recruited 75 Italian agents and American officers to accompany the Salerno landing forces. Taking a leaf from Donovan—the OSS chief once told J. Edgar Hoover: "I know they're Communists; that's why I hired them"—he did not shun the services of Irving Goff, who, according to congressional allegations, would become chairman of the Louisiana Communist Party and of the Veterans Committee of the New York Communist Party, nor those of Vincent Lassowski, both of whom had served in the Lincoln Brigade during the Spanish Civil War. Downes was also assisted by Peter Tompkins, who had studied at Harvard, Columbia and the Sorbonne; Tompkins spoke Italian and had been a reporter in Rome for the *New York Herald Tribune* and knew the Italian royal family. Tompkins' services might have been especially valuable had the British let him land before the attack (which they did not because it was feared that if he was captured he might reveal what he knew about the landings). But Tompkins did go in at H-Hour aboard a British motor torpedo boat, as part of a MacGregor unit led by a former New York reporter Marcello Girosi, who later produced Italian and American motion pictures starring Sophia Loren. The plan was to get through to the Italian naval staff and persuade the admirals to surrender the Italian fleet—a task that had in fact already been accomplished by diplomatic means.

[Nevertheless, OSS was in on the first great Allied landing on the continent of Europe.] [Deletion]

Salerno. The two advance OSS teams landed on D-Day (9 September 1943) near Paestum. [Deletion] They soon began tactical line-crossing missions for ten- to fifty-mile penetrations, using natives, chiefly members of pro-Allied resistance groups, hired and briefed on the spot. Most agents were recruited for one job and no more. They could be sold on going through the lines once or twice but very seldom more than that. They were paid off and left behind after debriefing.

In the course of placing men through the lines, the team leaders frequently found themselves up to twenty miles ahead of forward American positions. One team entered Agropoli shortly before the scheduled American assault and accepted the "surrender" of the town, while sending back urgent messages that the town was unoccupied by the enemy.

On 15 September, two Americans and sixteen Sicilian recruits were forwarded from the SI/Italy section in Sicily. Operating as three six-man radio-equipped teams, they conducted three reconnaissance missions southward and eastward from the beachhead, to confirm the evacuation of German units above Potenza. One team then headed northward for Avellino, but was caught in an enemy cross-fire which killed two agents and seriously wounded two others. A new team was formed to penetrate Naples. Two agents of this team succeeded in reaching the city but lost communication, since they abandoned their radio to evade German road patrols. [Deletion]

[As the campaign developed,] OSS field headquarters were formed at nearby Amalfi.

[The labyrinthine nature of OSS politics were demonstrated at Amalfi to the extreme displeasure of Mr. Downes. General Donovan arrived at Amalfi, announced that there would be a new OSS commander in Algiers, a job Downes expected to get. But no, Ellery Huntingdon, a rich Wall Street lawyer and a product of Yale, would have that job and control all OSS operations in Italy as well as French North Africa. Donovan informed Downes that he could remain in Italy, but only as chief of counter-intelligence. Moreover, he could recruit Italians who were loyal to the King, whom Downes despised. Downes was angry at what was tantamount to demotion and told Donovan that he would not serve under Huntingdon. He was conscious perhaps that Huntingdon had served as a fund-raiser in Donovan's campaign for the New York governorship in 1932 and was nothing more than a "good-natured incompetent" for all his political importance in New York. Moreover, Downes rejected Donovan's political directive concerning the King on the grounds that it betrayed the Italian democrats, who also despised the Italian King. Then came the third and conclusive incident: Donovan took Downes with him aboard an MTB on a day's outing to Capri, ostensibly to inspect a MacGregor team which was preparing to kidnap an Italian admiral from the British. On his arrival Donovan announced that it was his intention first of all to inspect the villa of Mona Williams, a leading New York society woman whose husband, a multi-millionaire, had made one of the largest contributions to Donovan's 1932 campaign. Donovan had assured Mrs. Williams that he would protect her villa from being "ruined by a lot of British enlisted personnel." Donovan gave the task to Downes, who rejected it with the words: "I don't want to fight a war protecting Mrs. Williams' pleasure dome." Downes, who was a left-wing idealist, was fired that night at a meeting with Donovan, and seems not to have played an active part in OSS affairs thereafter.] [Deletion]

Naples. Upon establishment of the Salerno beachhead, Naples became the principal Detachment target. The stream of refugees from that city, and from the rest of Italy, grew as German evacuation of the city became imminent. Using fishing boats, many who chose not to risk crossing the lines sailed across the bay to the Islands of Capri, Ischia and Procida. There, all available OSS personnel joined in a general interrogation program.

The original OSS advance units were shifted to Capri, where a temporary Allied PT boat base had been established. In addition to interrogation work on that Island, they set up bases on Ischia and Procida, where they recruited numerous islanders, fishermen and refugees from the mainland, and briefed them for short-range penetration of Naples. A total of five teams were sent into Naples harbor by fishing boats, which also carried arms for Neapolitan patriots to organize guerrilla warfare within the city. Two teams failed to reach the mainland due to machine gun fire from the German shore patrols. Other agents, infiltrated in this manner, had orders to pass southward through the German lines and to report to OSS headquarters on the mainland.

[Donovan's insistence that Italian recruits into OSS be checked for their loyalty to the Italian King, whom the left-wingers regarded as inept and politically bankrupt, to say nothing of being a coward, soon collapsed—a demonstration of Donovan's incapacity to see the truth of any politics but those of the Anglo-Saxon powers. Major Malcom Munthe, the son of the Swedish novelist Axel Munthe and an officer of the British special operations organization SOE, rescued the Italian historian and philosopher, Benedetto Croce, from behind German lines around Naples. Croce, a devout antifascist, had openly defied Mussolini and was equally candid in his distaste for the King. The Italian project was turned over to Peter Tompkins, who presented it to Colonel Huntingdon, the officer who had just been appointed to the key Mediterranean post in OSS to which Downes had aspired. Tompkins would recall that Huntingdon was "very pleasant" but "spoke not a word of Italian and understood less of intelligence." Huntingdon avoided any commitment to Croce's proposal that the OSS form a left-wing Italian Legion to act as a rallying point for the Italian nation against the Germans—until Donovan issued a pronouncement in what was another demonstration of his political unpredictability: OSS must support Croce. Within days, Croce's nominee, General Giuseppe Pavone, was located, and the embryo of the Legion was formed—despite London's and Washington's enthusiasm for the King.

[The neat change of heart did not, however, bring Downes back. Downes requisitioned a villa owned by a Director of the Bank of America, established OSS HQ in Italy, and then departed for that special, bitter limbo reserved for OSS men whose opinions failed to appeal to the chief. This may have meant the end of business for Downes, but not for the Legion. The British, who supported the royal family, intrigued against the OSS, which tended to support the left-wing. Huntingdon lost the battle of wits and was replaced by Colonel John Haskell, one of the more fortunate of General Donovan's high officers of secret service. The Legion collapsed. The stated reason: loss of morale and initiative among the Legionnaires. The real reason: so intricate and bitter had become the differences between OSS and the British services that Huntingdon decided to liquidate the Legion in the interests of Allied harmony. Haskell, a brilliant man whose brother Joe was chief of OSS/SO London, was a born intelligence officer who was conscious of the issue of class in intelligence work: he saw, wisely, that the royalists made the best intelligence officers, and the Communists and liberals the best wireless operators. Haskell proved too valuable a man to waste in arbitrating over a snake's nest, and at the precise moment his wisdom and patience were most needed in the political efforts to reconcile royalists and leftists and keep Italy out of a civil war, he was replaced by yet another perceptibly bewildered OSS colonel.]

The occupation of Naples began on 1 October. [Deletion] Fifth Army Detachment headquarters was moved promptly to Naples, and training, holding and communications areas were requisitioned and established.

Tactical line-crossing infiltrations by the OSS unit on the mainland were carried out and increased in number up to twenty a day. [A remarkable number of missions in such a dangerous game.] In one two-day period short-range OSS intelligence material provided objectives for nine Air Force bombing missions. [Deletion]

Anzio. The OSS Anzio unit, consisting of two officers and two enlisted men, landed with the Rangers on 22 January 1944. It made radio contact with OSS headquarters at Caserta for the relay of intelligence to G-2 on the beachhead, and with OSS agents and station VITTORIA in Rome.

Messages from VITTORIA were decoded and passed to G-2 on the beachhead as soon as they were received. Since one of the sources was an Italian "liaison officer" in Kesselring's headquarters, much of the information from VITTORIA was of great value in supplying data on the movement of German troops.

[The Italian "liaison officer" was Colonel Giuseppe Lanza Cordero di Montezomolo, an ardent royalist from Piedmont, where one of his relatives had been made a marquis by the House of Savoy. This man represented the OSS's first major human intelligence victory in Italy, and as Colonel Sir John Hunt, then a high officer of intelligence with the British in Italy would state: "...he was the only man in that line of business [in Italy] who was of any use at all." Montezomolo had first come to the attention of MI-6 in Cairo when a Colonel Revetria with the Italian army in the desert deserted to British lines with a wireless set. Revetria told the British that Colonel Montezomolo, a well-placed and extremely competent Italian staff officer at higher Italian headquarters in Rome, had the mate to Revetria's cipher and radio set. Revetria explained that Montezomolo wished to organize a revolution against Mussolini with British help, and bring Italy into the war against her ally Germany by joining the Western powers. Under MI-6 control, Revetria was permitted to call Montezomolo and, indeed, Montezomolo replied in the mate code. Thereupon, the British seem to have used Revetria's equipment to plant deceptions upon the Italian high command.

[After the capture of Naples, Montezomolo appears to have contacted OSS. By this time he had become eminent in the Italo-German high command and was liaison officer between the Italian General Staff and Field Marshal Albert Kesselring, the German C-in-C in Italy. Montezomolo was an intimate of the King and of the Chief of the Italian General Staff, General Vittorio Ambrosio, and had interpreted for Mussolini at various strategy conferences with Hitler. As Hunt would comment: "He was therefore a man who knew the sort of information that was wanted and could interpret it properly....In [this] position he was naturally able to find out all about the movements of German troops through Rome to the front." As important as all else, he was able to communicate with AFHQ quickly because of his wireless and cipher. "For some time, therefore," Hunt would state, "he passed us a great deal of information which was completely correct." As Tompkins and the Allied high command plotted to take over Rome, Montezomolo was given the job of chief of staff of the Italian corps responsible for the defense of the capital. At the same time he was a central figure in an Italian military plot to join the Allies that was so complicated it seemed directed against everybody except OSS. In mysterious circumstances—as Tompkins, who became Montezomolo's controller in Rome, would state, "almost as though someone wished to be rid of him so as to seal his mouth forever"—Montezomolo was caught by the Sicherheitsdienst. He was executed with 335 other captives in the Ardeatine caves, after two months of brutal interrogation which failed to break him. Tompkins would come to believe that he was sold to the Germans by an Italian leftist working for (and at the parachutists of) the British services.] [Deletion]

Perhaps the most significant item of information produced was the report, early in March, that the enemy planned a diversionary feint from Cisterna, prior to a heavy armored attack downward from Albano. Based largely on this information and subsequent confirmatory reports, an American armored regiment was moved from one sector of the beachhead to another. Two agents, dispatched independently on tactical infiltrations from the beachhead, returned after three days behind enemy lines and confirmed German preparations for the armored assault. Due to the timely move by the armored regiment, the German attack lost its advantage of surprise.

Twenty-two successful tactical intelligence missions through the lines were completed from Anzio by OSS/Fifth Army Detachment. The agents were, for the most part, ex-Italian officers with anti-Fascist records; others were members of the Italian San Marco (Marine) and Nembo (Parachutist) Battalions. Agents were kept at the OSS headquarters at Anzio, in an old fortress surrounded by a moat and heavily guarded. Most were sent on only one trip behind the lines, although two agents went on three missions each. Upon their return, they were sent to Caserta for rest. [Deletion] One agent, a former sergeant of the Italian San Marco Battalion, was seriously wounded, upon his return through the lines, by an American soldier on front-line guard duty. He was not picked up until dawn and, upon being brought to the field hospital, insisted on reporting to the OSS commanding officer before receiving extensive treatment. Periodically revived by injections of plasma, he gave a report and a rough but accurate plan of German fortifications at Littoria. A few days later, prior to evacuation to the American general hospital in Naples, he repeated his information, but by this time American dive bombers had already knocked out the enemy guns.

In April, a team of two men was sent, at the request of G-2, through the lines toward Cisterna and Cori, to report on soil conditions in order to ascertain the feasibility of using tanks and armored vehicles in the sector. The American attack that finally broke out of the beachhead followed the route surveyed by these agents.

Rome. The Fifth Army, following the occupation of Naples, gave top priority to the Rome area, and expressed additional interest in the development of intelligence sources as far north as the Swiss and Yugoslav borders. With these requests, and in view of the unprecedented opportunities for recruiting and penetration afforded the Fifth Army Detachment on the Salerno beachhead and in Naples by the aftermath of the Italian collapse, Donovan directed that primary attention be given to placing agents in Rome, and that contacts be initiated wherever else possible within Fifth Army's field of interest. SI/Italy meanwhile would concentrate on northern Italy.

The first strategic intelligence team was dispatched by Fifth Army Detachment across the lines on 12 October. Its target was Rome and it consisted of: "Coniglio," one of the leaders of the Neapolitan resistance; "Cervo," who had just arrived from Rome, where he had been a junior officer on the Italian General Staff and had served as Assistant Military Attache and on the Italian-German Armistice Commission; "Corvo," another leader of the Neapolitan resistance; two other officers; and a radio operator. "Coniglio," head of the team, [a former SIM agent, who was eventually to be shot by Germans] was instructed: (1) To develop an informant service in the Italian capital; (2) to arrange for the reception of supplies and radio equipment for resistance in central Italy; and (3) to dispatch other agents and sub-agents with radio sets from Rome into northern Italy. "Cervo" had the additional assignment of finding and evacuating a certain Italian scientist and inventor. Two men accompanied "Coniglio" across the lines on 12 October 1943; the others followed four days later.

On 17 October several high-ranking Italian naval staff officers and "Carlo," a prominent industrialist, arrived in Naples, after crossing American lines, and supplied extensive up-to-date military and economic information on northern Italy. "Carlo" immediately volunteered to return to Rome to build up a network of agents, and, after intensive briefing, was dispatched across the lines on 1 November, accompanied by two other agents and a young woman trained as a radio operator. After a successful crossing of the lines, "Carlo" was wounded by a German land mine. He dispatched one agent back to OSS headquarters at Naples, while the other agent and the radio operator proceeded to Rome. He himself was picked up by the Germans. But his knowledge of their language was sufficient to convince them, and he was carried to a hospital and given the usual first aid. During the night he escaped from the hospital, despite his wounds, and hitchhiked to Rome on a German truck. When he arrived in the capital, a friend hid and cared for him. He recovered after twenty-two days in bed, and contacted "Coniglio."

Aided by "Carlo's" acquaintances, "Coniglio" succeeded in reaching the leaders of the major political parties—Socialist, Communist, Social Democrat and Partito d'Azione—and the senior general of SIM in German-occupied Italy. "Coniglio," however, was unable to communicate by radio with the OSS base station. It had not been possible to train his radio operator adequately in Naples, prior to crossing the lines, so that the latter was unaccustomed to the SSTR-1. A local radio technician was called in to assist but was likewise unable to make contact. "Corvo," therefore, was dispatched overland to Naples to report and to deliver the information already procured. He reached OSS headquarters on 27 November. After his departure it was found that an insufficient aerial had been used for transmitting. This defect was remedied, and from then on radio VITTORIA in Rome operated without difficulty until its capture in March 1944. By the time the front became stabilized in November 1943, initial contacts in Rome had been established, as well as a reliable means of communicating intelligence from that city to OSS and military bases farther south.

A mass exfiltration mission from Italy was carried out for the first time in January 1944. Late in December, radio VITTORIA had requested that a sea pick-up be arranged on the west coast where a safe landing point had been found near Fossa del Tafone. "Coniglio" and "Corvo" wished to report in person on their position and capabilities and receive instructions for further operations. Furthermore, the Italian scientist, found by "Cervo" through Italian naval intelligence channels, had to be exfiltrated. The landing point was out of range for Naples-based surface craft, and an urgent radio message was sent to the OSS advance base in

Bastia, Corsica, on 31 December requesting that pick-up be made from there. Two evenings later, a U.S. PT boat from Corsica reached the pinpoint, successfully exfiltrated "Coniglio," "Corvo," the scientist, three Italian naval intelligence officers and the SIM general, all of whom were dispatched immediately to Naples by air. This operation, called RICHMOND I, was the first of a series of clandestine maritime landings successfully run for Fifth Army Detachment by OSS/Corsica.

OSS preparations in Rome for the liberation, which was expected to come with the landings at Anzio, were made by "Pietro," a young American foreign correspondent fluent in Italian, especially recruited for the mission by General Donovan [Peter Tompkins]. His specific orders were to contact OSS radio VITTORIA, act as intelligence officer for the Fifth Army in Rome and give the signal for sabotage and counter-sabotage measures to coincide with the Allied landings at Anzio.

"Pietro" was landed from Corsica at the Fossa del Tafone pinpoint, on the night of 21 January, along with four other agents and a radio operator assigned to the Milan area. Exfiltrated on the same mission were several agents returning to the base and one Allied prisoner of war. In addition, there were three political leaders from the Rome underground movements, on their way to urge unity of all Italian resistance at a meeting to be held in Bari at the end of January.

"Pietro" was brought to Rome, where he immediately conferred with "Coniglio" and representatives of resistance groups from a part of the Central Committee of the CLN. At the meetings, "Pietro" relayed the instructions of the Allied commander and alerted all groups to preparedness for an uprising in support of Allied landings at Anzio.

The five-month stalemate of the Allies at the beachhead necessitated postponement of OSS plans. The groups which "Pietro" had alerted for resistance and sabotage were transformed in February and March into a series of comprehensive intelligence networks regularly reporting specific details on the movements of German units, armor, equipment, etc. in the Rome area and to and from the Anzio beachhead. Among the sources of information tapped were the various political parties, industrialists and leading Roman citizens still enjoying German confidence, and officers on the "Open City of Rome" staff, including one actually assigned to Kesselring's headquarters [Montezomolo].

Elaborate precautions were taken to maintain the security of both VITTORIA and a second clandestine radio transmitter, which had been set up to handle the heavy flow of traffic between

"Coniglio's" and "Pietro's" agents in Rome and the armies on the Anzio beachhead. Nevertheless, in March 1944, security of the OSS stations was blown and their sole means for secret wireless traffic from Rome severed.

On 13 March the VITTORIA operator encountered by chance the same local radio technician who had been consulted in October 1943 when the station was established. This man had subsequently entered the pay of the Germans as a spy on resistance activity in Rome. "Cervo," in charge of finding safe houses for radios, at once ordered the VITTORIA operator to hide and, with an orderly, set out to change the location of both OSS stations. By the time he reached the houseboat where one station was located, the VITTORIA operator had been denounced to the Germans by the technician-spy and had, under pressure, revealed "Cervo's" identity. Despite five days of torture, "Cervo," who knew virtually all OSS agents in Rome, revealed no single detail. He was shot by the Germans on 23 March, along with 320 other Italians [including Montezomolo], at the Ardeatine Caves, in reprisal for the attack on a German police truck in the streets of Rome. The capture of "Cervo," who managed both radio stations, cut off direct communication between Rome agents and OSS, but the remainder of the agents were still safe.

The problems of hiding against the threat of further denunciations, reestablishing intelligence chains, and reopening contact with the base were further complicated by the overlapping jurisdictions of "Coniglio" and "Pietro." "Coniglio" had received no briefing from his base about "Pietro's" mission or his status. "Pietro," on the other hand, had not been instructed that "Coniglio" was "chief OSS clandestine agent in Italy." The need for security precautions prevented their meeting in person often enough to discuss conflicting points, and communication between them was carried on only through messengers and cut-outs. After VITTORIA's capture, they found separate means of relaying intelligence. "Pietro" contacted a British SIS circuit in the area being operated by two Italians. Unfortunately, the SIS receiving base in southern Italy did not relay "Pietro's" messages to OSS/Naples until they were over a month old. "Coniglio" sent his intelligence on events in Rome by courier northward, for relay by other OSS radios in northern Italy.

On 27 April another team was dispatched to Rome to contact agents there. The team, consisting of an agent and two radio operators, was landed on the Adriatic coast by the British. The agent utilized a forged pass, "signed" by a high-ranking German Organization Todt officer, which he presented to the German commander at Ascoli. He was immediately given a German staff car, and he and his two operators were driven safely to Rome. In his briefing he had been ordered to take control of radios which, he was told, were already in Rome. When he finally contacted "Coniglio" and learned that there was no means of direct communication, he joined with "Coniglio" in reorganizing information services, dispatching messages by courier to an OSS radio in Milan. [Excision]

Friction between agents in Rome, resulting from insufficient coordination and control by OSS operations officers, had prevented the evolution of a long-range intelligence organization from a tactical mission in support of a military operation. The initiative for action inside Rome was placed in the hands of agents themselves rather than retained by operations officers at the base. The latter were inadequately informed on conditions inside Rome after the Anzio landing failed to drive the Germans from the city. Thus the officers responsible for the operations did not know the facilities and resources of the teams inside the city. When contact was lost, the agents were forced to look to sympathizers inside Rome for funds and support. Several prominent Italians virtually liquidated their fortunes to make sufficient funds available to the OSS agents. [In July 1944, Donovan ordered a special committee to investigate the circumstances of the Rome operations as well as to liquidate the financial claims arising from the agents' activities. (footnote)]

To contact the agents in Rome and the CLN Committee headquarters there, a radio-equipped team led by an Italian professor, a key figure in the Communist organization in Rome, was dispatched. The professor volunteered to parachute, but because of his advanced age (53) and a bad knee condition, was not allowed to take any practice jumps. He and two radio operators were parachuted in the vicinity of Tivoli, in two feet of snow. Although they landed safely, they were dropped forty miles off pinpoint and lost their radios and most of their other equipment in the snow. They reported their condition by carrier pigeons which were dropped with them. Despite these difficulties, they succeeded in contacting the CLN in Rome, but only shortly before the liberation of the city.

Meanwhile, OSS agents there had passed to the Anzio and other fronts intelligence of considerable value, and had succeeded in organizing patriot forces in Rome into secret brigades for the prevention of German "scorched earth" programs. As a result, when the Allies finally broke out of the beachhead and the Germans evacuated Rome on 6 June 1944, the major electric and telephone centrals were maintained intact and one of Rome's radio stations preserved from destruction.

The nine months from the occupation of Naples until the capture of Rome in June 1944 were a developmental period for OSS in Italy. [Operations were under the control of Colonel Clifton Carter, son of a professor at West Point and brother of the aide de camp to the chairman of the Joint Chiefs of Staff. He would become a deputy director of the CIA and then director of the National Security Agency (NSA), the U.S. code and cipher breaking agency. His second-in-command was Major James H. Angleton, who had been an American businessman in Milan, where he owned the subsidiary of the National Cash Register Company. Later he became chief of OSS/Italy CI and chief of the CIA's counterintelligence service until he was dismissed over a policy disagreement with the then director, William E. Colby.] Strategic infiltrations and the first teams were placed in central and northern Italy. By parachute, PT boat and submarine, or by direct penetration of the front lines, agents, radio operators and supplies were delivered deep into enemy-held territory. Intelligence was received in steadily increasing volume, reliability and detail. Close liaisons were established with the principal centers of Italian resistance throughout occupied Italy and their activities progressively coordinated with the operations of the Allied Armies in Italy. Recruits, for both intelligence and sabotage work, were procured from resistance groups and from volunteers both in liberated territory and behind the lines. AFHQ, the armies in the field, the air forces and naval headquarters all became customers of OSS intelligence and research activities. [Deletion]

FIFTH ARMY

During November and December 1943, concurrent with its overland operations, Fifth Army Detachment established liaison with the Allied air forces at Brindisi, to obtain air lift during light moon periods (most favorable to parachutage) and maritime transportation during dark moon periods. Due to the difficulty of obtaining clearances for clandestine shipping activity, contact was made through American liaison officers with the Italian Naval Ministry at Brindisi, and approvals were finally received to use an Italian submarine, the "Axum," based in Brindisi. With transport thus assured, operations and intelligence officers of the Detachment could plan for long-range infiltration and exfiltration missions in the Rome area and in North Italy.

Only two line-crossing missions north of Rome had been carried out—on 22 October and 2 December—to contact resistance groups in Florence and Milan. On 5 December, by means of the "Axum," a total of sixteen agents and radio operators were landed on the Adriatic coast at Castel di Mezzo for missions in Rome, Ravenna, Genoa and Florence. Throughout December attempts were made to send additional radios to the agents by air and by sea, but the constant unfavorable weather prevented further long-range operations until 1944.

Early in January "Coniglio" in Rome was designated chief of OSS/Fifth Army agents in German-occupied Italy. He was instructed to establish new radio stations in Rieti, Perugia, Florence and Milan, and to intensify his reporting of German order of battle and military movements, as well as to maintain liaison with Italian political parties in Rome. Upon further briefing, he and "Carlo" were supplied with nine radio sets and ten million lire (credited to the account of "Carlo's" company in Naples for use in enemy-occupied Italy). Along with four other agents, including a young woman, "Vera," who was assigned to the Florence region, they were landed without incident on the night of 17 January in the RICHMOND II operation by PT boat from Corsica.

Typical of these early Fifth Army missions were CASSANO, MARIA GIOVANNA and NADA, dispatched during December 1943 and January 1944.

CASSANO was originally briefed to join a resistance movement reported in the Valle di Comacchio of the Ravenna region. When the team reached Ravenna, it learned that the resistance had been mopped up by the Germans. Reporting this to base, CASSANO was ordered to Venice to establish an intelligence service in that city, from which it transmitted successfully from the beginning of the year until May. On 1 May four more agents, with supplies, were sent to the team by submarine. The landing took place at Cortelazzo near Venice, just as a Fascist patrol passed on the coast. Of the agents who had been landed, two were killed and two others captured, who, under interrogation, revealed the details of the operation. The Germans attacked the original CASSANO team, killing an agent, a native assistant and a civilian passer-by. The radio operator escaped, hid his radio and ciphers, walked to the Anzio beachhead and crossed safely into American lines on 31 May.

The MARIA GIOVANNA team, headed by agent "Corvo," reached Genoa late in December. It transmitted successfully until the middle of February 1944, when it was instructed to prepare for Corsica operations RICHMOND IV and V to take place on the Ligurian coast. The team was ordered to the pinpoint to maintain an hour-by-hour contact at the beach and to act as reception committee for the landing. At the gate of the Genoa railroad station, the customs officer insisted on inspecting the suitcase containing the team's radio set. "Corvo" took the suitcase out of the hands of the radio operator and told him to escape, shot the guard and himself managed to escape over a fence into a crowd. He was forced to abandon the radio set, but sent an urgent message over another radio circuit to cancel the RICHMOND operation. Another radio was parachuted to him at a pinpoint north of Venice, which enabled his team to continue coverage of German convoys and ship movements from Genoa. In mid-September 1944, the operator and an agent of team MARIA GIOVANNA were surprised and captured by the Germans. "Corvo" was away, but his assistant and the operator were presumably killed, and the Germans took over the radio as a deception. Handling of this enemy-controlled station was turned over to X-2 officers and maintained by OSS until March 1945.

The key member of NADA was a woman, agent "Vera." "Vera" carried a radio set in a suitcase, on a 200-mile rail trip, to the leader of the Tuscan resistance movement. She then established contact with guerrilla groups in the Spezia area and with the CLN in Florence. Through her efforts, 65 supply operations by parachute were arranged.

One of her radio operators was found untrustworthy, since he was living with a German chorus girl in the pay of the SS and had been seen boasting in public about his radio work and his cipher plan. Members of the resistance in the neighborhood abducted and executed him.

On 2 July a group of German SS men broke into the room where "Vera" and her radio operator were making contact with the OSS base. The major was wounded, and two Germans were killed by hand grenades thrown by "Vera," who succeeded in destroying the radio and escaping out of a window with the operator. They joined a patriot group a few miles outside of Florence and, within eight days, found means of reopening communications with OSS. By September "Vera," a price on her head, was obliged to escape. She crossed into American lines during an artillery battle.

An especially effective network was developed by a key agent for the Milan region who landed from Corsica in late January 1944, carrying papers prepared for him by OSS and "signed" by a German general. In Milan he built up a large network of industrial and resistance contacts extending throughout North Italy. Forty-seven sub-agents reported to him at various times. On 20 May German SS troops raided the apartment in which he and an agent were operating. Armed with Sten guns, the two men resisted capture throughout the evening and into the morning, reportedly killing over thirty Germans. In the morning, out of ammunition, they leaped from the roof of the apartment house to commit suicide. The agent was killed and the radio operator survived, although seriously injured. Another agent, "Como," a Milanese doctor who had witnessed the gun fight, secured the crystals and papers in the apartment, hid the radio and escaped into Switzerland to report and to maintain contact with the resistance movements.

In addition to such intelligence operations from Fifth Army, a sabotage team was parachuted north of Rome to attempt interruption of communications between Rome and Florence. The team, dropped from British planes on 13 March 1944, consisted of one officer and twelve men recruited from the Italian Nembo (Parachutist) Battalion. Poor landing conditions scattered the team and equipment over a stretch of several miles, and some of the men were injured.

By the following morning, however, much of the demolitions equipment had been recovered, and on 17 March the team set out to cut the rail line between Terni and Perugia. It was attacked by a German patrol in the village of Appennino. Several of the men were killed and wounded, while the officer was captured by the Germans and shot on the spot. A few managed to escape. According to pre-arranged plan, another radio was dropped to them, but unfortunately was broken in landing. The remainder of the team dispersed and was finally overrun in June.

Concurrent with these long-range penetrations from Fifth Army, two other units were carrying out similar operations on a smaller scale—OSS/Corsica and SI/Italy.

CORSICA AFTER LIBERATION

Upon its liberation early in October 1943, Corsica was the northernmost Allied salient toward southern Europe, and became an important OSS advance base. It served as headquarters for the OG/Italy unit, as a dispatching station for SI operations into central and northern Italy and southern France, and as a forward field communications base.

OSS headquarters were established at Bastia, the northeast Corsican seaport, 35 miles from the Italian mainland, and approximately 90 miles from the strategic Ligurian coast. Administration and communications headquarters, as well as the OG training and staging area, were located at Ile Rousse, while a supply center was maintained at Ajaccio.

[One of the leaders of an OG on Corsica, an Italian-American who was a born businessman, heard that the French would land shortly to occupy the island—and promptly cornered all available supplies of wine and cognac. He is said to have made a fortune, selling the supply to the French when they came in. This same officer, who came to be called Trader Horn, fought with great distinction and courage later on in the partisan warfare around Spezia. This fighting became so violent that the Germans shot all OGs upon capture, burying the corpses in the roots of the trees along the waterfront of the city. Not without reason, the Germans considered the OGs, who were in uniform, terrorists and therefore beyond the rules of war.

[The violence of the operations conducted would become legendary, as would be those of similar organizations such as Company D of the OSS, and the 2677th Regiment OSS (Provisional). There was, at the time, considerable misgiving at OSS/Washington, especially that these organizations were recruiting and arming —and thereby increasing the possibility of revolution in postwar Italy, especially in the North—Communist partisans. There was also some concern that OSS was recruiting Mafiosi and, on a smaller scale, hit men from the ranks of Murder, Inc., and the Philadelphia "Purple Gang." Some OG group leaders engaged in blackmarketing on a large scale and as one OSS training officer for OGs would recall, the OGs consisted of "tough little boys from New York and Chicago, with a few live hoods mixed in.... Their one desire was to get over to the old country and start throwing knives." By 1945, these groups were considered to be so dangerous that OGs returning from operation were, on the orders of the Allied High Command, confined to a castle near Spezia until they were either returned home or were sent back into the field. There were several murders and much brawling and they proved to be only slightly less bothersome to the Allied High Command than they proved to the enemy. Officers whom they disliked had some reason, often, to feel that their lives were imperilled. It should be stressed, however, that by far the majority of these men in OSS private armies were perfectly civilized human beings who behaved most honorably both in and out of action.]

Corsica served primarily as a maritime rather than as an air base. American PT's of Squadron 15 and a flotilla of British motor gun-boats and motor launches of the African Coastal Forces moved up from Sardinia and had begun to operate out of Bastia by the end of October, both for naval sorties and for clandestine operations. In addition, a flotilla of five Italian MAS boats, manned by volunteer Italian crews from Maddalena, was also made available for the latter. Although the Italian boats had the advantages of low silhouette, high speed (up to fifty knots) and special auxiliary engines to permit silent maneuvering off pinpoints, the American PT's were used for the majority of operations. The radar of the American boats was important for defense and navigation, and their range made it possible to reach as far west as Toulon and as far south as the Tiber River. [The Italian boats were withdrawn from clandestine work in March 1944, after the crew of one boat had mutinied in the course of a joint British-French mission, killed the British and French officers and agent personnel, as well as their own officers, and sailed into an enemy-held port. (footnote)]

British SIS and SOE and the French services also opened advance operating stations in Bastia. Close coordination between the intelligence organizations was essential to prevent dangerous overlapping of pinpoints or sorties, and to plan and schedule future operations. The British senior naval officer, in command of naval forces, accepted and encouraged clandestine maritime operations, and established a procedure for determining sea transport priorities between the various organizations. In addition, a joint Intelligence Pool was organized by OSS and other services to centralize and make available all operational intelligence relevant to clandestine maritime activities, and to plan details of individual operations.

A chain of observation posts was projected on islands off the Italian coast, astride the German shipping lanes, to report enemy sea and air activity. Coastal shipping was particularly important to the Germans, due to the constant interruption of land supply routes by Allied air attack.

The first operation took place two weeks after the liberation of Corsica. On the night of 16 October 1943, twelve OG's landed on the island of Capraia, north of Elba, from a British minesweeper, the only craft then available. The landing was unopposed, and the OG's remained to establish an observation post in the former Italian naval semaphore station atop the Island. Direct radio contact was maintained with OSS/Bastia. A "crack" code [using a series of letter symbols to indicate weather and shipping developments (footnote)] permitted rapid reporting of observations to Bastia, where a direct private telephone line made possible instant relay of information from OSS headquarters to the Allied Forces War Room. Regular supply missions from Corsica maintained the garrison and rotated OG personnel.

The second post was established on the night of 8 December, when nine OG's landed unopposed on the Island of Gorgona, twenty miles off shore from Livorno. A high-powered telescope af-

forded direct observation of enemy port and shipping activities in
Livorno. For example, considerable activity was reported at large
fuel storage tanks in the harbor, believed by the Air Force to be
unused. Results of successful Air Force attacks on the tanks were
reported by "O.P. # 1" within two hours of the subsequent raids.
[The Observation Posts were designated numerically from north to
south: Gorgona "O.P. # 1," Capraia "O.P. # 2," Elba "O.P. # 3."
(footnote)]

Enemy plane spotting from the O.P.'s was particularly important for the security of Allied airfields on Corsica, making it impossible for enemy pilots to take advantage of the islands as a
screen against Allied radar on Corsica. [Planes on Bastia/Borga
airfield could be dispersed or in the air five minutes after an alarm
from O.P. # 2 (Capraia), itself about five minutes flying time from
Corsica. No radar was placed at the O.P.'s, due to lack of sufficient equipment or personnel for adequate protection from attack
by air or sea. (footnote)] In addition, weather reports covering sea,
precipitation, visibility, wind direction and velocity were sent at
least three times daily.

A third observation post was established on the German-held
island of Elba at direct AFHQ request. In December an SI team
was clandestinely infiltrated and maintained on the summit of
Mount Cappane, the westernmost peak on Elba, overlooking the
harbor of Porto Ferraio. Reports were sent by line-of-sight radio
direct to Bastia, and covered not only ship movements but conditions on the Island. The team was detected by the Germans after
six weeks but was successfully withdrawn on 1 February.

The O.P.'s were raided repeatedly by German assault groups
and strafed by enemy planes. Off Capraia, a MAS boat bringing
new equipment was sunk by mines planted within the harbor during a German attack of 20 February 1944. A strong German force
overwhelmed the small garrison on Gorgona on 27 March, but
withdrew after destroying the semaphore station. OSS casualties
were two killed and three wounded. The O.P. was abandoned but
soon ordered reoccupied at AFHQ request and maintained until
after the Allied capture of Elba in June.

Reconnaissance and small-scale attacks on coastal installations
were carried out by OG units. In October, November and December, a series of feints were ordered by G-3, AFHQ to draw fire
from enemy coastal defenses and to simulate commando landings
along the Italian coast south of Livorno, in order to give the impression of Allied interest in the region. Three such operations
were completed between 28 October and 5 December. [This is a
very rare admission on the part of either American or British gov-

ernments that special forces were used as live bait during World War II. By June 1944 such tactics had become routine, but aware that nobody likes to be sacrificed in some larger scheme, cover targets were always given to the troops involved so that they would think that there was *actual* need for the mission. The British conducted many such operations along the coast of northern France during the first months of 1944, suffering small but nasty casualties. Their object: to enable intelligence officers to locate real guns, weed out dummies, and test general enemy reactions.]

In an attack on the coastal highway near Castiglioncello on 2 January, eight operatives blew a stone bridge near the shore. Air reconnaissance the next day showed the bridge damaged and probably unsafe for traffic.

An American pilot was forced down on the Island of Pianosa later that month. Two OG reconnaissances explored the northern tip of the Island, and a joint OG-French raiding group of 150 men overran the bulk of the Island in a night attack in March, capturing prisoners (not including the pilot) before withdrawing.

A final amphibious raid by an entire OG section in late March 1944 was the GINNY mission, ordered as part of Operation *STRANGLE* [a very large-scale air operation to cut the two German armies facing the Anglo-American army group in Italy off from their reserves, supplies, and from Germany] to cut the coastal rail line south of Spezia. GINNY, consisting of fifteen operatives, was landed successfully, but the passage of German coastwise convoys forced the PT's to leave the pinpoint. The difficulty of the terrain delayed the mission, and it was discovered and captured by the Germans the next day. After "special" interrogation, [they revealed details on OSS explosives and training methods, and on the Allied military position in Corsica. (footnote)] all were shot, even though they were in uniform and prisoners of war. [German General Dostler, directly responsible for the shooting order, was tried, convicted as a war criminal, and executed in 1946. (footnote)]

Meanwhile SI/Corsica placed five strategic intelligence teams in northern Italy, principally in the Genoa-Spezia-Milan area. [Deletion]

The most active team, YOUNGSTOWN, was landed on 18 February. It consisted of an Italian officer and radio operator, who for seven weeks transmitted data on enemy shipping movements in the harbor of Genoa and details of German convoy procedure. The team had been landed with insufficient funds, [in line with an economy move by the OSS/Corsica Executive Officer, and despite the protests of the SI operations staff. (footnote)] and seven attempts to land more money for it failed. The Italian officer was captured but succeeded in escaping.

In April AFHQ sent a high priority directive to secure fresh intelligence on Elba preparatory to the French invasion of the Island. The leader of the original "O.P. # 3" was re-infiltrated. His communications failed, as did three SI attempts under fire to rescue him. Although pursued by the Germans, he succeeded in observing installations and disposition on the Island and managed to escape by stealing a boat and rowing back the 30 miles to Corsica.

SI infiltration operations were carried out both for the SI/France Desk in Algiers and for the Fifth Army Detachment (subsequently OSS/AAI) in Italy. [Deletion] Several successful maritime operations in southern France were completed in winter and spring of 1943-44, at a time when continuously unfavorable weather conditions had grounded all air lift from Algiers for a stretch of four months. The first entailed a successful landing of two agents near Cap Camarat on 29 December. Among the last operations, in June, two agents, who had been successfully landed, radioed from their pinpoint that barbed wire and mines made it impossible for them to leave the beach without detection. They were recovered by a second maritime operations five days later.

Between January and May a series of landing operations, designated RICHMOND, were successfully conducted in support of OSS/Italy. More than thirty agents were exfiltrated and over fifteen others successfully infiltrated in a series of trips to a pinpoint north of Civitavecchia. Many of the agents subsequently operated in Rome while others had assignments in various parts of North Italy. [Deletion]

In May and June the advance of the Allied armies in Italy and the capture of the Island of Elba sharply restricted the coast available for clandestine landings. Upon establishment of German radar installations along the Italian shore and concentration of the area covered by fast German E-boat and corvette patrols, operations became progressively more difficult. German precautions along the southern coast of France increased following the Normandy invasion. At the end of the June moon period maritime operations from Corsica were discontinued. OG headquarters moved to the Italian mainland, and the control of agent chains in northern Italy was transferred to Company D. By October 1944 liquidation of the remaining OSS/Corsica activities was complete.

SECRET INTELLIGENCE (SI)/ITALY

While the Fifth Army detachment landed at Salerno and Anzio to dispatch short-range missions in direct support of the ground armies, SI/Italy was directed to mount long-range operations from bases in South Italy.

In Sicily, SI/Italy had organized few through-the-lines missions and had dispatched an unsuccessful team to Sardinia. Subsequently, it committed all of its personnel to assisting occupation forces in locating enemy agents, documents and equipment, and developing liaison with local political forces such as the renegade Mafia. In Italy proper, it continued its political reporting and dispatched several teams, many of which were unsuccessful, to North Italy. As a result of its failures in both fields, it was reorganized in July 1944 during the general organization of OSS bases in Italy at that time.

Agent Teams. Two SI/Italy agents were landed on the Island of Giglio, the night of 1 November, on an operation requested by the PT Commander at Sardinia to establish an observation post for enemy convoys. When after three weeks no signal had been received from the men, they were recovered by PT boats. Their presence on Giglio had been discovered and they had been hiding from German and Italian patrols. For radio communication the team had had only an SSTR-1, with which it had been expected to contact a similar set at the SI base in Maddalena. The SI officers had not ascertained, before the mission, whether two SSTR-1's would be able to communicate with each other over so great a distance.

After two more months of recruiting and preparation, a series of missions were run by SI/Italy from Brindisi, using Italian submarines or Allied air lift. On 26 January 1944 the first three of these were dispatched by submarine. The PEAR team, consisting of an Italian Air Force officer and a radioman, was assigned to the Venice-Padua-Trevisa region. It reached its objective successfully and contacted the base on 9 February. The other two teams were unsuccessful: one assigned to the Trieste region fell into the custody of the Yugoslav Partisans; the other reached its destination in the Bolzano area but was captured.

On 14 February a team of three men was parachuted into the Udine area. It landed safely, contacting base on 22 February. Transmissions stopped, however, on 12 April, when the team was also taken into custody by Yugoslav Partisans.

On 21 February three additional teams were landed by submarine. RAISIN began to operate from the Bologna area on 19 March. In May this team was instrumental in arranging the recovery of five Allied general officers and an American consular officer who were subsequently ex-filtrated by "A" Force [British organization for exfiltrating Allied POW's, and for deception work]. The second team was captured by the Germans in a raid, shortly after reaching its destination in the Florence area. The third team, LEMON, made contact on 21 March, but its transmission was irregular. Its signals were carefully watched, and it was subsequently ascertained that the team had been captured and executed, while the radio was being operated by the Germans.

On 16 March three more SI/Italy teams were parachuted successfully. The first, APRICOT, opened liaison with CLNAI headquarters, the central committee of Italian resistance for North Italy. ORANGE consisted of two Italian Air Force officers who landed in the French Italian Alps and began regular contacts on 26 March. The third team consisted of an Italian professor assigned to the Milan area. When the Germans raided his station, he escaped and crossed into Switzerland.

On the night of 23 March three more teams were landed by submarine, assigned to Bologna, Milan and Spezia, respectively.

Throughout these operations, [deletion] SI/Italy was preoccupied with maintaining the independence of its operations from any control except that of the distant desk head in Washington. Due to a series of actions which the staff interpreted as interference with its operations by the British, direct contact with AFHQ was avoided insofar as possible.

Political Reporting. Meanwhile, as it had in Sicily, SI/Italy again diverted many of its resources to political reporting. When a rump Italian Government under Marshal Badoglio established itself at Brindisi shortly after the Allied landing at Salerno, a small group of officers joined the Allied Military Mission to the Italian Government. Liaisons were developed with available Italian leaders to obtain such political and economic information on Italy, on the situation inside Germany and on the intentions and capabilities of German military, political and economic leaders, as might be available through interrogations of men recently in close relation with high German authorities. [Deletion] SI/Italy established liaison with directors of SIM. While many of the regional SIM offices had defected to the Germans and the Italian "Republicans," some, including ones in Rome, Bologna and Florence, had gone underground and retained contact with the SIM chiefs who remained with the Badoglio regime. SIM agreed to supply agent recruits to SI, as it was already doing for the British. Few, however, were thus acquired.

It soon became clear that the Italian Government would not be able to move to Rome for an appreciable length of time, and that the interim regime in Brindisi had little to offer in the field of intelligence. By the end of October 1943, only an SI/Italy liaison officer remained stationed in Brindisi with the Italian Government, while other members began to develop contacts with various political groups in liberated Italy.

For this work, SI/Italy suffered several handicaps. It established liaisons with Italian political groups in connection with its principal function, the recruiting and dispatch of clandestine agents into enemy territory. This policy tended to compromise the semi-official atmosphere essential for political reporting. In addition, due to Italian sectionalism, the Sicilian ancestry of several of the SI officers was deprecated by Italian political leaders from central and northern Italy.

Furthermore, informal or semi-official contact with foreign political elements entailed an overt intelligence procurement function, clearly more in the province of trained R&A personnel. Political reports forwarded by SI/Italy might more aptly have been classified as unevaluated propaganda.

[By July 1944, it was clear in Washington that the OSS executive in Italy—despite some strategic intelligence coups of importance and a large number of excellent individual exploits—was not effective. On a cost-effective measurement it seemed to Washington to have achieved little, except experience. This, of course, was invaluable in long-range terms. Peter Tompkins in Rome had, for example, demonstrated admirably that strategic agents could exist and function at high levels in a police state. But OSS's record could not be compared with that of the British or the French services, and seemed incapable of functioning objectively. Its staff seemed always to be allying itself with one political faction or another, and, when such conduct might prove dangerous to the armies, playing all sides at once.

[Donovan came to Rome and began the shake up after he had had a private audience with the Pope. Colonel Carter, who had taken over the villa given by Mussolini to his mistress Clara Petacci, was sent home. He was replaced by Colonel Edward Glavin, a product of West Point and Magdalen. Glavin's assistant was Colonel Thomas Early, whose cousin was one of Roosevelt's oldest friends. Both were said to be political appointments made by Donovan to ensure that OSS survived the war. The real brains was Norman Newhouse, a Long Island newspaper editor and a Jew—one of the few Jews brought into high position by Donovan. SO was given to William Davis, a Philadelphia banker; X-2 went to James Angleton, a thin Yaley "with an amazing capacity for Byzantine intrigue." Morale operations went to Frederick Oechsner, once a Berlin news bureau head. William Maddox, the Princeton political scientist who was SI chief in London, was transferred to

Rome, and he was given Dr. Milton Katz, a professor of law at Harvard. A special SI division was created to arrange the penetration of Germany, Hungary, Austria and Czechoslovakia, and Colonel Howard Chapin, of the General Foods Corporation, was placed in charge. Above all, John O'Gara, executive vice-president of Macy's, New York, was appointed OSS Inspector General. His first job was to send an accountant to Rome to check OSS accounts. He found a state of authentic confusion, but no evidence of fraud.

[There were many changes among the smaller fry; but in principle the team was considered to be able. Donovan went home to encounter press comment about his visit to the Pope—the Pope had received the Sicherheitsdienst chief only a month before. It remained to be seen whether the Glavin team would prove any more effective than had Huntingdon and Carter against an enemy that was at once—despite the assertions of propagandists at the time and since—clever and vicious. To use an Australian expression, the SD and the Abwehr had not yet lost their balls.] [Deletion]

X-2/ITALY

In the Mediterranean Theater, as in the European, X-2 worked in intimate liaison with its British counterpart, and originally acted principally as a complement to the British effort. This tended to produce within OSS a lack of confidence in the Branch's "security," particularly on the part of SI/Italy, confronted with apparent British resistance to the development of independent OSS clandestine networks. SI argued that separate and unrelated clandestine intelligence chains were indispensable to the security and protection of both British and American operations, and feared that close X-2 relations with the British would jeopardize this separation. In addition, the development of initial SI agent chains required close personal supervision by operations officers, who were not at first appreciative of the X-2 system of control through close coordination and lateral liaison between field stations all over the world.

These objections were not overcome until after the capture of Rome in mid-1944, when the relative positions of British and American intelligence were defined, and when the X-2 staff and facilities became adequate to fulfill their assigned OSS functions of vetting SI agents and protecting OSS clandestine operations in the field.

Sicily. The first X-2 station in the Italian zone was in Sicily. An X-2 operative reached Palermo in August 1943 as a field representative reporting directly to X-2/Algiers. His activities were hampered by inexperience and by the hostility of the SI/Italy staff. The latter took strenuous exception to X-2 criticism of the close relations built up by SI during and after the Sicilian campaign with such native groups as the renegade Mafia. In North Africa and Sicily, the part played by X-2 was relatively negligible, and, except for the fact that an X-2 observer had been sent into Italy with a British intelligence field unit, X-2 had no experience on which to base a mobile unit's operations.

Naples. In December 1943 a forward X-2 station was opened in Naples. [Deletion] As with the rest of OSS, X-2 at first received from the military authorities, both British and American, little confidence, and consequently no responsibility for any but minor cases until it could show proof of its capabilities.

Between January and May 1944, progress toward recognition of the unit's usefulness was gradual but sure. In Naples, the principal function of the X-2 staff consisted of assistance in the clean-up of [German] stay-behind agents for the Army, but in addition good starts were made toward longer-range counter-espionage operations. A small group of X-2-briefed tactical agents were put through the lines by Fifth Army Detachment, with the result that some fifty agents in the area north of Monte Cassino were identified and captured before the fall of Rome.

The first exclusively CE operation undertaken was the running of a double-double agent in support of an important double-agent being run by the British. The technique applied here was to "blow" the American-run agent—to have him send to the Germans his W/T signal that he was under control—in order to give the Germans the impression that the Americans were so new at the game that they would not know about such signals, and that, therefore, all German agents who had not sent the signals were operating freely. Consequently, the German evaluation of the British-run agent rose, and they accepted his reports, chiefly because they differed from those of the "controlled" agent. The field experience of handling this type of case was valuable to the unit in its later work, and also won X-2 most useful recognition in Allied intelligence circles.

In cooperation with MO/Naples, leaflets in the form of funeral memorials were prepared, giving the names and identifying details, including pictures, of Italians who had worked as agents for the Germans and had been captured and executed by the Allies. Large numbers of the leaflets were dropped into enemy-occupied northern Italy, and subsequent reports from many sources testified to their deterrent effect on the enthusiasm of Italians for work with the German Intelligence Services and on the morale of those al-

ready assigned missions. By 1944 there were virtually no cases of
Germans crossing the lines. The short-range agents were almost
always Italians who tended to accept the training and money given
them, but who, for the most part, when captured, told all they
knew. Throughout the Italian campaign, a large percentage of the
Italian agents working for the Germans surrendered immediately
on crossing the Allied lines.

Rome. In May 1944 an S-Force, consisting of British and American intelligence groups of both positive and counter-espionage
sections, was formed for the Allied entry into Rome. The chief of
X-2/Naples directed all OSS personnel attached to this Force.
[Deletion]

After the disorganization resulting from the defeats at Sicily and
Salerno, the German Intelligence Services had made use of the
period preceding Cassino to set up schools for training agents in
Rome and Florence, and to send saboteurs for training to Scheven-
ingen in Holland. Valuable information as to the exact location,
organization and personnel of these schools was gained from captured agents before the S-Forces went to Rome. This information
helped considerably in the planning of definite targets for the occupation of Rome, resulting in the capture of 47 principal stay-
behind agents and 17 wireless sets in the first three weeks. [Dele-
tion]

Operation of Captured OSS Teams. SCI/Z worked closely with
intelligence and operations branches of OSS in watching the security of agent circuits in the field. It collaborated on the briefing of
all agents dispatched to partisan areas. In addition, certain agents
were assigned specifically to collect counter-intelligence information. Further, X-2 observed all agent communication traffic and
took direct supervision of such OSS teams as were ascertained to
be definitely operating under German control. [SCI/Z teams
formed to catch, turn and then employ German agents against
their controllers without the knowledge of those controllers are
among the trickiest of all intelligence operations and are admirably
described by Sir. J. C. Masterman in *The Double-Cross System in
the War of 1939 to 1945*. The process is also described at great
length, mainly upon American documentation, in my *Bodyguard
of Lies*.]

The outstanding case in Italy of an OSS clandestine station being doubled and forced to play back for the Germans was MARIA
GIOVANNA. Another team in Genoa, ZUCCA, occasionally
made use of the MARIA GIOVANNA radio. When a Gestapo
plant succeeded in becoming one of ZUCCA's informants, a series
of arrests were carried out among members of that chain, and

papers were found revealing the identification and location of
MARIA GIOVANNA. At the same time, German D/F-ing pinpointed the MARIA GIOVANNA radio and made it possible for
the Germans to capture one agent and the radio operator, together
with codes, crystals and transmitters. The leader, "Corvo," was
away at the time and eluded arrest. However, contrary to his briefing, he had not destroyed any of his back traffic files, which, along
with his procedure tables, were seized.

The Germans decided to play back the station, since all the necessary data were at hand and the radio operator professed himself
willing to collaborate. The first controlled message was sent in late
September after a week's radio silence. This lapse was not considered abnormal by the OSS control station, as the operator explained that he had been encountering radio difficulties. MARIA
GIOVANNA did not have a prepared signal to send to indicate
that it was being played back. [This was an incredible lapse, and
one that is very difficult to explain—unless it was sheer sloppiness
in the preparation of the agent, his wirelessman, and the mission.
SO learned the trade from SOE, and with the British the system—
security checks—was drummed into wireless operators from the
first minute of their training. Without such checks, it is obvious,
the operator would have no way of warning his home base that he
was operating under control or duress, and this, in turn, rendered
the headquarters dangerously liable to deception. Security checks
took many forms, but in general they consisted of arrangements by
which the operator would, if working his set under enemy control,
incorrectly transmit, shall we say, the tenth, twelfth and fourteenth
vowels. The Germans soon learned of this system, and so made it
their first target during interrogation. The British soon knew that
they knew, and so they refined the system in such a way that the
agent might give the Germans his bluff check while keeping to
himself the true check—perhaps the use of a four-letter swear word
at a place to suggest that the field operator had stumbled during
transmission. The Germans soon knew that the British knew, and
so the game started all over again.] The operator, however, whose
code radio name was "Falco," commenced signing his name as
"Falso" on all messages. Unfortunately this was considered to be
an error in transmission by OSS Communications Branch, which
corrected the name each time in the decoded message before it was
passed to SI.

The first message transmitted from the OSS base station, after
MARIA GIOVANNA came under control, contained a security
breach which entailed serious consequences. An agent, connected
to both MARIA GIOVANNA and ZUCCA, had returned

through the lines to report. He drew up a message to inform all future OSS line-crossers of proper methods and routes, and gave the name of a certain priest who would arrange for guides. Thus, the Germans were able to close down the escape routes and arrest the priest in question. [This tragedy—for the priest was almost certainly executed—shows the great dangers of failing to arrange a security check or, if such check was arranged, failing to employ it or to spot it. More often than not it was the base operators who failed to spot that the security check was being employed. One SOE officer was to complain that, when his operator had put in the bluff check, at great risk to himself, to warn that he was controlled, all that London replied was, "My dear fellow, you only left us a week ago. On your first messages you go and forget to put your true check." The SOE officer told also that when, after the Germans had tortured the operator to the point of near death and had obtained the true check and used it in a deceptive message to London, London replied: "Now you are a good boy, now you have remembered both of them."]

At least one parachutage of materiel was sent MARIA GIOVANNA in good faith, but, after about a month, the station began to arouse OSS suspicions. The station was coming on the air more frequently than in former times, details of intelligence messages declined and messages contained an inordinate number of requests for information, additional agents and supplies. Certain personal questions were framed and transmitted to MARIA GIOVANNA. The controlled agents recognized these questions as tests, and managed to answer them erroneously, thus indicating to SI satisfaction that they were being played back.

In late November, as soon as German control had been definitely established, X-2 took over operation of the case as a triple-cross. This was continued for some three and a half months, with the basic object of endeavoring to secure the dispatch of German agents back across the lines. From the post-VE-Day interrogation of German officers connected with the playback, it was ascertained that the Germans never recognized the case as a triple-cross.

It was AFHQ's desire that the cross be maintained until after the winter Allied offensive in Italy. Finally, some indiscreet messages were sent to the Germans which might have indicated to them that an offensive was being contemplated. AFHQ became alarmed at the risks inherent in the triple-cross and requested that it be closed down. A last OSS message was sent to MARIA GIOVANNA in February 1945, instructing it to discontinue sending, as it had been discovered that the signal plan was insecure. The Germans believed that OSS had finally discovered the playback, but considered that "Corvo" had probably managed to inform his superiors of the doubling operation.

After the circuit was cancelled, the radio operators were placed in a concentration camp, and were set free when the camp was overrun by Allied forces.[Excision]

German Intelligence Service "Keys." In the fall of 1944, SCI/Z began the publication of an extensive series of reports, called German Intelligence Service "Keys." These were expert summaries of all available information on the German services in general and on the specific divisions of the SD and Abwehr in the areas ahead, targets giving the locations of all GIS schools and establishments in northern Italy, and lists of all known SD and Abwehr members and of their relationships. These handbooks, periodically revised, gave a nearly perfect record, from all sources, in a form usable by the lowest echelons of the army CI staffs in the field, and provided fully cross-referenced data for the use of CIC and British FSS interrogators. In this way it was possible for SCI/Z to utilize the services of over 200 interrogators in the accumulation of still further data from the rapid interrogation of captured enemy personnel.

For these "Keys," considerable source material came from the exploitation of the Italian Intelligence Service itself. Although Italy ultimately had the status of a co-belligerent, all of its services had worked hand-in-hand with the Germans for a long time. X-2 had access to the complete Italian counter-espionage files, which included not only information on German intelligence personnel and operations, but also on those of the services of other countries all over the world. The data, in addition to those obtained from the British, French and Norwegian services, gave X-2 a wealth of information to supplement that which its own units were able to obtain in their short period of wartime operation.

MORALE OPERATIONS (MO)/ITALY

Morale Operations into Italy began in 1943 from the Algiers base. [Deletion] [The first project involved] the establishment of the first MO "black" radio in Tunisia in late June 1943, just prior to the invasion of Sicily. This was "Italo Balbo," so-called because the famous Marshal had been anti-Mussolini, and many Italians believed him to be still living. [Balbo was killed in North Africa, shot down over Tripoli by the guns of an Italian warship.] The objective was to undermine Axis military capacity by promoting discord and dissension between Fascists and Nazis and between Fascists and the Italian civilian population, urging resistance against the Germans and against those Italians who had "sold out to the

Nazis." The speaker himself was an Italian recruited in Tunisia. Allied monitors reported enemy "jamming" of the station on at least five occasions and numerous Italian prisoners of war, upon later interrogation, were surprised to hear that the station was not authentic.

"Italo Balbo" faded out after the conquest of Sicily, and a new "black" radio was established briefly at Anzio until subjected to artillery attack.

In central Italy, where adequate radio facilities were not available, emphasis was placed on the preparation and dissemination of printed material. MO instituted a poster campaign with the slogan "Wie Lange Noch?" (How much longer?) to provide evidence that a strong underground movement operated inside Germany. A series of sixteen leaflets, posters and stickers, using a large "W" as its symbol, was placed in German vehicles, on walls, on doors and windows, in books and other appropriate places, by agents operating behind enemy lines.

The most ambitious program in this field was the underground newspaper "Das Neue Deutschland." This purported to be the instrument of a German peace party the aims of which were to end the war, liquidate the Nazi Party and set up a new German state on democratic principles. Its platform included educational, religious, reconstruction and veteran planks, all couched in semi-religious language. In general, the doctrines of the movement reflected liberal principles which sounded quite specific but which were, in fact, so broad as to appeal to men of widely differing political beliefs.

"Das Neue Deutschland" produced a sharp reaction from the enemy. [Deletion] Himmler's publication "Das Schwarze Korps" carried a front page denunciation of it.

Another MO leaflet was designed for German frontline troops on the Eighth Army front in August 1944. It took the form of a Feldpost (V-mail letter or circular) purporting to come from a "League for Lonely Women." Soldiers on furlough had only to pin an entwined heart symbol (given in the leaflet) on their lapels to find a girl friend. The missive ended with the "reassuring" admonition: "Don't be shy. Your wife, sister and sweetheart is one of us. We think of you, but we think also of Germany."

These leaflets were delivered to the Maquis in France and the partisans in North Italy for dissemination by them. Italian agents and SAUERKRAUT missions infiltrated through the lines to distribute them in forward areas. Three days after the first infiltrations, copies were found on German POW's in Italy and France. G-2 believed them to be authentic German documents, and gave the information to "Stars and Stripes." "Time" magazine and many newspapers also carried the story, believing it to be true.

The greatest difficulty which faced MO was that of distributing printed material, for no matter how cleverly calculated its subversive propaganda, its effectiveness was nullified if it could be traced to Allied sources.

Usually such material was passed to resistance groups or to Allied agents by secret air drop. Partisan units at the front lines could often make it possible for MO to exploit an immediate tactical situation:

> An example of a precision morale operation was a joint PWB/MO job on Italian fascist divisions fighting for the enemy. SI at Siena first reported the appearance of the Monte Rosa Division at the Brenner Pass, and the desertion of several hundreds the moment the train struck Italy. It was made up of Italians interned by the Germans in the Balkans and given the alternative of slave labor or the Army. Their morale obviously was soft, yet the Germans needed them badly and intended to use them on the lines.
>
> I took this tip to PWB at AAI. SI and SO followed the Monte Rosa, and later the San Marco, Littorio, and Italia divisions until they settled near La Spezia. PWB opened up with aerial leaflets; and through a Partisan band nearby, MO surreptitiously distributed a "pass" from a self-styled "Patriots' Committee" inviting them to join the Partisans. (Actually we didn't know whether the Partisans would honor that pass, but we didn't give a damn; the idea was to make the Italians completely useless to the Germans.)
>
> The effects were cumulative. The appearance of the MO leaflets aroused the German suspicions. Kesselring was forced to interlard the Italians with German units he badly needed elsewhere. When the Italians reached the front lines, they deserted in whole platoons armed with surrender passes dropped to them by PWB. They were withdrawn in 15 days.

MO improvised another effective way of reaching German soldiers in a given locality at a given moment. The SAUERKRAUT operations utilized carefully screened POW's who were infiltrated in German uniform behind enemy lines. This plan was first used following the attempt of 20 July 1944 on Hitler's life, when MO wished to post a forged military announcement by General Kesselring to the effect that he was resigning his command, knowing that the "war is lost to Germany," and that senseless slaughter would be the only result of Hitler's Last Stand Order. The usual method of agent infiltration by parachute drop was dismissed as too slow for this purpose, and the SAUERKRAUT teams were quickly recruited, briefed and dispatched. The operation was highly successful, and Kesselring found it necessary on 13 September to deny authorship of the proclamation. Subsequent fakes were equally effective and provoked strong German counter-measures. None of the POW's used in these operations were captured by the Germans nor, so far as is known, were any of them "turned" against MO. In addition to their distribution of subversive material, the agents brought back valuable tactical intelligence.[Deletion]

A third device for the infiltration of "black" propaganda was the CORNFLAKES project, which exploited the disruption of the German postal system resulting from Allied bombing of the railways. Fake German mail bags were made and filled with copies of "Das Neue Deutschland" and subversive letters stamped, postmarked and directed to real addresses taken from directories. These were dropped by the Fifteenth Air Force in straffing missions over marshalling yards and railroad stations, in the hope that they would be picked up as stray mail bags scattered from wrecked railroad cars, and sent on through the regular mail. In twenty sorties, 320 mail bags were dropped.

By the close of the campaign the MO print shop had turned out some 30,000,000 items. An attempt was made to evaluate the effectiveness of "black" operations through investigations conducted among German prisoners of war. Conclusions were that about half the German POW's had heard of the "Das Neue Deutschland" movement; the CORNFLAKES project to infiltrate the Nazi mail system had not been suspected; German troops had deserted in tens and twenties to the partisans all over northern Italy during the last phases of the campaign, and Italian Fascist troops had deserted in blocks numbering up to 400, most of them carrying MO pass notes. The total of known desertions directly affected by MO subversion was estimated at 10,000.

It was, however, impossible to evaluate the net over-all effects of "black" propaganda. Demoralization was cumulative, resulting not only from propaganda, but also from bombings, hardships, defeats and from countless other conditions and events. To add to these, and in many cases to bring them to a head, the "black" propaganda supplied by MO constituted a significant supplementary weapon in Allied hands. The frequent and violent German reactions to specific MO themes and plants formed perhaps the best concrete measure of MO effectiveness.

OSS COMPANY D

On 3 July 1944 OSS/AAI moved to Siena, immediately upon the capture of that city, and on 20 July was activated as Company D. [Deletion] Twenty-eight long-range OSS teams were active inside northern Italy at the time of Company D's activation in July 1944. A total of 63 agents had been infiltrated, not including teams or personnel on short-range tactical operations immediately behind enemy lines. [Deletion]

In the two months of Allied advance from Rome towards Florence, extensive intelligence was obtained at the front from overrun agents and partisan groups, many of whom were recruited on the spot for further missions into North Italy. In addition, numerous key figures from North Italian resistance groups, prominent scientists, engineers and businessmen crossed into Allied lines to volunteer their services. Those recruited were at first sent to Caserta for training and briefing. Later, personnel were sent to OSS training and briefing areas near Brindisi for instruction in parachuting, intelligence, sabotage and communications.

A few early individual sabotage missions were dispatched. EAGLE, for instance, consisting of three American officers, was sent on 3 August 1944 to block approaches to the Brenner Pass. The officers were active inside northern Italy, despite unusual difficulties, for a period of four months. Subsequently, the leader of the mission ordered his two colleagues to return through the lines while he made a final attempt. A supply drop to him was arranged through an OG mission late in December. He did succeed in blasting one section of an escarpment approaching the Pass, and completely blocked traffic for several days. Shortly therefore, however, he was captured and, though uniformed, was tortured and killed.

In September, plans for further ground sabotage operations were suspended at the request of the Air Force, on the grounds that if intelligence agents could be infiltrated to report on targets for sabotage, the sabotage itself could be more effectively accomplished by subsequent bombing than by individual clandestine demolitions operations.

Teams were placed inside enemy-occupied Italy throughout the winter 1944-45. The flow of intelligence increased progressively, and in February over 2,000 items of information were received from teams in the field, covering order of battle, bombing targets, transport, lists of collaborators and war criminals and economic and political data. Teams were placed or reinforced in the regions of Venice, Udine, Bolzano, Milan, Como, Turin, Genoa and Lake Garda.

Among the numerous reports received were those of mid-December which warned of a contemplated German offensive on the sector held by the 92nd Division, new to the front. Subsequent reports of German movements gave confirmation. When the attack actually came on 26 December, the 92nd Division recoiled, but, as the Germans began to advance, resistance groups on either side of the German spearhead attacked the flanks. The Germans, fearing a trap, withdrew. Had they effected a break-through, the entire Allied position, due to the lack of reserves on the Fifth Army front, might have been seriously threatened.

[These results were not obtained without OSS casualties, and occasionally severe and/or mysterious casualties. One such case involved Major William Holohan, a Harvard man who had been a lawyer with the Securities and Exchange Commission. Colonel William Suhling, commander of Company D at Siena, a southerner in the tobacco business, had been instructed to infiltrate an OSS party to strengthen links with the CNLAI. With Donovan present, Holohan was briefed and given an Italian-American deputy, Lieutenant Aldo Icardi, a graduate of Pittsburgh University. At the last moment, the Holohan-Icardi mission was reinforced by an OG of Italian-Americans who were to go into the same area as Holohan, near Milan. The mission jumped on the night of 26/27 September 1944, 50 miles north of Milan. They were received by a Communist intelligence organization led by Ferruccio Parri, a Communist idealist.

[At some stage or another, Holohan revealed that he was carrying $16,000 in lire, U.S. money, diamonds and bullion. Holohan and his party were well received by Parri, who had been having serious difficulties over supply with SOE. With the delay in the liberation of Milan, Holohan's new purpose—his old was to secure Milan for the Allies—was to organize arms supplies to the partisans. This was a difficult assignment, for there were not sufficient supplies for all partisan bands and the Italians, especially the Communists, had shown themselves capable of menace if they suspected that one political force as being favored against another.

[Holohan received such a complaint from Vincenzo Moscatelli, a Communist who had been trained in guerrilla warfare in Moscow. Holohan assured Moscatelli that he would distribute arms, food, clothing and money with regard only for who were fighting the enemy—not the political color of the partisan. Tragically, two aircraft dropped 44 automatic weapons into the hands of a right-wing organization the same night of that assurance. This served to increase Moscatelli's suspicions that the West was arming the right against the left. Four days after his meeting with Moscatelli, Holohan disappeared.

[Captain B.M.W. Knox was dropped in to investigate the disappearance, and it soon became clear that Holohan had been murdered and robbed of his operational funds. Lieutenant Icardi became suspected, for he had radioed that Holohan had been killed in an enemy ambush. A case was brought in Italy and Icardi and his OSS sergeant, a New York Sicilian, were found guilty *in absentia* of the murder. The Italian court heard evidence that Icardi stole the operational funds and then poisoned and shot Holohan, dumping the corpse into the lake. The case then became the object of a series of trials in the United States. Icardi was depicted as a devout Catholic who wanted the right-wing partisans to receive their share of the supplies. Icardi accused the OSS of being pro-Communist, and that the OG with Holohan had engaged in the buying and selling of arms. The case against Icardi was never proven.] [Deletion]

Fifth Army Detachment. The Fifth Army Detachment of Company D had a staff of ten at the time of activation. At its peak, it included forty officers and enlisted men and forty additional personnel regularly assigned, together with another thirty temporarily attached or on loan from the OG 2671st Special Reconnaissance Battalion. It reported to G-2, Fifth Army, for direction.

Until the capture of Florence, the Detachment's main activity consisted in mounting short-range intelligence penetrations ahead of the lines for tactical and combat intelligence similar to operations begun after the Salerno landings. Further data were received from refugees and resistance members who crossed the American lines or who were overrun in the Allied advance.

Agents were placed in enemy territory either by plane through Company D channels or by direct line infiltration. Several of those parachuted had radios in direct contact with the Detachment's mobile radio station. In July, two such teams were dropped to points north of Pisa, near Spezia, from which point they retreated northwards with the Germans, reporting details of enemy movements, supply dumps, headquarters and strategic emplacements. Subsequently, additional teams were parachuted northwest of Spezia, south of Cremona and near Parma. At one time, four agents teams were reporting directly to the Detachment, and frequently answering specific questions from G-2, Fifth Army [Deletion]

Eighth Army Detachment. The Eighth Army Detachment of Company D consisted of one officer and four enlisted men at the time of its activation. It remained a small unit in comparison to the Fifth Army Detachment, with the complement at peak not exceeding four officers and fifteen enlisted men. [Deletion]

The front covered by this Army, including the Adriatic coast and the approaches to the strategic Po Valley, was static and strongly held by the Germans. The most successful technique of obtaining tactical intelligence proved to be the dispatch of carefully selected field missions by parachute or by clandestine maritime landing on the Adriatic coast, with radios reporting either directly to the Detachment or to the main OSS station in Italy. OSS agents joined active resistance groups and were able to give the Eighth Army comprehensive tactical intelligence coverage as far north as the Venice area. In the taking of Ravenna, for instance, the Detachment set up a mobile radio station in the British V Corps area to work directly with two of its radio teams in the tactical zone. The speed of transmission of intelligence enabled the Corps to use the station as a means of locating targets and directing artillery fire. [Deletion]

An indication of the success of the Eighth Army unit can be obtained from the fact that the British concentrated all clandestine line penetration activities in their sectors under the Detachment instead of under SOE. [Deletion]

Maritime Unit. In February 1944 an arrangement had been concluded between OSS and the Duke of Aosta to make available to OSS the techniques and services of the Italian San Marco Battalion, an "elite" corps of Italian naval personnel specializing in amphibious operations and maritime sabotage. A volunteer group of five officers and fifty men from the Battalion was assigned to OSS, along with the latest items of Italian maritime equipment. Included were swimming gear, two-man "mattresses" with silent electric motors to permit clandestine landings, and other assault, reconnaissance and demolitions equipment.

The San Marcos were placed under the direction of OSS Maritime Unit Branch personnel. In May they were based at Fasano, south of Bari, subsequently moved to Falconara, north of Ancona, and, after the capture of Ravenna in December 1944, set up an advance base near that city. U.S. PT's and British MTB's were used alternately [deletion] under British Navy control. By the spring of 1945, the MU staff had been reconstituted as the Maritime Detachment of Company D, and had added various locally procured fishing craft and speed boats to its equipment.

The first mission took place on 19 June 1944, a sabotage operation which succeeded in blowing a railroad bridge along the coast one hundred miles behind enemy lines. A second such operation was carried out late in July. In the August moon period, the first operation for intelligence purposes was run, at Eighth Army request, to exfiltrate agents and an Italian with plans and photographs of a section of the Gothic Line in the Pesaro region. Several carefully briefed partisan guides and San Marco officers were infiltrated and returned successfully four days later. The material reached Eighth Army four days before its attack on the Gothic Line in the Pesaro sector.

A total of ten clandestine maritime patrols on Lake Comacchio were accomplished, several small islands in the lake occupied, and a series of small offensive forays run against the enemy-held northern shore of the lake. By mid-April partisan groups south of Chioggia were contacted and, with the more clement spring weather conditions, rapidly supplied both by air and by sea. Several other operations were run jointly with the Eighth Army Detachment to infiltrate and recover agents and couriers.

CHAPTER 7

Sub-bases on the Swiss and French Borders

Lugano. OSS/Bern's first channels into Italy were established in December 1942, through contacts among political refugees living in the neighborhood of Lugano, just across the frontier from Italy. These men formed the nucleus of the committee, representing the major underground parties, which was secretly established as the CLNAI in Lugano in May 1944. [The senior Allied delegates were Allen Dulles, the OSS chief at Bern, and his SOE counterpart, John McCaffery, whose cover was that of assistant press secretary at the British embassy in Bern. The principal Italian delegate was a Communist, Ferruccio Parri, who had fought Mussolini from inside and outside Italian political prisons ever since 1927. He was, Donald Downes thought, "the perfect symbol of the resistance to police-ism, state-ism and brutality." It was the failure of Dulles and McCaffery to obtain more arms and gold for the Italian partisans that led Donovan to send the Holohan mission to Milan.]

The cleavage in Italian diplomatic and consular ranks, as a result of the fall of the Fascist Government, opened a broad field for the penetration of Italy through official channels. Many of the high-echelon personnel were pro-Allied. Those who were not were either dismissed or assigned to unimportant posts. SIM, the Italian secret service, not only became an SI source, but served as a medium for the release of Italian military personnel interned in Switzerland. Prisoners thus freed were sent back to Italy to organize SI chains, and to act as liaison with the partisans. Several of the smaller Italian consular posts afforded valuable cover for SI and SO operations, and at OSS insistence they remained open, despite initial orders from the Badoglio Government to terminate them.

At first, OSS/Bern was hampered in organizing its activities in Italy, both by the lack of Italian-speaking personnel and by inadequate cover. An American, resident in Lugano, was made OSS representative [He was Donald Jones, a former newspaperman.] Since his status was unofficial, he had periodic difficulties with the Swiss, who on several occasions virtually terminated his operations. Since diplomatic cover was essential, the State Department authorized, at the end of 1943, the establishment of a Vice-

Consulate at Lugano. [This man was Emilio Daddario of Connecticut, an SI officer at Brindisi.] Although the OSS representative could now operate more securely, sub-agents continued to be hindered by unpredictable Swiss controls. But the Vice-Consulate protected caches of arms and supplies and a clandestine press for printing identity cards and passes. [Deletion]

On 28 January 1944, a "revolution" was staged in the Italian enclave of Campione, a small village across the border from Lugano and peacetime gambling center for visiting tourists. In the "revolution" (which was unopposed) Campione declared its allegiance to the Badoglio Government, and an OSS base was established on Italian soil.

At OSS suggestion, it was determined that the Commune should be placed under the control of the Italian Legation in Bern, which by this time was cooperating with the Allies. The Swiss agreed to insure the food supply for the 600 inhabitants. Swiss francs replaced the lire. It was also decided that OSS would assume Campione's expenses until the Italian Government could again meet them.

Campione at once became the base for operations difficult or impossible to conduct from Lugano. In December 1944 a radio station was installed, and some of the intelligence which had formerly been routed through Bern was radioed directly from Campione to Caserta. Efforts were made to maintain contact with the resistance forces in the Como region, using small sets with a limited range, but, due to technical difficulties, the system never functioned reliably.

To coordinate air targets and air supply and to handle the volume of Italian intelligence coming from Bern, a Swiss Desk was established [at OSS] headquarters in Caserta in July 1944. The speed and importance of Swiss intelligence rose sharply with the establishment of radio contact on 28 August, and the opening of the French-Swiss border for pouch delivery. By 31 September, pinpoints, complete with ground signals and BBC call phrases, were on the air supply schedule for Italy. [Early in the war, the BBC established a system of communication with Allied agents operating in enemy-occupied Europe and with resistance movements. After the news broadcasts in the evening a special "voice" would begin to broadcast apparently nonsensical and meaningless phrases. For example, "The cow jumps over the moon at Milan" meant that four heavy aircraft would make an arms drop that night at 0200 hours at a prearranged point 42 miles northwest of Milan. "The apples are ripe and ready for plucking" meant that an MTB would land three agents as arranged at a pinpoint near Leghorn. There were literally thousands of these messages. Their security strength was that their meaning was known only to the controller in London or Caserta and the agent in the field. The agent was usually given a string of these messages before infiltration and provided he had not disclosed them—or their meanings—to anybody else it was impossible for the Germans to deduce what they meant and thereby take counteraction.]

The need for further coordination became apparent with the premature partisan uprisings, such as those in the Val d'Ossola and the Val d'Aosta. While these effected a temporary diversion of German troops, nevertheless the gain from the abortive attempts was not considered equal to the loss of well-organized resistance centers deep in enemy-held territory. In addition, the chief of OSS/Bern desired strongly to shift Italian contacts from inside Switzerland to Annemasse and Campione in order to avoid Swiss annoyance and to preserve the operations into Germany. Frequent border violations, both by partisans and by OSS agents, emphasized the need.

In November it was decided that all operations into North Italy would be under Company D control, and that OSS agents there would not contact OSS/Switzerland except in emergencies or when full information on their operation had been given to its chief. Lugano would maintain operating courier and supply routes into North Italy, but these would be coordinated by a Company D liaison officer established there in January 1945. Wherever possible, patriot groups or intelligence chains would be supplied with radios to report to [OSS Caserta], direct rather than by courier through Switzerland, in order, not only to concentrate operations, but also to expedite the transmittal of intelligence to Allied forces in Italy.

Annemasse. At the time of the campaign in southern France, the extensive coverage of German order of battle along the French-Italian frontier by the partisans and the Piedmontese resistance groups kept Allied forces informed of all German military movements which might have constituted threats to the Seventh Army flank. The PAPAYA mission of nineteen men was dispatched to the region of Annemasse, just inside France, to contact these patriot organizations. [Deletion]

PAPAYA's position was complicated by French annexationist aims across the Italian border. The French resented any potential interference with, or observation of, their plans to obtain possession of the Tenda and Briga regions, and feared that political reports sent out from the area would place their activities in a bad light.

PAPAYA reached Annemasse in the last week of September. The mission leader did not wait for the "proceed" signal, but crossed the border into Italy on his own initiative, accompanied by several other mission members. All were quickly captured by German border patrols and interned as prisoners of war. [Fortunately the Germans did not interrogate them closely. (footnote)] The remainder of the mission stayed on the French side of the border. Like the base at Campione, it assisted the detachments at Fifth and Eighth Armies and the Maritime Unit on the east Italian coast in the exploitation of Italian resistance to support Allied forces.

CHAPTER 8

The Italian Resistance

AIR DELIVERY TO PARTISANS

Air drop was the principal method for agent penetration and the only means of delivering supplies in any quantity into enemy-held territory. Infiltration by sea had become progressively difficult as the front moved up the Italian mainland, while maritime operations on the west coast were impracticable after June 1944. The east coast had been heavily mined offshore and operations, such as those of the Maritime Unit on the British Eighth Army front, entailed a considerable element of uncertainty and, at best, could transport only limited quantities of supplies.

Air containers and packages for partisan groups were prepared at a British-operated base near Brindisi. The OSS packing station, established in Algiers, had been dismantled after the South France invasion and the closing of the OSS base in Algiers. To meet the urgent supply requirements in North Italy, a new OSS packing staff was assembled, and its nucleus initially assigned to assist the British complement.

Air dispatch was effected by long-range RAF planes based in the Brindisi area. Due to the distance from the Italian front, weather factors frequently forced cancellation or postponement of agent and supply operations from Brindisi, despite reports of perfect conditions by the resistance groups. In addition, with RAF planes serving both the British and OSS, it frequently appeared to OSS officers that partiality in priority allocations was shown at times to British over OSS operations.

When weather prevented operations from Brindisi, the Twelfth Tactical Air Force, based near the front at Cecina and in the Arno Valley, was often able to carry out small-scale operations to fill immediate requirements of the Fifth and Eighth Army detachments.

Special Operations Section of 15th Army Group began its task as coordinator of all special operations into North Italy in February 1944. To this Section was delegated responsibility for the equitable allocation and control of airlift for personnel and supplies. In effect, the dispatch of all missions, both for operations and intelligence purposes, required clearance from "Special Ops" whether infiltrated by air or by sea. [Deletion]

At first, "Special Ops" attempted to set up British and American spheres of influence in North Italy and arbitrarily to establish the ratio of supplies to be dropped between these zones as two-thirds of the total monthly lift to the British zone and one-third to the American. This ratio approximated the number of resistance contacts that had been made in North Italy thus far by SOE and OSS. However, SOE had been more able to initiate long-range operations into North Italy, beginning immediately after the Salerno landings, basically because it was accepted as an integral part of the British military effort and did not have to divert part of its efforts to establishing its role in the Theater. Only by mid-1944 was OSS in a position to embark on a full-scale Special Operations program for North Italy. [Deletion] The effect of this was to raise the monthly allocation from the original one for the month of March 1944 of 45 tons for OSS and 90 tons for the British, to an allotment of 142 tons for each agency in August. [Deletion]

In September, all available long-range aircraft were diverted from Mediterranean targets to Poland, in a Strategic Air Forces move to support the underground inside Warsaw. This severely affected the partisan supply program in Italy at a crucial moment, preventing adequate re-supply of several major partisan groups suffering under concentrated German mopping-up campaigns.

In October, a wing of American four-motored bombers arrived at Brindisi to supplement the RAF but weather conditions held up all but fourteen percent of the scheduled 1,600 ton drop for that month. On the few good days, mass drops were attempted, but although increased tonnage was lifted, the margin of error in this method was great and the material was scattered over a wide territory. Out of 223 tons delivered, only 92 were recovered in usable condition. [The first "Air America" was the 885th Bombardment Squadron (H) (Special), which was organized, equipped, trained and commanded by Brigadier General Monro MacCloskey. MacCloskey, who flew fifty missions in support of clandestines, became Chief of the Air Intelligence Policy Division at USAF headquarters, and played a large part in the evolution of advanced air supply techniques to support guerrillas.]

Throughout the winter, OSS and SOE bent all efforts to deliver as many supplies as possible despite unfavorable weather and despite the Theater Commander's order to the partisans to "lie low." Total tonnages dropped were 149 in November, 350 in December, approximately 175 in January and 592 in February.

In March 1945, the American four-motored bombers were moved up to Cecina, where a field had been specially prepared during the winter. [Deletion] With American planes, improved weather, and the high output of the OSS packing station, which exceeded all schedules, new highs were reached in successful missions and amounts of supplies delivered to the partisans. The March allotment of 700 tons had been flown by the 23rd, and 190 more were delivered by the end of the month.

In the spring of 1945, OSS had more clandestine radio circuits successfully in operation and active liaisons with a greater number of effective resistance groups than did its British intelligence and operations counterparts. In the last two months of air supply, the OSS allotment was set higher than that for the British, and by VE-Day the total of American supplies, handled by the OSS packing station and successfully delivered inside North Italy, appreciably exceeded corresponding SOE totals. [Deletion]

RESISTANCE AID IN NORTH ITALY

Partisan bands, which had developed spontaneously to resist the German occupation of Italy, grew stronger and more united after the capitulation of the Italian Army in September 1943. This was particularly true in North Italy, where Italian anti-Fascist as well as anti-German sentiment was at its strongest. Many former Italian Army officers joined the civilian resistance groups and imparted to them the formal organization of military units. Early activities were principally in the form of aid to Allied airmen who had bailed out, passive resistance to occupation directives, minor acts of sabotage, and service as intelligence sources for the Allied secret agents whose presence became known to an ever-widening range of partisans.

In North Italy the six principal anti-Fascist political parties, Partito d'Azione, Communist, Socialist, Christian Democrat, Liberal and Republican, banded together to form a unified resistance movement with headquarters in Milan. This organization became known as the CLNAI (Comitato di Liberazione Nazionale per l'Alta Italia), and was both a political and a military organization. Its president was Pietro Longhi, a prominent banker and former president of the Credito Italiano of Milan. Its military activities were concentrated in the CVL (Combattenti Volontari di Liberazione).

By April 1944 CLNAI had constituted itself the supreme authority for resistance in North Italy, and, as it gained in strength, it assumed the stature of an underground government. Contact had been made with the Rome headquarters of the organization in the winter of 1943-44 by OSS agent chains there. In September 1944 a combined SI/OG mission, MANGOSTINE, was dispatched from Company D to serve as the permanent liaison between OSS and the northern headquarters of CLNAI. Two of the three officers had charge of intelligence and operations respectively. (The team leader was killed shortly after arrival.)

In November 1944, several of the CLNAI leaders (including President Longhi, Ferruccio Parri, later Premier of Italy, and Raimondo Craveri, son-in-law of Benedetto Croce), were exfiltrated through Switzerland and brought to Caserta for conference. They sought a tripartite agreement with the Allies and the Italian Government, to supply them with the funds necessary for their operations and to extend to them recognition as the de facto government in North Italy. They proposed placing into the field 90,000 partisans, and estimated the monthly expense per man at 1,500 lire, which, combined with a further sum necessary for couriers, transportation and the relief of bereaved families, came to a total of 160,000,000 lire a month. The sum was to be distributed to partisan groups all over Italy, according to regional priorities established by the Allied Command, but only to units under the control of CLNAI. This would avoid the passing of Allied funds to unauthorized or brigand groups, and would serve to unify patriot activity.

On 7 December 1944 an authorized agreement was signed whereby OSS and SOE would each allocate 80,000,000 lire per month for five months to CLNAI. [The total was raised in March 1945 to 350,000,000 lire, still shared by SO and SOE. (footnote)] This money would be repaid to the British and American Governments by the Italian Government after the war. No other Allied funds of any size were to be given to individual resistance groups without specific approval from CLNAI.

The Italian Government was at that time in a political crisis from which it did not emerge until shortly before Christmas, when [Ivanhoe] Bonomi became Premier. On 26 December Bonomi signed an agreement recognizing CLNAI as the provisional government of North Italy, which would subordinate itself to the central Italian Government upon the liberation of North Italy. The CLNAI delegates were successfully returned on 29 December. [Parri, future Premier of Italy, was arrested by the Germans one week after his return. OSS/Bern, however, arranged for his release in March 1945. (footnote)]

In the summer, fall and winter of 1944, OSS was instrumental in harnessing resistance groups throughout North Italy and forging them into a weapon that created a major diversion of the German military effort on the Italian front. [During the critical period of Allied operations in France, from May until September 1944, the Germans had two armies in Italy, with several important paratroop, SS, and Panzer divisions. In all, they had about a million personnel engaged in the Italian campaign, at least a fifth of whom were tied down by partisan operations during the autumn of 1944 and the spring of 1945.] In the interior, partisan bands were equipped and trained, and their operations were coordinated for maximum effectiveness in driving the Germans from whole areas and in making German movement, except in large convoys, dangerous at best. On sectors of the front itself, partisan support made it possible for thinly spread Allied forces to hold the line.

As the Allies advanced, partisans were organized by OSS to operate directly in support of the U.S. Fifth Army. This presented certain problems with respect both to partisan groups at the front and to those overrun by the advance. Food, clothing and equipment for hundreds of men were provided initially by supplies forwarded from OSS supply depots. Subsequently, through the cooperation of army, corps and divisional supply units, supplementary standard items of equipment were obtained. For clothing, the partisans were given GI uniforms dyed a dark green. A hospital for partisan wounded was established near the Fifth Army front.

The principal organized resistance group in the Florence region had early been contacted by OSS agent "Vera" of the NADA team. A series of supply operations had permitted the partisans in the resistance group to equip themselves and, by means of their communication with OSS headquarters, to carry out operations of immediate aid to the armies. For instance, an enemy staff car carrying Japanese naval and military attaches was demolished at a road block, and highly classified papers were seized and delivered to OSS. When Allied troops entered Florence, the operations of this group alone accounted for some 500 German casualties and the blowing of seven major highway and rail bridges to impede the German retreat.

On 10 June two leaders of another resistance movement in the Apuan Alps, northeast of Genoa, crossed into American lines and supplied extensive, detailed information on the German Gothic Line. [The Gothic Line was a line of fortifications across the northern throat of Italy. They were of great strength, they were manned by the best of the German infantry divisions still in the west, they were designed by the best military architects, they were built by a hundred thousand engineers and laborers, and their construction was a grave drain on the resources available to Hitler with which to repair the bombed industries and to create lines of fortifications on the eastern and western fronts. The line held from October 1944 until April 1945, and gave the exhausted Allied armies some of the worst fighting of the entire war. When the line did finally break under the weight of a combined assault by the American and British armies, the Germans in northern Italy surrendered, as will be seen shortly.] They immediately volunteered for a second mission and refused parachute training as being too time-consuming. After demolitions and communications briefing, they were parachuted "cold," late in August, to the FAUSTO resistance group, which at that time was reported to number 4,000 men and to have captured 450 German prisoners.

The group operated between Genoa and Piacenza, and in September captured a German courier carrying top secret documentation from Kesselring to the German commanding officer on the front facing the Fifth Army. The papers, weighing over 100 lbs. in their cases, were brought through the lines and delivered to OSS. Considered highly significant by 15th Army Group, they also included identification of German espionage agents in Italy which proved of interest to CIC.

The Germans began a major assault on the guerrillas in August with the objective of clearing Route 45 between Genoa and Piacenza, in a drive which extended through early September. Just at this time Warsaw resistance priorities diverted air lift from Italian operations and it became impossible to provide adequate re-supply. Axis forces cleared the highway, and subsequently opened a second offensive on the partisans, who had withdrawn into the hills. The resistance dispersed after an appreciable diversion of German troops had been accomplished, and soon re-formed on the Fifth Army front along with other patriot groups of the Tuscan resistance, which had remained active north of Spezia.

When the general German retreat from Rome to the Gothic Line was at its height in the summer and fall of 1944, several major partisan groups deep inside North Italy, supplied with communications and weapons by OSS, engaged in open warfare against the Germans, aided by OSS/OG teams sent in to coordinate and lead specific units.

One of the principal uprisings was in the Val d'Ossola, where a large group of partisans, one of whose leaders was OSS agent "Como," attacked German garrisons along the Lago Maggiore and sought to clear the enemy from a stretch of the Swiss-Italian frontier. "Como" had frequently contacted OSS/Switzerland and had established a supply base at Campione. From there he made frequent trips into Switzerland to procure equipment and arms and transport them across the border to the Italian patriots. On 11 August an OG mission, CHRYSLER, consisting of two OG officers and three enlisted men, parachuted to join the partisans, along with seven tons of supplies.

Early in September the Germans were reported to have committed up to two divisions to eliminate the Val d'Ossola bands. On 9 September they occupied the town of Cannobio. Two weeks later, the guerrillas notified OSS/Switzerland that they could recapture the town if they could be supported by Allied air attacks on certain specified targets, including enemy barracks and lake boats being used as transports.

Bern relayed the message to Caserta on 22 September, and on 25 September, the day of the partisan attack, the Tactical Air Force bombed as requested:

> The bombing was a complete success. Landing stages at Luino were destroyed and six lake steamers damaged at the pier. A large steamer carrying 500 Fascist troops was sunk ... the bombing took place at the same time as the partisan attack, the re-capture of Cannobio being successfully accomplished. The partisans are now in control of the whole region to a point north of Intra. As a result of this operation, morale has been greatly raised in all of North Italy.

The news that a partisan operation had been successfully supported by Allied air operations was considered by the Germans a severe blow to their military prestige. They staged a heavy counterattack, and the partisans requested further Allied air support for an additional drive to be staged in October. However, with Allied aircraft diverted to support the Warsaw resistance, it was impossible to comply, or even to deliver adequate supplies. Thus it was inevitable that the German attack should succeed.

"Como" made a final trip to Switzerland, obtained a quantity of Swiss arms and ammunition and loaded them secretly on a freight train. When the Swiss border control discovered the contraband, he took over the train, crashing it across the frontier into Italian territory occupied by partisans.

His operation was embarrassing diplomatically, and the Swiss took direct exception to it, particularly in view of the fact that the smuggled arms were of Swiss manufacture. "Como's" wife, who served as his assistant in Switzerland, was arrested, but made her escape from jail by tieing sheets together and letting herself out of a window. Because of his connection with "Como," the OSS representative in Lugano lost his passport, and his travel from Lugano was restricted. "Como's" departure, not only from Switzerland but from Campione, became imperative, but considerable subterfuge was necessary to get him, via Geneva, into France and back to southern Italy, where he was detained for the duration.

Meanwhile on 10 October the Germans had recaptured Cannobio, and most of the valley was again in their hands. The remainder of the resistance dispersed or retreated into the hills. The OG CHRYSLER team, along with numerous resistance members, crossed into Switzerland. Two key OSS operations officers were dispatched to Switzerland to obtain a firsthand report of the situation and to establish procedure for supporting North Italian operations near Switzerland.

An additional uprising, although on a somewhat smaller scale, took place in the Val d'Aosta, but, before appreciable supplies could be delivered by air to reinforce the partisans, the German mop-up had forced them to disband.

On the eastern end of the front, Ravenna partisan groups were contacted in September and supplied in a series of night maritime landings. A radio, BIONDA, served as liaison between the partisan group and Eighth Army headquarters. Both the intelligence supplied through BIONDA and the guerrilla operations of the partisan group were of direct material assistance in the capture of Ravenna.

On the western coast, meanwhile, another Allied action was supported by partisan action. When the 92nd Division attacked towards Spezia in October, the "Apuan patriots," located in enemy territory, struck at the enemy from the rear, making it possible for the 92nd to overrun Massa, while another partisan brigade actually occupied Carrara. Partisans continued to support the Division in its drive for Spezia, while an additional brigade operated to the north and east of the Division's right flank.

For the Brazilians, the partisans acted chiefly as an advance unit to report German attack preparations, and held mountainous sections of the line on a par with regular troops. At the time of the IV Corps Christmas offensive, the commanding general of the Corps credited OSS-directed partisan groups with having prevented a far-reaching enemy break-through.

Further operations and OG teams were dispatched throughout the winter, and liaison was effected with the major organized centers of partisan resistance. Conferences were held in the fall with commanders of the two leading resistance movements on the French Italian frontier, and a program was outlined to pass supplies to these groups both by air and through Annemasse. The two leaders were re-infiltrated by parachute to their respective groups.

In November two members of the resistance command in the Parma zone, one of them a priest, came out through the lines to contact the Pope and the Italian Crown Prince. The priest had been charged by the Bishop of Parma with informing the Pope of the activities of the Church in the clandestine movements in North Italy, and obtaining ecclesiastical authority for the Bishop to appoint chaplains upon request from partisan bands. Until late 1944, the Vatican had discounted the resistance movement, first because it considered it dominated by revolutionary and anti-clerical elements, and second, because of unfamiliarity with its effectiveness and strength. It was significant that, shortly thereafter, the Vatican reversed its position, and religious leaders were encouraged to support the patriots. [Deletion]

In November the Theater Commander issued a directive to all partisan groups in North Italy to "lie low" for the winter. The extended stretches of bad weather, that had repeatedly made flying impossible, and the danger of further diversion of Theater aircraft aroused fears that it would not be possible to give adequate supplies to the partisans during the cold months, particularly in view of the fact that open resistance groups would have to be fed, clothed and equipped. The effect of this directive on partisan morale was naturally depressing. OSS, SOE and AAI vigorously protested these measures, and all efforts were made to deliver as many supplies as possible.

The Germans capitalized on the "winter lull" by conducting another series of severe counterattacks and mopping-up operations. An interesting commentary upon their respect for partisans came to light from prisoner of war interrogations, when it was learned that German soldiers had to be given special inducements for days of service in anti-partisan operations (Baenderkampftage). Nevertheless, the combination of supply shortages and German counter-measures forced many of the partisan groups to disband for the winter.

Starting in December, however, the Maritime Unit undertook to organize other partisan groups in the Po Delta. The entire Po Valley had proved the most difficult part of enemy-occupied Italy for agent infiltration, due to the heavy concentration of German forces in this highly populated area.

In the Comacchio region radio BIONDA and partisan leaders from Ravenna were re-infiltrated, and a partisan group of several hundred Italians was maintained and operated in close liaison with the Eighth Army Command. Weather conditions throughout the winter made re-supply at times extremely difficult. Nevertheless, the intelligence produced through BIONDA remained an effective and important source both for Eighth Army and, more specifically, for the Polish Corps.

[The impact on the Germans of partisan activity is shown in a telegram of 26 February 1945 from the southwest commander-in-chief Kesselring to the Supreme SS and Police Chief in Italy, the Commander, 14th Army, and the Commander, Army of Liguria. (It appears in the official report.)

["Activity of partisan bands in the Western Appennines, and along the Via Emilia, particularly in the areas of MODENA, REGGIO and PARMA, and south-west of them, as well as near the neighborhood of PIACENZA, has spread like lightning in the last ten days. The concentration of the partisan groups of varying political tendencies into one organization, as ordered by the Allied High Command, is beginning to show clear results. The execution of partisan operations shows considerably more commanding leadership. Up to now it has been possible for us, with a few exceptions, to keep our vital rear lines of communications open by means of our slight protective forces, but this situation threatens to change considerably for the worse in the immediate future. Speedy and radical countermeasures must anticipate this development.

["It is clear to me that the only remedy, and the one which is unavoidably necessary to meet the situation, is the concentration of all available forces, even if this means temporary weakening in other places. I request you therefore to combine with 14th Army and the Army of Liguria, in carrying out several large scale operations which will nip in the bud the increasing activity of the partisan bands in Northern Italy. Please let me have your proposals as to when these measures can be carried out, and with what forces."

[One of the key figures behind the Modena operation was B.M.W. Knox. After a remarkable career behind German lines in Brittany, in which he helped raise a private army of some 30,000 Bretons, he was sent to Italy to raise a partisan army in the Po Valley. By the time Kesselring wrote this telegram, he was not alone in his fear of the OGs. The commander of one such group went in constant fear of his life from his own men and, indeed, discovered just in time that his car had been wired with a bomb. Knox's group was not strictly speaking OG but it operated in much the same way. While supporting a corps advancing across the Po Valley, Knox's job was to cut the single main road in the area. Following the armor into Modena, Knox and his men were constantly being held up by delirious Italians who would not let them proceed until they had quaffed some of the wine of the region, the highly-intoxicating Lambrusco. Almost to a man, Knox's team was under the influence when they entered Modena, a town infested by

hundreds of snipers left behind when the Wehrmacht retreated
before the American armor. The snipers' fire was dangerous and
intense and Knox was caught by fire coming from the belfrey of a
church while on the roof of a villa directing counterfire. Realizing
that if he remained there he would be hit by machine-gunfire, he
jumped through a fanlight—and found himself in a high-class
brothel. He left as soon as the courtesies permitted, cleaned out the
town, and then occupied it in the name of the Western powers.

[There were a thousand such stories which at once demonstrated
the violence, the high adventure and the low humor which marked
this aspect of World War II.]

By March the weather had lifted, and the flow of supplies successfully dropped to partisans exceeded allocation schedules.
Groups that had dissolved in the winter reformed in numbers
stronger than ever. At this point AFHQ, however, desired to prevent expansion of the resistance movement, to avoid repetition of
the bitter post-liberation experience in Greece. Again OSS, SOE
and "Special Ops" protested, requesting instead 1,200 tons as the
monthly allotment. They argued that the strain on the resistance
throughout the winter made it unwise, as well as a breach of faith,
to withhold supplies just when the partisan effort was reaching its
full potential for the final drive in North Italy. The directive was
revised. Recognizing the wide potential strength of the partisans in
support of the final drive, AFHQ decided that there should be no
limit on supplies to partisans in the Apennine area, whose activities
formed a part of 15th Army Group's tactical plan. Supplies to partisans in other areas, however, were limited to 250 gross tons, and
an increasing percentage of non-military supplies, such as food,
clothing and medicine, would be included in supply drops. [In
Greece heavy British arms supplies over the years to guerrillas had
resulted in a violent and prolonged civil war between left and right
factions. The British supreme commander in Italy thought the situation in Northern Italy was very similar to that which had existed
in Greece before the civil war, and he was not so very wrong. The
Communists were extremely well equipped and organized by partisan standards, and their belligerency and ambition for a postwar
Soviet in northern Italy was unmistakable.]

To avoid the difficulty feared by AFHQ, special American Liaison Officer Teams (ALOTS) were formed to assit in maintaining
partisan discipline. They were to enter specified areas and establish
liaison with the local or zonal partisan command, in order to coordinate and assist in operations and act in an advisory and instructional capacity, as well as transmitting directives from 15th Army
Group. In addition, each ALOT was given specific plans of action,

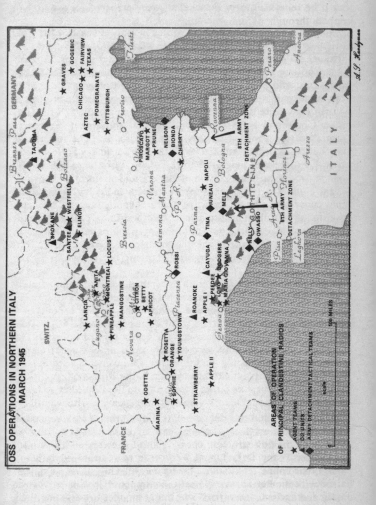

OSS OPERATIONS IN NORTHERN ITALY
MARCH 1945

both positive and counter-scorch [preventing enemy destruction of vital installations], to be executed in support of the Allied spring offensive. But the principal assignment, from the point of view of the Theater Command, was to prevent friction with and between partisan bands. Four of these teams were prepared for dispatch in the spring.

In April 1945, when Allied Armies in Italy unleashed the final offensive across the Apennines, there were over 75 OSS teams active behind enemy lines, working with resistance groups, organizing sabotage and harassing operations, planning counter-scorch measures, and sending intelligence by radio to Company D or to the detachments with Fifth and Eighth Armies. Entire regions in North Italy were actually cleared of German troops, and the German Commander-in-Chief admitted that movement, except in large, heavily armored convoy, was impossible. [The formidable OSS effort is to be compared with the extraordinary SOE infiltration of France and Belgium before D-Day. With these figures, SO had arrived as an organization of menace and stature.]

So close was partisan cooperation with individual army units that coordinates for artillery fire were frequently reported to corps, division or battalion headquarters. At other times, partisan groups established road blocks on German supply routes behind the front, and sent word by radio of the development of German traffic congestion, to permit bombing and strafing by Army Air Force planes.

On 5 April all partisan units in tactical positions immediately ahead of American lines were alerted by General Clark to support the impending Allied offensive [against the Gothic Line]. On 9 April the Eighth Army attacked in the east, and on 14 April the Fifth Army opened its offensive in the center toward Bologna. The army detachment teams were quickly overrun. Six agent teams, reporting directly to the Eighth Army Detachment, were able to furnish significant tactical information to the British on conditions along the east coast as far as Venice and up the Po Valley as far as Bologna. Additional teams were sent into enemy territory both for Fifth and Eighth Army detachments. Fifth Army teams were parachuted as far north as the area east of Lake Garda to observe movements along strategic enemy retreat routes, and all stations reporting to the Detachment were ordered to transmit bulletins every four hours instead of on the former schedule of once a day.

MU personnel on the Adriatic continued offensive patrols on Lake Comacchio and carried additional supplies to partisans along the entire coast from the Po to Venice. Between 22 and 27 April, OSS officers, with personnel from the San Marco Battalion and from SOE, coordinated the general rising of partisan groups to liberate a stretch of fifty miles of Italian coast including Chioggia on the Venice Lagoon.

OG teams, operating in the area south of Piacenza and Parma, organized successful road blocks on the key transport routes in their region and conducted extensive harassing operations against German columns and concentrations.

Orders to the partisans included not only the immobilization of enemy columns but the cutting of potential enemy escape routes to the north and the prevention of demolitions, particularly of municipal, industrial and transport installations. Specific missions ordered by "Special Ops," including orders to march on Parma and Fidenza, were carried out by over 4,000 patriots active in the region. Fidenza fell on 23 April three days before the arrival of troops of the American 34th Division. The German 148th Infantry Division was trapped through partisan operations between Pontremoli and Parma, and surrendered to the Allies on 29 April. Direct support, in the form of a strong road block and sudden flanking movement, was given to the 92nd Division in the capture of Pontremoli.

Allied Liaison Officer Teams and OG's took the lead in organizing partisan groups to cut potential enemy escape routes. Missions in North Italy were not alerted by 15th Army Group for all-out attack until 25 April, and, with the rapidity of the Allied advance, it was not possible to develop the full partisan potential before the attack order. Nevertheless Route 38, leading from Lake Como northeastward to the Brenner, was cut and held near Stelvio Pass and a by-pass route east of Sondrio, Route 39, was closed at Colle d'Aprica. Route 42 leading to Bolzano was also closed. Other teams operated successfully in the regions north of Udine and near Belluno. [During these operations, OSS became involved in the deaths of Benito Mussolini and his mistress Clara Petacci. Strangely, the circumstances of the couple's deaths are not dealt with in the OSS report, but the association seems indisputable. All northern Italy was in bloody tumult at this time, largely with the arms and instigation of the Western powers. During the afternoon, OSS agents Donald Jones and Emilio Daddario, both of whom were working for Allen Dulles, heard that Mussolini and his party were hiding in a villa near Lake Como and that the local mayor was trying to persuade Mussolini to surrender to the OSS. But for an order to Dulles—"don't meddle"—Jones and Daddario would probably have gone to capture the former Italian dictator and his party.

[As it was, they went instead to rescue General der Waffen SS

Karl Wolff, who had been talking surrender with Dulles and was now in danger of capture and execution at the hands of the partisans. Having rescued Wolff, they then ran across Marshal Rudolf Graziani, one of the heroes of the Fascist revolution and Mussolini's former War Minister. They took him prisoner, went to Milan, and the OSS men commandered the Hotel Milano as OSS headquarters, as full-scale revolution raged around them. Mussolini and Petacci, who had been captured by an OG-trained partisan group led by "Colonel" Walter Audisio, were shot with the others in their party. Audisio then called at the hotel and demanded that Jones and Daddario—they had been joined by Lieutenant Icardi, a central figure in the Holohan death—surrender Graziani's person.

[They knew that Graziani would be killed on the spot and so they refused, posting themselves outside the marshal's room to prevent the Communists from seizing him by force. They succeeded and, at the same time, talked Audisio out of establishing a Soviet in Northern Italy. A few hours later, General Wolff surrendered all German forces in Italy, thus forging the first major strategic intelligence coup of OSS history. This would not have come about with such speed had Jones and Daddario not succeeded in rescuing Wolff under exceptionally dangerous circumstances.]

Several widely separated counter-scorch operations were notably effective. An OG unit, directing 15,000 partisans in the Genoa region, interrupted German demolitions of the city's roads and took 3,000 German prisoners. AFHQ and the Allied Control Commission placed great importance on this operation, since it had been planned to use Genoa as a principal port for bringing food and supplies to North Italian cities. By the time the American 92nd Division reached the port, order had already been restored in the city, and enemy prisoners and equipment were turned over to Fifth Army. Other teams in the region between Lake Garda and the Swiss border were directly instrumental in preserving from destruction several key dams and power plants which provided twenty percent of the electrical supply of Milan. One team captured intact a large German communications center at Corvara.

Perhaps the most spectacular counter-scorch operation took place in Venice where team MARGOT, in liaison with the CLNAI, opened contact with the German commandant of the city, and received a guarantee that installations in Venice, threatened with destruction by the Germans, would not be touched, in exchange for a promise by the partisans not to attack or molest the German garrison prior to Allied arrival. In addition, using the partisan threat, MARGOT secured plans of mine fields in the harbor and nearby waters.

[The campaign over, the OSS command behaved with surprising parsimony. OSS had contracts with its Italian agents. These provided $200 a month pay and $5,000 life insurance policy. When the agents came to collect their money, or their widows did, the OSS paid up, but only at the legal exchange rate, which was one-fourth the real rate. When the agents protested, they were told by the OSS paymaster that it would be illegal to pay at any rate other than the official one. This was the first time that the OSS command had considered the question of legalities in their schemes; and the niggardly treatment did nothing good for American postwar intelligence nets among the Communist bands in the north.]

CHAPTER 9

Secret Surrender Negotiations

The existence of an undercover agency provided a logical channel for secret negotiations. Wavering enemy or satellite leaders and groups could thereby make known their desires to appropriate Allied authorities without incurring the prohibitive risk of public exposure. Such authorities, in turn, could probe vulnerable points in enemy morale without the possibility of official embarrassment.

OSS, in Bern and other areas, received frequent feelers of this nature from 1943 on. Acting as a secret channel only, it reported the instances to the appropriate authorities, and in view of the "Big Three" unconditional surrender formula, took no affirmative steps to continue negotiations. Early attempts, therefore, did not lead to peace negotiations or satellite defections; it was not until late in the war that two of these feelers were, with the approval and participation of policy-making authorities, carried to successful conclusions.

The availability of an organization such as OSS made it possible to extract valuable results, however, from many abortive negotiations. In the first place, the knowledge that certain leaders or factions had been driven to the point of contemplating surrender, revolt or negotiation constituted valuable intelligence in itself. Allied authorities could thus gauge the morale of the enemy and the effect of military operations, at the same time finding a basis for the direction of its political attack. In the second place, OSS could, while holding out no offers of negotiation and making no promises, exploit the weakening leaders and groups for purposes of intelligence and subversion.

Several early negotiations were handled in the Balkans. In 1943, OSS/Bern had suggested to Washington that a distinction be drawn between Germany and its satellites in applying the unconditional formula. In November of that year, JCS authorized efforts to encourage the detachment of satellites from the Axis, and high level contacts were developed in both Hungary and Bulgaria. The negotiations were handled from OSS/Istanbul and both came to nothing.

On Germany itself, OSS/Bern felt that there had been a serious Allied over-estimate of the German will to resist. Extensive effects might have resulted from following up sudden Allied military successes with agent surrender missions to enemy commanding generals. Bern reported evidence, dating from the early months of 1944, and cumulatively as the Normandy and South France invasions progressed, of a real opportunity to drive a wedge between the Hitler-SS group and the old-line military forces of the OKW. Full information was forwarded on the plots against Hitler, and on the defections in the higher ranks of German army and intelligence (Abwehr) services. No encouragement was, however, received from Washington to use the defecting contacts to split the Germans.

In the fall of 1944, Bern urged on 12th Army Group, and later SHAEF, a concentrated program to induce certain German generals on the West Front to surrender. General Bradley and his G-2, General Sibert, expressed great interest in this project and gave it their support. A member of the staff of the Bern mission went to 12th Army Group and then to London and was given access to certain German generals who were POW's. Several were selected for possible use in contacting pliable German generals on the West Front. [The principal German officer involved was General Bassenge, who was wounded by German troops when he tried to talk the German garrison in the Channel Islands into surrender in September 1944.]

The project however, was dropped at the time of the Ardennes counter-offensive, and, by December 1944, the opportunity to effect a surrender on the West Front had largely been lost. The Battle of the Bulge was, in fact, evidence that it was already too late to act. The attack, spearheaded by SS Panzer divisions, confirmed final seizure of control by the Nazi Party. Most of the OKW generals on this front who might earlier have been willing to surrender, including Rommel, Kluge, Schwerin and Stuelpnagel, had been removed, executed, or had committed suicide, and had been replaced by fanatical Nazis and SS. [After the end of the war, General Schwerin, who had been in command of the German forces at Aachen, stated that he had waited for several days to surrender the city to American forces under General Patton, which were then only a few miles away but held up because they had outrun their fuel supply. Before he could establish communication with Patton, Schwerin was replaced by an SS general, and the city was defended until it was reduced to rubble. (footnote)]

[Deletion] In November, an OSS team in Venice reported a German feeler indicating a desire to surrender. This was the first of a series of such feelers received throughout the following month both by Company D and OSS/Switzerland. Elaborate requests for conferences were made by the Germans and extensive conditions set for surrender. Late in January, all teams were warned that no terms could be offered except unconditional surrender to competent Allied commanders and that no negotiations could be entered into by the teams themselves, but that Company D would be prepared to transmit to the Allied Command all requests as received from the field.

On 25 February 1945, a Swiss intelligence officer conveyed word to OSS/Bern that an Italian industrialist wished to establish contact with the Allies on behalf of SS General Karl Wolff. When contact was established, Baron Parrilli, the industrialist, stated that Wolff was ready to arrange the surrender of the German and Fascist forces in North Italy. [Baron Luigi Parrilli was a Papal Chamberlain. His motive was a combination of humanitarianism, patriotism, pro-Westernism, and self-interest—he owned a big slice of the industry in North Italy.]

A meeting was held on 3 March with two of Wolff's emissaries, at which it was emphasized that Allied policy required unconditional surrender. At the same time, the release of two Italian POW's was stipulated as evidence of good faith. Ferruccio Parri, resistance leader and later Prime Minister, and an Italian officer, one of the key OSS agents in Milan, were shortly delivered to the Swiss border.

The next meeting held was between Wolff himself, the OSS mission chief at Bern, one other OSS representative and a Swiss intermediary. At that time, Wolff confirmed his understanding that only unconditional surrender would be considered by the Allies, and stated that he believed Field Marshal Kesselring could be won over to this position. He further asserted that he was acting entirely independently of Himmler. [Himmler had been making similar overtures through MI-6, SO and SOE in Stockholm.]

Washington, London and AFHQ agreed to the OSS/Bern proposal that, if Kesselring were prepared to sign, AFHQ representatives should be present. OSS was informed that two staff officers were preparing to leave for Switzerland. [Major Generals L. L. Lemmitzer (U.S.) and Terence Airey (Br.) arrived in Bern under the assumed identity of two OSS sergeants—probably the only occasion of the war when OSS was used as cover. (footnote)]

At this point, Wolff ran into his first serious difficulties. Kesselring had been summoned to Hitler's headquarters and it appeared unlikely that he would return. [Ernst] Kaltenbrunner, head of the SD, had heard of Wolff's trip to Switzerland and had ordered him to break off all contacts there. Wolff asserted nevertheless that he was prepared to carry out his plan, agreed on further meetings and appeared on 19 March at Ascona, a town a few miles from the Italian frontier. At this time, he met first with the Bern mission chief and later with the Allied generals. He reported that Vietinghoff, Kesselring's successor, would be difficult to win over, and felt that this could best be achieved by obtaining the backing of other Wehrmacht officers. He proposed a trip to the West Front to see Kesselring.

After Wolff departed on this trip, a period of twenty days passed, during which he returned to Italy but failed to appear in Switzerland. Himmler had forbidden Wolff to leave Italy and indicated that he would check on Wolff's presence there almost hourly. In view of this development, the Allied generals returned to Caserta. To maintain dependable contact, however, Wolff offered to hide a radio operator at his headquarters. A young Czech "Wally," who could pass for German and had been trained at the OSS school at Bari, was picked from an OSS advance outpost near Strasbourg. With his radio and ciphers, he was smuggled into Milan and lodged with Wolff's aide, Zimmer. One of "Wally's" messages gave the location of Vietinghoff's headquarters with an obvious invitation to bomb it. This was promptly done, and Vietinghoff nearly lost his life. A few days later, "Wally" radioed that Mussolini was in Milan, lodging a few blocks away. He again suggested a few bombs, but asked that care be taken not to drop one on himself. The invitation was not accepted.

By mid-April, the news from Wolff was slightly more encouraging. He was in telephonic communication with Kesselring, and a Luftwaffe General had joined his group. At this juncture, two "agents provocateurs" turned up, one in Bern, the other in Italy where he tried to get in touch with Vietinghoff. As a result, Vietinghoff grew fearful and doubly cautious. Himmler ordered Wolff to report to him in Berlin. Wolff stalled as long as possible, but finally decided to go. This disturbing news, brought to OSS/Bern by Zimmer on 17 April, seemed to spell the end of SUNRISE. It was followed, on 21 April, by a message from Washington, instructing Bern in the most definite terms and from the highest authority to break all SUNRISE contacts. [There had been acrimonious and insulting messages from Stalin about the negotiations and, with one eye on the harmony of the postwar world, which he believed rested with himself and Stalin, Roosevelt personally forbade further talks. Meanwhile, the Italian partisans in North Italy rose in full-scale and murderous rebellion that threatened the Allies with an even greater civil war than they were experiencing in Greece. At the same time, Tito and his partisans in Yugoslavia were proving threatening and truculent and it seemed that the whole Balkans might explode. As the Allied representatives argued with Washington, the only way to prevent this was to permit the German army to assume some form of control in the areas they occupied, until the American and British armies could get through to take command of the situation. Recognizing the extreme danger, Roosevelt soon changed his mind.]

On 23 April, however, Wolff, his adjutant, and Vietinghoff's envoy arrived in Switzerland to sign the surrender, but were informed that orders from Washington still prohibited any contact with them. Wolff, after waiting for two days in Luzern, finally departed, stating that he could not take responsibility for the actions of German or Fascist forces if he were not in Italy to keep them in line. He delegated full authority to his adjutant to sign.

On his return trip, Italian partisans surrounded the villa in which Wolff had taken refuge and made him a prisoner. OSS/Bern realizing that, if he were shot, the surrender, even if authorized by AFHQ and Washington, could not be implemented, decided he must be released. Accordingly, a rescue party was organized to persuade the partisans to free him. This was effected and Wolff, now in civilian clothes, reached the new headquarters at Bolzano on 28 April. On the same day, his two assistants left for Caserta to sign the surrender.

At this point communications became crucial. "Wally's" radio location at Bolzano was poor. Caserta, in the hope that "Wally" could pick up the signals, sent out the text of the signed surrender. "Wally" received the message, but for some reason was only able to decipher the first 65 groups. Wolff became suspicious of "Wally," and the latter's position was not strengthened when Allied bombers shortly thereafter dropped a bomb not many yards from Wolff's headquarters. Caserta repeated the message. Its arrival coincided with the return to Bolzano of the two assistants with the signed surrender documents.

It was now 1 May. Only 24 hours remained to put the terms of the surrender into effect, and still no confirmation came from Bolzano. AFHQ sent an urgent message to "Wally," and Wolff kept promising a reply within a few hours. Finally, in a message which reached Caserta only on the morning of 2 May, Wolff explained that, as a result of betrayal, Vietinghoff had been removed from his command, but that, at long last, the order for the cessation of hostilities had been given and would take effect at the stipulated time, 2:00 p.m. on 2 May.

The negotiations carried out through OSS/Bern for the surrender of the enemy armies in northern Italy and southern Austria had underlined one of the unique contributions an undercover—and hence quasi-official—agency could make in the course of modern war. With OSS personnel in Bern operating under cover, preliminary dealings could take place clandestinely without risking embarrassment to the U.S. Government. At the same time, OSS had the advantages of prompt access to the White House, the JCS, the State Department and high military authorities in the Mediterranean Theater. Moreover, the facilities and techniques of a clandestine service were readily available. A communications net existed, equipment and personnel for undercover radio transmission could be provided, the secret transportation of personnel was a familiar and well-organized technique, and means could readily be devised to procure any special documents or equipment desired.

While the unconditional surrender formula postponed their successful conclusions until victory in the field was a certainty, OSS could gather valuable intelligence through secret negotiations and could, finally, make possible the cessation of hostilities at an early date.

CHAPTER 10

Resistance Movements in Other Countries

OSS joined British services in organizing, supplying, directing and exploiting resistance movements in Greece, Albania, Yugoslavia, Czechoslovakia, Denmark and Norway. (Underground groups in Belgium, Holland and Poland were handled principally by the British with OSS/SO support at the London base.)

In five of the six countries, [an] SO/SOE agreement gave SOE control of coordinated operations in connection with resistance, and guerrilla groups had long been organized. SI, SO and OG's helped SOE to support, and to gain intelligence from, the various groups, in some cases establishing liaison with resistance units which had refused British overtures. In the Balkans, U.S. personnel soon became involved in the internal political conflicts, often disagreeing with British policy. In Scandinavia, on the contrary, where resistance was unified, native agents were principally used, and SO worked in closest coordination with SOE.

[U.S./U.K. disagreements were especially marked in Greece. Here OSS played an important but not the superior role. Such operations as it performed did not add to its luster. It was charged that after the war some OSS veterans had deposited operational funds in their bank accounts. Dr. Henry Murray, of Harvard, Donovan's psychological chief, reportedly remarked, "The whole nature of the functions of OSS were particularly inviting to psychopathic characters; it involved sensation, intrigue, the idea of being a mysterious man with secret knowledge." Some of the intelligence snafus caused roars of laughter at postwar OSS reunions. In particular, one MO officer was sent into Greece to spread the false rumor that the Germans were withdrawing. Soon another agent of another branch of OSS operating in Greece reported this information as "an intelligence 'scoop.'"

[Relations between SOE, which had operational responsibility for Greece, and OSS, the Greek section of which was staffed either by Americans of Greek descent or by American Hellenic scholars, were rarely harmonious. George Vournas, a Washington lawyer who was a senior and influential member of a Hellenic-American brotherhood, would record: "Speaking for myself and my fellow officers on the Middle East, we had no [political] favorites a priori [in Greece]. We were in favor of the group that fought the enemy and thereby advanced the hope of victory. As the fight progressed you would find fellow officers to be for [the Communists] or [the royalists] depending upon their performance." But the British, Vournas believed, "were not interested in Greek liberation or even effective prosecution of the war, but in naked imperial interest.... The plethora of British bureaus [sic] and agents [whose numbers were such that they were literally stepping on each other's toes] played Greek cabinet ministers [whose very subsistence depended on the salaries advanced by the British] one against another.... It happened that [the Communists were] the most numerous and effective organization. Had it been the [right wing]...that, too, would have been undermined instead of being showered with gold sovereigns, unless it faithfully toed the British line." This, of course, was dismissed by the British as the blatant misconceptions of people who did not understand the intricacies involved. There was some justification for this attitude, for the OSS was never politically harmonious, which was one of its fundamental weaknesses, one of the root causes for its political and human instability. History would tend to the opinion that Greece was a British show, that they did well, and American naivete concerning Greek affairs almost caused a successful Communist revolution.]

In Czechoslovakia alone, no large resistance group at first existed, and there was no SOE preemption. In August 1944, according to arrangements by the Czech Government-in-Exile in London and Moscow, Czech Forces of the Interior began an insurrection with headquarters at Banska Bystrica. Apparently no arrangements for supply had been made, and OSS/MedTo rushed to dispatch quantities of its Cairo stocks, but was largely prevented by bad weather. At the same time, Russian forces failed to break through to the resistance group as promised. The result was a disaster to resistance and OSS personnel.

A rough estimate of enemy forces detained through 1944 by these small-nation [not including Belgium, Holland, Poland, and Czechoslovakia (footnote)] resistance groups would total, together with the continuous losses in German war materiel and soldiers, some forty divisions.

GREECE

Between August 1943, when the first two SI agents disembarked from a submarine, and November of the following year, over 300 OG's and SI, MO and SO agents were infiltrated to Greece and the Greek Islands. These were dispatched by air from Italy and Cairo, by land from Turkey, or by sea from Turkey and Italy. Special operatives worked with guerrillas in harassing German troops, destroying vital installations, and reporting enemy battle order. Agents worked undercover in Greek cities, running extensive chains to collect political, economic and military intelligence. They gathered many of the shipping reports which made it possible for the RAF to clear Axis shipping from the whole Aegean. [This is a very doubtful claim. It is far more likely that Ultra, *the* main source of intelligence in all theaters during World War II, provided the information that enabled the RAF to clear the Aegean, just as Ultra contributed so vitally to the clearing of the Atlantic, the Pacific and the Mediterranean. What is also likely is that the Ultra security authorities attributed the acquisition of this type of intelligence to OSS in order to deflect German attention away from their cryptanalytical insecurity. This happened all the time, to Americans, Britons, Canadians and, especially, to the small European resistance movements who were used ruthlessly by London and Washington for cryptanalytical security and strategic deception purposes.] From 1943 on, OSS provided the State Department with the only independent American information on Greek political affairs and the moves and intentions of other powers in that country. [Here, as elsewhere, America was spying upon her two most important allies, England and Russia, both of which had strategical and political interests in Greece. A similar case was that of Yugoslavia. This type of activity was one of the root causes of the interminable friction between England and America over Mediterranean operations, and resulted, on occasion, in England refusing to provide facilities for clandestines entering these areas of sensitive operations.]

Two OSS representatives had arrived in Cairo in April 1942 to survey possibilities for operations across the Mediterranean. In December JCS approved establishment of a base, and in March 1943 the first SO officers for Greek operations arrived, followed in May by the first SI officers. The SO/SOE agreement gave SOE in Cairo direction of SO operations, and SO teams were ordered to use British communications under the command of the senior SOE officer of the area of operations. Since it coordinated air transport over the Balkans, SOE similarly attempted to assert control of SI activities. The independence of U.S. intelligence was however maintained, although SI thenceforth had to rely chiefly on sea transportation.

On the other hand, SIS offered every kind of advice and material support to SI, including all documents from 1943 up to the outbreak of the Greek Civil War at the end of the following year. SIS furnished also money (gold), arms and maritime conveyance for SI teams, until OSS/Cairo was able to supply these services independently. In return, OSS afforded considerable assistance with the clandestine boat service it later built up. SI agents penetrated several areas on which British coverage had been insufficient (e.g. Evros, East Thessaly, Corfu and Euboea), supplementing Allied order of battle intelligence. [MI-6 will not, probably, appreciate this contention; SOE certainly will not. For it is said that Oxford ran northern Greece while Cambridge ran the Peloponnesus.]

Assistance also came to OSS from the Hellenic Information Service of the Greek Government-in-Exile; HIS recruited all service personnel for the SI/Greek Desk, as well as some agents. In return for this, OSS supplied HIS with selected intelligence reports on political and economic conditions inside Greece.

Recruiting and Training. Agents were recruited principally in and around Cairo, although some arrived from the United States. They were mostly Greeks at first, but it was early decided to use Americans to lead the teams. Reasons given for the decision were: (1) That American agents would provide less biased intelligence coverage; and (2) that native agents would find it more difficult to gain the necessary respect and assistance from guerrilla groups.

Initially, agents received rudimentary instruction from the desk heads only, but, by August 1943, a training school was in operation, originally out in the desert at Ras el Kanayas, later on the outskirts of Cairo. A nine-day briefing course for English-speaking agents included instruction in order of battle, reporting, cover, code, maps, escape and security. Sixty-eight agents, who were to parachute in, went to the British school at Ramat David in Palestine, where in ten days they made six day-jumps and two night-jumps. Here, also, they received British training in demolitions, field craft, close combat and associated arts. Radio operators went on field trips to other cities in Egypt, for practice in setting up clandestine sets and operating unknown to the control authorities. Finally, the agents waited in the holding area at Ras el Kanayas, taking refresher courses, pending the laying on of transportation.

Infiltration. The greatest handicap to operations from Cairo was inadequate transportation. Parachute training, followed by the long wait on the priority list of the Balkan Air Force, took months. The question of a small air unit under OSS control was unsuccessfully raised. MTB's were requested repeatedly but never arrived. Of the means available, Greek caiques, which usually transported agents in about one and a half months, proved to be the fastest.

Caiques were small fishing and cargo vessels, from two to eighty tons, manned by crews of from two to six men. The larger ones were fitted with antiquated auxiliary engines, producing a speed of three to four knots. Thirty-six of these boats were at one time or another operated, first by SI, later by OSS/Maritime Unit. The port of Alexandria was embarking point from Egypt; from there, the larger (fifty to eighty ton) caiques sailed to Karavostasi on the northwest coast of Cyprus, where OSS hired crews and built up a large store of supplies. The next stage, accomplished in twenty to forty ton caiques, went to Kusadasi, Turkez, and the final jump-off post was Rema Bay, Turkey, whence the smallest of the vessels transported agents to occupied Greece.

SIS facilitated the organization of this service, not only in the charter of caiques and the supply of the Cyprus base, but also in making arrangements with the Turkish secret police for permission to operate U.S. caiques in Turkish waters and ports.

Secret Intelligence. Between May and October 1944, 30 SI teams totalling 80 U.S. agents left the bases at Cairo, Bari and Istanbul, a maximum of 23 teams being in Greece at one time. [Among the OSS agents who came was Thomas Karamessines, a Greek-American lawyer. Karamessines later became CIA station chief at Athens and then the controversial head of what the American press came to call the "dirty tricks" branch of CIA, Plans. The agents were controlled by the Greek desk of SI/Cairo, which was headed by Dr. Rodney Young, a Princeton archeologist who had attended the American School of Classical Studies in Athens and became curator of the Museum of the University of Pennsylvania. His successor was Stephen Bailey, who was a political scientist with an Oxford background and went on to become President of Syracuse University. They worked well with the British, perhaps because of their innate Anglophilia, a characteristic rarely observed—or at least demonstrated—by the more youthful and less experienced of those in OSS. Later, when Donovan perceived the magnitude of the Soviet threat in the Balkans, which was not until long after Churchill and Menzies understood it, Donovan gave instructions that the new main target for OSS in the theater was not the German threat to the Middle East but the Russian to the Balkans. This caused a wail of concern amongst the youthful, idealistic branch of OSS. There was a very strong liberal or left-wing strain in young OSS politics; when tied to Washington's failure to acknowledge the realities of political developments in the Balkans, this proved dangerous and—the British would contend at the time, and the Americans would agree later—inept.] Of these 23, 5 were performing liaison with guerrilla groups (four with EAM/ELAS in Thrace, Thessaly, Euboea and the Peloponnesus, one with EDES in Epirus), while 18 were undercover in enemy-controlled territory, including Athens, Salonika, Khalkidike, the Dodecanese and Aegean Islands and Corfu. [EAM and its army, ELAS, formed a leftist resistance group, eventually taken over by Communists. EDES was a smaller anti-Communist resistance group. (footnote)]

The only British or American mission to reach EAM headquarters was SI team PERICLES, which accompanied this Hq. from 29 April 1944 almost to the outbreak of civil war at the end of the year. Through its connections with the Greek labor movement in Cairo, the Labor Desk/SI had established contact with EAM and arranged for the reception of three men (one U.S. Army officer, one Greek naval officer, and one Greek labor leader) to act at liaison. PERICLES' principal contribution consisted in independent U.S. political intelligence on EAM, its composition, strength and leadership, its reactions to the Greek unity conferences in the Middle East, its organization of a National Council in April 1944, and similar information of value to the State Department. PERICLES also signalled the unexpected [and, at least by MI-6 and SOE, unauthorized] arrival of a Russian Mission in July 1944, at a time when the British were contemplating denunciation of, and withdrawal of all their missions from, EAM; PERICLES provided exclusive news of the personnel and apparent purpose of the Russian drop, and of its reception by EAM.

Of all the SI teams, probably the most successful was the three-man HORSEBREEDERS, whose leader, prior to his enlistment in the U.S. Army, had been in British employ as an agent in Crete. HORSEBREEDERS was assigned the penetration of Volos, an important port from which little, if any, worthwhile intelligence had been produced. SIS had particularly requested this penetration, inasmuch as it was not satisfied with the SOE agent there and did not wish to compete directly with him.

Establishing himself in Kerasia, a village near Volos, the leader of HORSEBREEDERS established a network of some 500 subagents, covering Volos and the Thessaly plain northward. Recruiting a second radio operator, it provided a radio and set him up on Skiathos Island to report ship traffic on the important Piraeus-Salonika route through the Straits of Skiathos. Using this information, combined with intelligence from U.S. and British agents in

Piraeus and Salonika, squadrons of the RAF joined the Royal Navy in clearing the Aegean of German shipping.

Two other radio operators were trained in the field, one to assist the original operator, and the other to establish a set near Lamia. The job was facilitated by the help of the EAM organization outside Volos, which provided contacts over the whole area.

Some idea of the operation of this extensive undercover chain may be obtained from the returnee report of its leader:

The network was composed of cells. Each cell consisted of about ten to twenty men who were working into a certain area. The organization plan of two cells was about as follows:

Number 15 and number 23 were the cut-outs, that is, the persons to disappear in case of accident to some near person in the cell in order to cut the connection between the cell and central agent and not permit the enemy to pass from one side into the other. In that case, the reconnecting agent, number 07, would help in reaching the other central agent by going backwards through the other cell. The first organizer, number 01, was only to pass on the mail and follow the work of the cell in general. The numbers 02, 03, 05, and 06 with their helpers a, b, and c were doing the main work, and I was corresponding with them and the first organizer. The helpers were to report and receive orders and instructions each one from his superior. A central agent was in each town, where the mail from all cells was concentrated, on the same day of the week or when there was something urgent, and from there it was forwarded to me. . . . Each report had to have in succession the number of the cell, the number of the agent and helper, its evaluation and the date of the information. For instance, 1605b5619 meant that in the 16th cell, the helper denoted by the letter b of the agent 05 saw with his own eyes (5) so and so to happen on June 19th.

In a special branch belonged persons who held positions very close to the enemy intelligence as interpreters, generally to German officers. They could inform us when the Germans suspected Greeks or were going to arrest certain people. In this way we could protect the network. Sometimes they also had the opportunity of obtaining valuable information or dealing with the Germans themselves. In this way we were able to buy secrets and to make sabotage against their army. . . . In addition, to this same branch belonged persons who gave shelter to other members of the organization in time of emergency or when they were passing through their villages.

I answered each of their reports and remarked on each point of information they sent me. I also specified what else I needed and gave them instructions on how to obtain the additional information....

In addition I established five observation posts with which I was in direct touch by phone. Thus I knew immediately every shipment into Volos Port and from Euboea Island to the Thermaic Gulf. Two of the above posts were also observing car movements on the road from Volos to Larissa and from Volos to Almyros and the railroad line from Volos to Larissa....

Agents had been put at all entrances of each town to observe what enemy war material was going in or out of the town. The same thing was done in the ports and aerodromes and railway stations. I had reports of all enemy transportation or movement with exact times everywhere in my area. The reconnaissance men were reporting about the quality and quantity of the enemy war material, and men were sending plans of the aerodromes, ports and every other enemy installation on the coast....

The branch of sabotage also did a very good job. My agents were putting sand and emery dust in the grease boxes of the trains passing along the main railway betwen Lamia and Pirgetos....

It should be remembered that HORSEBREEDERS operated under the advantageous conditions of an occupation, where there is less danger of being given away to the government than in neutral territory, and more recruits available than in an enemy country. Nevertheless, the accomplishments were spectacular.

Every method was employed by the occupying forces to capture such teams. Fifteen Germans tracked down an SI agent at Calchi, took hostages in the village and demanded his surrender. The agent secured his ciphers and documents and killed himself.

Morale Operations. MO meanwhile carried on operations to terrorize German garrisons, discourage collaborators and bolster resistance in Greece. Several media was used. From Cairo, in January 1944, the "black" radio MORSE broadcast in Morse code four times nightly to Greece and the Balkans. The programs consisted of newscasts, interspersed with rumors which MO wished planted, some of which were published in underground newspapers. The cover used for German broadcasts was that of a Nazi wireless operator giving the "inside story" to his fellow operators; for Greek, Hungarian and Rumanian broadcasts, it was an underground station sending out the truth to resistance groups.

In August 1944, the "black" radio station BOSTON was set up near Izmir with the cooperation of the Turkish secret [and, the Germans protested, the supposedly neutral] police. It transmitted on a daily schedule of six ten-minute programs; the voice posed as a "reformed" Greek collaborationist, trying to convince his former partners of the folly of continuing their collaboration. This station was the target of a Nazi sabotage attempt and jamming operations. All radio broadcasts were discontinued after the liberation of Greece and the invasion of the Balkans in October 1944.

MO also dispatched special missions to Greece and Crete. One such team was infiltrated in June 1944 to Volos, under HORSEBREEDERS' care, for the purpose of distributing subversive MO material. The two men printed a Greek newspaper designed to bolster Greek morale, and distributed pamphlets urging resistance. They sent out poison-pen letters, posted fake military orders and spread rumors.

MO originated a campaign to convince German troops that their commanders believed the war was lost and that soldiers should be saved to rebuild Germany. The British had kidnapped General Kreipe, German commander in Crete, and MO circulated the story that he gave himself up in protest against the "useless slaughter" of his troops. When General Krech was killed by Greek Andartes near Sparta, MO's version was that the Gestapo killed him while he was trying to escape to a British submarine; according to MO, he left a letter justifying his escape by pointing out that Germany had lost the war and that it was criminal to sacrifice further lives, and stated further that he was taking this action in conjunction with General Kreipe. This campaign was implemented by rumors, "black" and "white" radio, planted letters and newspaper releases.

Special Operations. SO and OG sabotage was coordinated and directed by SOE according to the SO/SOE agreement.

The first SO sabotage operation was a dramatic one. At the request of the U.S. Joint Chiefs of Staff, following a letter from Secretary Hull, SO undertook to cut the flow of crome ore from Turkey. R&A furnished important information on bridges in the Evros district. A four-man team crossed into Evros from Turkey on 29 March 1944, and walked five hours to the local EAM Hq. There it stayed two months, training and equipping (with parachuted arms) a force of 220 guerrillas and warding off attacks by troops of the quisling Greek Government. Bridges on the only two rail lines were selected:

Svilengrad bridge (Bulgaria): 210 feet long and twelve feet high. Two U.S. officers and 170 guerrillas. 1,400 lbs. of plastic explosives.

Alexandroupolis bridge (Greece): 100 feet long and 45 feet high. Two U.S. non-commissioned officers and fifty guerrillas. 550 lbs. of plastic explosives.

On 27 May the detail for the first bridge arrived at the location.

Our plan was: (1) To place sufficient guards to eliminate any interference from the German guard post of ten men and the Bulgarian post of 21 men; (2) to prevent any reenforcements from reaching there in time; (3) cut all telephonic communications; (4) carry out the demolition of the bridge.

The first step was very easy because the Germans were caught napping and did not interfere until the last five minutes of the operation. They fired a flare and opened up with a machine gun and sub-machine guns in the general direction of the bridge. Luckily the bridge was already mined and we were making the connections with prima-cord. Steps two and three were easily carried out.... After the demolition of the bridge we began our forced march, crossing the Arda river at 0400 hours. There a German post noticed us and notified the reconnaissance battalion.

The next evening the reconnaissance battalion was hot on our trail.... Captain _____, Lt. _____ and the sabotage crew broke away from the main body and proceeded south to get the news of the southern bridge leaving a Greek officer in charge. This young officer after three days of maneuvering finally ambushed the CO of the German battalion and his staff and killed all of them.

The detail for the Alexandroupolis bridge was equally successful, and the economic sabotage mission completed.

OSS activity was complicated by Greek politics. The strongest resistance group was the Communist-led EAM, with its army, ELAS, consisting in 1944 of an estimated 20,000 regulars and 10,000 irregulars. Next was the Socialist EDES, with an estimated 6,000 regulars and 4,000 irregulars. British policy maintained consistent support of the Government-in-Exile in Cairo, at the same time sending military supplies to both resistance groups. U.S.-British relations were complicated by the constant appeals of EAM/ELAS and EDES to U.S. agents for assistance in combatting British influence in Greek affairs.

In this connection, a major SO achievement was the negotiation of the so-called "Plaka" agreement of February 1944 between EDES and EAM. This temporarily ended internecine fighting between the two guerrilla forces and directed their combined energies against the Germans, allotting different areas of combat for the two groups. The senior American officer on the Allied Military Mission to Greece was credited by the British Mission Chief with major responsibility for the agreement.

Other SO operations included train holdups and road-mining, accompanied frequently by skirmishes with the Germans. A total of 25 SO agents entered Greece between September 1943 and November 1944; most of them were attached to guerrilla bands (principally EAM), leading them in sabotage operations, arranging for supplies by air and sea and for evacuation of U.S. flyers.

The first 4,800 pounds of military equipment arrived at a secret airfield on 21 October 1943, the same plane evacuating the first 10 airmen. Using guerrilla labor, SO completed four clandestine airfields, at Paramathia (EDES territory), Neohorion, Grevena (Macedonia) and Mavreli; these served through 1944 as supply and evacuation points. An over-all agreement was finally made for EAM to deliver all U.S. fliers to Euboea, whence they would ship out on OSS caiques.

The climax to Allied sabotage in occupied Greece carried the code name *Smashem*. According to plans of the SO/SOE Allied Military Mission, *Smashem* was to be the final and operational phase of activity, with OG's and British Commandos cooperating with guerrillas to hamper the German troop withdrawal.

Beginning 23 April, 190 OG's, in groups of from three to fifteen, entered Greece by caique and joined guerrilla bands at strategic points. September 8 was fixed as the opening date for *Smashem*, with orders to sever rail lines and highways to impede the German withdrawal northward toward Yugoslavia. One Operational Group, stationed thirty miles from Lamia, near the Athens-Salonika railway, blew up over 7,400 yards of track. Another cut the Larissa-Volos line, causing a seven-day interruption of train service. OG's ambushed convoys and trains, destroying locomotives, trucks and cars, and fighting numerous actions with German garrison troops. They were withdrawn in November 1944, having accomplished the following:

(a) Trains ambushed—14
(b) Bridges blown—15
(c) Trucks destroyed—61

(d)   Railroad lines blown—6 miles (total)
(e)   Enemy killed—349 (definite count)
(f)   Enemy wounded—196 (definite count)
(g)   Estimated killed and wounded—1,794

An unusual SO feat was the establishment of a clandestine hospital in Greece by a dental officer, who parachuted into Greece in December 1943. By June 1944, it had grown so large that 134 mules were required to move it from one location to another. The staff was international, consisting in that month of four Americans, three Russians, four Greeks and two Italians. The hospital cared for, in the following priority: (a) Members of the Allied Military Mission (U.S. and British); (b) EAM guerrillas; (c) local civilians. Following a drive against EAM, in the course of which the Germans burned 127 villages, the hospital provided 800 pounds of typhus and typhoid vaccines, sulfa drugs, atabrine, bandages, etc. This material had been flown in for the purpose and was distributed through Greek doctors.

Between the time of the arrival of the first SI agents in Greece in July 1943 and the outbreak of civil war in December 1944, OSS had undertaken extensive operations, handicapped to some extent by the absence of any faster transportation than the one to two month caique service. Supply of guerrillas by SO, and the delaying operation *Smashem* by OG's aimed at detaining as many German troops in Greece as late as possible. SI networks gathered information on enemy battle order, shipping, rail and other communications, and industrial production in Greece. SI also supplied the State Department with its only on-the-spot American intelligence on the national and international political developments in Greece. Ambassador Lincoln MacVeagh wrote that OSS had:

> ...at all times been of great assistance to me in the conduct of this Mission. In addition, the number of written reports to which the Embassy has been accorded access has given it precious assistance in its attempts to evaluate conditions correctly in the enemy occupied countries to whose Governments it is accredited.

UNRRA and FEA offered similar appreciation. At the outbreak of the civil war on 3 December 1944, extensive OSS networks were well established and afforded the State Department independent American coverage of military and political developments and, in particular, of EAM-British relations.

The German retreat from Greece moved slowly. It began in

August, but did not clear Athens until 12 October, Salonika until the end of October, Crete and the Dodecanese several months later. Four members of the City Team for Athens arrived the day the Germans left, preceding British forces by three days. Another OSS group arrived in November and, by 10 December, there were 38 army and civilian personnel in Greece plus 6 men maintaining a supply base on the Island of Elba.

Control of Greek operations was transferred to OSS/Athens, and the advance bases at Izmir (Turkey), Edirne (Turkey) and Bari (Italy) were disbanded. SO, MO and OG personnel left for operational activities elsewhere in Europe or in the Far East. Meanwhile, the total of ninety SI personnel still in Greece was cut sharply. Eight teams were maintained in territories held by the two main rival guerrilla groups, ELAS and EDES. A ninth team made a one-month photographic tour in November, covering war damage, German atrocities and general economic conditions. Finally, the base office in Athens acquired SI, X-2, R&A and Services personnel. Thirty-three OSS representatives were thus in Greece itself at the outbreak of Civil W/r on 3 December 1944.

The Civil War lasted about two months, with the British forces, supported to some extent by small Royalist and EDES groups, beating back the Communist-led army of the EAM.

OSS maintained eight teams in the field, five in EAM-controlled territory, one in EDES territory, and one each in Salonika and Patras, cities whose control was disputed. OSS team PERICLES provided the only Allied liaison with EAM headquarters. Carrying messages to and from EAM leaders and reports of political and military developments, the leader of PERICLES crossed the lines in civilian clothes almost daily. The other field teams were cut off from pouch communication with Athens and depended on W/T alone. Although OSS agents tended to support whichever faction they accompanied, the resultant bias did not approach that of the reports by the participants. Since General Sir Ronald Scobie would not permit war correspondents to interview EAM leaders, even in the presence of British officers, OSS provided the only independent coverage of the Civil War.

An OSS team was further instrumental in the evacuation of 965 British prisoners in EAM hands. In late December this team located the group near Lamia without adequate food, clothing or medical care. The team obtained EAM permission for the parachutage of supplies by RAF planes to the prison camp. On 20 January, the OSS officers brought two representatives of EAM to Athens for conference with the British concerning an exchange of prisoners.

At this conference, EAM refused the services of the International Red Cross (although this organization received public credit for the operation), and consented only to allow OSS officers to make arrangements for the delivery of the prisoners at an exchange point at Volos. On 23 January, the OSS party of three officers entered EAM territory with a British convoy of fifty trucks and nine ambulances, and by 24 January the evacuation had begun.

In Athens, meanwhile, the City Team operated under unusual difficulties. An R&A analyst reported:

> During the first week the combination office-billet was situated a half block from the front lines. After the British managed to extend the area of their control, the front was pushed away from the office another block and a half. However, with a British-Greek police machine gun, which fired through the day and night, next door, and Greek militia barracks and a main military thoroughfare, which were targets for ELAS mortar shells, one-half block behind the office, there were few days when quiet prevailed enough to concentrate on a long report.

Despite these difficulties, OSS continued to service the State Department, Foreign Economic Administration and U.S. General Sadler of ML (Greece). Selected reports were also forwarded to the British intelligence services.

Following the cessation of hostilities, OSS personnel was further decreased to 23 members. This allowed for a base staff at Athens, and for three two-man teams, complete with W/T sets, to cover the Greek-Yugoslav border. In June, one field operative was murdered by agents of the Okhrana (a movement for Macedonian autonomy). Trips by Athens personnel further augmented OSS coverage of Greece, Cret and the Dodecanese. An R&A representative maintained contacts with leaders of the Popular Party, Populists, Liberal Party and the Socialist ELD-SKE, and with various members of the cabinet.

A three-man X-2 unit had been working with the British and Royal Hellenic security services since October. At the time the Civil War broke out, these had formed an Anglo-American advance base in Salonika· arresting German agents and collecting German sabotage and W/T equipment. To avoid involvement in the Civil War, these men returned to Athens in December, but continued their cooperation with British SIME and ISLD after hostilities ceased.

The main cells of the Abwehr sabotage section (IIH) had been left at Athens and Salonika to run some 120 agents in post-occupation sabotage and resistance. X-2 and the British identified the complete enemy group: seventy agents were apprehended; six more were killed; twenty-five left Greece and were traced to their hideouts elsewhere; four defected to the Allies; and ten served as controlled informers for the identification of like infiltrators. Several caches of wireless and sabotage equipment were uncovered. Two groups of parachutists, totalling 26 men, were rounded up and their equipment taken. Up to the termination of OSS in October 1945, no single enemy sabotage plan had been successfully effected.

X-2 also serviced other U.S. agencies, vetting Embassy employees, World War II pension applicants, Greeks in the American merchant marine, ML and ATC personnel, and applicants for visas to the United States. It cooperated with the State Department in studies of economic collaboration for the "Safe Haven" project.

OSS/Athens was also busied with the problem of agent release. Every step was taken to recompense the Greek agents. Death benefits were obtained for the next of kin of four Greeks killed in OSS service. Some 74 certificates were distributed. One hundred and seventy-six names were given to Hellenic Intelligence. OSS helped several of its former agents and sub-agents to find employment.

In the light of the new July [1944] budget [which reduced OSS appropriations from some $50 million to $10 million], personnel was again decreased, this time to a total of thirteen, with one roving SI team (plus W/T), and two SI, one R&A, and three X-2 representatives in Athens. All communications were handled through the Embassy.

YUGOSLAVIA

Fifteen Reichswehr divisions, aided by some 100,000 well-armed native occupation troops, were detailed to maintain order in Yugoslavia against the large-scale resistance activities. It was of importance to Allied forces in Italy, confronted by twenty-six German divisions, that the fifteen in Yugoslavia remain there. SO teams, with OG aid, joined British forces in effecting military supply of resistance groups by sea and by air, while SO and SI liaison officers attached to guerrilla units radioed enemy battle order, bombing targets and other strategic intelligence to bases in Bari and Cairo.

[From the start, Yugoslavia was a highly-charged, most complicated affair that often seemed to defy definition. Donovan himself was caught in its meshes from his first association with the country —early in 1941 when, as the President's agent, he was in Belgrade to urge Yugoslavian leaders to resist Berlin and support London. Only a few days after he left the city, those same leaders revolted against the Berlin-faction, which was leading the country into the German camp. The revolution was organized by Menzies of MI-6 at Churchill's orders and led to the massive aerial bombardment of the capital by the Luftwaffe. It is said that 17,000 people perished in this attack. The fact that Donovan had been in Belgrade so soon before the coup d'etat led to Isolationist charges in America that Donovan had organized the revolution on behalf of the White House.]

U.S. officers were recruited in Washington and Cairo to act as uniformed liaison with units of the Partisan (Tito) and Chetnik (Mihailovich) [also spelled Mihailovic] resistance groups. They parachuted from Balkan Air Force (British) planes and were received by British groups already operating with the resistance. Trained in SO, they were to lead guerrillas in the destruction of strategic installations.

Arrival in the field soon showed that the Partisans already had efficient officers (many of them Communist), not disposed to U.S. leadership, and desirous only of the weapons to work with. The SO men became in effect intelligence officers and were instructed to send in enemy battle order, economc information, and political and military intelligence on the resistance.

Lack of SI training was evident on political and economic reporting. In general, the SO officers had little conception of economic intelligence, and sent none. Their political appreciations compared unfavorably with those prepared by their British colleagues. Understandably, they usually supported the groups they were living and fighting with. Liaison officers with the Chetniks favored the Chetniks, while those with the Partisans supported the Partisans. Even more unreliable were agents of Yugoslav descent, who usually were predisposed to one side or the other and reported the situation in moral black and white. [This, of course, was the inevitable consequence of clandestine service with one side or another in dangerous circumstances behind enemy lines—one's life depended upon one's loyalty and, as often, upon one's beliefs.]

But military intelligence was valuable. The Partisans at first knew little of battle order reporting and needed the aid of OSS liaison officers to build up efficient and widespread intelligence units with each Partisan Corps.

The first officers were flown from Cairo and parachuted 18 August and 22 August 1943, to the headquarters of Mihailovich and Tito, respectively. As in Greece, both were SO officers attached to the British missions already there and had to use SOE communications and SOE code.

[Major Linn Farish, an Olympic competitor while at Stanford and an oil geologist by profession, went to Tito's headquarters; Walter Mansfield, newly graduated from Harvard Law School and a future Federal Court judge in New York City, went to see Mihailovic. Mansfield was reinforced later—in a world of marshals and generals, brigadiers and colonels, he was only a lieutenant—by Colonel Albert Seitz, an engineer from West Point who had served with the Royal Canadian Mounted Police. Seitz was never in doubt about his position. He was there, he would state, to give the appearance of reality to the illusion that this was a joint Anglo-American political expedition. The show was British, he said, and the whole show would remain British. So that nobody slipped a few words to Mihailovic, the British contingent commander insisted that everybody speak English, that nobody speak French—until this moment the language of diplomacy. Moreover, dependent upon British wireless for their communications, they were not able to communicate their real impressions about Mihailovic until they had been rendered obsolete by Churchill's and Roosevelt's decision to back Tito and to abandon Mihailovic to his fate.

[Donovan, angered by British blocking measures, and disposed to support both Tito and Mihailovic on the grounds that both were strategic factors in the war with Germany, decided to launch his own, independent mission. As we shall see, he escaped the limits placed on SO activity in the various agreements with SOE by a neat little bureaucratic trick. He transferred the SO men who were going into Yugoslavia to the staff of SI; and since SI was not covered by the accords with SOE, they could, at least in Yugoslavia, carry their own wirelesses.

[Meanwhile the Farish-Seitz missions were endangered by an act of OSS idealism that might have resulted in Mansfield being brought before a Mihailovic firing squad. The central figure was Major Louis Huot, an OSS officer who had been a reporter in Europe for the Chicago *Tribune*, formed a high regard for Tito in September 1943 and, quite without his government's authority, planned and launched a maritime operation to supply arms, ammunition, food and gold to Tito's forces. Huot is supposed to have sent in over 400 tons of such equipment and supplies—more than had been officially supplied to Tito by the U.S. and U.K. governments—before he was caught. Huot was merely transferred out of the theater and his accomplices placed under house arrest.

[What was dangerous about this exploit was that at the time Huot was smuggling, neither Britain nor America had made up its mind which side it must support; and neither did Huot know any better. Huot was, it seems, guided entirely by his personal political beliefs, which were what the Americans call "liberal." The danger was—and it was very real—that Mihailovic might have interpreted Huot's smuggling as a hostile act authorized by the U.S. government, and acted accordingly against Mansfield—after all, Mihailovic and Tito were fighting a war between themselves. Moreover, it was precisely this type of misuse of authority that made the British so reluctant to permit OSS to work in certain areas of politically complicated trouble.]

Using British facilities meant British control plus unnecessary delay in transmission of messages. However, the agreements signed in London in June 1942 between SO and SOE gave the latter the right to coordinate SO activity in the area. Furthermore, the British in Cairo controlled air transportation to the Balkans, and had the network in the field which must arrange for the arrival of new agents. Considering, perhaps, that their own organization was successfully carrying out the job required, or for other reasons, they opposed any independent SI operations in Yugoslavia—the Americans would be under British command in the field and would have to remain at base in order to wire through British radio. SO teams arrived successfully, once having agreed to use SOE communications, while SI teams found it difficult to obtain air priority from the (British) Balkans Air Force.

Donovan's trip to Cairo in November 1943 established the right of U.S. operatives in the Balkans to independent communication. Later, [deletion] in September, command of OSS teams in the field was transferred from the British Military Mission to the Independent American Military Mission to Marshal Tito.

On 26-27 December 1943 the first two OSS/Yugoslavia teams (ALUM and AMAZON) to carry their own radios were dispatched to Slovenia by SI. Faulty navigation resulted in the parachutage of three of the seven men directly into a camp of White Guards (pro-Axis native troops). Fortunately, the White Guards concluded that an Allied air invasion was upon them, and the three were able to make a quick retreat, returning later at considerable personal danger to retrieve their secret code books.

ALUM sent in volumes of intelligence collected by the two teams. While the political information lacked balance (the leader

of ALUM was of Yugoslav descent and 100% pro-Partisan), the
military reporting was excellent. Locations of anti-aircraft fields,
[fighter] fields and locator points in Slovenia were cabled out. Battery sites, gun calibres and serial numbers were given. [OSS
learned from MI-6 that all agents should be instructed, whenever
possible, to obtain the serial numbers of such military equipment
as airframes, aeroengines, artillery pieces, tanks, heavy machine
guns, radar and wireless sets. This information was to be sent to
MI-6 London, where a young British scientist of great ability, Dr.
R. V. Jones, had worked out a system of assessing German production capacity based upon serial numbers. The system proved
remarkably accurate not only in order of battle intelligence but also in strategic intelligence matters such as the function of the Peenemünde missile establishment on the Baltic. Jones already suspected that Peenemünde existed as part of a German missile program,
but to prove the point he had to establish whether certain types of
advanced radar were being used there. This he was able to do by
matching the serial numbers of radar equipment captured in Tunisia at the end of the North African campaign with serial numbers
of advanced radar equipment obtained from Ultra intercepts.
When the sequence was obtained satisfactorily, Jones and his colleagues in the MI-6 scientific branch had only to go and look at the
captured equipment to be able to form an idea of the performance
of the new missiles—trajectory, operating altitude, speed, etc.]
From a captured German, the men obtained the complete AA and
locator system of southern Austria. They worked out two safe
flight paths, one northeast to Wiener-Neustadt, and the other
northwest toward Munich.

During 1944 the group expanded to fourteen men, a fifteenth being killed when his parachute failed to open.

A spectacular achievement was the crossing of an advance section of the group, consisting of one American and two Partisans,
over the border of the Greater Reich. Arriving on 23 June 1944,
the section survived 44 days. The men constructed a bunker of
logs, cut by themselves, on the side of a hill overlooking the main
rail line from Zidani Most to Ljubljana. Transmitter, battery and
pedal generator were installed underground and the whole camouflaged, so that it was invisible from ten yards. Villagers, contacted
by the Partisans, left food baskets nearby twice a day. Railroad
workers turned in daily manifests of traffic on the line and also on
the Zidani Most-Maribor line.

A railroad guard discovered them, and they moved several
times, continuing to transmit daily railroad intelligence. After 5

August 1944, they were not heard from.

SO's and OG's worked together with British forces to supply the Partisans. Following the Italian surrender in September 1943, Tito's forces had advanced and occupied the whole Dalmatian coast, opened up the port of Split and appealed for an Allied landing and/or military aid. On 5 October, a mission from Tito arrived at Algiers and was contacted by members of the Yugoslav Desk from Cairo. On 11 October, one of the Americans reconnoitered Vis Island (where the Partisans proposed to unload military supplies), in a Royal Navy gunboat provided by the Allied Naval Command and camouflaged as a fishing smack. On 15 October, at OSS initiative, the first load (200 tons of coal), provided by the same Command, left for Vis on board a Partisan vessel.

OSS organized the shipping operations at Bari, negotiated for the supplies and obtained the ships. By 25 October, there were 25 vessels smuggling goods the 120 nautical miles to Vis; and by 31 December, there were 40. These consisted of small vessels owned by the Partisans, and of ships in Italy, formerly belonging to the Royal Yugoslav Government.

Following the German raid on Bari in December, the base moved to Monopoli. [Sterling Hayden, the American film actor, was put in command of the OSS supply base at Monopoli, and had at his disposal some 15 schooners, supplied by the OSS Maritime Unit at Cairo, of which a Wrigley's chewing gum executive was commanding officer.] Normally the ships left Monopoli at daybreak and arrived at a checking station at Manfredonia at 2000. Here they lay until 1300 the following day. The Italian Adriatic could be traversed by daylight. By nightfall the ships would enter the danger zone, and by 0300 be at Vis, in time to be camouflaged before daybreak brought German air reconnaissance.

In January 1944 the British, who had contributed all the military supplies, took over the operation. During the period of OSS direction, the following had been accomplished:

Number of loaded ships sailed from
  Italy 155
Total tonnage shipped . . . . 11,637 tons
Partisan troops shipped 2,000
Partisan wounded evacuated 700
Partisan refugees evacuated 20,000
Number of ships repaired and
  operated 44

It is estimated these supplies made possible the activation of 30,000 guerrillas. Two thousand Yugoslav guerrillas were equipped in Italy and shipped into Yugoslavia.

On 20 December the Germans diverted three divisions (the 1 Mountain, 114 Light and 755 Infantry Divisions) to clean up the coastal activity. They recaptured all the Dalmatian Islands but Vis, which was defended by a large force of Partisans, British Commandos, and 211 OSS OG's. Fifteenth Air Force bombings of Mostar Island and of the ports of Zara and Fiume assisted its defense. The holding action was intended to maintain the flow of material, but the three Reichswehr divisions directed against the supply line closed off the coast.

OG's and Commandos remained to harass enemy forces on other Dalmatian Islands and to obtain enemy battle order there and on the coast. [Deletion]

A typical attack was that on Solta Island, carried out by a force of 600 troops, principally Commandos, but including an OG detachment of 150. A landing on the southern coast was effected from LCI's [landing craft, infantry] at 2400. Troops proceeded to move into position around the town of Grohote under cover of darkness. Due to the extremely difficult terrain, positions were not taken up until 0600 and the presence of Allied troops was prematurely disclosed to the enemy, who opened fire. Troops moved up under fire to assault positions, and at 0700 the RAF dive-bombed the town with P-40's, according to plan. The bombing accomplished its purpose of softening up resistance, the enemy was attacked and the town taken. The enemy garrison of approximately 110 men was killed or captured. American casualties were one killed and five slightly wounded.

This and other operations were commanded by the much larger British force, and served mainly as initiation for the OG's in preparation for action in Greece, Italy, France, Norway and the Far East. The Group was withdrawn in July 1944 upon the retreat of German occupation troops.

Meanwhile, on the mainland, the U.S. network in Partisan country spread. Along with its British counterpart, the Yugoslav Desk had moved, at the time of the shipping operation in October 1943, from Cairo to Bari. There Serbo-Croatian-speaking agents could be recruited in greater numbers than in Cairo. A training school was established. In April, control of OSS operations in Yugoslavia and Central Europe, was transferred from Cairo to [Caserta].

By October 1944, forty OSS officers and men were running fifteen intelligence teams, attached to the various corps of the Partisan army. Intelligence included daily battle order cables, with map locations of important targets. The teams served as liaison to coordinate air attacks with Partisan operations.

In December 1943, the two-man Air Section had moved up from Cairo to Bari to take over the job of transmitting Partisan bombing requests to the Fifteenth U.S. Air Force. Since targets were cabled without integration from American and British officers accompanying all Partisan corps, some priority system was necessary. Conference with Marshal Tito's representative in Bari produced a decision to use only those bomb requests approved by him. Target bombing in support of Partisan offensives commenced in late March 1944, and, besides offering tactical assistance, served to raise Partisan morale.

The Fifteenth Air Force was of considerable assistance to the Partisans in late May. The Germans attacked Tito's Hq. at Drvar on 25 May, with glider troops landing in the area itself, and with armored columns closing in on all sides. [The Germans seem to have been as mystified about Tito as were the British and the Americans before they met him. For a time the German intelligence services reported that he did not exist at all, that Tito was the name of a group of partisan leaders. In another notable and widely-circulated dispatch it was reported that Tito was a woman. When the Germans attacked Tito's headquarters, they were confused even further. Under the codename Rosselsprung (Knight's Move), the Germans landed on Tito's birthday, hoping no doubt to catch him carousing unawares. For a time Tito was trapped, but cut a hole in the floor of his hut and slid down a rope to the river bed below. All the Germans found of him was a marshal's uniform, draped over a dummy. The British and Russian officers attached to Tito's staff helped him escape through forests, and he was exfiltrated to Bari by MI-6.] Due to the surprise of the attack, request for air support was not cabled out until the 27th. On 28 and 29 May, B-17's, B-24's, P-38's and P-47's of the Fifteenth Air Force bombed and strafed German troop concentrations around Drvar, and, on the following day, the Partisans broke through German lines to the South. Marshal Tito noted this in an order of the day: "American and British prestige is now equal to that of the Russians." [In February 1944 a Russian military mission arrived at Tito's headquarters, and from time to time a few Russian planes came over with small loads of parachute supplies. In comparison to the Anglo-American loads, these supplies were minute. Nevertheless, the Russians managed to claim the credit for

the supplies by claiming that the U S stamped on the sides of the
cannisters and bales meant "Unione Sovietica."]

The Air Section of OSS/Bari also served A-2, Fifteenth Air
Force, in preparing a basic map survey of rail and water communi-
cations in the Balkans, and in selecting interdiction points, using
OSS, Photo Reconnaissance and other intelligence sources.

Drops of men and supplies were carried out by the Balkan Air
Force, which had earlier moved from Cairo to South Italy. The actual task of parachuting to guerrilla groups in Nazi-controlled territory was complicated and dangerous, the average experience being something like that of SPIKE team:

> After being recruited in Cairo [deletion] the first of March
> 1944, we moved up to Bari, 7 April 1944. At Bari we expected
> to stay only a few days before taking off for our job in Mace-
> donia.
> We made our first attempt to enter the country 25 April
> 1944. This attempt failed due to the plane having to turn back
> before reaching the pin point because of bad weather. We
> turned back that night and arrived in Bari being greeted by a bit
> of anti-aircraft fire, as the pilot thought we were over Brindisi
> and came in unidentified. We made several more attempts to
> get in until the night of 23 June 1944. We jumped into the Brit-
> ish Mission "Burlesque," headed by Major Saunders. This was
> a bad night for all. Major ____ hurt his ankle, Sgt. ____, his leg,
> and radioman ____, his back, in a fall from a tree he landed in. I
> drifted several miles away from the drop zone and after four or
> five hours of wandering around the mountains found some Par-
> tisans, and later the British Mission.... After being chased
> around the mountains by the Bulgarians, we made our way to
> Vueje.

Four secret meteorological stations, staffed by OSS, radioed
weather reports every six hours, sending measurements taken with
technical equipment which had been parachuted in; balloon runs,
for example, were made daily. The transmission of weather intelligence received special handling, and reached the 19th Weather
Squadron at Cairo on the average of seven minutes after it had
been put on the air in Yugoslavia.

Escape routes for U.S. fliers were organized. Partisans, under
OSS direction, brought in downed fliers, and housed them in bar-
racks near fields they had constructed. Working with the Air Crew
Rescue Unit (Fifteenth Air Force), OSS arranged for planes to

transport the men periodically. By VE-Day about 1,600 had been safely flown out.

The first "Safe Area" maps to be issued by any U.S. Air Force in any theater were prepared by the Air Section for the guidance of airmen over Yugoslavia. These showed areas under Partisan control, toward which downed fliers should attempt to make their way. [Deletion] First issued in January 1944, they assisted in the recovery of 467 airmen during the first four months of use. Beyond this concrete effect, they fortified air crew morale during operations over Yugoslavia, Bulgaria, Austria, Rumania, Czechoslovakia and northern Greece. [Deletion]

Subversive propaganda was sent in by MO. Specially packed leaflets, pamphlets and posters were dropped to U.S. representatives with Partisan forces. These were intended to demoralize German garrisons and terrorize native collaborators. An MO officer concluded, however, that the results were smaller than in more highly educated countries. The illiterate half of the population not only was unaffected, but could see little reason for risking lives to get the leaflets to the enemy. Many of the three million pieces delivered found other uses.

MO was also criticized by the Partisans for distributing surrender leaflets, which brought German deserters and German satellite troops flocking to Partisan strongholds. Inasmuch as the Partisans had inadequate food and clothing, no place to keep the prisoners, insufficient personnel to guard them, and a degree of inimical sentiment toward them, they shot them. The MO leaflets had the net effect of stiffening German soldier morale.

Meanwhile, of the two competitive resistance groups, the Chetniks had lost favor with the Allies. OSS liaison officers at the two Hqs. had submitted reports respectively favorable to the group to which they were attached and unfavorable to the opposing group. Allied policy was eventually settled in favor of Tito, and, in early 1944, all U.S. and British representatives with Mihailovich were withdrawn.

U.S. airmen, however, continued to bail out over Chetnik territory, where they could not be contacted and evacuated by U.S. agents. Further, it was felt that the U.S. should maintain intelligence units in all sections of Yugoslavia. With the support of Ambassador Robert D. Murphy, General Eaker (MAAF) and General Twining (Fifteenth Air Force), the point was finally won. On 3 August the HALYARD team parachuted to Pranjane, eighty kilometers south of Belgrade, where Mihailovich had collected, housed and fed 250 U.S. fliers. The three members of HALYARD directed 300 laborers, using sixty ox-carts, in the construction of an airfield 600 yards long and thirty wide. On 9 and 10 August, C-47's evacuated all 250 airmen. On 26 August, 58 additional U.S. fliers and two British came out. By the time the team left in November 1944, the total was over 400.

[This team was led by Lieutenant George Muselin, a University of Pittsburgh man of Yugoslavian parents. Muselin was pro-Mihailovic and had taken part in an earlier mission to Mihailovic's HQ. He was withdrawn only after a prolonged dispute with the British culminated in a demand by Churchill personally that the United States, like Britain, withdraw all representatives from Mihailovic's HQ. Muselin went back in on the personal orders of Roosevelt at least partly because of Donovan's desire to back both sides as strategic factors useful against the Germans—another example of Donovan employing his lawyer's nimble wits to gain his ends over British opposition.]

A six-man mission, intended for the acquisition of intelligence in Mihailovich territory, parachuted successfully to the air rescue team on 25 August 1944 [despite violent British opposition that a mission to Mihailovich at this stage of the war might cause Tito to be suspicious of the sincerity of the Anglo-American attitude towards him—this indeed occurred]. This move proved to be an unfortunate one. The Chief of Mission [Lieutenant Colonel Robert McDowell, a former professor of Balkan history at Michigan University], explained to General Mihailovich that his assignment was purely to collect military intelligence, and that his presence did not constitute political support of the Chetnik Government. Nevertheless, an imaginative leaflet in Serbo-Croatian appeared, reading in part:

> The delegates of the Allied American Government and the personal representatives of President Roosevelt, the tried friend of freedom loving small nations, have arrived.
>
> Immediately upon his arrival, Colonel [McDowell] and the members of his mission went to the headquarters of the Supreme Command. On this occasion he presented a written message from President Roosevelt....The whole meeting and the discussion at the headquarters of the Supreme Command was photographed by an American photographer, who was chosen to be present at this important event as an official war photographer for Fox Movietone News.

The false claims made by this leaflet had just the effect on the

Partisans which the British had wished to avoid. Tito, who had not been consulted, took the opportunity (coinciding as it did with the arrival of the Red Army) to cease active cooperation with U.S. and British liaison officers. One after another, teams at the various Partisan corps reported they were tied down to headquarters, could not travel without Partisan "guides," and received, together with their British colleagues, only the skimpy daily Partisan communiques. English and American representatives duplicated the radioing of this intelligence, and were able to collect little else.

On 1 November 1944, a month after arrival, the Mission returned (to submit reports favorable to Mihailovich). The Partisan attitude, however, never changed, and the OSS, unlike the British Military Mission, had few bargaining points. [To a certain extent, members of the mission to Mihailovich encouraged misunderstandings by speeches at Chetnik meetings and over the Chetnik radio. It may be argued, on the other hand, that Marshal Tito would have found some other opportunity, if this one had not occurred, to cease cooperation with the Western Allies. (footnote)] The British were able, as before, to obtain concessions from the Partisans due to their strong position: they had direct radio contact with the Balkan Air Force, and were able to produce air support for Partisan military operations more quickly and more often than could OSS teams; this same contact insured efficient air supply of British teams; finally, the British (like the Russians) spoke as official representatives of their Government, which the American agents did not.

To remedy this last weakness, the Independent American Military Mission to Marshal Tito arrived in Valjevo 9 October 1944, and took command of all U.S. teams formerly attached to the British Military Mission. [This mission was led by none other than Colonel Ellery Huntingdon, the lawyer who had replaced Donald Downes as chief of OSS in Italy. Huntingdon stayed in Yugoslavia even shorter a time than he had in Italy. He handed over to Colonel Charles Thayer, a State Department man who had served in Moscow and was a friend of Brigadier Fitzroy MacLean, the commander of the British mission to Tito. Both had played polo a great deal together in Moscow and, indeed, Thayer's appointment to the *independent* U.S. mission had been made at the suggestion of MacLean when the two met for drinks in London. Thus, the U.S. mission was not quite so independent as Donovan wished. Polo and Moscow apart, they had identical views concerning Russia and Communism—they were both implacable in their detestation of Communism, and both survived with Tito because they recognized that he was a nationalist first and a Communist second.] Negotiations with Marshal Tito, to improve intelligence coverage with greater freedom of movement for U.S. teams, proved relatively unsuccessful. Difficulties in obtaining permission for entry and movement of U.S. personnel continued on a smaller scale.

[Soon afterwards, a state of extreme tension developed between Tito, who was supported by the Red Army, and the Anglo-American military missions in Yugoslavia, which were, of course, supported by the Allied High Command. The cause of the tension was Yugoslavia's claim to the port of Trieste, which was occupied by the British as custodians for the Italians. At one stage in 1945, war threatened between the Western powers over Trieste, and General Patton engaged in a massive strategic deception scheme backed by MI-6 and OSS/SI to make it seem that the U.S. Third Army in Germany was preparing to move on Trieste "in order to teach Tito good manners." Some historians argue that this was the real starting point of the Cold War. In the event, Tito backed off. However, the incident was a tragedy, for there was a great and genuine admiration for Tito in London and Washington. After all, the Jugs—as they were called affectionately—had lost 1.7 million people (10% of their population) in the war against the Germans and Italians. This casualty figure was far higher than that of the French and Americans combined, and approached that suffered by England.]

The Mission prepared medical, economic and battle order reports, including one of the first American war intelligence reports on the Russian Army's combat methods. On 20 October, with Belgrade still half in German, half in Russian, hands, the Mission entered that capital and became a City Team, gathering political and economic intelligence, and acting as U.S. liaison until State Department representation arrived.

Prior to the Mihailovich set-back, OSS/Yugoslavia had turned in some outstanding successes. Continuous relay of German battle order was important to the armies in Italy. The coordination of air bombing with Partisan activities helped detain fifteen German divisions in Yugoslavia. It was always difficult to evaluate in tangible form the results of secret intelligence and operational activity. But the equipping of tens of thousands of guerrillas and the evacuation of some 2,000 downed airmen were concrete accomplishments.

In September 1944, command of the fifteen OSS teams in the field was taken over from Brigadier Fitzroy MacLean (British SOE) by the Independent American Military Mission to Marshal

Tito (IAMM).

The joint U.S. Chiefs of Staff authorized IAMM to:

(1) Establish military liaison with the Partisans;

(2) report to AFHQ on military developments;

(3) handle all U.S. supplies to the Partisans; and

(4) command U.S. personnel in Yugoslavia.

An IAMM base at Partisan Headquarters had been established in August on Vis Island. Four of its members arrived at Valjevo on 9 October and, from there, advanced with the Partisan I Corps. They entered Belgrade on 20 October, with the last German units still surrendering in that city. The group sent in reports on economic conditions, war damage, military developments, a breakdown of the Partisan I Corps, and analyses of Partisan and Russian battle techniques.

The Mission established itself in Belgrade and became a city team. By January, this consisted of thirteen men, including four SI, three R&A and two X-2 representatives. The fifteen teams accompanying the Partisan Corps in the field were cut to eight by May. Liaison with the Partisans produced little on German battle order, Partisan cooperation having been notably poor since mid-1944. Political coverage was somewhat better. OSS maintained contacts both in the various government ministries and with the more or less silent opposition groups. Since the State Department did not arrive for several months, these OSS reports formed the only U.S. coverage of Yugoslav political developments.

An X-2 hope for the exchange of information with Yugoslav counter-espionage services came to nothing.

Economic and medical reports were also prepared. Members of various U.S. agencies (Typhus Commission, Red Cross, ATC, State Department, MAAF) were at one time or another attached to the mission. Until the arrival of an OWI representative, OSS itself distributed OWI publications. While the principal commitment for supplies to the Partisan army was British, OSS arranged for a contribution of some ten tons of drugs and medical equipment, and of eighty jeeps. About one hundred additonal U.S. airmen, downed in Yugoslavia, were evacuated.

On 31 March 1945, the U.S. Ambassador arrived, and the Embassy took over many of the functions which the mission had been carrying out in the interim. Since the Yugoslavs refused clearance for a coexistent OSS unit, it was withdrawn in July. All field teams followed suit, excepting one in Trieste, which was transferred to SI/Italy jurisdiction.

RUMANIA

The anti-Nazi coup in Rumania on 23 August 1944 presented the two-fold opportunity of retrieving prisoners of war, and of gathering Rumanian intelligence on Germany. On 29 August, an OSS team of 21 men landed at Popesti airport in Fifteenth Air Force B-17's. [Deletion]

[The team was commanded by Frank Wisner, a CI expert who later became CIA station chief in London, chief of the CIA's Office of Policy Coordination, and CIA's Deputy Director of Plans. He suffered a nervous breakdown and committed suicide in 1965. Wisner used as cover the fact that the OSS unit was an Aircrew Rescue Unit. The codename for the operation was Bughouse, which was very unfortunate, and with the mission were three men of distinction: Russell Dorr, who had been one of Donovan's law partners in years gone by, became chief of the Marshall Plan Mission to Turkey, chief of the International Bank for Reconstruction and Development in Persia, and Washington representative of the Chase Manhattan Bank; Frederick Burkhardt, a philosopher of Wisconsin University, later president of Bennington and then president of the American Council of Learned Societies; Phillip Coombs, a professor of economics at Williams College, later an Assistant Secretary of State for Educational and Cultural Affairs during the Kennedy Administration, and then Research Director of the International Institute for Educational Planning in Paris.

[This team's contribution to intelligence about the German service's operations in Russia over a period of nearly ten years was of enormous importance.]

OSS preceded the Russians and had a free hand for several days. Until the first week of October, the British had only one representative there, an SOE agent who had parachuted in late 1943. [This officer was the fabled SOE Colonel Gardyne de Chastelain, a member of a Huguenot family long resident in England. He had been sales manager of an Anglo-American oil company in Bucharest before the war, and was said to have been a close friend of King Carol II. When Carol abdicated in 1940 and fled the country with his red-haired mistress Madama Lupescu, De Chastelain is said to have supervised the loading of the royal train with three motor cars (a Rolls, a Mercedes, and a Lincoln), four dogs, 152 trunks, the palace's gold plate, some Rembrandts, a large supply of gold bars, his treasury of $4 million, the couple's great wardrobes, and the valises containing the deeds to several chateaux, mansions and vineyards in France and Portugal. When De Chastelain was paradropped into Rumania to begin his SOE mission in February 1944, he fell into a reception committee that consisted of the guns, beaters and carriages of a nobleman's hunting party. Unfortunately, the secret police were there as well. They arrested De Chastelain as he was getting out of his parachute shrouds. De Chastelain, who was almost a caricature of the agent who had been born with a silver spoon, was not shot. Nor was he put into a dungeon. He was given a luxurious villa just outside the capital, had servants, and was allowed to go for walks. He was also permitted to transmit intelligence to the British naval base at Malta. He lived in vice-regal splendor until the Russians came in September 1944. Then he was ejected as a British deception agent. See my *Bodyguard of Lies*, pp. 452 et seq. for a full account of the part played by this interesting agent in Bodyguard, the strategic deception scheme for the Allied invasion of Europe through Normandy on D-Day, 6 June 1944.]

[Excision] The first task in Rumania was the evacuation of U.S. flyers. OSS/Bari had been informed by a representative of the prisoners (flown out in a Messerschmitt piloted by a Rumanian) that over 1,000 men were located near Popesti airport. Upon arrival of the team at Popesti, Rumanian officals obtained trucks at Bucharest to carry the releasd prisoners from their camp to the airfield. The evacuation began on 31 August, and, by the following day, over 1,100 men had been flown out in B-17's. Meanwhile fighting continued in the outskirts of Bucharest. OSS combed the Rumanian hospitals and with Russian help, once the Russians arrived, assembled and dispatched more U.S. flyers during the ensuing weeks, bringing the total of those evacuated to 1,350.

The second priority task was the examination of the Ploesti oil fields. Five R&A experts, entering with the first team, arrived at Ploesti on 3 September and commenced photographing damage and screening documents. The first of the sources to be tapped was Ruminoel, the official German oil mission in Bucharest. Although Ruminoel had been badly disordered after bombing, street-fighting and looting, documents were obtained detailing daily exports of oil products, monthly oil output since 1939, and the requirements and purchases of both the Wehrmacht and the Luftwaffe. From them it was learned that shipments of processed products to Germany had declined by sixty-two percent during the months when the Ploesti refineries were under air attack. Previously, thirty percent of all Germany's oil had come from Ploesti. Additional papers, obtained in the office of Schenker and Co. (German), revealed the destination of oil shipments to German territory, information which provided the Eighth and Fifteenth Air Forces with several new priority targets.

Further OSS investigations in and around Bucharest provided valuable documents. The general confusion occasioned by the German departure from, and Russian arrival in, Bucharest offered many opportunities for picking up manuals and equipment. Particularly remunerative were searches in Schenker and Co. (which proved also to be the center of German espionage in Rumania) and in the local Luftwaffe Hq. From these and other sources, OSS provided AFHQ, Italy, with ninety percent of its information on Rumania. This came from 24 personnel, including 11 SI, 6 X-2 and 2 R&A representatives. [The hiring of six Rumanians made for certain security weaknesses. In addition, the Rumanian liaison officers, attached to OSS and later to the Allied Control Commission, were reporting regularly to the Rumanian General Staff on OSS activities. It was not until August 1945 that all the liaison officers were dismissed. (footnote)]

A seven-man X-2 unit uncovered in September a large quantity of diplomatic documents of the former Rumanian Prime Minister, Mihai Antonescu, and transmitted them to the State Department. Some ten thousand dossiers were found in the office of the Nazi Party in Rumania and combed for information to be used in the War Crimes Trials. The German Gestapo files for Rumania were also acquired and transferred to SHAEF for disposition.

From these sources and from some sixty former Axis agents (some of them acting as doubles) X-2 identified over 4,000 Axis intelligence officials and agents, more than one hundred subversive organizations and some 200 commercial firms used as cover for espionage activity. Two hundred pages of such data were forwarded to General Deane of the American Military Mission in Moscow to be transmitted for Russian intelligence for action in Rumania.

Liaison with the Rumanian General Staff and with the 2nd Ukrainian Army produced a series of tactical targets, supply depots, airfields, enemy unit locations and communication centers, for OSS to cable back to the Fifteenth Air Force. Bombing and strafing lines were established, a liaison job which was subsequently taken over by a special MAAF unit, sent in for the purpose. After many setbacks, agreements were completed with the Russian NKVD and a sort of liaison effected. Counter-espionage information was exchanged, and OSS further obtained the right to interrogate German military and political prisoners.

Contacts with government and opposition leaders provided political and economic coverage of Russo-Rumanian relations. Trips to Slovakia, Transylvania and Debrecen (seat of the Provisional Hungarian Government) yielded reports on political developments, leading personalities and Russian occupation policies in those areas.

Examples of information obtained from the above-listed and other sources were:

(1) For ONI, reports on the Rumanian fleet in the Black Sea, navigation conditions, coastal defenses; an illustrated German analysis of naval and air operations at Salerno.

(2) For AFHQ, the first over-all coverage of Hungarian and German divisons in the area; unit identifications and composition.

(3) For the Air Forces, evidence that bombs used in raids on oil refineries should be fused no longer than 1/100th of second; information on a German radar control apparatus effectively countering "window"; targets at Moosbierbaum in Austria (chemical works manufacturing aviation gasoline), and at Wismar (Dornier factory assembling FW-190's).

The OSS mission had originally entered under cover of an Air Crew Rescue Unit. The U.S. section of the Allied Control Commission arrived on 9 November (until which time OSS had been the sole American representation in the country), and the unit became a sub-section of US/ACC. Lacking local [Russian] official approval, the station was closed in September 1945.

CZECHOSLOVAKIA

Lack of contacts in German-controlled Czechoslovakia hampered both British and U.S. subversive operations. Only two OSS units penetrated the country, the first in late 1944, when a Slovak resistance movement momentarily appeared, the other in 1945.

[The OSS man responsible for sending OSS agents into central Europe—this theater consisted of Germany, Austria, Hungary and Czechoslovakia—was Howard Chapin, in peacetime an executive of the General Foods Corporation. His deputy was Gilmore Flues, a lawyer from Ohio who became Assistant Treasury Secretary during the Eisenhower presidency. The team leader of the main OSS expedition, which landed in the lower Tatra mountains, east of Prague, and which met with disaster, was a young American, Holt Green. The disaster which struck the "Green Team"—as the OG was called—was due to the immaturity of the service, the affliction which had pursued Donovan ever since OSS was founded. As a former high officer of OSS would state 30 years later: "Green was the wrong man for the job and should never have gone in in the first place."]

Encouraged by the Russian advance in Hungary and Ruthenia, two divisions of the Slovak Independent Army revolted. Aided by partisan groups, they seized Banska Bystrica in late August, set up their Hq., and broadcast appeals for help over the local radio station. Contact with the Czechoslovak Government-in-Exile had been established by the insurgents in the planning stage, and it was through Czechoslovak Army Hq. in London that OSS made arrangements for the infiltration of a liaison group and an air crew rescue unit. The Slovak Army, together with the partisans, prepared the Tri Duby airfield (ten km. south of Banska Bystrica) for B-17 landings, and arranged recognition signals.

On 17 September 1944 six OSS personnel were landed at this airport by the Fifteenth Air Force. Five tons of military supplies for the partisans accompanied them. Thirteen U.S. fliers and two British were evacuated.

On 7 October six B-17's landed sixteen additional OSS personnel together with twenty tons of Marlins [light submachine guns], Bren guns, bazookas, ammunition, explosives, medical supplies, food and clothing. On this trip 28 U.S. aviators were evacuated.

The OSS purpose was to act as U.S. liaison with the Czechoslovak Army and the partisans, to arrange for their supply by air, to train them in the use of American weapons, to evacuate U.S. fliers in partisan care, and to collect intelligence on German and partisan battle order, industrial targets and military, economic and political developments. The mission was attached to Czechoslovak Army Hq. at Banska Bystrica and commenced cabling reports. Between 13 and 20 October, for instance, it cabled out over 1,000 words a day of enemy battle order and target information.

But the Germans could not risk the continued sabotage activity so close behind front lines, and commenced, in September, a powerful drive to wipe out Czechoslovak resistance. The commanding officer of the first six OSS men, realizing the danger, had wired an urgent request for increased supply of military materiel. He asked for only one more man, a radio operator. Five separate teams, however, had been prepared in Bari for reception at Tri Duby (SI, SO and medical survey teams plus agents for Hungary and Austria). These teams were ready to fan out independently of the original team, and the first group had agreed to receive them, with the understanding that it could not be responsible for their safety. One of them, the Hungarian pair, was successful. But the others were caught in the partisan flight before the German advance.

As the German troops closed in on the insurgents, resistance became increasingly disorganized. On 26 October the Czechoslovaks evacuated Banska Bystrica in favor of Donovaly. The American group of 37 men (OSS agents and U.S. fliers) divided into four sections to accompany separate units in the hope that casualties would be smaller. From then on, a nightmare, panicky retreat began, as the completely disorganized partisans threw away their weapons, stole the American supplies and fled through the snow-covered mountains toward the Russian lines. The Czechoslovaks starved and froze. On one day 83 of them, waiting for the return of a reconnaissance patrol, died of cold.

Reunited, the OSS group, losing men one by one, traversed the mountains. On 6 November, one OSS member and five U.S. aviators on patrol were captured. On 11 November, all the airmen, together with two OSS officers elected to stop in a village and surrender. On 26 November, one OSS man was surprised on a food-purchasing visit to a small village. On 12 December, two more OSS personnel were captured. At Christmas, the remnant OSS group had been for several weeks at a mountain hotel near Velny Bok, two of them sleeping in a house nearby. On the day after Christmas, 250 German and Hlinka guards attacked the hotel, on information supplied by a partisan guard. All the OSS personnel in the hotel were taken, sent to Mauthausen concentration camp, tortured for what information they could give, and executed on 24 January 1945. The other two OSS men, aided by a partisan girl, successfully escaped some fifty miles to the Russian lines.

The principal difficulty appears to have been incomplete planning on the part of the resistance movement and of its Allied supporters. Supplies and a swift military advance had been guaranteed by the British and the Russians respectively. As it turned out, the Russians took two months to get through the Dukla Pass, for which they had allotted two weeks. [This failure was not for lack of trying, inasmuch as some 120,000 men were reported lost in the attacks. (footnote)] Finally, in mid-October, the Russians flew in to Tri Duby airfields two brigades of Czechoslovaks trained in Russia. Unfortunately these were almost unarmed, and once landed, could only join in the general flight toward the Russian lines. Meanwhile the British apparently made no effort to help the insurgents. OSS rushed material from Cairo to Bari, but bad weather prevented most of the supply sorties.

One other OSS agent, "Cottage," penetrated Czechoslovakia. He was a native, with contacts in Prague, trained in Italy and parachuted near Prague in late February 1945. He never established radio contact, due to a faulty or possibly sabotaged set. He did, however, organize a small resistance group and participated in the Prague insurrection of 5 May.

BULGARIA

Like the other city teams, OSS/Sofia was the first U.S. representation in the country. The U.S. section of the Allied Control Commission (ACC) did not arrive in Bulgaria until November 1944, while British intelligence missions had been withheld until 21 September. On 23 August a two-man OSS team had been dropped on the Greek border and joined Greek guerrillas harassing the withdrawal of German troops. Advance through Bulgaria was hampered, however, first by the German troops and later by Bulgar celebrations; the team did not reach the capital until 17 September, where it found another one preceding it. This latter consisted of four men dispatched by car from OSS/Istanbul on 6 September 1944.

The first task was to arrange for the prompt evacuation of 335 airmen (mostly American). These were released from the camp at Shumen, Bulgaria, on 9 September and entrained for Sofia. Inasmuch as Sofia had not yet been occupied by the Russians, and was still subject to Allied bombing, OSS objected to this move. The chief of mission located the train some thirty miles beyond Gorna Orekovitsa, had it turned back and re-routed direct to Turkey. On the morning of 10 September, the Sofia railway station was severely bombed at about the time the aviators would have arrived. OSS cabled to Istanbul information of the trainload, and the aviators were met at the frontier by the U.S. Assistant Military Attache and a large Turkish reception committee.

The City Team provided the only independent U.S. intelligence during the critical and confused period of the Bulgarian transition from hostile to co-belligerent status. Besides political and economic coverage of Russo-Bulgar relations, OSS liaison with the intelligence section of the Bulgar operational staff provided daily reports on German battle order in Macedonia, plus several German and Hungarian military documents on training, weapons, etc.

The Russians, however, upon their arrival in mid-September, put a stop to further operations. On 24 September, the American and British intelligence missions were ordered to leave. Both parties demurred, stating that they would have to receive authorization from their respective headquarters. When the Russians repeated the order on 26 September, offering the alternative of imprisonment, the missions left. [Two explanations have been offered for this summary dismissal. The first (suggested by several members of the Bulgar Legation at Istanbul) was that the colonel commanding the British unit was suspected by the Russians of anti-Russian activity; in order to get him out of the country it was necessary to oust all missions. An alternative is that the Russians wished to establish their control of the area before any foreign missions were admitted. (footnote)]

On 5 November, the OSS team obtained permission to re-enter, and resumed its military coverage (through the Bulgars and Russians), its political and economic reporting on developments in Bulgaria and its assistance in War Crimes investigation. An X-2 unit vetted State Department and other U.S. personnel and visa applicants. In December, Russian ACC pressure on the State Department representatives, who had arrived in November, again forced OSS withdrawal, this time permanently.

ALBANIA

The German occupation aroused resistance, as it had in neighboring Greece and Yugoslavia, from several Albanian guerrilla groups. Because the latter spent much of their time and equipment in civil war, U.S. policy was early decided against the supply of weapons. While no SO unit therefore entered the country, SI sent five teams for purposes of intelligence only. By November 1943, when the first arrived, the Communist-led FNC [National Liberation Front] controlled most of the country, and it was to FNC units that the five OSS teams were attached.

The first SI representative arrived in Cairo in June 1943 to begin operations into Albania, but found no suitable recruits with facility in the language. In November the desk moved to Bari and began dispatching agents originally recruited in the United States.

The first SI team, TANK, was smuggled ashore at night by British motor boat on 17 November 1943. [The team was led by Thomas Stefan, who was smuggled in from Sterling Hayden's base. Stefan was an effective, if uncelebrated, OSS agent, for he managed to make what appeared to be friendly contact with Enver Hoxha, the Albanian partisan leader and, later, prime minister of his little country on the Adriatic.] The British SOE mission in Albania had refused to cooperate with OSS agents, unless they accepted British command and used British communications. The three men therefore, with FNC support, established themselves independently in a cave by the sea. They built up a network of agents

and, by January, were radioing German battle order, economic information and intelligence on the strengths of the rival guerrilla
groups. Among other services, they aided the return of a plane-
load of 26 Americans forced down over FNC territory; this party
(including eleven nurses) was helped by representatives of SOE,
SIS and SI to reach the coast, when an SO team evacuated them
by sea. A German drive through the Shushica valley, combined
with the ill health of the team members, forced evacuation of
TANK by British boat in February.

In March the BIRD team took over the same area. Surviving a
month-long attack by 800 occupation troops specifically detailed
for its destruction, the team remained until July 1944, and provided reception points for three further teams.

The first of these parachuted in March, the other two in July
1944. Despite repeated German attacks, they remained with their
FNC guerrilla units, maintaining intelligence coverage. Upon the
German withdrawal in October 1944, one team entered the capital,
Tirana, while the other two worked up into northeast Albania,
radioing military developments and data on industrial destruction.
All three stayed in the country, giving economic and political coverage and serving as liaison for State Department and other U.S.
agencies until the establishment of a city team in Tirana in February 1945.

Perhaps the principal difficulty encountered by SI/Albania was
its lack of control over transportation. Air supply of teams in
enemy-held territory depended upon the closest relations and identity of interests between those responsible for the teams and for the
required air operations. Support of U.S. teams by the Balkan Air
Force (British) was unreliable throughout. After months of waiting
had beset several missions, the head of the Albanian Desk unsuccessfully proposed, as had section chiefs in other areas, the establishment of an OSS air unit to obviate such delays.

Upon the withdrawal of German troops in October 1944, the
two roving teams were recalled from northern Albania to join the
base team in Tirana. Coverage of political and economic developments continued. A medical officer made an inspection tour of the
southern section of the country, reporting on hospital conditions
and on the spreading typhus epidemic. [Deletion] Enver Hoxha,
head of the Communist-controlled Provisional Government, delayed for some time the establishment of an OSS City Team, and
the admittance of new OSS personnel. Finally, in February 1945,
authorization was obtained, and the team was set up with eleven

members, including five SI and one R&A. An interesting move by
the Provisional Government was the refusal to accept any U.S. civilians. This order effectively prohibited the entry of the principal
OSS expert on Albania (until he later joined the Consular staff).

The City Team continued its intelligence coverage, besides performing services for various visiting American representatives
(State, Military Liaison, etc.). Until State Department representation arrived in mid-1945, OSS provided the only independent
American evaluations of developments, and formed the only
American link with Albania. Pressure from the Albanian Government necessitated the Team's departure in September.

[One agent, codelettered T, an American of Albanian extraction, was infiltrated clandestinely towards the end of the war. He
vanished and was not heard from again. Even in 1975, his widow,
who was living in Washington, was still trying to find out what had
happened to him. At the time, General Donovan launched a full-
scale investigation, for there was every possible evidence that the
man had not defected. But the investigation came to nothing and T
was listed in military records as having "no known grave." The
Cold War—which to a degree resulted from Tirana's hostility for
the British and their naval operations in the Adriatic and from
Anglo-American plots to depose Hoxha—had started.]

CHAPTER 11

The Principal Neutral Countries

From three neutral capitals, OSS attempted the most difficult kind of positive intelligence work. Normal agent operations involved sending to the target area a quantity of observers to collect information which could be heard, seen, bought, or stolen. The process was a straightforward one, subject to relatively direct control. Less predictable was the indirect approach, by which intelligence operatives attempted, often from outside, to obtain information from a few highly-placed members of the target community. Through them it was possible to gain high-level intelligence of a type which could rarely be obtained by agents operating directly on a lower echelon.

Bases were established at Stockholm, Istanbul, and Bern, the first two with staffs approximating fifty personnel, the last with less than twelve Americans.

Poor direction in Istanbul resulted in almost complete failure. All contacts in Central Europe, instead of being operated individually by OSS/Istanbul, were handled through one sub-agent, whose activity was penetrated by the Gestapo. Stockholm and Bern, on the other hand, produced excellent high-level intelligence. One Stockholm item in 1943 was rated by British SIS "the find of the year," and one Bern agent "the best intelligence source of the war."

[This claim is difficult to sustain. While the agent concerned, Fritz Kolbe, the special assistant to Ambassador Karl Ritter, a very important official of the German foreign ministry who undertook special diplomatic assignments for Hitler and the Wehrmacht, did provide masses of information of a high grade, most of it had been rendered obsolescent by the time it arrived in Allied hands—London and Washington had already read it through Ultra. However, it did make Allen Dulles ecstatic, as this advisory to Washington shows: "Sincerely regret that you cannot see at this time Woods [Dulles had given Kolbe the cover name of "George Woods"] material as it stands without condensation and abridgement. In some 400 pages, dealing with the international

294

maneuverings of German diplomatic policy for the past two months, a picture of imminent doom and final downfall is presented. Into a tormented General Headquarters and a half-dead Foreign Office stream the lamentations of a score of diplomatic posts. It is a scene wherein haggard Secret Service and diplomatic agents are doing their best to cope with the defeatism and desertion of flatly defiant satellites and allies and recalcitrant neutrals. The period of secret service under Canaris . . . is drawing to an end. . . . The final death-bed contortions of a putrefied Nazi diplomacy are pictured in these telegrams. The reader is carried from one extreme of emotion to the other as he examines these messages and sees the cruelty exhibited by the Germans in their final swan-song of brutality towards the peoples so irrevocably and pitifully enmeshed by the Gestapo after half a decade of futile struggles. . . ."]

German authorities unsuspectingly conducted a Stockholm agent on a one-week tour of the German synthetic oil industry. Bern's greater quantity and quality included contacts in the German underground group which engineered the 20 July 1944 attempt on Hitler's life, and accurate reportage on German scientific developments in atomic and bacteriological warfare, and on the V-bombs, including both their assembly and firing locations.

[The Istanbul Affair was at once one of the great Allied intelligence triumphs of World War II in Europe and one of its greatest disasters; and the whole reflected once more on the fact that new intelligence services are very much more prone to error and defeat than established ones. Effectively the entire OSS in Central Europe being controlled from Istanbul was under Gestapo control, and when this fact became known to the Ankara Committee—the Allied intelligence authority responsible for controlling all intelligence activity out of Turkey—it led to a severe and serious collapse of relationships between the British and the American services. This was not restored until Frank Wisner, one of America's leading intelligence experts, was put in to restore security. With the help of the British, he turned defeat into victory.

[Cicero, the valet in the employ of Sir Hughe Knatchbull-Hugessen, the British ambassador to Turkey, who had been stealing documents from the ambassador's documents cases, was identified as an SD agent. He was then brought under control and played a useful part in Bodyguard, the strategic deception scheme being played out in the period November 1943-August 1944 to mislead Hitler about the direction of the Allied main attack against German-occupied Europe. Cicero was allowed to continue his espionage at the British embassy but was provided unknown to himself with information that was designed to reinforce the opinion of the German General Staff that the Allies might not land in northern France at all, but would attack Germany through the Balkans.

[Wisner's activities led finally to the complete neutralization of the German intelligence service activities in Turkey, at least for any purposes useful to the Reich, when Ludwig Moyzisch, Cicero's SD controller and the chief of the SD in Turkey and the Near East, was induced by the Allied services to throw in his lot with the Western powers. Moyzisch, whether wittingly or unwittingly is not clear, was by April 1944 providing OSS and MI-6 with strategic intelligence information of great value to the Russians—his information, passed to the OSS and then by Washington to Moscow, enabled the Russians to destroy a major network of German stay-behind agents in Rumania. He also provided the United States with intelligence of great value concerning Japanese networks in Europe.]

Control of such operations was a far more delicate task than that involved in the direct approach. Security and communications presented peculiar difficulties. Years of preparation, and experienced personnel would have increased the chances of success, but even then the risks were great. After Pearl Harbor, it became evident that the United States had few men trained in such work and little time for the long-range preparations which are normally essential to its success. Mistakes and losses (as was apparent in Istanbul) were inevitable; the achievements (particularly those of OSS/Bern) were surprisingly high.

TURKEY

Istanbul provided an unparelleled opportunity for the gathering of intelligence on Central and East Europe. Through Turkey travelled the main body of Jewish and other refugees from the Nazi regime. A stream of businessmen and government officials passed back and forth. Some seventeen foreign intelligence services were active, while the city itself teemed with professional international informants. Provided U.S. activities were not directed against the Turks themselves, the Turkish police was willing to cooperate in every way, even providing hotel and border registration lists. OSS/Istanbul, handicapped by unsatisfactory personnel, failed, with a few exceptions, to exploit this rich field of intelligence.

The first agent in Turkey was "Rose," an American businessman recruited in New York in April 1942, while on a trip home. The chain he established in and around Istanbul operated into

1945, gathering intelligence from important local residents and from travellers arriving from Europe. A contact in the Rumanian Embassy [Rumania was one of Hitler's two most important allies at this time] furnished him copies of the political and economic reports pouched to and from the Rumanian Foreign Office. Another sub-agent obtained a copy of the Reichs Telegram Adressebuch, listing telegraph addresses of all German firms. The majority of "Rose" intelligence, however, came from a newspaper reporter, turned international agent, and was unreliable rumor. An exception was the information on Rumanian oil developments and output, gained from "Rose's" excellent contacts in that business.

A year later, in April 1943, an OSS representative arrived to establish a mission for (1) organized interrogation of travellers, (2) counter-espionage, and (3) operations into Hungary, Bulgaria and Rumania. His cover of Lend-Lease representative was supported by his previous experience as an American banker. By mid-1944, the mission consisted of 43 members under State Department, FEA, Military Attache, business, press and other covers.

Besides the above-mentioned "Rose" chain, other local informants were picked up in Istanbul and Ankara. In December 1943 a special mission, recruited in the United States, held conversations with the Bulgarian Minister in Turkey and opened discussions for getting Bulgaria out of the war. A subsequent one-man team arrived to gather intelligence available on the Far East through the Turkish merchant marine. From arrival lists obtained by bribery of the Turkish police, OSS interviewers picked out the most important and likely persons; the interviews resulted in military targets, economic data and political coverage of developments in the various Central European countries.

Operations into Europe itself were channelled through agent "Dogwood." "Dogwood" was a Czech engineer, who had previously worked for British services in Istanbul and then had been handed over to OSS by them. He became chief agent of the CEREUS circle [named for a large cactus] of elderly well-connected individuals resident in Istanbul, and was given charge of all subsequent contacts passed on by the American Military Attache office and other units.

CEREUS consisted of the president of an Istanbul firm, an Austrian businessman (in radio), a rich and idle Austrian with many social connections in his home country, a German professor of economics—friend of Franz von Papen [German ambassador to Turkey], another German professor with widespread connections among German Junker families, and a Hungarian nobleman—manager of an American oil firm in Istanbul. It established contacts in four Nazi-dominated countries—Austria, Germany, Hungary and Bulgaria:

Austria. The Austrian businessman of the circle talked, in September 1943, to the assistant general manager of the Semperit Corporation (operating seven rubber and buna [synthetic rubber] manufacturing plants scattered from Duisburg to Krakow). The assistant manager volunteered at that time fuel and construction details of V-2, its exact size, speed and range, and the locations of various plants manufacturing or assembling the weapons, including Peenemuende. He gave similar details on synthetic rubber production, e.g. on the manufacture of experimental rubber plates to cover submarines in an attempt to nullify Allied radar. His information received special commendation from SIS/London.

Through this man, OSS communicated [with] [excision] "Cassia" [who was] a member of the Secret Committee of Fourteen, organizing an Austrian resistance movement. He maintained an intelligence network all over Central Europe through the personally picked managers of over twenty warehouses. On his trip to Istanbul in January 1943, "Cassia" turned in valuable industrial information, outlined the organization of Austrian resistance, and made plans for the reception of OSS liaison agents.

From these Austrian industrialists also came the first indication that the Messerschmitt factory complex at Weiner-Neustadt had largely transferred to Ebreichsdorf, Pottendorf and Voslau. Fifteenth Air Force photo-reconnaissance checked on this hint and verified it. [Destruction of the plant by bombing followed.]

Germany. Helmut, Graf von Moltke, a leader in the plot against Hitler, sent a message to OSS/Istanbul through a member of the CEREUS circle. He requested arrangements to confer, during his December 1943 trip to Turkey, with any of three pre-war acquaintances. Of the three with whom he would feel safe in discussing the anti-Hitler plot, only U.S. Ambassador Kirk in Cairo was available.

An OSS representative carried the message to the Ambassador, who refused to meet von Moltke and sent an unsigned note to the effect that he saw no reason to renew the acquaintance. OSS arranged for a meeting with Brigadier General Tyndall, U.S. Military Attache in Turkey, who talked with the Count for an hour and a half on 17 December 1943. The latter, however, felt too insecure to give any information, and returned to Germany, where he was arrested in February and subsequently executed as a ringleader in the 20 July attempt on Hitler's life.

Hungary. In September 1943, a CEREUS contact was approached by a well-known Hungarian double-agent with a proposal from the Hungarian General Staff for an exchange of liaison officers. OSS/Istanbul was aware of the character of the contacting agent, and suspected an attempt at penetration. The obvious course was, nevertheless, to effect the exchange, maintaining the closest security, gaining what intelligence was possible, and revealing nothing.

That each party might be assured that the other was bona fide, code signals were broadcast over the Algiers and Budapest radios at stated hours on a given day. [The Germans broke the code broadcast, since OSS/Istanbul sent the preliminary messages to Algiers without adequate communication security. (footnote)] An OSS agent of Hungarian nationality was infiltrated to Budapest, and a new Hungarian Military Attache arrived in Istanbul in November and contacted OSS through "Dogwood." The Attache, the Hungarian double-agent, and other Hungarian agents served as couriers.

As suspected, the operation turned out to be an attempt to infiltrate OSS. Although some of the Hungarian General Staff seriously wished to negotiate, on satisfactory terms, with U.S. representatives, the German Gestapo had the situation in hand. For instance, the new Hungarian Attache in Istanbul was, privately, also in Gestapo pay. Due to insufficient OSS security, the Hungarian agents gained knowledge of other Istanbul contacts, and caused the subsequent collapse of CEREUS operations.

[Throughout the first half of 1944, Hungarian dissidents maintained contact with the British services through the three main neutral capitals. Their object was to arrange a surrender and, indeed, they offered to arrange that the Hungarian army facilitate an Anglo-American march on Budapest from the south. The British did little with these overtures, regarding the Hungarians as only a shade less treacherous than Germany. But the contact did prove useful for Bodyguard, the large-scale strategic deception scheme to mislead Hitler about the time and place of the Allied invasion of Europe in 1944. The dissidents planted information that confirmed Hitler's fears of a British attack through the Ljubliana Gap in the Julian Alps on Vienna and thence to Budapest. Hitler came to regard this threat as a distinct possibility, and took steps to turn the Gap into another Thermopylae—thus extending once more his already over-extended armies.

[In February 1944, however, OSS evidently felt the time had come to place a team in Budapest. This was headed by Florimond Duke, a former advertising man for *Time* magazine, and his assistants were Guy Nunn, who had been at Stanford and was a free-lance writer, and Alfred Suarez, a radioman who had fought in

Spain during the civil war. The Duke mission was flown from the secret airbase at Brindisi on 15 March 1944, reputedly with a personal message from Roosevelt to the Hungarian government suggesting that unconditional surrender was not as unpalatable as it sounded and that if the Hungarians did revolt against Hitler they might receive Allied assistance. Word of this mission reached the Russian intelligence service, who had plans of its own for Hungary. It is believed widely that the Russians leaked news of the Duke mission to the SD in Budapest, the object being to prevent any form of understanding between the West and the semi-Fascist Hungarian government.

[The Duke Mission landed just as the Hungarians revolted against the Wehrmacht of their own volition, and Duke and Co. found themselves caught up in a vast *ratissage*. The Wehrmacht took control of Budapest in violent battles that destroyed much of the "Paris on the Danube." The Hungarians handed Duke over to the Nazis. This disaster led the British in Italy to accuse OSS of frittering away its resources, and fundamentally to a situation which was dangerous—OSS and MI-6 in Italy were in a state of barely-concealed hostility as each service went its own way.]

Bulgaria. Through a traveller, "Dogwood" recruited an agent resident in Sofia. Border control was too tight to permit the dispatch of a trained radio operator carrying his set, and OSS had to be content with sending the crystals. The agent recruited an operator with a radio, but satisfactory communication was never established.

Besides providing these contacts in Europe, circle CEREUS picked up occasional intelligence in Turkey. For instance, a Czech engineer, who had directed the construction of many of Bulgaria's water systems, supplied detailed industrial and tactical information with expertly prepared maps.

Through the latter half of 1943 and early 1944, CEREUS submitted over 700 reports from some 60 sub-sources on battle order, industrial targets, production data, political opposition and allied subjects. Although SIS in London rated a few items highly, all of the intelligence was undependable and much of it planted.

Since the mission chief exercised no control over "Dogwood," the latter would not reveal his sub-sources, merely assigning them various code names on his reports. The Reports Office in Cairo was therefore unable to evaluate the intelligence material. The large majority being vague hearsay, the Cairo Reports Officer at one point refused to process or disseminate the material as intelligence at all.

A further weakness in the intelligence resulted from the centralizing of operations through "Dogwood." Since the latter was not a member of the OSS office, he could not have available the facilities and data necessary for briefing and training. CEREUS members and contacts received therefore almost none, and their intelligence reports showed the lack. Had they been operated directly by OSS instead of through a doubtful sub-agent, many would have been released after X-2 vetting, and others might have been developed into excellent sources.

The careless handling of agents eventually resulted in the arrest of many of the OSS/Istanbul contacts in Europe. On 19 March German forces occupied Hungary, arresting all members of the General Staff and all OSS agents involved in the negotiations who had not previously committed themselves to German control. Two days later, the Gestapo apprehended "Cassia," [excision] leader of the Austrian resistance.

It was unfortunate for some members of the Hungarian General Staff that their group had been penetrated by the Gestapo. But the arrest of other OSS contacts was due to insecure OSS handling. There were two main possibilities. Agent "Dogwood" may have been German-controlled, in which case all operations were blown from the start. Alternately "Dogwood" was not a double-agent, but his self-confident garrulity, unchecked by the mission chief, was responsible. Both knew that the Hungarian negotiations involved double-agents, might be an attempt to infiltrate OSS, and required carefully insulated handling. Yet "Dogwood" had such extraordinary self-assurance that he apparently thought he need only take a double-agent into his confidence in order to gain his support. The mission chief exercised almost no control over him, and meanwhile himself gained fame around Istanbul for his talkativeness. Despite the presence of an X-2 representative from October 1943 on, the mission chief supported "Dogwood" in his refusal to allow X-2 vetting of CEREUS recruits.

In the end, the enemy-controlled Hungarian double-agents knew all about the Hungarian and Austrian operations, and the arrests followed.

There were other security violations. The Turkish Intelligence Service, after relations with the U.S. organization had improved, informed OSS that: (a) Two chauffeurs, one assigned to the mission chief's car, were in Russian service; (b) the X-2 chauffeur reported regularly to the Turkish police on X-2 activities. A further notable penetration of OSS was effected by one Mrs. Hildegarde Reilly, reputed to have been the most successful female agent working in Istanbul during 1944 and 1945. Mrs. Reilly came in contact with an OSS officer, and, although she was known to be a double-agent, the mission chief approved the association, hoping that some information on German activity could thus be acquired. The project backfired, inasmuch as Mrs. Reilly is known to have reported to the Germans on OSS personnel and activities. Other similar penetrations were accomplished by various female spies in the city.

In June 1944, a new chief [Wisner] arrived in Istanbul to salvage what of value remained. There were by then no contacts in Europe. A detailed investigation was undertaken, and members of the CEREUS circle, including "Dogwood," were summarily released.

Relations with British agencies improved. [Various British intelligence officers had privately voiced criticisms of the insecurity of OSS/Istanbul during the CEREUS operation. In May 1944, a meeting of representatives from all British agencies had decided to minimize relations with the mission, pending some improvement in security in both business and personal activities. (footnote)] An over-all rise in the quality of intelligence acquired from European travellers followed the creation of a Joint Interrogation Board with members from OSS, the U.S. Military Attache's office, British Naval Intelligence and SIS. A system of negative checks was evolved to avoid U.S.-British competition for, and dual use of, agents, without revealing the actual employees of either party to the other.

[Deletion] The CEREUS operation illustrated the multiple pitfalls of this type of intelligence. Disasters were likely to slow the early steps of a new agency in a treacherous field. Yet attempts had to be made somehow to acquire experience in indirect operations, one of the most remunerative approaches to strategic intelligence collection.

SWEDEN

Like Bern and Istanbul, Stockholm provided a neutral base close to German-controlled Europe. Here OSS interviewed refugees, sailors, travellers, officials, and businessmen from Germany, Denmark, Norway, and the Baltic countries, and reported infringemets of Swedish-German agreements. Some of the best intelligence finds of the war were acquired through liaison with representatives of Baltic countries in Stockholm. From Swedish sub-bases in Malmoe, Haelsingborg, and Goeteborg, OSS agents penetrated Norway, Denmark, Finland, Lithuania, and Germany. Bases along the Norwegian frontier dispatched supplies across the border to/Norwegian guerrilla groups.

Secret intelligence. The first agent (dispatched by COI) arrived in March 1942 to lay the groundwok for further intelligence activities. By the end of the year there were three men, including the prospective mission chief.

[The first OSS mission chief in Stockholm was Bruce Hopper, of Harvard, who went by sea to Liverpool and then from the RAF special operations base at Leuchars, Scotland, by RAF Mosquito, a fast, light intruder bomber which ran scheduled flights to Stockholm across enemy territory as regularly as any peacetime air service. The chief of operations at Stockholm was Wilho Tokander, a Chicago lawyer of Finnish extraction. There, too, was Taylor Cole, a political science professor at Duke University, and Walter Surrey. Agents included Stanton Griffis, chairman of the board of Madison Square Garden and Brentano's book chain, and Therese Bonney, an American journalist in Paris who was friendly with Field Marshal Mannerheim, the Finnish leader in the war with Russia in November 1939.

[Hopper's mission was distinguished primarily for its long battles, successfully concluded, with the State Department. The American ministry in Stockholm was reluctant to provide cover and the Passport Division refused to give passports to OSS officials going to the Scandinavian capital on operations that were not clearly and boldly stamped with the letters OSS. The American minister in Stockholm, Herschel Johnson, reportedly considered American intelligence operations as satanic. No doubt there was some truth in this suspicion: Calvin Hoover, the economist of Duke University who controlled SI operations in Scandinavia at OSS headquarters in Washington, actively encouraged Hopper's men to spy carefully on the Russian intelligence services.

[This sort of activity was hardly likely to engender good relations between the Russian and American embassies, nor was it likely to encourage a spirit of cooperation between the Russian and American intelligence services throughout the world. However, espionage against Russia receded when Tokander took over from Hopper in the autumn of 1943. From a practical point of view, however, the attack on Russia produced admirable yields, including the order of battle of both the Red army and navy—priceless material that was obtained for a price from Finnish military intelligence sources, then engaged in war on Germany's behalf against America's ally, Russia. It is worthy of note that when the State Department was successfully brought to heel, up popped the old hostiles—the old guard of the British intelligence services. Here, the engagements were long, loud and acrimonious, especially over OSS intentions concerning German-occupied Norway. It was not until Joseph Haskell arrived to take command of SO/London

that the OSS Scandinavia was able, at long last, to get down to the
business of fighting the actual enemy—Germany.]

[Excision] The State Department had the controlling decisions
in the entry of new OSS representatives, and also in communications. It was therefore with some misgiving that the new OSS
mission chief listened to the U.S. Minister's first ultimatum. A
week after his arrival, the Minister called him in to inform him
that any espionage activity for the U.S. on his part would result in
the Minister's personal request for his recall.

Relations, however, slowly improved. State Department cable
facilities were used, with the Minister retaining the right to inspect
all outgoing messages. And in mid-1944 it was the strong stand
taken by the Minister vis-a-vis the Swedish Government that allowed OSS to remain in that country. As the Axis defeat became
more obvious during 1944, and Swedish cooperation with the
Allies improved, the Minister made high-level arrangements
through the Swedish Under Secretary of State for meetings between OSS and the Swedish secret police. [Presumably these meetings were amicable because OSS was permitted to establish intelligence bases at Malmo, Halsingborg, and Goeteborg in the
summer and autumn of 1943.]

[Excision] These ports line the Kattegat sea-lane between Denmark and Sweden, and provided excellent vantage points for (a) in-
terviewing sailors, refugees, travellers, officials, and businessmen
coming out through Denmark, and (b) spot intelligence on German
traffic to and from Norway. By contacting leaders of transport
workers in these ports and in Stockholm, OSS procured the first
consistent flow of accurate information on the German transit traffic to and from Norway through Sweden. The information showed
that the personnel and materiel traffic was far heavier than the
Swedish-German agreement permitted, and than believed by the
U.S. State Department. OSS reports covering the shipment of
troops resulted, in late 1943, in the suspension of the Swedish Government's permission for German troops to be moved through
Sweden. [Excision] It was [name excised] at Malmoe who collected, from a Swedish official in the seamen's union, the most telling
evidence on German troop movements via Oresund, Sweden.

Through contacts with the Danish resistance, he also recruited
two young men who were dispatched to Denmark. They came back
some weeks later with intelligence on German troop movements,
installations, and morale, and returned again to Denmark. By the
time of their second return, the Swedish secret police had learned
of their activities and arrested them. Through the tacit assistance
of a Danish-born police officer, however, they were released and

returned to Denmark, whence one of them went to Germany to return eventually with more German military intelligence.

Other agents were subsequently dispatched on round trips to Denmark from Stockholm. In the same way, travellers from Goeteborg established networks of SI agents in Norway, Finland, and the Baltic states. An SO contact with a Gestapo group in Norway produced, in early 1945, the number and location of German divisions there, including those which had just moved in from Finland.

An outstanding espionage accomplishment was the coverage of SKF ball bearing shipments to Germany. [As David L. Gordon and Royden J. Dangerfield pointed out in *The Hidden Weapon; The Story of Economic Warfare*, (Harper, 1947, pp 88): "Bearings are essential in the production of planes and all kinds of mobile equipment, and German aircraft and ordnance designers used exceptionally large numbers. If their supplies could be knocked out it would create a major bottleneck in the production of military and transportation equipment, and ease immeasurably the planned invasion of France."] During early 1944, one of the main objectives of the strategic bombing program was the destruction of the German ball bearing industry. As the supply of enemy ball bearings became more stringent, due to the success of the air program, acquisition of Swedish ball bearings became increasingly important to the enemy. Despite strenuous efforts by the Economic Warfare Divisions of the American and British Governments, including extremely liberal preclusive buying arrangements with SKF, it was estimated that five to seven percent of the total German supplies were coming from SKF Goeteborg, with the percentages running considerably higher for certain types of bearings.

During 1943, the OSS [agent] in Goeteborg obtained from his transport worker contacts the approximate tonnages of ball and roller bearings leaving the harbor, the names of the ships loading bearings, the times of departure, and ports of destination. This intelligence, wired to London, caused the sinking by air attack of one such ship.

In order, however, to gain even more accurate information, the SI representative contacted through cut-outs, an individual, "B," who was working in the SKF shipping office in Goeteborg. "B" had considerable moral misgivings, being divided between loyalty to his company and his government on the one hand and, on the other, belief in the Allied cause. He would accept no payment.

From December 1943 to May 1944, he supplied reports on the ball bearing shipments, serial numbers and quantities; also on the export of ball bearing tools and machinery, such as the lathes made at the SKF subsidiary plant in Lidkjoeping and shipped to

Schweinfurt. To avoid discovery, the OSS cut-outs were constantly changed, but on 13 May 1944 "B" was arrested by the Swedish secret police.

The data he had supplied showed that the exports were larger than the Swedish Government had admitted. In May, a U.S. Economic Warfare Mission arrived in Stockholm, and, using these figures, extracted an agreement to stop all ball bearing shipments. Agent "B" was given a three-year jail sentence, lost his position in his firm, and for some time his rights as a Swedish citizen.

Agent "Red," recruited in Washington, acquired some excellent intelligence. [This man was Eric Ericson, whose exploits received much undue fame through the film *The Counterfeit Traitor*, which starred William Holden. The operation was a joint OSS/SOE affair.] An oil dealer, he had been blacklisted early in the war for trading with the Germans. He was given a chance to prove innocence and went to work for OSS in Stockholm. As a Swedish citizen, he affected a sympathetic interest in maintaining the German oil supply. He pretended to plan a synthetic oil plant in Sweden and contacted August Rosterg, who owned the controlling interest in the German firm of Wintershall. From him he obtained considerable information on German oil manufacture and supply.

In October 1944, he arranged a week's tour of the synthetic oil industry in Germany, visiting and inspecting many plants. His subsequent report received favorable comment from British MEW and American experts. In particular, the information on the Ammendorf plant was considered valuable. German officials finally became suspicious and avoided further contacts with him.

The Japanese next approached "Red" independently, in the fall of 1944, with a proposition that he buy ball bearings for them. He accepted the assignment and actually bought some. In the meantime, however, the Russo-Japanese negotiations for shipping the bearings via Russia broke down, and the Japanese began laying plans for smuggling them into Germany. The Swedish secret police uncovered the negotiations, and the attempt was given up, but not before "Red" had obtained valuable evidence of the types and amounts of bearings most desired by the Japanese, incidental information on Japanese and German personalities and activities in Sweden, and clues which helped the Swedes arrest a group of smugglers. Through VE-Day, the Japanese continued their close relations with "Red," who exploited them for much counter-intelligence information.

One double-agent, "Phillip Morris," was taken on by OSS/Stockholm. He presented himself to SI in April 1943 and offered information on members of the Italian Intelligence Service and bombing targets in Italy. A Washington report (based on information from the British, the FBI, and X-2/Italy) described "Phillip Morris" as one who would sell his services to the highest bidder or bidders. The chief of mission, however, elected to hire him and laid on an operation to take place in Italy. The agent was unfortunately arrested for espionage by the Swedes in late 1944, and escaped with German assistance to enemy territory, where he reported the contacts given him in Switzerland and in Italy.

The best intelligence of all came from liaison with foreign services in Stockholm. The intelligence service of the Polish Government-in-Exile in Stockholm gave OSS top priority in reports, in return for assistance in supplies, transportation, etc. A notable item was its report on a new underwater detection device ("schnorkel") installed on German U-boats [actually an air-intake device, now spelled snorkel]. [Deletion] A similar liaison with the Hungarian Minister in Stockholm began in December 1943. Estonian, Latvian, Lithuanian, Belgian and Dutch refugee groups provided further intelligence. In return for an OSS/Stockholm pledge not to establish independent networks in Denmark, British SIS and SOE relayed all their reports on the area.

Good relations with the Swedish Government proved remunerative, particularly after the termination of German transit traffic in the fall of 1943. [Excision] The release from jail of several SI sub-agents was secured. [Excision] [Moreover, with Hopper's departure, relations with the Russians improved.] The First Secretary of the Soviet Legation approached an SI official in late 1943 with a proposed barter arrangement. In return for SI reports on Baltic shipping, the Russians would supply certain Japanese information. SI soon discovered that this exchange was a one-way street, and the relationship was converted into a social one. It was suspected that the Russians hoped merely to ascertain the extent of American penetration into Finland. [Excisions and deletions]

Special operations. Sweden offered possibilities of direct infiltration by boat either to the North German ports or through Denmark. Since the time was short, however, OSS/ETO maintained in London the facilities already established there. A document section was, for instance, never set up in Stockholm, with the result that agents had to wait long periods for the arrival from London of papers, which were often outdated by that time. A Labor Desk agent, "Goethe," could not leave when his documents came two months late and incorrectly prepared. No air transport was available. At the same time, Swedish ships ceased traffic to Germany in late 1944, when insurance companies withdrew their coverage [under U.S./U.K. government pressure]. This left OSS only two possibilities, German ships to Germany and Swedish fishing boats to Denmark.

The latter route proved simpler, since Danish resistance contacts offered a degree of safety in the trip to the German border. The WESTFIELD Mission, SO, sent one team through Denmark, but at a time when the SFHQ lines had just been blown, and most of the members were hiding out.

. The team was divided into two sections. "Birch," the leader, who had friends in Berlin, was to go in first alone, establishing, if possible, a safe route through Denmark and Germany. The radio operator and one assistant were to follow as soon as they had word from him outlining the route. An allied courier had deposited two radio sets, explosives, cameras, film, food, cigarettes, and liquor for them [excision] in Berlin. Pending the arrival of his radio operator, the leader would use the bi-weekly [Allied] courier service.

"Birch" left Goeteborg by Swedish trawler on 22 February 1945, but had to turn back because of Gestapo seizure of the fishing hamlet in Denmark where he was to land. On 5 March, a second attempt succeeded in landing him at Skagen. Here he arranged for transportation by car, through a Danish resistance agent, known to the fishing group which had brought him ashore.

From Skagen, he was driven to Aalborg, where he contacted a dentist as a safe address for his two assistants. He took a train to Kolding, passing several control searches, and in Kolding contacted a fish dealer, one of the members of the old SFHQ underground.

The fish dealer took him across the German frontier between Krusaa and Flensburg at midnight, 13 March; midnight was the usual hour for a delivery of fish, and the controls were not too strict. They drove to Hamburg, where "Birch" went to a safe address provided by SFHQ, and arranged for the trip of his successors. Moving on to Bergedorf, he looked up a gasoline dealer, whose name had been given him by the fish dealer, and made similar arrangements.

At Bergedorf he met a Danish [excision] chauffeur who agreed to take him to Berlin in return for American cigarettes and coffee, plus gasoline from the dealer. "Birch" was in Berlin by 15 March.

Living with friends in Bernau, a few miles northeast of the capital, he prepared a report which he sent back. [Excision]

He slowly legalized his status, obtaining the various necessary papers, licenses, and ration cards. He recruited a noted physician, who treated, among others, Ribbentrop and Goebbels; the doctor provided, besides intelligence, two guns with ammunition, and lodgings in both Berlin and Potsdam.

Subject to constant Anglo-American bombing, and eventually to Russian artillery, "Birch" covered the whole Berlin area and sent back [excision] three more reports. He took a car trip to Hamburg in early April, principally to see if his two followers had yet arrived. His trip took him within six miles of the front, where he found and reported the degree of disorganization and wreckage. Returning to Berlin, he spent nearly all of the last half of April in an air-raid shelter with the rest of the starving Berlin population. The Russians entered his sector of Berlin on 2 May, and he was returned to the U.S. occupation zone on 20 May, carrying one of the first reports on conditions in the Russian zone.

The radio operator and assistant, who were to follow along the underground route to Berlin, never arrived. The two men did traverse Denmark in late April, aided by fake documents, cigarettes, and pornographic pictures. Crossing the German border [excision] on 2 May, they spent four days in Luebeck, surrounded by British troops. When they were overrun on 6 May, they supplied counter-espionage and tactical information.

"Birch" was the only successful direct infiltration from Stockholm. Even this mission came too late for the reports, relayed by [excision] courier, to contain any outstanding items. OSS/Sweden did not have the facilities (documents, transport, staff) available in London for such direct operations.

Morale operations. A two-man MO unit arrived in April 1944, and, using OWI equipment, began production of black propaganda. Some 250,000 pamphlets, leaflets, stickers, posters, letters, and seductive booklets and postcards were turned out. The unit produced and distributed [deletion] *Handel und Wandel*. This was a weekly business publication containing largely financial news, together with editorial matter frankly angled from a German industry viewpoint. Its purpose was to hold out the hope to German businessmen that if they acted to throw out the Nazi leaders, Allied business interests would cooperate with them in building a bulwark against Bolshevism. [To propagandize for a "bulwark against Bolshevism" was not then part of Allied policy; MO, however, was free to do so, since its publication pretended to emanate from enemy sources. (footnote)] Limited distribution of this publication was made mostly through SO agents in Norway, Denmark, Sweden, and Germany, the bulk being distributed through OSS/Stockholm, the remainder through Lisbon. One pamphlet in late August 1944, following the Finno-Russian armistice, was distributed among the German troops in North Finland urging them to escape to Sweden. Swedish officers stated that a large number of soldiers deserted, many of them carrying the leaflet. Rumors were also spread in Stockholm, some of them reaching, through friendly news reporters, the front page of Swedish papers.

X-2. The three-man X-2 unit, under State Department cover, performed the only U.S. counter-espionage in Scandinavia.

Upon arrival in April 1944, the first X-2 agent was presented by SI with visa information (including photos) on every German citizen who had entered or left Sweden for the previous several months. SI further assisted in the penetration of two embassies: a Bulgar contact furnished regular coverage of developments, personnel and reports in the Bulgar Legation; through a Sudeten-German trade unionist, a representative of the SI/Labor Desk contacted a code clerk in the office of the German Military Attaché, and, from March 1945 to the end of the war, obtained copies of German cables even before they were sent. With such SI aid, and in cooperation with the British, Swedish, Norwegian, Danish, Dutch, and French counter-espionage services, X-2 acted to protect both Sweden itself and U.S. agencies in Sweden from Axis espionage.

Maximal attention was given to the technological field, in view of Sweden's outstanding industrial and scientific achievements and their possible use by the enemy. The best defense being offensive penetration, information was collected on the intelligence services of the northern European states at home and of the external intelligence organizations active within each of these countries. Penetration of these services, including those of underground movements, pseudo-governments, and governments-in-exile, was carried out through controlled and double-agents. X-2 gave valuable assistance in the neutralization of over 150 active German agents (all confined or executed) and the identification of over 3,000 agents and officials of intelligence interest. Of paramount importance in mid-1945 was the information obtained on the collaboration between German and Japanese intelligence organizations and between the Axis and neutral countries.

X-2 also frustrated enemy activities directed at the United States. It was initially responsible for keeping out of the United States several technologists, formerly in German espionage, who could have greatly endangered the security of the U.S. scientific program, particularly in the field of nuclear physics, and numerous others who, on the basis of CE files and the X-2 vetting interviews, were found to be more than undesirable. Toward the end of hostilities, the number of visa applicants increased to such an extent that, by early summer 1945, the Stockholm office was handling close to 1,000 monthly.

In conjunction with the British, X-2 ran several double-agents into Germany to obtain information on German rocket developments. For the State Department, in addition to vetting all visa applicants, it checked its non-American employees (with a resultant dismissal of five), and helped on "Safe Haven" work. [Deletion]

SUPPORT TO NORWAY AND DENMARK

Secret operations in Norway and Denmark differed markedly from those in any other Nazi-dominated territory, resistance in both countries being well unified and the native intelligence services in effective control. Since the principal effort from London was directed toward France, OSS attempted no large-scale coverage.

It was the task of SO and SOE to arrange for supplies, training and communications with the resistance groups, and for this purpose SO and SOE base offices in London were integrated after 1942 in an organization later known as Special Force Headquarters (SFHQ).

SFHQ/Scandinavia, though theoretically a joint operation, was in the main British-run, SOE having supported Danish and Norwegian resistance movements for over two years before SO set up an operating establishment in London. The agents were native Norwegians and Danes, under the orders of the Norwegian Government-in-Exile or of the Danish Freedom Council. They were recruited in the area of operation, over 100 being secretly brought to England for training in SOE schools. SO and SOE cooperated in arranging for supplies and transportation.

An exception to this British control of the operation was the advance SFHQ base in Stockholm. Although it was directly under SFHQ/London, it had to be separated, for purposes of cover, into British and American units. Activities of the American unit, WESTFIELD, began with the arrival of the chief in November 1943, and supplemented those of the SOE mission, which had been in Stockholm since 1940. [The leader of this mission was George Brewer, who had taught English at Yale and had become a Broadway playwright. The head of the OSS/Norwegian desk at London was Commander George Unger Vetlesen, an American of Norwegian origins who had two aces—he was a millionaire and a friend of King Haakon.] By July 1944 there were eight SO staff members, [excision]. Some 70 sub-agents were employed.

SHAEF's directive to SFHQ called for a two-fold task, first a counter-scorch effort to preserve installations, and second, sabotage of transportation to delay the German troop movement south-

ward. During 1943 and early 1944, SHAEF had requested little ac-
tion in order to avoid reprisals and useless waste of lives. But on 26
October 1944, extensive rail sabotage was authorized, and on 2
December 1944, as the West Front advance slowed to a halt,
SHAEF requested the strongest delaying action possible.

Both WESTFIELD and SFHQ/London were divided into Norwegian and Danish sections:

Norway. Except for a small Communist resistance group,
operating in southeast Norway, all resistance was centralized
under the national "Milorg." Section F.O. IV of the Norwegian
High Command in London controlled "Milorg," and it was with
F.O. IV that SFHQ cooperated. By January 1944, nineteen teams
of from two to six Norwegian agents each had been equipped with
W/T in England and dispatched by air and sea to lead resistance
groups in Norway. By VE-Day there were 62.

SO worked with SOE in supplying these teams. When one-half
of the Norwegian fishing boats, used to transport agents from the
Shetland Islands, were sunk by enemy action, OSS procured in
November 1943 the use of three 110-foot U.S. subchasers, which
operated from then on without loss. SOE had been unable to supply its teams by air during the summer months due to the length of
the Arctic day. In 1944, however, OSS obtained the services of
Colonel Balchen of the USAAF, who, with six B-24's based at
Leuchars, Scotland, volunteered to risk the long daylight hauls of
summer. [Colonel Bernt Balchen was a Norwegian-born arctic ex-
plorer who was a friend of Trygve Lie, the Foreign Minister of the
Norwegian government-in-exile in London. Balchen had been refused permission by the British to fly unmarked planes to Norway,
and so he asked Lie to take the matter up with Churchill. Churchill
intervened on Balchen's behalf and within two months the first of
Balchen's aircraft was dropping supplies to the guerrillas in the
Norwegian mountains.] Americans in SFHQ also developed, in
early 1945, the use of double hessian bags for drops of clothing,
bandages and other soft materiel. The bag cut container weight by
100 pounds, and the use of light flare parachutes, also developed at
that time, produced a further decrease in the auxiliary load.

In Sweden, the SO WESTFIELD mission initiated the supply of
resistance groups north of the 62nd parallel, an area which the
SO/SOE agreement assigned specifically to SO. Three supply and
communications bases, code-named SEPALS, were established
along the far northern Norwegian frontier. Swedish permission
was obtained, with the excuse that they would serve as weather stations.

First W/T contact with a SEPALS base was received by London on 9 August 1944. From this date, the fifty Norwegian agents manning the bases worked across the border, leading local resistance groups, establishing supply caches in Norway for their use, gathering intelligence and fighting off attacks from German frontier patrols. Sabotage operations included the demolition of one regimental supply depot filled with highway construction machinery, nine German border guardhouses and barracks, two mountain snow-ploughs, one 17-truck highway ferry, a smaller ferry and a 1500-ton Finnish steamship.

The demolition of the supply camp, for instance, was carried out by a party of five men on 12-13 January. The purpose was to prevent the construction by the enemy of a new road between Storfjord and Theriksrosen, to be used for the withdrawal of German troops from northern Norway and Finland. The party left base in the early afternoon of 12 January, and reached a sheltered position near the depot three and a half hours later. Here they waited, and performed a final reconnaissance. At 2345 hours the group cautiously approached the camp, placed explosives and escaped. The first charge detonated in ten minutes, and the others followed. Later intelligence, furnished by the Swedes, disclosed that the entire supply depot had been destroyed, and the road construction abandoned.

The SEPALS parties organized and armed a northern resistance group of some 6,000 men. This group supported OSS operations, and was of considerable assistance after VE-Day to the 1,200 Allied troops who invested Norway to take control of the 130,000 German troops still there. Members of the resistance also gathered intelligence for cabling through the bases back to London. They covered the German escape from Finland and movement to Narvik, shipping activities, laying of minefields, and other military and naval developments during the last six months of the war. The bases also provided meteorological data for use by the British-based air forces and by ATC. [Excision]

SO activities in South Norway supported SOE activities with the resistance groups there. WESTFIELD sub-agents provided safe addresses. Both sea and land routes to the Oslo area were worked by the British and American groups. An SO chain of some 400 agents in Oslo distributed over half a ton of propaganda material prepared by OWI and MO.

WESTFIELD also sent five men into Norwegian territory to receive an SFHQ mission. The RYPE team consisted of twenty American OG's, dispatched from London on 24 March 1945 to cut the Nordland rail line at two points in the North Trondelaag area. The purpose was to prevent German re-deployment of 150,000 troops in northern Norway, which was being accomplished over these lines at the rate of a battalion a day. Fourteen members of RYPE landed at the reception point at Laevsjoen, while the fifth plane lost its course, and the men were mistakenly ordered by the pilot to parachute into Swedish territory. An arrangement with the secret police, however, soon released them from internment, and they crossed the frontier to rejoin the main body of the team. Further efforts to reinforce the group from London resulted in two plane crashes and the death of ten OG's.

[The OG team leader for the RYPE operation was Major William E. Colby, who became director of the CIA and station chief in Rome and Stockholm. He was not a member of OSS initially but a volunteer from the U.S. airborne corps. It has been stated that the British kept the OSS out of Norway for fear that "American amateurs" might upset their own "difficult relations" with the Norwegian resistance. In later years, Colby would not discuss this contention publicly. However, it seems there was a bad attitude towards U.S. airmen on the part of many Norwegians, caused by the bombing of civilian targets when the USAAF was raiding the Norsky Hydro-Electric Power Plant, which was being used by the German atomic bomb project for the production of heavy water.]

Trekking on two long trips through the snow, RYPE carried out both of its rail-demolition tasks successfully. The first, involving the blowing of the 18-foot railway bridge at Tangen, was accomplished on 15 April. And on 23 April, the group, reinforced by the returnees from Sweden, blew up a 2½ kilometers of rail with 240 separate charges of plastic. Although attacked by German rail guards, they escaped without losses. The two operations reduced the German rate of troop movement south from one battalion a day to approximately one battalion per month.

Like the SEPALS parties, RYPE was also of service in taking over control on VE-Day, being the first Allied troops in the area.

Denmark. In Denmark, even more than in Norway, SFHQ directed all operations, and the area remained under the British control which had been established prior to the arrival of OSS. The WESTFIELD mission carried out some independent work, including management of the only clandestine boat service (bi-weekly) carrying agents, supplies and microfilmed messages between Malmoe and Denmark, and conduct of the only wireless telephone link from Haelsingborg to Denmark. The mission further handled from Sweden all radio communication from SFHQ teams in the field.

When the Germans terminated local self-government in Denmark in the summer of 1943, the Freedom Council was organized, with a headquarters in Sweden. SFHQ worked through the new

Council, cleared agents (all Danish) with it and exfiltrated only a few to England for training. Supplies were parachuted by Britain-based planes, or carried by boat from England and Sweden. Between January 1944 and April 1945, SFHQ parachuted 268 tons of supplies.

SHAEF requests for increased sabotage of transportation, in October and again in December 1944, resulted in a large-scale effort. The railroad attacks between 25 January and 12 February were particularly effective, blocking completely, for that period, the main eastern railroad in Jutland. Movement southward of the 233 Reserve Panzer and 166 Reserve Infantry Divisions was considerably delayed. Other sabotage was directed against industrial targets. For example, on 2 January eight guerrillas attacked and destroyed the Charlottenlund factory making radio parts for V-2; the factory was subsequently abandoned.

An unusual example of air support for a resistance movement was the bombings of Gestapo files. In October, German counterintelligence had been taking a serious toll among members of the resistance, particularly in the Jutland region. On the basis of urgent W/T requests, SFHQ arranged for the bombing of Gestapo and Sicherheitsdienst headquarters in Aarhus to destroy the files on resistance activities and men. Twenty-five [RAF] Mosquito bombers, dispatched on 31 October, demolished the headquarters, and it was reported that 150 German Gestapo and counter-espionage officials were killed in the attack. Similar operations were repeated at Copenhagen on 21 March and at Odense on 17 April.

In general, individual credit could not be divided between the SO and SOE organizations. Since SOE had been operating for some time prior to SO arrival in London, maintained a much larger staff in SFHQ, and had actual, if not nominal, control of all the operations, the larger share of credit for the accomplishments of SFHQ should go to SOE.

In Norway, the signal accomplishment was the organization, in cooperation with the Norwegian Government-in-Exile, of a resistance group counting 31,980 effectives. These were armed with 450 tons of equipment, delivered by parachute drop from the British Isles, boat from Scotland and Sweden, and cross-country gun-running from Sweden. Some fifty agent teams, trained in England, provided leadership and communication with the London base. About 200,000 German troops occupied Norway until February 1944, when the Germans started to move southwards for the defense of the Continent. When, in October 1944, SHAEF requested delaying sabotage in Norway, in order to ease the situation on the

SUMMARY OF AIR OPERATIONS
Denmark

	Successful	Unsuccessful	Agents successfully dispatched	Radio sets delivered	Tonnage
1941					
December	1	..	2	..	..
1942					
January	..	..	..	..	..
February	..	..	..	..	..
March	..	..	..	..	..
April	1	2	2	..	..
May	..	..	..	..	..
June	..	..	..	..	..
July	..	..	..	..	..
August	1	..	..	..	.75
September	..	..	..	..	..
October	1	1	1	..	..
November	..	..	..	..	..
December	..	2	..	..	..
TOTAL	3	5	3	..	.75

	Successful	Unsuccessful	Agents successfully dispatched	Radio sets delivered	Tonnage
1943					
January	..	2	..	..	..
February	1	5	3	4	.50
March	1	..	4	..	.50
April	2	..	..	2	1.00
May	..	..	..	..	..
June	..	..	..	..	..
July	4	..	3	..	1.50
August	6	..	..	..	6.00
September	..	..	..	..	..
October	3	..	..	..	2.00
November	..	4	..	..	..
December	3	1	3	..	1.00
TOTAL	20	12	13	6	12.50
1944					
January	..	..	..	..	..
February	4	2	2	..	3.50
March	..	..	..	..	..
April	6	4	3	..	6.50
May	4	..	..	..	5.00
June	..	..	..	..	..
July	..	..	..	..	..
August	10	5	2	..	10.00
September	26	17	..	..	30.50
October	24	15	9	..	32.75
November	65	32	1	..	86.00
December	6	11	..	..	7.00
TOTAL	145	86	17	..	181.25
1945					
Jan.-Feb. 23	46	31	1	..	65.00

West Front, "Milorg"/SFHQ sabotage of rail lines, roads, boats and port installations was so effective that on VE-Day German forces in Norway still numbered over 100,000 men, composing twelve divisions.

In Denmark, the total effect produced by SFHQ was the organization and arming of a resistance group numbering by VE-Day some 13,000. The flat terrain of Denmark made the suppression of resistance a much easier task than it had been for the twenty German divisions in mountainous Norway. Nevertheless, in March 1945, Denmark still held 35,000 Nazi troops, constituting three and one-half divisions.

In general, all these operations were British-directed. The principal SO activities were those involved in effecting radio communication, obtaining supplies and documents, packing them and laying on air or sea transportation. The attached exhibit gives some idea of the quantity of supplies dropped to Denmark by air alone.

SWITZERLAND

In both World Wars, Switzerland was the main Allied listening post for developments in European enemy and enemy-occupied countries. Switzerland's geographical position and its neutrality made it the happy hunting ground for the intelligence services of all the belligerent countries. In this respect, it was chiefly of use to the Allies since Switzerland opened no doors to the outside world for the surrounding Axis forces. British, French, Polish, Czech, and many other services had long been established and had combed the field for useful agents, and there were few high calibre men equipped for this work who had not already been impressed.

OSS, too, exploited the espionage opportunities of Switzerland. An exceedingly small staff located there succeeded in producing the best OSS intelligence record of the war. Some one hundred chief agents, many of them leading chains with hundreds of sub-agents, provided early information on such items as V-1 and V-2, atomic and bacteriological research, the German counter-offensive at Bitche and the planning for the 20 July attempt on Hitler's life. Members of the staff handled negotiations with various satellite governments and for the surrender of Axis forces in North Italy on 2 May 1945.

Intensive planning in OSS/Washington for the establishment of an office in Bern began in the spring of 1942, and, in May, the first representative of OSS left for Switzerland, where he was attached to the U.S. Legation.

[The spymaster was, of course, Allen W. Dulles, brother of John Foster Dulles, the future American Secretary of State during the most intense of the Cold War phase of international politics. A.W. Dulles arrived at the French-Swiss frontier only minutes before the German army closed the frontier in what was one of their first ripostes against the Anglo-American invasion of French North Africa.

[Dulles, who had been an American spy in Switzerland during World War I, took a flat at 23 Herrengasse in Bern, and the press announced that "Allen W. Dulles, Special Assistant to the American Minister," had arrived in the Swiss capital. His main task immediately was to seek out and encourage elements in Germany who were seeking to overthrow Hitler and end the war. Largely because of Roosevelt's unconditional surrender proclamation at Casablanca in January 1943, this proved fruitless. No understanding could be reached between Washington and the Schwarze Kapelle, the Gestapo's codename for the small element in the German General Staff and in the Abwehr (the German secret service) who were trying to destroy Hitler and Hitlerism with just as much devotion as any other resistance movement in Europe. Dulles was not able to give the SK any moral encouragement, or, for that matter, any other form of encouragement.

[Dulles' principal assistant was Gero von Schulze-Gaevernitz, whose father, an official of the Weimar Government, had been known to Dulles after World War I. He was extremely well connected in Germany, being an in-law of the great industrial chief, Stinnes. One of Dulles' most important advisors was Wilhelm Hoegner, another prominent figure in the Weimar parliament, who had once brought Hitler to trial for treason. Nor did Dulles neglect contact with the left wing in Germany. Here one of the main contacts was Noel Field, a former State Department man with a Harvard education who had become intoxicated with communism during the Popular Front phase between the world wars.

[The first of the go-betweens with the Schwarze Kapelle was Hans Bernd Gisevius, a former Gestapo man turned Abwehr field agent with direct and undeniable contacts with the chief SK plotters, Admiral Canaris, General Beck (the former Chief of the General Staff), Count Wolf-Heinrich von Helldorf (police president of Berlin). Gisevius had been rejected by MI-6 as a contact on the grounds that he was probably a deception agent, an assessment that proved incorrect in the long term.

[Dulles' main contact with the Kreisau Circle—an anti-

Hitler group whose philosophy was violent revolution to rid
Germany of Hitler to be followed by the elysium of a Christian
socialist state based upon sound democratic principles—was
Adam von Trott du Solz, a former Rhodes scholar who was well
connected with middle-of-the-road elements in higher London
society and within the British intelligence service. Dulles even
had contact with the SD: that organization's delegate to OSS
Bern was Prince Max von Hohenlohe-Langenburg-Rothen-
haus, a very elegant figure in European society. Through the
prince, Dulles sought to provoke Himmler into a *coup d'etat*
against Hitler. Dulles was certainly in sympathy with the German
opposition, and especially the group around Canaris. When Dulles
became director of the CIA, he is said to have arranged a CIA pension for Frau Canaris, whose husband was executed by Hitler for
high treason.]

[Deletion] [Dulles opened an office in buildings occupied by
OWI, where OSS enjoyed diplomatic immunity. Meetings with
sub-agents were held, after blackout, at the mission chief's
house, where surveillance was almost impossible. Sub-bases
were established in Geneva, Zurich, Lugano, Ascona and Basel
with similar security precautions. Knowing that telephones
were tapped by the Swiss, no secret information was passed
over the phone. [This rule was violated once in a crisis which
left no alternative, and the agent involved, to whom a rendezvous was given, was picked up by the Swiss within a few hours.
(footnote)] No messages of a secret character were sent by
Swiss post. In conjunction with the Legation, a courier service
was arranged with the outlying sub-bases.

As all mail or courier communication between Switzerland
and the outside Allied world was cut off, OSS/Bern had to rely
solely upon commercial radio over the Legation stamp, supplemented for certain purposes by the trans-Atlantic telephone.
The first and most serious communication difficulty was a mechanical one, namely the task of enciphering the multitudi-
nous reports which had to be sent every day to Washington,
and often to London and Algiers as well. Two of the key
members of the staff, who were vitally needed for other work,
had to spend their entire time in ciphering and deciphering,
Fortunately, relief came from the skies. As American aviators
made forced landings in Switzerland, permission was obtained
from the Swiss to attach a certain number of these aviators to
the Legation staff. Soon the OSS mission had six or seven of
them working as cipher clerks on a 24-hour shift.

During the period of Switzerland's isolation, attempts were

made, from time to time, to get pouch material through to London or Algiers. These efforts were largely unsuccessful until the liberation of Corsica in October 1943, when a complicated but nonetheless reliable scheme was worked out. Maps, drawings and the full texts of reports were microfilmed in Bern and sent to Geneva, where they were given to a locomotive engineer on the Geneva-Lyon run. The film was hidden in a secret compartment built over the firebox. If the train were searched by the Germans en route the engineer had only to open a trapdoor at the bottom of the box and the film was immediately destroyed in the flames. In that event, the engineer would notify OSS on his return to Geneva, and a duplicate film would be given him. At Lyon, the film was turned over to a courier, who took it by bicycle to Marseille. Here it was entrusted to the captain of a fishing boat bound for Corsica, where, finally, it was picked up by plane from Algiers. Over this involved route, only ten to twelve days elapsed between Bern dispatch and Algiers receipt of the film.

In November 1944, after the French border had been opened, a clandestine radio post was established at Bern. Up to this time, the use of commercial channels had lost time and limited the stations which could be reached, since the messages had to pass through diplomatic or consular offices. Earlier efforts which various of the foreign missions in Bern had made to establish clandestine radios had always been balked by the Swiss. They had no difficulty, of course, in D/F-ing them, and their practice then was to interrupt transmission by cutting off the electric power at the appropriate moment. If this hint were not taken, formal diplomatic action would follow. By the end of 1944, however, OSS/Bern had established such good relations with Swiss intelligence that it decided to try out a radio post, and was not molested.

While deeply attached to maintaining their own neutrality, the Swiss really had one serious fear, invasion by Germany. In 1940 the Germans had been poised to strike France through Switzerland. It was only the quick break-through in the north which had avoided this. In March 1943, the Germans again came near to invasion to open up better rail communications with Italy, for the purpose of provisioning their hard pressed armies in North Africa.

To avoid possible incidents, Switzerland had passed stringent legislation directed against any persons operating in its territory in the interests of any of the belligerent powers. This legislation, of course, did not apply to the official representatives of the belligerent powers, except insofar as they might be found guilty of suborning Swiss nationals or residents. Allied intelligence officers, therefore, had to exercise the greatest care and circumspection. Those directing the various Allied services were officially attached, under various covers, to their diplomatic missions. The agents whom they employed, to escape the scrutiny of the Swiss police, had to use ingenuity and guile and observe the rigid rules of security, both in their contact with the officials for whom they worked and in carrying out specific missions.

OSS/Bern, however, established close relations and personal friendships with many Swiss officers, particularly in the intelligence service. An exchange of information was initiated on German troop movements, in which the Swiss were particularly interested, and the U.S. secret radio station was allowed to operate.

Joint OSS/OWI operations were worked out in the field of propaganda warfare. The OSS mission had early established contact with a Frenchman, known under his cover name of "Salembier," who had been one of the French Deuxieme Bureau's chief propaganda artists in World War I. He knew his trade, and was set up in business, operating from Geneva, by OSS and OWI jointly. Millions of pamphlets, leaflets, cards, postage stamps, and every form of literary propaganda were printed and smuggled into Germany and Fascist Italy. When the Frankfurter Zeitung was suppressed by Hitler, a small edition was printed in Switzerland and sent into Germany. Much material was also dispatched to the French resistance to aid them with their own publications. The speeches of de Gaulle were reprinted in vast quantities and smuggled into France.

OSS/Bern also maintained close contact with the intelligence operations of the diplomatic staff and of the Military Attache's office. There was a free exchange of battle order information between OSS and the latter, and, at one time when he was not permitted to communicate other than to G-2, Washington, a certain amount of his material was incorporated, with clear source indication, into the reports sent by OSS/Bern to SHAEF.

Relations were established with several prominent dissident diplomats of satellite states. They included the Hungarian and Bulgarian ministers to Switzerland, Baron Bakach-Bessenyey and Georges Keosseivanoff, and the former Rumanian Minister, who had severed official relations with his country and was living in retirement in Geneva. The anti-Nazi elements in Hungary were particularly anxious to make contact with the Allies and, in September 1943, maneuvered the transfer of Bakach-Bessenyey from Vichy to Bern, and from that time on, he was in secret contact with OSS. These sources provided considerable economic and some military intelligence, but their reports were especially interesting for the light they shed on their countries' political dilemmas.

Another valuable channel of information became available as early as December 1942, when the French Embassy in Bern, upon the total occupation of France by Germany, ostensibly terminated its military and naval information services. The well-trained and long-established Deuxieme Bureau personnel, which, over the years, had developed a large network into Germany and had as well prime contacts in France, was threatened with disbandment for lack of funds. OSS/Bern agreed to finance the service under its old head, a French major of long training in the Deuxieme Bureau, and the latter managed to retain his position at the Embassy. Working in cooperation with the American Military Attache, the Deuxieme Bureau service was maintained and expanded. In order to give its personnel the feeling that they were working for their own Government, the material they collected was sent by radio through OSS channels directly to the military services of the French in Algiers. From this source, OSS received weekly some one hundred pages of intelligence on Germany, France, Italy and the Balkans.

Such was the general background in which the small unit at Bern operated. Some of its more interesting activities follow:

Hungary. In February 1943 Kallay, the Prime Minister of Hungary, sent an emissary to Switzerland to establish contact with OSS. His purpose was to give information on the position of his country, and to request the initiation of informal and confidential conversations between Hungary and the United States. While the Hungarians were apprehensive of an open break with Germany, they feared the Russians far more. In July, the emissary informed OSS/Bern that his Government was prepared to liquidate its existing commitments toward Germany and refuse to enter into new ones, thereby attaining a de facto state of neutrality, contingent, however, upon certain guarantees from the United States regarding Hungary's frontiers and assurances concerning Russia's Hungarian policy.

Although discussions of this nature were out of the question, Bern felt that Hungarian good faith might be tested by requesting cooperation in an operation. It was suggested that the Hungarians make arrangements to receive an American agent, whom they would furnish with military information, for transmission by a secret radio to be sent in by Swedish courier from OSS/Stockholm.

SPARROW, as this project was called, might have been successful if it had not taken almost eight months to put into effect. The Hungarians were in agreement in principle, but, for various reasons, stalled for several months before actually getting down to details. Innumerable difficulties had to be ironed out with OSS/Algiers. It had been decided to send a team of three men, and considerable time elapsed before the qualified personnel could be found. Finally, on 15 March 1944, SPARROW, consisting of a colonel, a major and a lieutenant, parachuted into Hungary close to the Yugoslav border. [This mission was that carried out by Florimond Duke.]

Plans had been worked out with the head of the Hungarian intelligence service, General Ujszaszi. The agents were to be treated as prisoners of war, and go through the routine questioning by the military authorities. Then, instead of being interned, they would be taken to a secret hideout from which they could operate their transmitter.

At first, all went according to schedule. The men gave themselves up at the nearest village. Shortly thereafter an English-speaking major appeared, stating that he had been waiting for them for several days. Together with their equipment, he took them by stages to Budapest, where they arrived on the evening of 17 March. They were then taken to General Ujszaszi, who received them cordially, and apologized for the necessity of keeping them in jail. The two cabinet ministers SPARROW had come to see were out of town for a few days, but he would arrange an interview as soon as they returned.

Less than 48 hours later the Germans occupied Hungary, and the men were turned over to the Wehrmacht. For two weeks they appeared to be getting away with their cover story, that they were on a mission to the Yugoslav Partisans when their plane was hit by anti-aircraft fire, and that they had been forced to bail out. Then the Gestapo took over with interrogations lasting for six weeks. During one of them, the colonel was shown a twenty-page signed statement by General Ujszaszi which told the whole story. The men had no recourse but to admit the obvious details, but were able to conceal the OSS origin of their mission. Eventually they were returned to the jurisdiction of the Wehrmacht, interned in Germany and liberated by the American forces nearly a year later.

Austria. The effect in Austria of the Moscow Declaration furnished excellent proof of the value of psychological warfare. The announcement, in October 1943, that the United Nations would guarantee the independence of Austria, encouraged the growth of resistance. In December 1943, OSS/Bern was contacted by envoys of an underground organization claiming a membership of 5,000 made up largely of Socialists and Communists. They wished to set up a channel through which to send intelligence and receive instructions.

At about the same time, relations were established with the coordinating committee of the Austrian resistance movement. This group had already contacted OSS/Istanbul, and had been given a transmitter and code for communicating with Algiers. However, on their return from Turkey, the couriers had been forced to abandon their radio in Sofia. As communications were far easier to maintain with Switzerland, the group had sent two envoys to establish a link there. Plans were worked out with Algiers to send agents and a transmitter, but the project fell through when the Germans occupied Hungary, where much of the activity was centered.

The leader of the group, "Oysters," came to Switzerland in March 1944, where he had a wide variety of contacts in industry, government, commerce and police, even to top-ranking Gestapo officials, and was able to give Bern a quantity of valuable information. To counteract Russian influence, "Oysters" was anxious to have the Allies undertake a radio propaganda campaign directed at Austria. Fifteen to twenty experienced Communist agents, he reported, were being parachuted every month into Austrian territory.

Due to OSS indiscretions in Turkey, plus data secured by the Germans when they occupied Budapest, many of the Austrian resistance leaders were arrested, including "Oysters." Although an Austrian by origin, "Oysters" was a naturalized Brazilian. Bern therefore initiated steps to have him exchanged for a German in Brazil. This was never effected, but the negotiations served to stay his execution, and he was taken over by the Russians when they occupied Budapest.

Bern had numerous other channels into Austria, and one source, an Austrian industrialist, was of particular value. It was he who first gave OSS/Bern the location of the V-bomb laboratory at Peenemuende, and much of the technical information on the rockets.

Late in 1944, the Austrian resistance established a secret post in Zurich, and arrangements were made for a courier service between Zurich and Vienna. [Excision] "K-28" [excision] considered himself an envoy of the resistance, an operations man, although he was willing and did furnish Bern with some of the best intelligence obtained on Austria during the last months of the war. The fact that SI and SO operations were handled by the same U.S. organization, rather than by two as in the case of the British, proved a great advantage. OSS/Bern could fit "K-28" into its scheme of operations without any difficulty, and used him both for SI and SO activities. [Excision]

"K-28" travelled back and forth frequently, from Switzerland to Milan and over the Brenner to Vienna and back, disguised as a German courier. In 1945, in order to check details on the Austrian underground organization, Bern arranged with OSS/Paris to send with "K-28," to Vienna, an Austrian agent who had been working with the exile group in Paris, to the great mutual advantage of both parties. Those inside were encouraged with the knowledge that they had outside help, and the exiles were strengthened by establishing this direct contact with internal resistance.

Germany. Intelligence on Germany, from the end of 1942 when the Swiss mission was established, was gathered from a wide variety of sources. It came from officials in confidential positions inside Germany; from businessmen who occasionally visited Switzerland; from political and labor leaders once prominent under the Weimar Republic, who had fled to Switzerland after Hitler came to power and who maintained contacts with Germany; and from various church organizations.

This work had an unexpected measure of success, largely because of two circumstances: (1) A highly placed agent [Kolbe] working inside the German Foreign Office gave OSS/Bern unstinted cooperation for eighteen months, and (2) the German military foreign intelligence service, the Abwehr, contained anti-Hitler elements.

The Foreign Office Contact. The best of all Bern's sources was established in August 1943. "Wood" held a most confidential post in the German Foreign Office. He had entered the foreign service before Hitler's rise to power, and from the beginning had been a staunch opponent of the Nazi regime. Despite his refusal to become a Party member, because of his abilities he was attached to several German diplomatic missions abroad. After the outbreak of war he was recalled to the Foreign Office, where he was rapidly promoted to a position which gave him access to the most secret information.

The inside view "Wood" thus obtained increased his opposition, and he embarked on his underground career. Since he was unable to leave Germany to make personal contact with the Allies, he had secured the cooperation of a member of the French resistance, an

Alsatian doctor. Through this channel he sent information to both the French and the British. Finally, with the help of a woman who had charge of the Foreign Office courier service, he received permission to make the trip to Bern as official courier. The initial contact with OSS was made through a friend of "Wood's," resident in Switzerland.

"Wood" brought him several copies of top secret Foreign Office cables, and, from copious notes he had made in Berlin, gave OSS/Bern many additional items of vital information. Secret and top secret messages were being mimeographed in several copies for various German Foreign Office bureaus, and it was "Wood's" task to destroy the copies which came to his office. The liaison position of his bureau provided him with the most important ones. At the first meeting, "Wood" told OSS/Bern that it would be possible for him to secrete the significant messages and to arrange either to bring or send them to Bern from time to time.

For several months, "Wood" managed to go to Switzerland every few weeks. Soon he was bringing cables by the pound, officially packaged and sealed by him in the Foreign Office. The problem of handling this periodic flood of material was a staggering one. The security angle alone was perplexing enough, and the task of translating and encoding took the time of the entire staff at Bern for weeks after each batch of telegrams was received, until the frontier opened in September 1944 and the material could be sent out in bulk.

Toward the end of 1944, both because of the increasingly difficult conditions in Berlin and to facilitate transmission, "Wood," furnished with an OSS camera, began to photograph his documents and send long rolls of film. He sent this film to OSS in an envelope addressed to an imaginary Swiss sweetheart, by German couriers who had no idea of the material they were carrying. The photographing of these messages was generally done in the basement of a hospital in Berlin with the help of the Alsatian doctor. During the frequent air raids, the work had to be done with flashlights. [One of "Wood's" more trying experiences occurred when Himmler requested a file which, at the moment, was being filmed. "Wood" had to rush back to his office and pretend to pull out of his files what he was actually extricating from his coat pocket. (footnote)]

As Allied interest shifted to the Far East, the material received from the German Air Attaché in Japan became increasingly important. Bern lacked any established route for passing to "Wood" the urgent requests from OSS/Washington. Deciding that the simplest and most direct way was least likely to cause suspicion,

OSS/Bern dispatched a post-card from the Swiss sweetheart. On the reverse of an Alpine scene was a message, stating that one of her friends, prior to the war, had kept a shop selling Japanese trinkets, toys, etc., and had found a considerable market for them. Now her friend could get them no more. In view of Germany's close alliance with Japan, was it possible to find any of this Japanese material in Germany, or to get it through Germany? Her friend wanted more of it. This tip was all that "Wood" needed. The next batch of material contained dozens of up-to-date reports, direct from the German Embassy in Tokyo.

Over a period of a year and a half, OSS received from "Wood" more than 1,600 true readings of cables to and from the Foreign Office and some forty German diplomatic and consular missions. They included reports from the military and air attaches in Japan and the Far East, data on the structure of the German secret service in Spain, Sweden and Switzerland, and espionage activities in England and in the British Embassy in Istanbul. Each step in the German efforts to bribe wolfram from Spain, to squeeze more raw materials and commodities from satellite states, and to get more manpower from France was laid bare. "Wood" also informed Bern about Allied codes which had been broken by the Germans.

Until his escape to Switzerland some months before VE-Day, "Wood" was never suspected. British SIS rated him the best intelligence source of the war.

The Abwehr Contact. Through contact with members of the Abwehr, OSS/Bern maintained close touch with the underground elements in Germany who plotted the overthrow and the assassination of Hitler.

Early in 1943, direct contact was established with one of the chief Abwehr personnel in Switzerland, Hans Bernd Gisevius, Vice-Consul in the German Consulate General in Zurich.

At one of the first meetings between the mission chief and Gisevius, the latter, who had just returned from Berlin, drew from his pocket the texts of several secret telegrams which had been sent by the American Legation in Bern. The Gestapo had broken the State Department code, which, because OSS was so under-staffed, had been occasionally used for long reports from that office of a political nature.

One of the enemy-deciphered cables was a report, based on information previously furnished by Gisevius, on the political situation in Italy, and mentioned that certain leading Fascists, including Ciano, were possibly open to approaches from the Allies. This cable had been shown to Hitler, who promptly forwarded it to Mussolini. A few days later Ciano was removed from his post as

Foreign Minister. [He was executed by the Fascists soon afterwards.]

To what extent the cable may have been responsible for his dismissal has not been revealed by any Axis documents thus far uncovered. The information brought by Gisevius was immediately passed on to the American Minister, and the code was gradually discarded. To have ceased using it abruptly would have aroused German suspicions, and naturally it was used only for innocuous reports, or to furnish the Germans with misleading information.

This initial proof of good faith marked the beginning of a long and close association. Gradually Gisevius revealed the names and the plans of those involved in the plot to overthrow Hitler, to which Bern gave the code name "Breakers." Until Gestapo suspicions were aroused, nearly a year later, Gisevius constantly travelled back and forth between Zurich and Berlin and kept OSS currently informed regarding "Breakers." When, finally, it became unsafe for him to return to Germany, his place was taken by another Abwehr conspirator, who also operated under the cover of Vice-Consul in Zurich. [The position of the Abwehr in Germany was badly upset by the various defections from its service engineered by British and U.S. counter-intelligence in Istanbul. (footnote)]

"Breakers," as Gisevius revealed it during the eighteen months preceding 20 July 1944, comprised a group of high German officers, the chief of the Abwehr and some of his staff, Foreign Office officials, Goerdeler—former Mayor of Leipzig, and Socialist and trade-union leaders. They were anxious to enlist American support for their plans, and even proposed to cooperate with American forces behind the German lines. In particular, they wished to secure American and British collaboration against Russia. "Breakers" was always told, however, that, while Washington was glad to know that there were Germans who were trying to oust the Nazis, and sympathized with this aim, it was first up to the Germans themselves to take action against Hitler. Moreover, under no circumstances would America break faith with her Russian ally.

Gisevius returned to Berlin about the middle of July 1944, and took part in the abortive putsch on the twentieth. He escaped the Gestapo dragnet after its failure, and for six months remained in hiding in Berlin. He informed OSS/Bern of his whereabouts, and, to help protect him, OSS circulated the rumor that he had escaped to Switzerland. The Gestapo combed the country for him. Finally, with a complete set of Gestapo papers prepared by OSS/CD in London, Gisevius did make his escape to Switzerland in January 1945.

Industrial Intelligence. "Breakers" and "Wood" were the two most striking of the operations of OSS/Bern directed against Germany. There was, however, a constant flow of intelligence from many sources. Important German industrialist centers were penetrated, and detailed information regarding production in various lines of German industry, particularly aircraft, was forwarded to Washington. Swiss industrial circles were in close touch with German business, and, by discreet contact with pro-Allied members among them, it was possible to obtain the most detailed information on the German situation. The German Legation and most of the German consulates were also thoroughly penetrated, and little went on there which was not known.

Among other items, Bern reported on the midget or "beetle" tank, a year before it made its short-lived appearance at Anzio on the Italian front. Much information on the locations of aircraft factories was also secured, including data on the first jet-propelled planes.

Bern gave a considerable amount of intelligence on the factories manufacturing parts for the rocket bomb, including the Rax Werke at Wiener Neustadt, which was raided toward the end of 1943. The first inkling of the nature of V-1 came from a Swiss industrialist, who, as early as February 1943, informed OSS/Bern that the German secret weapon was possibly some sort of aerial torpedo. It was not until the end of May that Gisevius reported that the Germans had developed what he understood to be a new heavy missile employing the rocket principle. This, he said, was already in limited production somewhere in Pomerania. At the end of June, Gisevius and another source brought details on the rocket, and an Austrian source fixed the location of the assembly plant and testing ground at Peenemuende. Finally, on pinpoints furnished by Bern and checked by air reconnaissance, Peenemuende was raided by the RAF in the summer of 1943.

Hitler had hoped to have his rockets over England at the end of 1943, setting 30 November as the deadline for "Program A-4," as the Germans called it. The raid on Peenemuende upset the timetable, and the first rockets did not appear until June 1944.

Information on the rocket bomb installations was one of the major items covered by the French chains during the spring and summer of 1944. The first such reports reached Bern late in 1943, and, months before the Allied air forces took action, many of the launching sites, especially in the Pas de Calais region, had been pinpointed. One chain obtained valuable photographs of the emplacements themselves.

Until the launching sites were overrun at the end of 1944, OSS/Bern continued to receive intelligence from Germany and

France on the characteristics of the V-bombs.

Washington showed great interest in some Bern reports on bacteriological warfare and urged Bern to push investigation. However, while a certain amount of data was collected, no conclusive evidence was uncovered that the Germans were preparing for this type of warfare, although there were many indications that they had ample supplies of poison gas.

An outstanding Swiss physicist provided information on his fellow German scientists who were working on atomic development. This project in the United States was then so secret that what was going on in this field in other countries was not even assigned as a target to Bern. The only evidence Bern received that its cable had caused quite a stir in Washington was the immediate instruction to reclassify it as top secret, closely followed by a detailed questionnaire as to the location and activities of a long list of German scientists. From then on, contact with the Swiss physicist was closely maintained and much information sent.

Ascertaining that the headquarters of German atom splitting activities had been moved from the Kaiser Wilhelm Institute in Berlin, Bern was given the task of finding out where the German atomic energy scientists were really working. The first clue received on their hideout in South Germany came from several letters mailed by one of the atomic scientists to a Swiss friend in touch with OSS/Bern. None of the letters were mailed from the exact place where the scientific laboratories were established, but the telltale postmarks from little towns all near together in a particular locality, taken in conjunction with other information, enabled OSS to pinpoint the laboratory's location. Sabotage was planned and an agent sent to Bern for the purpose. Unfortunately, he was picked up by the Swiss, due to indiscretions on his part, before Bern could get him into Germany. However, information acquired through Bern and other sources had already satisfied atomic experts in Washington that the Germans were far behind in the race.

West Front Intelligence. In September 1944, when the French border opened, OSS established a sub-base at Annemasse, just over the frontier from Geneva, for penetration of Italy and the Alps. Two productive chains were also operated from Annemasse through Switzerland into Germany. Later, a base was established on the northern frontier of Switzerland, first at Pontarlier and then at Hegenheim in Alsace. Through it, operational military intelligence from Switzerland could be supplied directly to the 6th and 12th Army Groups.

The post was first used to relay directly to the 6th Army Group daily reports on the Rhine water level readings. Preparations were then being made for the passage of the Rhine, and it was feared that the Germans, as soon as Allied forces attempted to lay down pontoon bridges or to use river landing craft, would blow up some of the dams either on the Upper Rhine or on its tributaries, and create a temporary flood to wash away the facilities established.

Here speed was important. A flood, started in the Upper Rhine between Lake Constance and Bale for example, would take several hours to reach the critical points in the middle and lower Rhine, where U.S. forces might be trying to cross. Direct radio signals were worked out so that Bern could get this information through to 6th Army Group in a matter of minutes. In addition, the Army wished to be informed on any particular flood conditions in the Rhine arising from natural causes, and for this reason requested the daily readings. It desired them taken at various points along the river, which was not easy. Several Bern agents were picked up when the mysterious telephone calls, from points along the Rhine to Bern, were intercepted and analyzed. Readings at Bale, however, could be taken and communicated with relative ease. The OSS/Bale representative would merely take an early morning stroll across the Rhine bridge, read the gauge, and telephone his observations to Bern. A few minutes later the 6th Army Group would have them. [Bale is also called Basel.]

A Labor Desk was also opened in Bern, after September 1944, for the direction of labor union and similar contacts. Labor Desk policy was based on the experience that more useful results were obtained by taking advantage of the trade union and socialist elements who already had contacts in Germany, or the possibility of traveling to Germany, than by attempting to bring in outsiders to infiltrate them through Switzerland.

Union leaders produced useful recruits who had regular occasion to cross the border, and, by feeding them directives, equipment, and money, developed chains within enemy territory which produced regular and useful intelligence. In general, the attempts to bring in outsiders and pass them over the German border without the knowledge of the Swiss resulted in a high percentage of failures. Swiss counter-intelligence was extremely efficient, and the German frontier well guarded on the German side. At the end, travel within Germany was surrounded with so many confusing and ever-changing restrictions that it required a large staff to follow them and to keep the travel papers, passports, food cards, and the like, up to date. The Swiss, with all their facilities and their firsthand knowledge, were naturally much more quickly informed than any of the other intelligence services possibly could be. [Excision]

German preparations to flood the Belgian and Dutch coastal areas were reported by Bern, long before similar information reached Washington and London from other sources. Sufficient reliable information was also collected to forecast the German offensive in the Bitche-Wissembourg sector, launched on 1 January 1945. OSS/Washington was later assured that this information was of great assistance in stemming the tide of the German breakthrough in that area.

Japan. Despite the distance between Japan and Switzerland, the latter was nevertheless a good base for obtaining Japanese intelligence. The current information obtained through the German Foreign Office by the "Wood" contact was an example. In addition to that, there was a German refugee industrialist in Switzerland who had close contacts with the Japanese Navy and continued throughout the war to be in touch with high Japanese naval officials, both in Japan and in Germany. He proved a useful source of information, being out of sympathy with the war party in Japan.

As the war drew to a close, two Japanese officials, attached to the Bank for International Settlements, established, through a neutral member of the Bank, running contact with OSS/Bern. Prior to the Potsdam Conference, information came through this source, indicating Japanese willingness to surrender on the basis of the territorial integrity of the four main Japanese islands, provided the Emperor and certain basic features of the Japanese constitution be maintained. The whole background of Japanese reasoning, influenced as it was by the chaotic conditions of Germany resulting from its fight to the bitter end, was set forth in submitting this proposal. It was deemed of such importance that, at the request of Assistant Secretary of War McCloy, the mission chief took the information to Secretary of War Stimson, at the Potsdam Conference in July 1945. [Deletion]

CHAPTER 12

D-Day Preparations in London and Algiers

The principal OSS effort of the European war was directed toward France. Large OSS bases at London and Algiers provided extensive R&A, X-2, CD, R&D, Communications and other services. By the time of the invasions, OSS had gained some three years of experience, less than any foreign espionage agency, but sufficient to produce a creditable performance.

[As important, relations between the American and British service chiefs in London were excellent. Good sense prevailed over the petty phobias that existed in remote stations and formed the enduring liaison that existed between the American and British services for the next thirty years. Much of the credit for this remarkable liaison must go to the high sense of purpose displayed by the chiefs, General Sir Stewart Menzies (SIS) and General Sir Colin Gubbins (who replaced Hambro as chief of SOE for the invasion) on the British side, and Colonel David Bruce, Colonel William Maddox (OSS/SI) and Colonel Joseph Haskell (OSS/SO) on the American.]

SO operations from London and SI operations from Algiers presented a striking contrast. The support and exploitation of resistance, directed from ETO, were conceived to be paramilitary tasks. SO recruiting, training, dispatching and servicing were handled in a military and largely impersonal fashion, apparently modelled on SOE procedures. SO and SOE officers and men, many of them in uniform, parachuted into France and organized resistance groups, trained them, arranged for the large air drops of supplies, directed sabotage and incidentally transmitted intelligence. On and after D-Day, resistance was coordinated with the advancing Allied armies by an additional 276 personnel dispatched as liaison, and by SO/SOE detachments with each of the armies in the field. Generals Eisenhower and Patton, among others, paid official tribute to the remarkable resistance effort in causing diversions, covering undefended flanks, disrupting enemy communications, protecting vital installations and delaying and harassing enemy troops in transit. [Deletion]

THE LONDON BASE

The OSS establishment in London served not only as the base for clandestine activities in northern, western and central Europe, but also as a collection and dissemination center for intelligence of interest to U.S. and Allied agencies in Washington and London.

Early administrative arrangements were characterized by informality, since no elaborate chain of command was required. During 1943 and 1944, however, the base expanded to meet growing commitments, and administrative procedures became more complex. By mid-1944, OSS/London was an elaborate organization which included more than 2,000 personnel and 14 branches. All branches reported directly to the Deputy Strategic Services Officer, and through him, to the SSO. The chain of command represented a departure from the Washington arrangement, where the Director, OSS, controlled the various branches through three deputy directors for intelligence, operations and services. In London, the SSO and Deputy SSO were also supported, at the planning level, by a Plans and Operations Staff and a Secretariat.

[Beside the unenthusiastic reaction of Malcolm Muggeridge (quoted in my introduction) to the early OSS arrivals in London can be placed this more sarcastic appraisal by Kim Philby, another MI-6 counterintelligence man. He would write (from Moscow, whence he had defected, having been a Russian agent all along): "Our first visitor from the United States was a certain Kimball, of the FBI.... He talked with machine-gun speed, accusing the Navy, the Army, the State Department and the White House of having ignored FBI warnings of imminent Japanese attack....OSS were not far behind...we had assigned to us a small liaison party. Its head was Norman [Holmes] Pearson, a poet of Yale. He was hail-fellow-well-met, and have you heard the latest one about the girl on the train? He was terribly funny about his organization *Oh So Sexy*. It was a notably bewildered group, and they lost no opportunity of telling us that they had come to school."

[First OSS/SI chief was Dr. William Maddox, a political scientist who had taught international affairs at Harvard and Princeton. He was assisted by Russell D'Oench, grandson of the founder of the Grace Shipping Lines. The overall chief of OSS in London was David Bruce, a multimillionaire whose father had been a U.S. Senator, whose wife was a daughter of Andrew Mellon and was called the world's richest woman, and a man whose career had taken him into the legislatures of Maryland and Virginia. He had served on the boards of twenty companies; as a U.S. diplomat in

Rome, he knew Donovan well, and he knew Menzies better—an acquaintanceship that was valuable in those days. Bruce would go on to become ambassador to France, to Germany, to Britain, to China, to NATO; the chief of the Marshall Plan mission to France; and the American delegate to the Vietnam Peace Conference in Paris. The first chief of SO in London was none other than Donovan's friend, Colonel Ellery Huntingdon.] [Deletion]

Special Operations. In June 1942, OSS/SO and SOE had entered into an agreement which spelled out the basic terms of cooperation between them. As early as April 1943, there was a realization of the need for a joint SO/SOE headquarters in London to coordinate American and British teams in the field. The proposed headquarters must have responsibility for the dispatch of agents and the supply and direction of resistance groups. It was estimated that sixteen SO/SOE officers would be required for the headquarters, eight of whom would be detailed to an Operations Room. [The controlling center, where maps, charts, messages, and other data pertinent to all SO/SOE operations would be maintained. (footnote)]

On 4 September 1943, SO/SOE representatives met to discuss unification. Recognition of the need for additional personnel resulted in a statement of responsibility for D-Day procedure for the Operations Room "including the participation of OSS." On 7 September, SO pointed out that OSS representation ought not to be restricted to the Operations Room, but should include full responsibility for operations in U.S. sectors of the future front. The British accepted the suggestion, and also admitted American personnel to the controller staff in the Operations Room, where they would have charge of cables, incoming and outgoing, and responsibility for certain cases which had been inadequately handled by the country sections.

By December 1943, the combined headquarters of SO and of the London Group of SOE had virtually been established. Official recognition of the new arrangements was given in two documents, dated 10 and 14 January 1944.

The first, addressed to the regional directors and section heads of SO and SOE, originated from the SO/SOE headquarters, London, and was signed by the American chief, SO and the British chief, SOE. It stated that "integration between the London Group of SOE and the SO Branch of OSS, ETOUSA, has taken place." It went on to underline the joint aspect of the integration in the following provisions: (1) Duties would be assigned to officers irrespective of their American or British allegiance; (2) certain sections, of equal concern to both SO and SOE, such as Air

Operations and Planning, would be run jointly; (3) in the event of
an operation of concern to only one of the two agencies, the officer
of the organization concerned would make the decision; in the
event of an operation of equal importance to both organizations, a
disagreement would be submitted for decision to the Director
(British) or the Deputy Director (American) of the joint headquarters. [Deletion]

SHAEF approved the integration on 24 January. The principle
of dual control and equal responsibility between SO and SOE was
thus effected, and SO became fully merged with its British equiva-
lent. It was, however, physically impossible for OSS to assume
partnership on an equal basis, due to the lack of personnel. Thus,
joint control at the top, rather than full partnership down the line,
characterized the operation. [Deletion]

SO/SOE was designated Special Force Headquarters (SFHQ)
on 1 May 1944—a change in title which had no effect on the functions of the organization. The new designation clarified the relationship to the new Special Force Staff Detachments, SO/SOE
units to be attached to the armies in the field. [Deletion]

Transport. Air transport filled the greatest part of the demands
for dispatching agents and supplies. [Deletion]

Efforts to obtain U.S. Army aircraft for agent drops began in
October 1942 and continued unsuccessfully for a year. A shortage
of planes made Eighth Air Force priorities difficult to obtain, even
though both Admiral Stark and Ambassador Winant supported
the requests. It was not until October 1943, when JCS approved
the allocation of aircraft for the support of the Polish underground, that the Air Force agreed to supply air lift, and it was
not until January 1944 that it became available. From that point
on, however, squadrons of specially converted B-24's, and later A-
26's, stationed eventually at Harrington, carried out agent and
supply drops for SI and SO, along with similar planes pooled by
the British. By March, some 200 flights were being run per moon-
period. [Deletion]

X-2/London. A Counter-Intelligence Division of SI, organized
in March 1943, became the Counter-Espionage (X-2) Branch of
OSS by June of that year. Despite the late start, by 1945 the
United States had acquired an experienced group of professionals
in the complicated techniques required for the protection of U.S.
services abroad. [Deletion]

From the beginning of the war the British had urged creation of
such a service either in OSS, or jointly between OSS and the FBI.
After it had been formed, the British carried out a thorough policy
of offering the new section complete access to files in London,

sources, secret methods, procedures and knowledge of the personnel, organization and operations of what was probably the world's
most experienced and efficient, and therefore most carefully safe-
guarded, security system:

Characteristic of the apprentice training offered OSS by the
British was that given to some X-2 members in the double-agent
section of MI-5 (B). These officers were assigned desks in the offices of that section and had free access to the files of double-agent
cases, to the traffic of current ones, and to the officers who had
directed or were directing such cases. Normally, in the course of
their study, they met both double and controlled enemy agents
whom the British were operating, helped to gather the "chicken
feed" which was to be transmitted to the Germans, and learned the
relationships between the sections to which they were attached and
the other intelligence organizations which shared the exploitation
of double-agent networks. One American officer was given a desk
in the room of the director of the double-agent section, and was
made party to all conversations and conferences on problems arising in connection with the management of current British cases,
some of which were of a long-range character and therefore involved the highest security. When the secret methods of the British
agencies were fully understood, the importance of the security risk
they took was appreciated as overwhelming.

It was on this basis that X-2/London opened offices adjoining
those of the British, and began in March 1943 to learn the job. It
early became obvious that London would have to be the center of
X-2 operations in Europe, North Africa, and the Middle East, due
to the presence in London of other Allied counter-espionage services and the sources of intercepted material which were available
only there. [Excision]

Preparing Special Counter-Intelligence Teams (SCI). In preparation for the invasion of Europe, the X-2 intelligence sections for
the areas to be occupied had two main tasks: the gathering of as
great a store of basic counter-espionage files as possible from the
registries of the British and other Allies; the preparation of a machine, consisting of Special Counter-Intelligence teams, for work
with the invading armies, and a headquarters War Room to support their operations.

These tasks were clearly parts of the one main purpose: the liquidation of the enemy intelligence and subversion services. The earlier operations, from neutral countries and newly gained footholds
in Africa and on the Continent, aimed at drawing a tight intelligence ring about the periphery of enemy occupied and dominated Europe; those that accompanied the attack of the armies

applied in the field the stores of intelligence so far gathered toward the neutralization and control of enemy services.

There was in London a startlingly large and accurate mass of data on individual enemy agents and their organizational relationships, on channels of communication, and the like; it was possible not only to list and map enemy offices and operational stations, communications chains and training schools, but also to pinpoint the location of individuals and of related groups of the German satellite undercover agencies. This information had been gathered from the activities of Allied CE stations in neutral countries, the surveillance of known enemy chains, the operations of double-agents and controlled enemy agents, the interrogation of defected or captured enemy agents, censorship sources and various other means. The SCI teams carried this information to the field with them—information, which they, and the CIC teams of the armies, exploited with results that expanded at times in almost geometrical progression: the swift capture and interrogation of one pinpointed agent led to the identification and location of one, two, or three others, who each might yield like identifications in his turn.

Members of the SCI teams to accompany American armies in the field were trained and briefed in the X-2/London office, and, for a group of selected officers, in the double-agent section of MI-5 (B). The training consisted of formal lectures on enemy organizations and their relationship; the study of CE files of invasion areas; classes in codes and communications procedures; work with desk personnel in the preparation of SHAEF cards, target lists and the like; and discussion and study group meetings with experienced British and American officers. [Excision]

War Room. In late April 1944, the training of the SCI units and the Western European Desk's arrangements to serve them, were tested in a three-day field exercise carried out, together with SI and SO units, at Horsham under simulated battle conditions. An analysis of the weakness of the liaison and communications methods, brought out under this test, indicated the need of more standard procedures, which were accordingly prepared and published in May. The document fixed the terms under which a joint British and American headquarters' Western European Desk, to be known as the SCI War Room, was to operate, and defined the relationships between SI, SO, and X-2 with respect to the handling of agents, the interchange of information and the interrogation of certain categories of persons. The plan established two separate organizations in COSSAC. One of these was the Evaluation and Dissemination Section (EDS) to compile, analyze, edit, and distribute

(a) the semi-overt type of counterintelligence (on collaborationists, police, political papers, etc.), and (b) [deletion] the so-called SCI War Room, an unofficial arrangement [excision] for the purpose of servicing SCI units in the field and EDS in London.

The SCI War Room contained master maps pinpointing all known German agents and espionage centers, including "national" sub-agents of Allied-controlled German agents. It was a headquarters desk, geared to serve as the operational and intelligence base for the units with the armies. In the period before the liberation of Paris, it handled all requests, even for supplies, from the field.

Besides the normal desk work of receiving, processing, carding and distributing the mass of information from all sources and preparing target lists and studies for the units, it answered queries for checks on arrested or suspect agents, assisted with fuller information for field interrogations, and arranged with the field units for shipment to the U.K. interrogation centers of enemy agents of importance or special promise as double-agents. [Excision] Until a special Vetting Desk was set up at the end of 1944, the War Room had also the task of carrying through security tracings on an increasingly large number of SI agents recruited in the field as military operations progressed.

In early March 1945, a reorganization of the War Room and desk system was accomplished, which (a) made of the War Room a broader and less secure agency, and (b) gave to the desks the job of handling double-agents. The desks were now organized, not according to countries within the SHAEF area of responsibility, but according to branches of the German intelligence services.

The new SHAEF G-2 Joint Counter-Intelligence War Room was to work directly for the SHAEF Counter-Intelligence Branch (CIB) staffs during the last phase of military operations and through the liquidation period that would follow the collapse of Germany. [Deletion]

The French services were also admitted to participation. The Director and Deputy Director were attached to SHAEF and were not responsible to their respective Services. The War Room had no concern with the running of agents, although it did receive relevant information produced from such operations; nor was it responsible for German activities outside the SHAEF area except for Austria, which by special agreement, was to be the concern of the War Room during the occupational phase.

The new War Room was looked upon by the CIB staffs as part of their own machine, and they had recourse to it constantly for information on the German intelligence services, and guidance in the conduct of their operations. This relationship made for a diffusion of information on enemy intelligence personnel and organizations to lower field units, which had hitherto known little or nothing about them. The War Room assisted in training and briefing interrogators assigned to the American Interrogation Center, a number of whom came to London for study and conference. It also sent to the field over-all studies on enemy sabotage activities and methods, although none was prepared on such general topics as types of agents employed, missions, cover stories, etc. [Reports on the extreme vulnerability to enemy saboteurs of Allied supply lines were unfortunately ignored by Services of Supply. (footnote)] [Excision]

The most striking of the new features was that the desks were assigned, not to the study of the GIS in certain areas, but to that of highly particular sections of the Abwehr or the Sicherheitsdienst themselves. Thus the several desk officers could become final experts on assigned sections and sub-sections of GIS. Given that concentration of specialty, an officer could have at his command all the information available on his subject, and could, therefore, handle more business more effectively in a day than he could if his interests were more dispersed and the necessity of refresher reading on various kinds of scattered cases necessary. Such functional arrangement of targets was an ideal one for a CE agency since the targets were, not areas, but enemy undercover agents and operations themselves. [Deletion]

An X-2/London Desk. A typical desk history, through the various reorganizations, was that of the German Desk, which began its work in January 1944. As was true of all the London desks, its first activities centered chiefly on the job of building up its basic file of records from the large accumulations of the counterpart British desk. It focussed on the enemy undercover organizations in Germany, which for the purposes of the Desk, included Austria.

In August of 1944, the Polish, Czechoslovak and Swiss desks were incorporated into a German Desk, in preparation for a German War Room to service SCI teams and the field stations, before and after the German surrender. Actually, no such War Room came into full operation for the reason that the joint X-2/MI-5/MI-6 SHAEF G-2 Counter-Intelligence War Room came into being in time to deal with the mass of work on the arrests, interrogations and the like, that came with the decline and collapse of the German military strength. The new arrangement left to the Desk the management of all special cases, and the processing and distribution to Washington of the reports transmitted to it by the War Room on German cases. Lists of suspect persons, organization studies of the GIS, area target lists and similar material, made in preparation for the support of the field teams in Germany, were, despite the change, distributed to the field.

Target lists, worked out from sources ranging from top secret material [i.e., Ultra of SIS communications] to German telephone books, were found to be highly useful to T-Forces and CIC teams, which went into towns and cities with the first army units. Such raids yielded in turn, from captured documents and the speedy interrogations of captured GIS personnel, fuller and more recent information of targets ahead. A staff of the German Section in the Paris office worked on this project exclusively. Its lists, produced and distributed at top speed, were, when time allowed, supplemented and corrected by cabled and pouched notes drawn from the London files of the German Desk and of the War Room. Headquarters could, by this time, draw on fully checked and detailed interrogation reports of captured or defected German officers and agents of high grade. Toward the end of the fighting and after, only the more highly placed and more knowledgeable members of the GIS could be given thorough interrogation. They would yield more information of the significant personnel in the echelons below and above them, with the least expenditure of time and energy.

The German Desk collaborated with the War Room, not only in making target lists, but in the preparation of studies and reports on the methods and techniques of German intelligence services, recent changes in the relationships among branches of the various German services, their plans for long-range resistance, sabotage and intelligence operations and related activities.

During the period of settlement after VE-Day, the Desk served the X-2 staffs at Wiesbaden, Frankfurt, Munich, Salzburg, Berlin, Stuttgart and Bremen. All special cases handled by these stations were directed by the London German Desk. [Deletion]

Liaison with foreign intelligence services. One of OSS/London's more important intelligence responsibilities lay in maintaining relations with the non-British foreign services also operating in ETO. As the center for most of the exiled governments, London was a giant "marketing place" for all intelligence activities. The various foreign services offered, not only a wealth of information from their own underground sources, but also a rich reservoir of personnel and contacts for agent operations. The return, to be given for these assets by OSS/London, was in money, equipment, facilities, techniques and the exchange of appropriate OSS-gathered intelligence.

There was no set pattern for OSS relationships with these foreign services. Some of the contacts were initiated through General Donovan at the highest level. Others were arranged by the

Strategic Service Officer through the good offices of the Embassy or armed forces. Some simply grew out of informal personal relationships at branch or sub-branch levels.

As a result, there was rarely any particular coordination and often some confusion. For example, trouble arose when—as in the case of liaison with the Poles—two uncoordinated OSS contacts were in touch with two different political factions of the foreign service.

At times, efforts were made to integrate liaison more closely, but none was particularly successful, since many of the informal contacts were on a personal basis which brought a quicker, more satisfactory service than could be obtained through channels. The advantages of informality and ready access outweighed the disadvantages of inconsistency and duplication. Qualified analysts were available to sift and weigh conflicting intelligence, and any irreconcilable conflicts could always be handled on a case-by-case basis by the Commanding Officer.

French. The French were the first of the foreign intelligence agencies with which OSS/London developed liaison. Contact was arranged through the U.S. Embassy in July 1942, and, by 1943, SI was in close touch with BCRA [Bureau Central de Renseignements et d'Action, commanded by André Dewavrin, a deadly little elitist who had been at St. Cyr. BCRA's interrogation tactics once caused Scotland Yard to investigate strong reports that two Frenchmen had been beaten to death in the basement of the BCRA offices on Duke Street, Mayfair], various French officials of the FFI, and numerous individuals outside the DeGaulle movement. Most helpful, outside of the political intelligence obtained, were the ground reports of bombing results in France for A-2 and the information on names, descriptions and locations of Allied airmen who had been shot down. OSS/London's closest relations with the French were in the development of the SI *Sussex* and SO *Jedburgh* plans. [Deletion] There were difficulties, particularly when De Gaulle occasionally evinced displeasure at Anglo-American policy by cutting off all intelligence contact. Relations, however, were always somehow reestablished and continued throughout the war.

Polish. Contact with the Poles began in August 1942. SI soon developed a Polish Section for liaison with both the Polish Intelligence Service, which concentrated on military intelligence, and the Ministry of Interior, which handled political, psychological and social intelligence. From the latter source, SI received intelligence reports on conditions in Italy, Rumania, Bulgaria, Yugoslavia and Germany. Simultaneously, SO made connections with London representatives of the Polish resistance program through a liaison officer at SOE. Meanwhile R&A was in touch with some of the leftist Poles in London.

In the summer and fall of 1944, SI requested information for G-2 on the Russian-Polish crisis. Polish dispatches, however, proved to be so heavily slanted against Russia that they were often valueless. Moreover, the Poles were so divided among themselves that information on any subject varied according to which Pole had provided the data. Finally, it became apparent that the Poles were not only sometimes using resistance supplies against the Russians, but were inflating their share of available materials through identical requests made simultaneously of OSS/London, OSS/Washington and the British. The OSS Polish investment, in the long run, appears to have been largely unproductive, but justified by the necessity of playing all possibilities.

Dutch. Although occasional reciprocal services were performed by OSS and Dutch intelligence officers, after the dispersal of the latter's network by the Nazis in the summer of 1942, regular contact between OSS and the reconstituted military (MID) and secret intelligence (BI) branches of the Dutch service was established only in October 1943. Relations were greatly facilitated by the intelligence OSS could offer on Far Eastern areas, where the Netherlands had an interest.

Five elaborate maps on coastal defenses in Holland were made available by the Dutch to SI and turned over to ONI. Summaries of W/T reports from Holland on German battle order were supplied SI regularly, and , after June 1944, on the same day they were received from Dutch MID by BI. Via this rapid relay of Dutch W/T messages, SI received information on German plans to inundate Holland, and, for the Army Air Force, on V-bomb sites, bombing results, etc. Two complete maps were prepared from aerial photographs, showing all areas in Holland of actual or probable inundation and results of daylight bombing attacks. They were sent to Washington. Documents and personal articles, currently in use in Holland, were also made available for SI agent use by the Netherlands services. [Deletion]

Belgian. Belgian intelligence officials were first contacted by OSS/London in August 1942, in order to discover, for the Eighth Air Force, civilian reaction to Allied bombing in Belgium. Further intelligence from this source was sporadic and disappointing; the Belgian services were bound, by an agreement with the British, to limit relations with other Allied organizations.

SI did arrange, in early 1944, to receive from the Belgian Surete raw military intelligence reports—Air, Naval and Battle Order—simultaneously with the British. Cabled spot intelligence began arriving in February 1944. These cables, in increasing numbers, reported V-1 and V-2 emplacements and other vital military targets, of special interest to the Eighth and Ninth Air Forces. Through initial contacts, SI was able to establish at Brussels, in September 1944, its ESPINETTE outpost which recruited agents for the penetration of Germany. [SI was receiving a peak load of one hundred operational cables a week from Belgian sources in September 1944, just prior to the liberation of the Low Countries. (footnote)]

R&A obtained from the Belgians a wide collection of clandestine newspapers and a large volume of economic and administrative material including, later in 1944, information on Lithuania, Esthonia, Poland and Denmark. Twenty-four administrative maps of occupied Belgium were prepared by R&A in collaboration with Belgium intelligence representatives.

Norwegian. Contacts with Norway's intelligence services and with the Foreign Minister were first made by SI in September 1942. Until a year later, however, when arrangements were made for SI to receive directly secret military intelligence from Norway, rather than through the Military Attache at the U.S. Embassy, little other than occasional political-economic reports were received. Following this clearance, SI procured reports on submarine bases and activity in Norwegian waters, as well as ground estimates of AAF bombing results on Norwegian targets, and reports for COSSAC on supply and transportation needs there. Access to the files of the "E" [for espionage] office of the Norwegian Royal Ministry of Defense assured up-to-date data on shipping, defense installations, etc., in that country. SI reciprocated with supplies for British-Norwegian intelligence teams, and with underground intelligence reports from Sweden of interest to Norwegian officials.

Czechoslovak. In July 1942, OSS replaced the U.S. Military Attache as sole American liaison with the Czechoslovak Intelligence Service. CIS had no intelligence sources of its own in Europe, until 1944, and its reports, although regular, were often duplicated elsewhere or of dubious value. In July 1944, however, CIS teams began operating in Czechoslovakia, and SI was able to receive prompt answers to requests by the War Department, SI Labor Desk, R&A, X-2 and OSS/Washington on such items as rocket experiments on Rugen Island, mining operations in western Bohemia, an underground arms factory and air targets in Slovakia. Through contacts with leading Czechoslovak political figures and the Political Intelligence Section of the Ministry of Interior, SI obtained information on political developments, economic data on Central Europe and dossiers on individuals in the underground—Poles, Austrians, Hungarians and Sudeten Germans.

Both SI and R&A were in touch with Danish, Yugoslav and Greek officials. Liaison was carried on with the last two for OSS/MedTO. The intelligence flow from all these sources, however was scanty, and no agent operations directed toward them were mounted from London.

Throughout the period, OSS/London attempted in vain to develop closer relations with the Russians. During the spring and summer of 1944, a few selected intelligence items were submitted to them by SI, and the Reports Division developed an informal contact with one Russian source. Nothing important, however, was ever received in return, and the tenuous relationship finally dissolved.

Reports Division/SI. In the early days of OSS/London, when the flow of intelligence was small and the list of customers short, items were handled by the appropriate geographic desks, and, on urgent occasions, by the Strategic Services Officer, ETO. But with the gradual shift in emphasis from service for Washington to support for the Theater, intelligence specialists came into demand, and, in the summer of 1943, the Reports Division/SI was established to process and disseminate intelligence. At the end of 1944 the Division included over one hundred personnel.

By July 1943, material was being processed from British and other Allied intelligence sources, from OSS offices in Algiers, Stockholm, Bern, Lisbon, Madrid, as well as Washington, and from other OSS branches. Later, many of the sources were OSS espionage agents reporting directly to London from behind enemy lines. The intelligence from all these sources poured into the Division by cable, pouch or courier.

On arrival, the material was broken down by subject matter and processed by military, political, economic and scientific experts. These specialists first evaluated the information on the basis of source and other known intelligence concerning the subject. The material was then translated, if necessary, edited, mimeographed and distributed to all interested agencies within the Theater. [Deletion]

Adequate dissemination to all these customers without duplication, contradiction or embarrassment was complex and delicate. For instance, the greatest care had to be taken to keep OSS intelligence, hostile to an ally, from falling into its hands. Such material was classified "Control," signifying that dissemination must be restricted to U.S. customers. Particular caution was also required in disseminating material received from one ally concerning the internal affairs of another.

Likewise, special precautions were needed to prevent material originating with an ally from returning to it or one of its own customers via OSS channels. Such an event not only made for duplication but also might lead to false confirmation—an apparent, but actually unjustified, affirmation of intelligence previously received. Similar care had to be taken that OSS material should not reach customers via some shortcut before expert analysis, editing and evaluation by the Reports Divison. In this event, aside from the risks of duplication and false confirmation, there was the collateral danger of two contradictory reports emanating from OSS at the same time.

Security posed another problem. Some items could safely be disseminated to some customers but not to others. For example, special care had to be taken, in April 1944, on disseminations of certain psychological warfare material to OWI, which that agency sometimes revealed to the Germans in propaganda broadcasts. All the material involved was useful to OWI analysts, but some of it was too confidential for broadcast purposes. The Reports Division worked out with OWI a system of special symbols on disseminations, indicating which material forwarded them could be used on the radio.

Speed was another problem. Occasionally information arrived of such urgency that the usual Reports procedure had to be bypassed. On these occasions, the Chief of Division and the SSO usually went personally to the interested customers and indicated that a regular dissemination would follow. During the invasion of France, a special teletype machine was installed to relay hot items direct to the appropriate military HQ.

A by-product of its work in disseminating information was the Reports Division's important role in intelligence target selection. From 1943 on, the Division's customers submitted lists of new subjects in which they were interested. In turn these requests were noted and passed on to operational desks for relay to other bases or agents in the field. In 1944 the Reports Division, on its own initiative, took up the work of collecting lists of such intelligence objectives, and in the fall became the Division of Intelligence Direction, selecting targets for and briefing German agents. In this way, the Division developed closer liaison between the various SI Desks and outside agencies.

Clothing and documents. While an agent's positive record depended on such personal factors as ingenuity, he could not be expected to succeed without such basic essentials as clothing and documents, correct to the minutest detail. Furthermore, agent morale depended to a considerable extent on confidence in cover, in the authenticity of clothing, suitcase, cigarettes, matches and the like.

It was decided, in Washington, that the most efficient operation of R&D and CD must necessarily be at the operations center of London, rather than in Washington. Representatives of both Branches arrived in April 1944. Theoretically, CD would collect the requisite data, while R&D would manufacture the items. In practice, the two pooled their resources.

R&D in Washington had compiled a list of equipment and machinery necessary for a complete printing, lithographing and photoengraving plant, to be delivered to London as soon as possible. However, the delay in arrival of the equipment was so great that, to all intents and purposes, the branches had to equip themselves on the spot, on either a loan or purchase basis.

The work could not have been carried out at all without considerable British cooperation. One British company supplied a lithographing press which was installed on 4 July. Another plant loaned, privately and without charge, a photoengraving camera and a routing machine, with the sole proviso that the machines be marked as the property of the company—to be returned at some future date. At the end of May, suitable arrangements were made with a British firm for the purchase of paper of the most specialized nature. The mill's output was only nine tons a week, but it produced under ideal security conditions. CD/R&D concluded that it was already working for SOE, which agency had quietly permitted OSS to benefit from the mill's experience.

In April 1944, the two Branches began combined operations with a staff of five. The number increased steadily, so that by the end of the year there was a total of thirty-six personnel, including five civilians. By that time the procedural pattern was set. In two separate buildings near the OSS/London office, CD/R&D handled the production of clothing and documents.

Clothing. For the clothing shop, OSS supplied a tailor, while Polish Intelligence furnished a cobbler. Relevant clothing data came from careful study of actual examples of the uniforms to be duplicated. For example, a trip to a British POW camp produced valuable information not only on enemy uniforms, but also on articles suitable to be carried in an agent's pocket. At various times personnel were dispatched to the Continent to obtain German uniforms, accessories and equipment.

In clothing, complete anonymity was desired, but it was hard to locate inconspicuous garments. An additional hazard was provided by laundry marks, which proved almost impossible to remove. The British applied a cleansing method, but this affected the dye of the cloth so that a suspiciously light spot remained.

No detail was too insignificant to escape notice. Buttons had to be sewn on by threading the holes in parallel instead of criss-cross fashion. Inside pockets were fitted on each side, and, if the suit were tailored to order, a tailor's slip would be on the inside of the left pocket. Sometimes a strip of cloth matching the material of the suit would be placed along the rim of the inside pockets of the jacket. Normally, plain bone buttons were used, but suspender buttons were sometimes marked "elegant" or "for gentlemen" or "mode de Paris," as was found to be customary on both German and French clothes.

Accessories were varied in origin. For example, shoelaces were German, handkerchiefs were British imitations, and towels were made in Ireland. Since the stock of genuine articles was insufficient, a Camouflage Section was established in August 1944 to manufacture additional accessories, as well as lead pencils to be used as concealment devices, belt buckles for the same purpose, letter drops and the like.

In the fall, when the SI demand turned to German equipment, field trips to the Continent produced sufficient material for use as models. The stock of second-hand items soon gave out, and CD/R&D resorted to the normal British methods of manufacturing clothing and subsequently soaking, dirtying and subjecting it to several cleanings and pressings.

Documents. In May 1944 CD/R&D began [rubber stamp and document production. The French] furnished background intelligence, while OSS/Washington sent blank documents. In addition, field detachments, other American agencies and T-Forces supplied valuable data and blanks from time to time.

The problems of letterpress, lithographic press and photoengraving equipment were early solved, but the question of print was recurrent. Continental type was varied and its supply was short. The solution lay in printing from photoengraved plates. A suitable photoengraving plant was established, which could turn out work of a refinement and character necessary to produce plates that would duplicate enemy documents perfectly. It was, of course, often hard to find an original document that was not faded or discolored, and R&D had to develop various chemical processes to sharpen outlines.

Papers, even when perfectly matched in form, color and texture, differed greatly when examined under ultra-violet light. This difficulty was never corrected, but appears not to have been discovered by the enemy. Watermarking, it was found, must be effected simultaneously with the actual manufacture of the paper, a procedure with which the British paper mill, mentioned above, was familiar. Unfortunately, perfection required time; SIS had spent, on one occasion, two years to produce a single document, but, since time was important, perfection often had to be sacrificed to expedience. In such duties as paper matching, filling in by hand and matching colors, the fatiguing detail and accuracy required was extreme. Nevertheless, CD/R&D achieved notable success. A very small percentage of agents were discovered because of unsatisfactory papers or clothing.

Message Center. Prior to the establishment of an OSS Communications Branch, radio traffic for all OSS sections in London was handled by the Message Center. This central routing point was formed, after the OSS/OWI split in June 1942, from the staff of the original COI code room, which had been established at the U.S. Embassy in December 1941. It moved, on 1 September 1942, to OSS Headquarters on Grosvenor Street.

Through teletype links (for local purposes), and cable lines and wireless (for long distance), the OSS Message Center maintained contact with other official agencies in London, both U.S. and foreign, and, after August 1943, with points all over the globe. Where it did not have its own facilities—such as cable channels—OSS arranged to use State Department, Army or commercial circuits. The first OSS link was over a commercial trans-Atlantic varioplex circuit to Washington which served the increasing amount of administrative traffic.

[While England had Ultra and America had Magic, Germany had no comparable cryptanalytical triumph against the Western powers in World War II, although until 1943 they were extremely successful against Russian traffic. Germany did not penetrate any of the SHAEF main ciphers, although they did excellent work against British naval ciphers until late 1940. This success resulted in heavy British naval losses, especially during the Norwegian operations of 1940. They were very successful, too, against U.S. and U.K. merchant marine ciphers until late 1942. These abilities caused terrible losses among both British and American convoys, especially down the east coast of the U.S. On a tactical level, German agencies were successful against the U.S. armies—especially the 3rd and 9th—when they were on the Continent. But in general high-level ciphers were not penetrated, and this accounted for a good deal of the surprise that the Western powers enjoyed on D-Day in Normandy and for destroying whatever chance the Abwehr might have had to operate effectively in England and America after 1940-41.]

Because the major portion of all messages passing through the OSS communications center in London was classified, each network had a special cipher system—double transposition, confidential machine, etc.—depending on the nature and extent of the traffic. Cryptographic procedures and other security precautions at the Message Center were strict. Incoming messages were given a prefix number indicating, for cipher clerks, the code system employed. The deciphered text was then paraphrased before distribution, to prevent comparison by enemy interceptors of the clear text with its coded counterpart and possible compromise of the cipher system itself. The original coded text and deciphered copy thereof were filed for permanent reference in the code room. Outgoing cables, sent through the OSS Message Center, had to be encoded exactly as received, a paraphrased version being returned to the originator for filing.

Efficiency of London-Washington traffic was increased considerably with the addition, in January 1944, of an Army teletype scrambler. This unit enciphered messages at the same time that they were transmitted to the mouth of the trans-Atlantic cable, thus avoiding two time-consuming processes; encipherment and paraphrasing. Its high security permitted its use even for top secret messages.

Meanwhile, arrangements for large communications bases to accommodate prospective field operations were being worked out between OSS officials and British in London. SIS and SOE already operated independent secret networks in many parts of the world. As in similar discussions involving OSS and these organizations, SO and SOE—admittedly restricted to wartime duration—were anxious to pool their resources and experience, while SI and SIS guarded the independence of their respective long-range secret intelligence networks. During the summer and fall of 1942, it was agreed that SO should handle its commitments through British-controlled communications links, while SI might establish its own station on a separate site.

Station CHARLES. On 22 September 1942, an OSS Communications Branch was officially established, and, soon afterwards, projected OSS W/T arrangements in London received G-2 and Signal Corps approval. A new station—53C, or CHARLES, the third radio base in SOE's London network—would be built, equipped and staffed by American personnel.

By November 1943, Station CHARLES could begin operation. Intended at first to cover only the northern, or Scandinavian, sector of the three into which the British had divided Western Europe for communications purposes, Station CHARLES was given, as Normandy invasion plans were formed, responsibility for SO/SOE operations in France as well. To prepare for its more extensive commitments—which were to include *Jedburgh* agent

teams and mobile detachments with armies and army groups—
Station CHARLES called for more personnel and field equipment, tied in its training with the highly-developed British programs at SOE stations 53A and 53B, and set up a Technical Maintenance section devoted, among other things, to experimenting with new radio equipment and techniques. Since the personnel problem remained unsolved, the British loaned 36 high-speed radio operators and 50 additional female personnel to CHARLES until an allotment of Americans could take over, and permanently assigned 22 skilled cipher clerks. By 1944 the station was manned by 300 personnel.

In February 1944, Station CHARLES began a series of trial exercises to prepare field and base operators alike for actual operations. And on 13 March, it undertook its first "live" commitments—Norwegian teams, transferred from SOE Station 53A. By the end of March, procedures had evolved in the radio rooms, and new trainees were gaining confidence in the techniques of indicating call signs, "break-ins," requests for frequency and schedule changes and other signals. The field exercises were continued with *Jedburgh* and mobile unit personnel, so that, by D-Day, the operators at CHARLES were familiar with, and could work simultaneously, three types of commitments, each with its special problems. They learned for instance, never to repeat coded messages in full, always to map out and rotate schedules (skeds) on an hour-to-hour basis, and to tune transmitters over wide frequency ranges (usually high during the day and low during the night).

Profiting from all that was learned of internal procedures, routing of messages, etc., in the first seven months of its development, Station CHARLES, just prior to D-Day, was physically remodeled to ensure the greatest efficiency. At that time its six principal departments consisted of:

Radio operators (Received and transmitted)

Coders (Enciphered and deciphered; trained clerks for other theaters)

Perforators (prepared call signs and broadcast tapes, for routine or mass signalling)

Teleprinters (Contacted SO/SOE Hq. and other stations)

Registry (Kept message files, logs of contacts, etc.)

Technical Maintenance (Maintained receiver and transmitter sites, tested, repaired and experimented)

These departments reported to a centrally located Control Room and a directing Chief Signalmaster.

Garbled or indecipherable messages were reduced almost totally by a system of interpretation, in which the duty signalmaster and skilled cipher supervisors joined to analyze problem messages on the basis of Morse (transmission) errors, context, agent's language faults, past messages and other data. Repetition was rarely requested. Code groups which had been missed entirely, due to static or other causes, were provided either by recordings or by monitoring reports from other SOE stations (made on contacts where the operator was not highly proficient). If an operator's capture by the enemy were suspected, his transmissions were "fingerprinted": during a contact undulator tapes were run to obtain a visual picture of the sender's "fist," and checked with tapes at headquarters made by the SO or SOE agent prior to dispatch.

After the cipher system to be used had been determined, different signal plans were prepared for each agent group by OSS and SOE planning boards. Each plan included: the operating frequencies to be used for both regular and emergency contacts (selected from lists of workable frequencies provided by SHAEF, after consideration of the location of the agent in relation to London and other agents, season and anticipated ionospheric conditions); contact times; call signals (variable or fixed three-letter groups), a signal system for arranging alternate or additional skeds, using a Day Indicating Table for the day of the week and a Transposition Table for hour and minute; base broadcast periods; and the "Q" signal system of three-letter combinations with specified meanings to facilitate and shorten contact time.

An early and elaborate plan was that for the Norwegian agents, who were scheduled to make at least one contact every other day, always at a different time according to a prearranged schedule, and never on the same frequency. Frequencies could be changed during a contact, by either the base or the outstation, by so signalling in accordance with the signal plan's tables and codes. Contacts were limited to one hour—not for security reasons alone, but because the number of agents to come on the air each day were closely scheduled.

The later *Jedburgh* plan was simpler, allowing two daily contacts at different times on odd and even days. Frequencies could be changed but, because of a limited 8-channel arrangement, agents were requested not to ask for different schedule times. Each *Jedburgh* plan was, nevertheless, provided with one of two 24-hour emergency channels, to be used when communication outside the regular sked time was urgent. Nightly broadcasts from CHARLES to all *Jedburgh* teams were also listed on the plan. Although many *Jedburgh* communication links were weak, comments of returning agents were generally favorable. All frequencies, and particularly the emergency frequency, on which 832 contacts were passed, were satisfactory. [Deletion]

Station CHARLES worked altogether 64 *Jedburgh* teams, 24 mobile circuits and more than 32 Norwegian commitments. Heaviest traffic during July and August was with the mobile army units. Upon the liberation of France, main traffic at CHARLES reverted to the Scandinavian sector. By the middle of October, CHARLES had closed, the few remaining *Jedburgh* and detachment channels being transferred to SOE Station 53A, and the Norwegian commitments to 53B. Station CHARLES personnel moved to the new OSS base in Paris or to SI station VICTOR.

Station Victor. In the attempt to meet priority needs of the SO/SOE stations, Theater allocations of specialized communications equipment, personnel and frequencies for an independent SI station were postponed. Station VICTOR (SI) was not established until March 1944, at which time it undertook responsibility for half of the joint SI/SIS *Sussex* missions and for four mobile detachments. In April, there were already several WeT-equipped SI teams in France, while only temporary base facilities existed to serve them. All operations at VICTOR, until well after D-Day, were conducted during a period when permanent installations were still in the process of assembly, and an adequate complement still being acquired. By July there were as yet only 100 personnel. The consequent differences in performance of Stations CHARLES and VICTOR were, under the circumstances, not surprising.

In contrast to the SO/SOE base, Station VICTOR did not constitute a self-contained unit. Although carrying on its own radio contacts with the field, it relied for ciphering and distribution on the main Message Center in London. The Center deciphered and sent, via its numerous teletype circuits, VICTOR intelligence direct to BCRA, SIS, X-2, Eighth Air Force, Director of Intelligence of the U.S. Strategic Air Force and G-2, SHAEF. The actual work with VICTOR was handled by a special operations staff at the Message Center. Only in July 1944 was this "ops" section, with its cipher facilities, moved to the VICTOR site, to permit greater speed in the coding and decoding of VICTOR messages.

Station VICTOR was handicapped in other ways. A month after its activation in March, and only a few weeks after its one large field exercise had been completed, actual operations were begun by *Sussex* agents in France. In addition, owing to an SIS security ruling, agents in training might not contact the same base with which they would be communicating from the field. VICTOR operators, as a result, did not have the benefit of the trial-and-error experience, and the knowledge of personal idiosyncrasies that CHARLES personnel were able to acquire before working their agents in the field. Furthermore, the late start of the *Sussex* program caused SI/London to dispatch some agents before they had completed training.

Signal plans used at VICTOR, for *Sussex* and *Proust* agents, called for one scheduled contact every other day, each on a different frequency, at a different time, and using a different call sign. Alternate contact times, frequencies and call signs were provided *Sussex* plans which were operated on five channels, four for normal schedules and broadcasts, and one for emergency use. These were rotated except for the low-frequency channel which was used exclusively for VICTOR's two nightly broadcast periods directed toward all agents.

Of the many complaints that came back to VICTOR from *Sussex* operators, most could be attributed to VICTOR's unfamiliarity with the agents and to inadequate *Sussex* training. Furthermore, SI agents lacked the resistance protection on which most SO agents could depend. For this reason, the former were often forced to set up aerials in locations that were physically secure, but unsatisfactory from a communications standpoint. When signals were not actually weak from these combined causes, they were frequently interrupted by enemy jamming.

Better luck was experienced with the light and heavy Special Signal Detachments with Allied armies and army groups. Standard U.S. Army Signal Corps equipment and procedures were used from positions of relative safety, and good atmospheric conditions permitted a high average of successful contacts. The SI/X-2 staffs operated, as did the corresponding SO/SOE units, on a 24-hour basis in the case of the heavy sections at Headquarters, and on hourly skeds in the case of the light detached units.

THE ALGIERS BASE

Algiers was planned to serve as the major MedTO base, corresponding to that in London, for operations into Europe. [OSS operations in support of the largely Franco-American landings in southern France in August 1944, for which the Algiers Base largely existed, were in the hands of Edward Gamble, the manager of a New York brokerage organization specializing in government bonds. His SI chief was Henry Hyde, a lawyer who had attended both Cambridge and Harvard, was married to the daughter of a prominent Frenchman, and whose father inherited a very large insurance fortune in the U.S.] In London were centered the main headquarters of OSS Branches X-2 and SO. SI and R&A also maintained large staffs there for liaison and intelligence correlation. Various other operating and supporting branches brought the London personnel total close to 2,000.

OSS/Algiers, on the other hand, was staffed by not more than one-third as many. R&A and X-2 activities were limited, and SO did not begin support of SO/London until early 1944. For SI, on the contrary, Algiers-offered greater opportunities than did London. Most important of its advantages was its location in a U.S.-controlled theater, where British services, in particular SIS, could not hamper SI operations, and where American units were more apt to give OSS the necessary supply, quarters and transportation support. For the penetration of France, SI could also find many suitable recruits, some of them fresh out of France, in the French colonies of North Africa.

According to orders approved in principle by the Theater Commander on 7 February 1943, the following OSS activities, among others, were authorized:

> SI activities in...south and southwest Europe...to the eastern boundary of Italy, and the islands adjacent thereto; SO activities in Italy, Sicily, Sardinia, Corsica, France, and other places as are required by the North African Theater Command.

Counter-intelligence and counter-espionage in these and certain other areas were also authorized.

Secret Intelligence. For operations into Europe, SI was divided into desks—French, Italian, Labor and, later, Spanish.

Activities of SI/France began with the arrival of its chief in late February 1943. Attention was first directed toward the struggles of the major rival French factions in North Africa. OSS officers associated by necessity with all political factions, Giraudist and De Gaullist, but principally with patriotic anti-German elements who had assisted OSS in preparations for the North Africa landings. The weight of information from these sources on various detailed aspects of the De Gaulle-Giraud conflict in the summer of 1943 frequently caused OSS reports to conflict with those of State Department representatives. That Department took strenuous exception to OSS political reporting on North Africa, as overlapping the work of its representatives on the scene, who were normally charged with such activity.

Donovan at the time placed less importance on political reporting than on military intelligence in direct support of the armies in the field, and ordered SI/France to redirect its emphasis accordingly. Thereafter, the SI/France staff trained, briefed and dispatched its agents strictly to obtain military and order of battle intelligence from inside enemy-held territory.

A Labor Desk was also established under SI, designed for eventual penetration of Germany through contacts with underground refugees in North Africa and France. Approvals for agent transport proved difficult to obtain, however, and the staff of the Labor Desk was transferred in March 1944 to Bari, Italy, for infiltrations through Yugoslavia.

The Chief Intelligence Officer controlled, in addition to these sections, the Reports Office. With the arrival, in November 1943, of specialists in battle order and coastal defenses, the first technical direction of intelligence was possible. The Algiers staff could then be divided into Operations and Intelligence and increase agent efficiency accordingly. Toward D-Day (15 August), liaison was established on a high level with AFHQ and Force 163 and specific suggestions, inquiries and criticisms were freely exchanged on incoming and outgoing reports.

X-2. Counter-espionage work in North Africa had first been carried out by OSS/Oujda, and its commanding officer had established the X-2 unit in Algiers, reporting to X-2/London.

In June 1943 a new chief, previously briefed in London, arrived and reconstructed several of the informant agent chains he had previously used during the *TORCH* opeation in Tangier, Araboua, Rabat, Casablanca, Fez and Oran. As of July 1943, the old OSS stations in these areas and at Oujda reported their CE activities to X-2. The central files in Algiers were organized to incorporate the scattered CE intelligence there, as well as that which began to come in from the field stations. In September, X-2 and the Communications Branch coordinated their activities for D/F-ing enemy stations.

Relations with the French were productive. [Deletion] X-2 units, particularly the Oujda group, worked with them in several successful operations against enemy parachutists in the Department of Constantine.

The new officer had, however, the difficult task of establishing close relations with British [excision]. While the latter received volumes of CE material from SIS, X-2 could not offer in exchange a similar quantity from other OSS sources. [Deletion]

Special Operations. A small SO group arrived in Algiers in January 1943. Because of the shortage of OSS personnel in North Africa at that time, most of these men had to undertake administrative and housekeeping duties at OSS headquarters in Algiers. Lack of adequate leadership and planning at this state, plus depletion of SO personnel through assignment to other work, appreciably delayed the start of SO operations based on North Africa..

According to the London SO/SOE agreement, activities of these two organizations in North Africa would be joint, and coordinated by SO. So well entrenched, however, was SOE in the Theater—including primary access to transportation, recruits and equipment—by the time OSS officers initiated their discussions, that SOE's acknowledged superiority in North Africa gave SO little opportunity to expand independently beyond its auxiliary contributions of administration, training and Operational Groups.

Massingham was the organization SOE established in Algiers, following the Allied landings, for operations into Europe. In accordance with negotiations between London and Washington, it was to be a purely British endeavor; however, OSS, with theoretical command of Special Operations in the North African Theater, might and did send an OSS observer.

At the *Massingham* camp at Ain Taya, the OSS representative assisted as an instructor. After understudying British SOE officers, he began training young recruits from the Corps Franc d'Afrique in demolitions, the handling of Sten guns and hand grenades, and unarmed combat. The instruction lasted from 9 December 1942 until Christmas, when Darlan's assassination by a student of the Ain Taya camp brought activities there to an abrupt close.

[The murder of Admiral Jean Darlan was one of the most mysterious events of this period of World War II. Under American pressure, this pro-Fascist Frenchman was made High Commissioner of French North Africa in November 1942 and promptly began to behave like a Fascist—concentration camps, political prisoners, anti-Semitic decrees and the like. The appointment caused a major political storm in Washington, and President Roosevelt was compelled to announce that Darlan's appointment was "only a temporary expedient, justified solely by the stress of battle." No "permanent arrangement" had been made with Darlan, the President insisted.

[Indeed, no "permanent arrangement" had been made, for less than a month after his installation as High Commissioner, Darlan was shot and fatally wounded in his office by Fernand Bonnier de la Chapelle, a Frenchman aged 20. Bonnier de la Chapelle was immediately arrested, tried and executed, all in 40 hours, leaving the world with the mystery: whose hit man was he? It was never established with any certainty. Everybody blamed everybody for the murder and the peremptory execution. An OSS agent, Carleton Coon, of Harvard, was, writes R. Harris Smith, suddenly posted out of the way "before he too could be accused of collusion in the murder." The enemy press accused the British intelligence services; the British intelligence service accused the Nazi intelligence services; the Gaullists accused the Giraudists. The information, released for the first time in the OSS War Report, that the assassin was undergoing agent training at the Massingham SOE establishment will, doubtless, provoke a new wave of speculation about whom Bonnier de la Chapelle was working for. On the evidence, however, it cannot be assumed that Churchill had any part in this affair; the most probable explanation is that, while Bonnier de la Chapelle was undergoing SOE training in a purely British establishment, he was acting for French rather than British interests when he pulled the trigger.]

Liaison, already established during the Tunisian campaign continued throughout the war in the form of a joint program of parachute training and supply packing operations at the OSS-organized Club des Pins school, near Sidi Ferruch, west of Algiers. Under the direction of experienced OSS officers, classes ranging from ten to seventy Spanish, Italian and French recruits were trained weekly for SOE, SIS, Deuxieme Bureau, Bataillon de Choc, and OSS missions. Their intensive instruction included practice parachute jumps into unfamiliar territory and paramilitary training, close combat, demolitions, small arms, etc. In mid-September, first recruits for the newly-formed Operational Groups began training at the Club des Pins parachute school.

A packing station was also established. Parachutes for personnel and supplies were rigged and various types of containers tested in experimental drops. This remained a joint British-American program until March 1944, when OSS set up its own independent supply and packing facilities. Modifications of American aircraft, once planes were obtained, were developed in various experimental tests to attain maximum efficiency in dropping both personnel and supplies.

A small independent SO training area (Station "P"), established in January 1944 near Algiers, was reorganized and moved in April to Chrea as an enlarged OSS paramilitary school. Here, until July, approximately fifty SO agents and saboteurs—mostly French recruits—were trained each month as organizers, instructors, and members of French Commando units. Courses at Chrea included: small arms, map reading, field craft, security, demolition, communications and industrial sabotage.

SPOC [This Anglo-American organization was under the joint command of Colonel John Anstey (SOE), who became chairman of a leading English tobacco company (John Player & Sons) and High Sheriff of Nottinghamshire, and Colonel William Davis

(OSS/SO), a Philadelphia banker.] In early 1944 it was agreed between SHAEF and AFHQ that the support and control of all resistance activity in southern France would rest with SHAEF. Responsibility for this function was delegated by SHAEF to SFHQ, and, under SFHQ, a joint American and British headquarters, known as G-3 Special Project Operations Center (SPOC) was established on 1 May at Algiers to conduct operations in France.

Prior to this centralization of control, SO/North Africa had arranged with French Army headquarters in Algiers to obtain the services of a limited number of French officers and enlisted men. In return, SO undertook to provide paramilitary and parachute training for a much larger number of French Army personnel. SO personnel in Algiers were rarely fluent in French or familiar with any special part of France. For this reason, it was felt in Algiers that SO operations before D-Day, because they involved living under an assumed name, with false papers and in civilian clothes, could be performed more effectively by Frenchmen.

Pursuant to this agreement, about one hundred Frenchmen were recruited and trained in Algiers for work as SO agents in France. These men were made available to SPOC, and it was arranged to procure 200 more. Six French Operational Groups and 25 *Jedburgh* teams sent from London came under the tactical control of SPOC, as did the SO Packing Station in Algiers, which had been established in March. An Air Operations Section, similar to that at SFHQ/London, was created to work with the Bomber Group which provided the air lift for body and supply drops from North Africa.

A total of 212 American SO and OG personnel were infiltrated into southern France by SPOC during the summer of 1944. Of these, 9 were SO agents, 21 were *Jedburghs,* and 182 made up the 14 combat sections into which the Operational Groups were divided for work in the field. In addition, 30 French SO agents worked for SPOC in France.

At the time of the *ANVIL* invasion (15 August 1944), G-3, SPOC controlled 10 Inter-Allied Military Missions, 17 *Jedburgh* teams, 10 Operational Group missions, a British Paramilitary Group, and special counter-scorch teams in the ports of Sete, Marseille and Toulon. Since 20 May, the SPOC Air Supply Section had dispatched more than 1,500 tons to Maquis and undercover Allied groups. At least seven Lysander and Dakota moonlight landing operations had been successfully completed in southern France, carrying heavy weapons, infiltrating Allied leaders for consultation with FFI chiefs, and exfiltrating agents, resistance leaders and Allied airmen.

A special staff known as Special Force Unit No. 4 (SFU-4) represented SPOC with the Seventh Army during and after the *ANVIL* invasion. Its purpose was to coordinate the activities of the various SPOC teams with FFI and with the Seventh Army and 6th Army Group in the field, and to provide a central wireless link between them and the Algiers base. SPOC agents in France sent situation reports, supply requests, etc. to Algiers via the SFU-4 link at Seventh Army Hq. or via advance OSS units with the Seventh Army. Upon the completion of their missions, agents contacted SFU-4 officers with the Army for further instructions, or proceeded to rear bases at Grenoble and Avignon for de-briefing and repatriation.

By early September, FFI action against the enemy had virtually ceased in most departments. However, Algiers continued to supply resistance groups covering the Allied flanks against by-passed enemy pockets in the southwest and on the Italo-French border. Lyon was taken by Seventh Army and FFI forces on 4 September, thus ending the need for further SPOC operations in southern France. The organization was officially liquidated on 9 September 1944.

Operational Groups. Donovan anticipated inclusion of radio-equipped guerrilla-type units as part of SO in the Mediterranean Theater, when he sent, in January 1943, the Chief of SO to discuss with Theater authorities the use of "auxiliary operational groups."

OG recruits were volunteers from U.S. Army units who spoke the language of the country where they would operate. Consisting normally of four officers and thirty enlisted men, each group was divided into combat sections comprising, as a rule, two officers and thirteen enlisted men, including a radio operator and a medical technician. They were trained at camps in the United States.

The first Italian-speaking OG recruits did not reach North Africa until late July 1943. The men were incorporated into an Operational Group command as Company A, and given final SO training and briefing for operations in Corsica, Sardinia and Italy. OG's for France, sent from Washington in February and March 1944, were organized in Algiers as Company B and used pursuant to SHAEF plans for the June and August invasions.

Communications. Following D-Day in North Africa, the OSS Communications staff consisted of a small group of Frenchmen, most of whom had assisted with preparations for Operation *TORCH*. The OSS station in Algiers provided the sole radio link with Gibraltar from North Africa and transmitted all Army and State Department messages there until an AFHQ Signal Corps unit was established at Algiers.

By March 1943, all Frenchmen had been replaced by American personnel. The small coding, transmitting and receiving office had expanded to include a message center at SI headquarters in Algiers, and a large Communications headquarters—including base radio and main receiving stations—at Cap Matifou, about twenty kilometers away. A communications school, where agent-operators were trained separately for clandestine radio work, was located some distance from the other bases. By May 1943, OSS/Algiers was in direct contact with OSS offices at Casablanca and Tangier, with clandestine stations in Corsica (PEARL HARBOR) and southern France (MEXICO), with the SOE/*Brandon* post at Le Kuif, Tunisia, and with a seldom-used but important station at Madrid. Besides those direct contacts, the Message Center also handled messages, through State Department and Army channels, to and from OSS bases all over the world.

An important sub-station was established at Ile Rousse, Corsica, in October 1943. This was used for servicing OG operations and as an alternate base for agent circuits in France, when Algiers could not be reached from the field. [Corsica was about 300 miles from the average French circuit, compared to Algiers' 600 miles. (footnote)] Forty percent of incoming field messages from France in the pre-invasion days of 1944 were relayed to Algiers via Corsica, which continued to serve as a sub-station until October 1944.

Transportation. [Deletion] Donovan arranged with General Eisenhower for OSS to go direct to the RAF command for aircraft, so that it no longer had to apply through British SIS, which was often slow in cooperating. [Deletion] In June 1943, Donovan persuaded General Curtiss, A-2, U.S. Strategic Air Force, to agree to assign a few planes for special operations. It was not until August, however, that two B-17's, a C-47 and seven B-25's were released to OSS and airmen transferred from regular bomber units to the OSS Parachute School. At Club des Pins, trap doors were installed in B-17's and experimental night landings made from the C-47 on improvised runways. B-25's, too fast for personnel drops, were adjusted for container and package use.

An experiment was attempted in March 1944, modelled on the successful British system of "Lysander" mail pickups. B-17's and C-47's were tried, but, because they stalled at low speed, could not be used for aerial pick-ups. Clandestine fields for receipt by air of documentary intelligence, "burnt" agents, etc., were, nevertheless, prepared by SI agents in France and a few serviced at infrequent intervals by British "Lysanders."

Finally, USN PT Squadron 15 was made available by AFHQ for agent deliveries from Corsica. [Deletion]

Major General Sir Stewart Menzies, the Chief of the British Secret Intelligence Service, who helped Donovan found the OSS.
Daily Telegraph, London

General Sir Colin Gubbins, the Chief of the British Special Operations Executive, who helped Donovan found OSS/SO.
Author's Collection

The enemy—Admiral Canaris, Chief of the Abweht, and Reinhardt
Heydrich, Chief of the SD. *Bilderdienst, Munich*

Colonel
M.J. Buckmaster,
the British O.C. in
the Anglo-American
Resistance Forces
in France during
the war.
*Associated Newspapers
Copyright*

The people of Amsterdam, Holland throng the cathedral square to celebrate VE Day. It marks the end of five years of German oppression and they are overjoyed that the war has come to an end. This aerial photograph made of the main square in Amsterdam by an 8th AF plane flying low over the city, shows part of the populous celebrating. *U.S. Air Force Photo*

Nazi Major General Erich Elster, surrounded by his staff, discusses terms for the surrender of himself and his 20,000 troops at the River Loire. Lt. Colonel J.K. French, an OSS official is second from right.
U.S. Army Photograph

Commandant Burgoin, "Le Manchot," "The One-Armed Man," who commanded the Jeds in Brittany, leading the Battalion of Heaven down the Champs Elysée in Paris in a Victory Day Celebration.
Author's Collection

A-20 Havocs of the
12th Air Force dropped
supplies by parachute
to stealthy French
Commandos who
preceded the main
waves of amphibious
fighters who landed
in Southern France
on D-Day. The
technique of dropping
supplies by parachute
was developed by
Major General Gene
C. Vance.
U.S. Air Force Photo

Supplies being dropped by parachute from Boeing B-17's to the Maquis in France.
Official U.S. Air Force Photo

This guerilla band composed of American Rangers, South Africans, Russians and Poles operated behind German lines in Italy, disrupting communications. Left to Right are: Brigadier General Rufus S. Ramey, Kansas City, Mo.; William La Rue, Columbus, Ohio question S/Sgt. Taylor and his group about their experiences back of the German lines. Campagnatico area, Italy.
U.S. Army Photograph

Group of men and
women partisans who
helped South African
troops entering
Pistoia to ferret out
German snipers and
pockets of resistance.
Fifth Army, Pistoia,
Italy.
U.S. Army Photograph

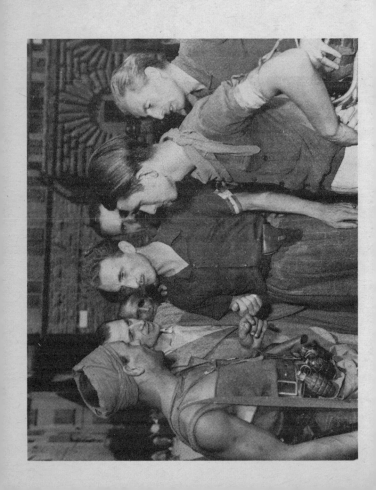

Members of the Partigione group at Florence, Italy, confer on strategy aimed to capture snipers. Some are armed. The man on the left wears a variety of equipment. British Eighth Army. *U.S. Army Photograph*

Partigione (Partisans), regarded as hoodlums before being recognized by AMG and supported in their noble actions, were great assistance to the Allies in Florence, Italy, in wiping out nuisance Nazis and Fascist elements who remained inside the city after it was captured by the Eighth Army. Shown is a demonstration of the Partisans in the Piazza Signoria in Florence.

U.S. Army Photograph

Crowds in Milano swarm around the filling station in the center of Milan from which the bodies of Mussolini, his mistress and other Fascists were hung by the feet after their execution by Italian patriots. *National Archives*

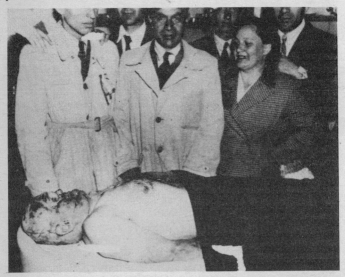

After the third day the great man began to stink but the odor of his rotting corpse did not keep curious citizens of Milan from crowding into the morgue to view Mussolini's body. Some of them were grim, others laughed, and still others gloated. *National Archives*

CHAPTER 13

Early Infiltrations into France

ALGIERS INTELLIGENCE

The first clandestine network organized by OSS for intelligence in metropolitan France was established three months after the North African landings and without benefit of any SI organization as such. Radio operator "Tommy," who had served Operation *TORCH* and run the OSS operation in Corsica (the first in enemy-occupied Europe), was assigned the task. Because he had both experience and extensive personal contacts in France, "Tommy" was asked, at the same time, to take radio sets and to re-establish W/T contact for SOE, whose station near Nice had been broken up by the Germans. In return for British air lift, OSS performed these services.

The mission proceeded in the first week of February via Corsica in the same French submarine, "Casablanca," that had carried "Tommy's" Corsican team a month previously. By the end of February, "Tommy" had succeeded in setting up a clandestine station for the Deuxieme Bureau in Marseille, a new British sabotage post in the Alps, and the beginnings of an OSS intelligence network and W/T station, MEXICO, in Toulon. He was given virtual independence in the recruiting and training of OSS agents and operators; security and on-the-spot policy were, for all practical purposes, in the hands of one man. Necessary as this delegation was at the time, lack of complete control from Algiers made for complications later on.

Although officially working in liaison with the Giraud-backed SR intelligence service, whose Marseille station he had organized, "Tommy" quickly contacted key figures in the underground movement. These patriots, fervent supporters of General de Gaulle and opponents of Giraud, were among the first to volunteer their whole-hearted cooperation to the OSS cause in France, and it was with their help that "Tommy" set up his secret radio station, MEXICO, in Toulon. An experienced radio operator was supplied him through the leader of all underground resistance in the Provence region. These same securely organized patriots volunteered to protect the new OSS station and construct a network of agents to provide it with information, military, political and economic, throughout the south of France, for transmission to AFHQ, Algiers.

In addition to maintaining contact with these competing French followers of Giraud and De Gaulle, "Tommy" kept in touch with the secret station of British SOE. For the sake of security, all three sources had to be kept separate and ignorant of each other. "Tommy" organized "Comite OSS." This was a liaison organization made up of SR and OSS agents, designed for exchange of information between the two organizations and nominally giving SR supervision over OSS activities. In actuality, SR claimed information from OSS sources as its own, and the main purpose of "Comite OSS," as far as "Tommy" was concerned, was to ward off SR suspicions of his other underground contacts.

Station MEXICO, operating clandestinely in enemy-occupied territory and receiving the cooperation of hundreds of individuals, ran grave risks every day of being blown. "Tommy," insofar as he was capable under the complicated conditions in which he operated, took precautions. A special committee of high officials supporting the underground movement was appointed to ensure the physical protection of the OSS station at Toulon. The committee consisted of a former counsellor of the prefect of Var, the police chief of Toulon, the head of the Toulon arsenal, a local pharmacist, and two police inspectors. When "Tommy" suspected in mid-April that SR officers were attempting, for political reasons, to dispose of MEXICO and its personnel, he organized a second radio station some sixty miles north of Marseille as a reserve base.

Despite these precautions, "Tommy's" three-way contact with rival organizations in a single limited area, however disguised, could not help in the long run but arouse suspicion and jealousy. Strained relations between SR and "Tommy" were a natural result of his extensive connections with the De Gaullist underground. The official liaison between SR and OSS in France, "Comite OSS," was discontinued although "Tommy" still obtained secret reports via one of his agents employed at the SR station.

Another blow to MEXICO's security came in early May when the newly-formed SI/France desk in Algiers decided to send a mixed mission to French, British and U.S. stations alike. "Tommy," who was to signal the submarine in and return with it to Algiers, made arrangements for the landing party and for the security of his own men. He gave instructions on the handling of the French, the British and the new OSS agents (the first to be sent to

France by the SI desk at Algiers), and on bringing the new arrivals to Marseille with the least possible contact between them.

On his first return trip from France to Algiers, "Tommy" brought bulky information, such as maps and documents, which could not be communicated by radio. Of chief interest to G-2 and the Air Force in North Africa was the full plan of AA defense in France, including the secret signal code which had been obtained from a German major in exchange for gold.

During the initial three-month period under "Tommy," MEXICO sent almost 500 messages to Algiers. While Allied forces were then active in Tunisia, they needed, for future operations, the intelligence which came to them on defense preparations, political opinion and Axis movements generally in France. MEXICO's detailed coverage of enemy shipping activity from Marseille to Toulon was especially appreciated by G-2, and resulted in the Allied torpedoing and sinking of at least five enemy ships attempting to leave for Tunisia.

S E C R E T
PARAPHRASE

April 5, 1943

FROM MEXICO
NO. 132
UN CERTAIN NOMBRE D'AVIONS BOCHES ETAIENT TEMPORAIREMENT A ISTRES LE TRENTE MARS X IL Y AVAIT DES MESSERSCHMIDTS DU DERNIER MODELE CENT DIX X IL Y DEUX PIECES ARTILLERIE DE MARINE DE CALIBRE 305 X X A PEYROLLES IL Y A DEUX PIECES BOCHES DE 280 SUR WAGONS ILS SONT SUPPORTES SUR LES WAGONS PAR SEPT TRETEAUX X X TOUS LES DEUX JOURS ON DEPLACE UNE DE CES PIECES
Received April 5, 1943
(Message from Station MEXICO, giving miscellaneous battle order intelligence.)

Back in Algiers, "Tommy" worked with the new executive officer of OSS/Algiers on plans for sending badly-needed supplies into France. At the same time, it was decided that sample U.S. weapons might be distributed to resistance groups, already organized, for later use. The method to be employed for getting the various supplies to the Maquis who could use them was the parachute drop.

"Tommy," who again would lead the expedition, took a parachute course at British SOE headquarters and became thoroughly grounded in the use of secret weapons, grenades, mortars, Sten guns, and the like. Between 12 May and 19 June, OSS/Algiers attempted without success to obtain from the American Air Force at Constantine (Algeria) a plane for OSS use. Eventually it turned to the British. Coincidentally, the SOE station in France had just been captured by the enemy. In agreeing to provide transportation for the OSS parachute mission, SOE asked "Tommy" to carry over radio sets and money to rebuild its station. On the same flight, "Tommy" was to drop an OSS agent who was to go, with underground assistance, to Switzerland and northern Italy. And he himself was instructed to set up additional intelligence stations for OSS in southern France, arrange secret landing places for future parachute drops and plane and submarine landings, extend his French underground contacts, and supply them with arms and other necessary equipment.

On 19 June 1943 at 2200 hours, "Tommy's" party left Algiers in a British Halifax, and parachuted to a reception group of Maquis agents near Mont Ventoux in the Vercors region at 0120 hours. So secure were the preparations at the landing point that "Tommy" was able to stay on for twelve days and start a new station—BOSTON—for sending intelligence to Algiers. "Tommy" then reinstalled the British SOE station, and supervised its operation and two supply drops over a period of two months.

From July to October 1943, "Tommy" worked at building up his OSS intelligence network under the nose of an increasingly active Gestapo, and without any additional supplies being furnished. The latter fact was attributable partly to bad weather, which made parachute drops difficult, and partly to OSS dependence for transportation on the British. OSS promises to "Tommy's" agents of money, weapons, food and personnel were broken on more than one occasion, and had the unhappy effect of losing much Maquis support.

In the midst of these difficulties, OSS station MEXICO was captured. "Tommy," much disturbed by what he considered the unsympathetic attitude of new OSS administrators toward the work he had done, blamed the incident on SI insecurity. His accusations may not have been entirely unwarranted; the SI/France Desk (being organized in Algiers) was admittedly laboring under a handicap of limited and inexperienced personnel in its first efforts at intelligence chain-building in France. Whether it was the attempt of the new and insecure SI agent to contact MEXICO that put the Gestapo on the trail is not certain. However, it was not long after this agent's arrival at the OSS station in Toulon (in disobe-